MONSTROUS TRAVELS AS WICKED AS SIN

MONSTROUS TRAVELS AS WICKED AS SIN

THE SINFUL CRIMES DUOLOGY
BOOK TWO

W. H. LOCKWOOD

CONTENT ADVISORY

Thank you so much for picking up **Monstrous Travels as Wicked as Sin.**

If you've already read **Sinful Crimes for the Artistically Inclined**, you know what to expect, but we go… just a little darker here. Please do check the full list of CWs on my website: whlockwood.com

Once again, this book is intended for an adult audience and includes scenes and themes that may be upsetting for some readers. These include but are not limited to violence, murder, explicit on-page intimacy, supernatural horror, and all the things that come along with Percy Ashdown being, well, Percy Ashdown.

And this time Percy is… He's maybe even more 'Percy'.

Deep breath.

Thank you, and if you choose to go ahead, I hope you love this book too!

WH

CONTENTS

BRUGES

"Disease, insanity, and death were the angels that attended my cradle, and since then have followed me throughout my life."

MUNCH

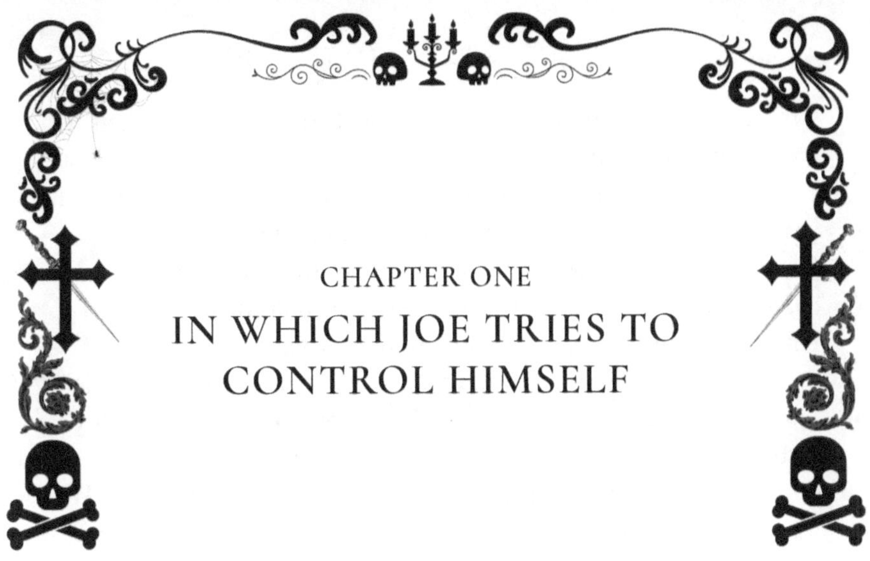

CHAPTER ONE
IN WHICH JOE TRIES TO CONTROL HIMSELF

Percy Ashdown pressed a glittering red ruby just beneath his shapely lower lip. He gently tapped it three times with the tip of his long left ring finger, keeping his face statue-still in the mirror as he reached for the next. All the while, he was well aware of the curious, slightly unsettled gaze that watched his every move.

He pretended he didn't notice.

"They look very real," came the voice from behind.

"Well-cut glass," he replied.

"Because I know it's none of my business," the voice continued, while Percy stifled a sigh, "but I would hate for you to lose them. If they *were* real."

"Then it's a good thing they're not." And he pressed the fourth tear-shaped ruby to his chin.

Joe Bruno, sitting on the elegant bed of the plush hotel room, wondered why he still cared. Since the day he took up with Percy, they had burned through more money than Joe would ordinarily see in a decade. Not his money, to be sure. A Catholic priest's wage didn't compare to whatever bottomless goldmine Percy seemed to have torn out of, and he had resolved not to trouble Percy with such quibbling concerns as the strength of facial glue versus however many carats those red jewels on his chin may or may not have been. Still, it pained him to think of a real ruby falling and sinking into the stones of some aristocrat's gravel drive, to be trod deeper and deeper into obscurity, when a single one could probably cover a month's rent for a normal person. If they were real.

But then Percy put down his eyeliner, turned, and Joe wanted nothing more than to lick those jewels from Percy's chin and swallow them down. Every last one.

Percy was dressed in full costume for a Halloween ball. He wore black from his perfectly polished shoes, over his expertly tailored trousers, to his black shirt that wrapped what Joe knew to be hard, delicious, irresistible manhood personified.

Joe's breath already came that little bit deeper, his trousers suddenly feeling a touch too tight, but it only got more trying from there.

Percy had affixed a laced corset vest over his thickly starched shirt. It featured a base of black, with red and gold trim, that sat quietly against a pattern of embroidered black roses. Joe had suggested it looked more eighteenth than nineteenth century. Percy had argued that it was an anachronism to suggest that no one from the nineteenth century had carried over taste from the eighteenth, particularly if the person in question was almost six centuries old, and particularly given that any man of taste would prefer fashion of the eighteenth rather than the nine-teenth century, anyway. Joe, in all honesty, hadn't been invested enough to argue any further, and now he was thankful for that. The corset was tighter than any regular vest could ever have been, and on Percy's ample frame, it swept over his abs and pectorals in sharp lines, leaving little to the imagination.

When he could finally raise his eyes to Percy's face, his lips dropped open. It was not the done thing at all, but Percy had left his dark hair wild, as he always did. That brought the tips to a curling frame of his blue, blue, insanely blue eyes, but now those eyes were shaded with dark eyeshadow, black and grey with a hint of malicious-looking gold, framed by deathly black eyeliner, adorned with a little blood-like splatter of tiny rubies across his right cheekbone.

His handsome fingers finished the tie of his cape, long and black and lined with red silk, the trim repeating the pattern of black roses in correspondence with his vest, and when he smiled, which he did, watching Joe's reaction, his divine lips pulled back to reveal the sharp, white tips of two very realistic-looking fake fangs. "Well?"

"You're the most beautiful man I've ever seen," Joe breathed, and following hot on the same statement was, *I will do literally anything you ask*, but Joe bottled it up with a nip of his own lip. He knew Percy well enough to know that if he said that, all their plans would be out the window, and they two would fall on the bed in a drunken orgy of pleasure, the rest of the world be damned.

But that night, they had work to do, so Joe only offered a sulky, "I don't see why I have to be Van Helsing."

"You're a *sexy* Van Helsing," Percy corrected.

"Van Helsing wasn't sexy." He raised himself from the bed to look down at his leather trousers, leather vest, leather holster, replete with a whip, knives and wooden crosses. Percy had insisted on him wearing a white shirt beneath the vest because it looked 'less evil', and he'd taken great care selecting an excessively large crucifix which he'd arranged to perfection against Joe's handsome chest. Joe's chestnut curls were getting longer, given how little time he had these days to visit a hairdresser, and they were now by his cheekbones, left free at Percy's insistence, to set off his golden-brown eyes behind his enticingly long lashes.

"He's sexy now," Percy said. "Or, you know, you could be Solomon Kane?"

Joe sent a half-hearted glare. "Are you fetishising my priestliness again?"

"I'm not." He was. "Just throwing ideas out there. You didn't want to be the Red Death—"

"Too hot."

"Or the Phantom of the Opera—"

"Too obvious."

"But there's something nice about this." Percy came to his side in front of the mirror. "We go together. We're a pair. It's romantic." He took Joe's hand to his lips and placed a gentle kiss there.

Joe watched on doubtfully. "But my sole purpose in life is to stake you."

Percy shrugged. "So it's a lot like reality then." He took a sly enjoyment of Joe's blush out of the corner of his eyes, then turned to him. "You look beautiful. Just like you always do." And Percy kissed him. Then he kissed him again. Then he kissed him again, and here found himself pushed back with some inexplicable yet arousing energy.

"The plan," Joe blurted out, turning away to still his fast-beating heart and settle his rising cock. "We need to go over the plan again."

"But we've been over it a thousand times," Percy moaned.

"But this is my first heist—"

"Second."

"First proper one, and I want to do everything exactly right." Joe took his hand and led him to their small and overcrowded dining table. "Let's go over it one more time, in excruciating detail, as though we're explaining it to someone who has no idea what we're doing or why we're doing any of this."

Percy looked across at him with a frown. "Must we?"

Joe looked back sweetly, but expectantly. "Please?"
And on a long, tired breath, "Of course, darling."

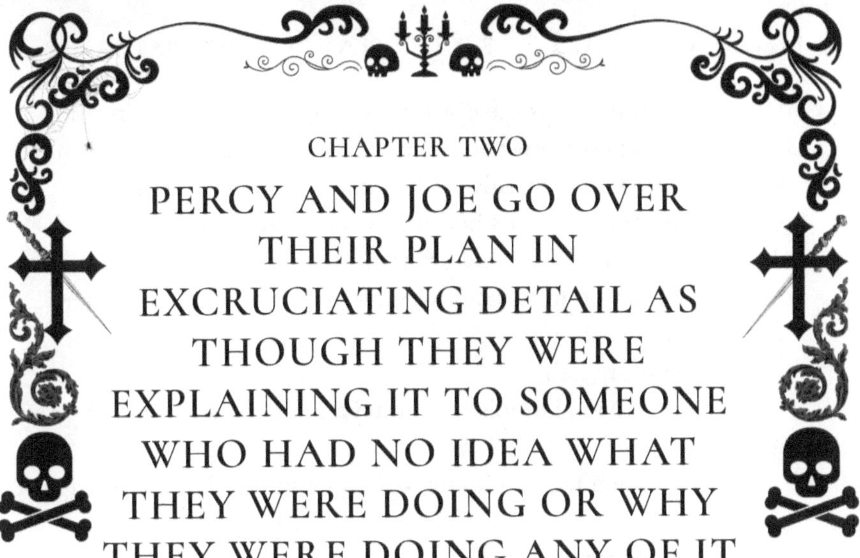

CHAPTER TWO
PERCY AND JOE GO OVER THEIR PLAN IN EXCRUCIATING DETAIL AS THOUGH THEY WERE EXPLAINING IT TO SOMEONE WHO HAD NO IDEA WHAT THEY WERE DOING OR WHY THEY WERE DOING ANY OF IT

"Our target is this man." Percy tapped his lovely finger on a picture of the smug face of a rich twenty-something. "Philippe Dubois, descendent of mediocre but wealthy aristocracy, drug kingpin, and former Eurovision winner for Belgium, who dabbles in stolen art he has no right to share a room with."

"Which explains what we're doing here in Bruges, Belgium," Joe put in.

Percy squinted. "That was a weird thing to say."

Joe frowned. "Was it?"

"Yes." Percy eyed him a little longer. "Are you sure you're feeling all right?"

"Yeah," Joe said slowly.

"Hmm," Percy huffed with one more uncertain glance. "Very well. This," and he pulled one picture from beneath another, "is where we're going tonight."

The image showed a three-storey palace, five misaligned windows spanning each floor, the top level set in a copper roof gone green, with a huge, round turret augmenting the left flank. The stone walls gave a fantastical pinkish glow, and the lot was ornamented with gothic spears and arches of iron, gargoyles, and the deathly sharp stake of a weathervane on top. Around the gorgeous building swept a greenish moat, and, all things considered, the château looked exactly like the perfect destination for a Halloween ball. Had it been anywhere near Halloween, but as Percy pointed out, such quibbles do not interest the filthy rich.

"This is Mr Dubois's country estate," Joe explained helpfully.

With a twitch in his left cheek, Percy muttered, "As you well know."

"And the reason we're going," Joe continued, excitedly draping a wide-open art catalogue over the top, "is to steal this."

The next image was full page and full colour. It featured a painting depicting two ghastly figures. In the background, laid out long on a bed, was a woman—sickly, gaunt, the paleness of her face almost indistinguishable from that of the pillow she lay upon. With dark hair and nauseating greenish sheets, it was the image of a woman either dead, or very close to dead.

In the foreground and centre of the painting stood a young child, upon a harshly, unevenly shaded orange floor. The little girl, even from the facsimile in the book, seemed to look directly into the eyes of the viewer. But then she also didn't. She stared out piercingly, but somehow her gaze was not quite there at the same time. They were the eyes of someone present but also vacant—in the room, but not. They were the eyes of someone who had been part of reality, then fled from it in madness. Tangible and intangible.

Percy had seen a very close reproduction of the painting in person, and found it disturbing enough, but Joe felt a sharp chill tap its way down his spine at the thought of being alone with the real thing, even if it hadn't been haunted.

But it was.

And they were going to steal it.

"Death and the Child by Edvard Munch," Percy announced. "Completed in 1889, it depicts Munch's own mother and sister. It captures, in vivid horror, the moment the little girl realised her mother was dead and gone forever. A moment so harrowing it haunted him for the rest of his life, and he painted it over and over in an attempt to come to terms with the trauma. He never did, of course, but whatever he distilled in this painting has gone rogue, and this particular version is said to be one of the most dangerous paintings in existence."

"One of?" Joe said, in a vague attempt to lighten the mood.

"One of," Percy replied seriously. "But this one has an added air of mystery. As you know, anyone left alone with this painting will be murdered by it. But is it the little girl or the mother who kills the victim? And why do they choose such a…" He gave pause over the correct wording, before settling on, "Such a *viscerally malignant* manner?"

Joe swallowed nervously. "You paint quite the picture."

"I do not." Percy grinned. "But I am very good at stealing them. And that's the task that now befalls us. Steal this priceless, deadly work of art, deliver it to an anonymous buyer, and receive seven hundred thousand dollars in exchange for our hard work."

"But," said Joe, "that's the brilliant part. You've had two fakes made. So we pass one of those to the buyer, they think they're getting a supernatural murder weapon, but all they really get is a nice copy."

"Meanwhile," said Percy, "we replace the real thing with the other fake and burn the haunted painting. No one gets hurt, and we walk away seven hundred thousand dollars richer."

"I've got to say," said Joe, and not for the first time, "for an art historian, you're pretty relaxed about destroying a completely irreplaceable work of art."

Percy blinked twice. "One of her victims was strangled with their own entrails."

"Good point," Joe rasped.

"I thought so," replied Percy. "But although this sounds simple enough, it's not going to be easy." A fourth sheet of paper, a blueprint of the palace, was pulled over the rest. "Dubois is giving one of his vile parties tonight. Luckily for us, it's a masquerade ball. Two of the real guests have been 'detained'—"

"In a shipping container."

"Yes, in a shipping container." And he added disapprovingly, "With blankets, soft lights, snacks, and a heater to make sure they're cosy."

Joe shrugged guiltily, so Percy continued, "And their invitations have come to us. Therefore, you are?"

"Ignatius Fürst Fugger von Durchdenwald, German lesser aristocracy. Though why I had to get the stupid nam—"

"And I am Windsor Cromwell Grosvenor Montague Smith the Third." Percy smiled. "Son of some upwardly mobile CEO or other. We enter, have a glass of champagne or two just to be seen, keep to ourselves, then quietly disappear. The party will take place in the grounds here," he tapped on the blueprint, "throughout the palace here and here, but we need to go here." The same finger slid to the far end of the map, to a circular room. "This is Dubois's murder room. Third story, at the top of a lonely turret, in a bedroom guarded by two large and dangerous men at all times. It's soundproofed, and beneath the expensive sheets of this very big bed is a lining of thick plastic to make cleanup easier. He's said to have killed eleven people in that room alone, all with the painting."

"That Belgian bastard," Joe spat.

"Quite right," Percy agreed. "He's a cold-blooded euro-trash psychopath, and you should never underestimate that sort of person."

Joe nodded. "You don't win Eurovision unless you have a ruthless streak."

"Or unless you rig it, which is the same thing, really. In this case we're dealing with the sort of no-talent sympathy vote that cheers for themselves the loudest when the expected score comes in. Keep your guard up at all times. If Dubois has even an inkling we're after that painting tonight, either one of us is liable to find ourselves thrown in the room with it. Then what do you do?"

"With a ghost?" said Joe, his confident, defiant raise of the chin making Percy a little weak at the knees. "You can't kill a ghost, as you know, so I'm going to talk to her. There must be some sort of suffering that's tying her to this life, whether mother or daughter, and I think if I can—"

"She's Norwegian," Percy replied, controlling any outward sign of his disapproval. "She won't know what you're on about."

"Oh."

"You're going to die is what you'll do if you try that, so *do not* get trapped in that room alone. Dubois's personal security are complicit, so don't hesitate to kill them if they try anything. But if worse comes to worst and you do get stuck with the picture, none of this 'saving the sad ghost' bullshit. Your only chance of survival will be to destroy the painting before she climbs out and destroys you." He reached across to a side table. "You have your cigarettes and your lighter, and here's some lighter fluid. Douse the painting well, burn it."

Joe accepted the long, slim tin hesitantly. "Do you worry that maybe starting a fire while locked in a soundproof room at the top of a turret would be a more terrible way to die?"

Percy locked eyes with him. "You remember I showed you how to pick a lock?"

"Yes, but it's hard. It takes time."

"The fire will give you more time than a murderous ghost would. You could try stabbing or shredding the picture, but I've never done that before and I can't guarantee it will work."

"Oh, but you've burned a lot of haunted paintings?" Joe quipped.

"Only two," said Percy, tidying their plans away. "And it worked both times. Might I suggest this isn't the best time for experimentation?"

Joe rolled his eyes. Of course Percy had experience burning haunted paintings. And of course he would casually drop that in at the last minute. Annoying, sexy Percy.

Annoying, sexy Percy walked around the table and settled himself back against it. He had chosen a dark, heady perfume to match his costume, and the scent drew Joe almost irresistibly, just as the rich silk of the settling cape and corset begged to be touched.

Joe held himself steady as Percy concluded, "We hid a copy of the painting in a copse on the grounds yesterday. Hopefully, it's still there. If we can winch it up and into the window of an empty bedroom, we can sneak it past the guards, and make the switch. But this part is important."

Joe scrunched up his face, because he knew what Percy was going to say, but he still couldn't understand it.

"We must try not to damage the painting on the way out. Treat it as the masterpiece it is."

"But we're going to burn it anyway," said Joe, for possibly the tenth time.

Percy sighed. Need he explain again? "This is a particularly vicious ghost, and I don't want to take any chances. Ideally, we'll exorcise the picture before we burn it to make sure there are no nasty surprises."

"Okay, but then what difference will a few bumps and scrapes make?"

"Do you want to piss her off?"

"I imagine an exorcism will piss her off."

"Joe, please." Percy sighed dramatically. "Can we just stick to the plan? It's all this going off piste during a heist that sinks everything."

"Fine." Joe also sighed. Less dramatically. "I'll be deadly careful with the precious painting before we set it on fire."

"That's all I ask, handsome." Percy leaned across and kissed Joe gently, just on the sharpest point of his impressive jawline. Joe closed his eyes and leaned into it, letting the tingle of Percy's kiss slip over him. Percy passed a hand around his neck and pulled him a little closer, taking the kiss a step up his jaw.

"Percy…" muttered Joe in half-hearted warning.

"It might go better," Percy mumbled, moving the next kiss to Joe's soft, full lips, "if I wasn't preoccupied," Percy slid a hand down over Joe's large, ever-firming cock, "with thinking about fucking you."

Joe slapped his hand away. "That's all you ever think about."

"Hmmm. True," reflected Percy, watching his handsome fiancé make for the door. His back, his ass, his strong thighs, all clad in the fanciful leather of a fictional vampire slayer.

The real crime would be to let that costume go to waste…

What a long evening it would be, especially if Joe was going to be so strict about things.

But then Joe turned and his whip slapped against his right thigh. "Well, Dracula?"

On the other hand, Percy considered, as he laced his mask over his heavily made-up eyes, maybe if he played his cards right, Joe would be stricter still.

"Anything you say, Van Helsing."

CHAPTER THREE
THE DUBOIS CHÂTEAU

Invitations and fake identifications were shown at the wide open, heavily surveilled, wrought-iron gates, and their hire-for-the-night black Mercedes drove through. It crunched to a stop, they stepped out, and as it drove on, Joe's shoulders and heart wilted. "You can't be serious."

"I told you it wouldn't be easy," Percy replied, stepping up the ancient stone stairs onto a long, grey, gothic bridge.

"You also told me it would be a moat," Joe whispered, catching up fast. "This is a lake, not a moat."

"Hence the boat," said Percy, raising a fake smile at a zombie who passed by with a slutty Freddie Krueger. Grimacing disdainfully, he followed slowly in their wake, saying quietly, "This is why we do a sweep first. Pictures and blueprints can't compare. Those documents are several years old and Dubois is just the sort of tasteless bastard to do an interior redesign—put in a home cinema and a shark tank where a three-hundred-year-old dining hall should have been. We carefully, discreetly, trace our intended path around the palace to make sure it's all as it should be, then if it is, we do it again for real."

Bolstered a little by his confidence, Joe's hand slipped beneath the folds of Percy's cloak and grasped his reassuring fingers. "Thanks for bringing me in on this."

His sweetly spoken words pulled Percy's attention almost entirely from the job at hand. "Are you having fun yet?"

Giving his slightly shy smile that Percy adored, "I think I am, actually."

With a flick of his wrist, Percy took Joe by surprise, twirling him into a cold, dark corner, wedged between the palace and the bridge's stonework, enshrouded by Percy's cape. Hot, heady perfume, Percy's warm lips on his own, the grind of Percy's thigh between his.

"You said, 'discreet'," Joe laughed, not at all inclined to leave the shelter Percy had created, wondering somewhere in the back of his mind how so very few weeks had turned him from virgin priest into sex-obsessed, high-class criminal.

Then Percy whispered, "I love you," and Joe knew exactly how it had happened.

Percy kissed him one more time, softly, tenderly, then released him from the delightful prison. Joe stepped unsteadily towards the light of the gigantic doors, slipping his fingers out of Percy's grasp seconds before they stepped through.

Wealth assaulted him like a Ming dynasty vase smashing his face to pieces. Shocking wealth that Percy was accustomed to, that set Joe on edge every time.

The ceiling was two storeys high in the entrance hall, blinding white, thickly adorned with elaborate cornices all around. A ponderous crowning mould lay in the centre, its grapes and leaves licking and lilting down to a spectacular chandelier, where thousands of perfectly cut crystals shone their orderly superiority over all below.

To their left, a wide staircase split and regrouped over and over to lead the guests to the recesses of the palace in a display almost as disorienting as a painting by Escher. In front and to the right, more arched stone doorways that led to who knew where.

Joe should have known, because he had studied the layout, but faced with the light and the statues, and the actual knights' armour that was too stereotypical to be true, and, worst of all, more people than he had imagined, all knowledge fled. So many people kissing cheeks and laughing through perfect teeth and too-high cheekbones, and all who apparently knew one another, and so many, wall to wall, shoulder to shoulder.

That was when Joe realised.

It was impossible.

How had he imagined they would sneak a priceless work of art out of a literal castle in the middle of a party? This was probably the time to inform Percy of the error of his ways—he must not have realised the enormity of the task any more than Joe had.

Yet Percy only surveyed the room with calculating eyes, plucked two glasses of champagne from a waiter's tray, and nodded for Joe to follow.

The guests were dressed in considered, tailored, flamboyant costumery—well, all except slutty Freddy Krueger—but the crowd still parted for Percy as though he had been the Red Death himself. Only sexier. Whether it was lust or envy, pause was given wherever he walked, as though they all sensed he belonged front and centre. He sipped from his crystal flute, threw a charming smile with a glitter of ruby wherever he thought it might work best, and he began a smooth reconnaissance of the mansion, pressing a hand back to Joe when they passed through an especially narrow or dark passage, to check he was still within arm's reach.

How, Joe knew not, but Percy led them unerringly through the exact procession of rooms they had practised in theory so many times. Richly adorned lounges, excessively decorated sitting rooms, disused but expensively stocked and tidy kitchens, and to a square living area at the far end of the palace, which sat at the base of the stairs that led to the turret.

Unfortunately, that room was neither empty nor depleted as they had hoped it might be. That room had become the drug den.

Half a dozen guests were making use of a large, rich, oak coffee table, polished to a glass-like finish, perfect for lining up and snorting lines of cocaine, while another dozen or more stood around talking. But even with the large gathering, terrible music played loudly, low lights illuminated very little, and, all things considered, it should have been a cinch to pass through the preoccupied group and up the stairs relatively unnoticed.

Percy took the chance and moved seamlessly through the space, but just as he approached the stairs, he diverted. Joe watched the dark shapes of two large men descend and take up position at the base of the stairs.

Security.

Not ideal.

Percy turned, and in a starkly atypical move (for anyone who knew him), he bumped clumsily into a man whose face had heretofore been dipped and hidden behind a rolled Belgian franc note. A man who, when standing, revealed bright blue sequined hot pants beneath a Belgian-flag-coloured body-suit, topped with oversized, red-rimmed fake glasses. A man they both recognised as Philippe Dubois.

"Oh, god," Percy couldn't help responding to the ocular onslaught.

"Watch it, Dracula," Dubois sneered.

"Please accept my apologies." Percy stepped deftly around him.

Joe followed Percy out of the room, and some hot, confusing time later, fresh, cool air swept over them, as they passed into the large courtyard. If it could be called a courtyard. The huge square was hemmed in on three sides by guesthouses, stables, and a garage for sixteen expensive cars, open, so everyone could see the contents. A wide, circular stone drive was heavily peopled by chatting guests, and in the middle sat a large, brightly illuminated pool. Beyond that, the wide moat-lake enclosed the lot.

"This is more like it," said Percy, finding a relatively quiet spot against a wall, pulling his golden cigarette case free and snapping it open for Joe.

"It's not going to work," Joe informed him immediately, loosening two cigarettes from their gentle clasp.

"Don't be like that," Percy grumbled. He accepted the smoke Joe shoved between his beautiful lips, and he flicked his richly etched, matching golden lighter open.

"Look around." Joe shared the flame, then took a desperately needed deep inhalation. "We cannot sneak a painting past this many people."

"I don't see anyone in the moat." Percy passed a glance towards the moss-laden water sparkling in the dark. "It's filthy. It's well-hidden. It takes us right beneath the bedroom we need." He turned towards Joe, leaning a shoulder into the building. "Don't lose your nerve now. We've been over this a thousand times."

"I still don't see why we can't just sneak in there, destroy it, and then, I don't know, jump in the lake or something."

"I'm not getting this corset wet. Do you know how much this cost?"

Joe grimaced. "I don't want to know."

"If you knew, you wouldn't want to risk the seven hundred thousand." Joe threw back some champagne to hide his irritation as Percy went on, "We've been hired to do a job and we're going to do it. If we burn the painting publicly, word will get out it's been destroyed, and our buyer will be off with the cash. But more importantly, while this is your first real criminal enterprise, please keep in mind that I have a reputation to uphold."

Joe watched Percy studying the courtyard, and Joe studied his chin and cheek to see that all his rubies were still present. He'd made a reasonable point. Percy had told him from the start that he, an art historian well respected in his field, also trafficked fine arts and artefacts. And Joe took that for what it was. High-class crime—rich people passing paintings between one another. None of it held much interest for him. But then he found out Percy was also, on occasion, a hit man. Though as far as he knew, he tended only to kill dreadful people. That was charming in its way, the way being that Joe adored Percy and could think no ill of him. But to hear the term 'reputation' set Joe's mind wandering. Who was Percy Ashdown to the world at large? To the criminal underworld? To museums and galleries and universities? To the elite world of princesses and billionaires he navigated as well as that of the small, privileged college where they'd first met over an exorcism.

Growing up, Joe's entire life had been one small village high in the Apennines of Italy. Then, following the incident, he had joined the Church. Demons, ghosts, all awful and dead and dangerous things became his obsession and his purpose. He had been sent to fight them numerous times. He had been to Hell and back. He had stolen, transferred and hidden protected supernatural objects, and here and only here his path intersected with Percy's. Percy was drawn to the same supernatural relics Joe was, and that was the spark that originally brought them together.

But for all the wealth of the Church, it was always cloistered away. Many a golden hall had Joe walked, but outside those secret rooms he was paid only a small stipend, living on Church-owned land, taking relative ownership of a beautiful cottage and cathedral only because it was one of the most dangerous locations of any church, anywhere, and no one else was stupid enough to accept it.

The world Joe inhabited day to day was nothing like Percy's, and he wasn't sure he would ever truly understand its inner workings. Or ever know any of the people who knew a different 'Percy Ashdown' to the one he adored.

So what could he do? Back out and leave Percy to face the murderous painting alone? Or trust that Percy knew his work well enough to have the reputation he spoke of? Well enough to be able to pull this off...

Percy spun around to him at that exact moment and thrust a shapely hand beneath his chin. Onto this he tap-tapped a small line of white powder, then raised his eyebrows suggestively. "Courage?"

Joe gasped, bulging eyes scanning the crowd. "Where did you get that?"

"I pickpocketed Dubois."

He may have been lightly shocked, but Joe couldn't hide the fact he was also impressed with how smoothly he'd done it. "Did you know that was him?"

"Actually, no." Percy laughed. "He was just the easiest mark."

"And how do you know what that even is?" asked Joe, eyeing the powder.

"Well, you're hardly going to bring speed to a party like this."

"That's it? That's your drug safety talk of tonight?"

"Look." Percy dabbed his finger hurriedly into the line and thrust it towards Joe's mouth.

"Get that away from me!" Joe snapped, slapping at his hand.

With a heavy sigh, Percy shoved up a lip, exposing his sharp fang, and ran the powder over his gums. He held up a finger for one, two, three seconds. "Numbing," he announced. "It's clearly cocaine. Just like I said."

Joe tsked in defeat, pulled Percy's hand close, and sniffed the line away, soon coughing on the rotten taste at the back of his throat, which he washed down with the good champagne. "You know, you probably shouldn't have stolen that."

"He'll never know it was me," said Percy, doing the same. "Now, I will escort you to the room—"

"I don't need an escort," Joe declared, already emboldened by the fast-acting drugs.

"I will accompany my compellingly sexy fiancé upstairs," Percy corrected. "Then I'll bring the fake painting across in the boat. Don't leave that window unless you have trouble, in which case, I'll know not to come. But if you're there, throw the rope down, I'll attach it, then I'll come and help you pull the painting up."

"This is almost too easy," Joe said on a wide grin.

Percy smiled back. "Drugs are doing their thing?"

With a happy nod, "We should bring this to every heist."

"All right, darling," said Percy, trying to refocus his attention. "Let's go insi—"

"You look really nice." Joe's head tilted to the side, his speech coming a little sheepishly. "I like your rubies."

Percy lowered a stern eyebrow. "Did you have dinner? That's gone straight to your head."

"It's not that." Joe let a hand slide softly down Percy's chest, moving his body closer. "I've been thinking it all night. I just thought I should say it. Out loud. I'm glad you wore them. You're beautiful."

It was a dangerous thing, Joe's allure. Enough to put Percy out of business entirely if he kept on that way. Percy might have considered him a natural flirt, charmingly artless as he was, but Joe's flirting was never directed at anyone else. Ever. Small as Percy thought the weakness in himself, there was something particularly captivating about that. Being the sole object of Joe's adoration was more intoxicating than their ill-gotten cocaine, and Percy was on the verge of losing his battle to keep his villainous professionalism, therefore he arrested Joe's hand before it could drift any lower. "One more word, and I'm taking you to the stables."

Joe felt Percy's palm settle across his challenging lips as he attempted to speak again. A promising thrill of vampire teeth nipped his neck, settled with the giddying tickle of Percy's tongue all the way to his ear, then he slipped away in a swirl of red silk and black roses, leaving Joe to chase breathlessly after him.

CHAPTER FOUR
PERCY COMPLICATES
MATTERS

Percy and Joe retraced their steps into the house, but were halted halfway through their journey by furious words shouted in a thick Belgian accent from deep within the house: "Find that bastard, Dracula!"

"Ignatius! This way!"

"Don't call me that!" snapped Joe, running full pelt after Percy, back outside, around the corner of the building and into darkness.

They pulled up, backs against a cold wall, where Percy proposed, "If we skirt the dark side of the lesser buildings, we can find our way to the back bridge, and hide out in the copse until this dies down a little. Then we'll cross together in the boat, scale the outer wall and break into the turret."

"Or," suggested Joe, "you could lose the rubies, teeth, cloak and corset, and no one will know who you are."

"Never!" And he was off again.

Behind the stables, the pair traced the treacherous edge of the moat, not a millimetre wider than Joe's tight, lace-to-the-top, brown knee-high boots, which were only marginally wider than Percy's black shoes. Remarkably, they both made it, step by tentative step, to the far end of the stables.

"Shit!" said Percy.

"What?" panicked Joe.

"We need champagne," said Percy.

"What?" panicked Joe.

"Champagne! If we have to wait that whole time in the copse, we're going to need drinks." Hiding himself in the shadows, Percy nodded for Joe to follow until they could see the courtyard again. "A waiter! Run."

"I'm not breaking our cover over a drink!"

"What cover? They're not looking for a sexy Van Helsing. You're my natural enemy. They'll never suspect we're together."

"But—then—what…" Joe floundered. "I didn't need to do that circumventing the moat thing? I could have just walked to the copse?"

"I mean, if that works better for you, I guess…" Percy looked down at his shoes, kicking in the dust. "It might be considered somewhat antisocial—"

"That works better for me." Joe strode off handsomely to obtain alcohol for copse sitting.

Percy frowned hard at his back, then continued his excruciatingly slow procession around the edge of the property behind the garage, and on and on, slipping and saving himself five times before he found the bridge. He clambered along the exterior edge, locked out of it as he was by a seemingly endless series of tall, sharp iron railings, until finally he had crossed the moat and stepped down onto the spongy, damp, muddy ground of the private woods. Leaves crunched beneath his feet as he crouched low and ran stealthily to where he soon discovered the scent of cigarette smoke, and a very smug Joe lying back beside one empty wine glass, halfway through a second.

"You might have waited," Percy muttered, dropping to the ground beside him and snatching his cigarette.

"Do you have any idea how long you took?" Joe protested. "But look. I got a whole bottle."

Appreciative eyes ran over both the bottle and Joe's reclining frame. "I forgive you."

He lay down, and there they enjoyed a quiet smoke, another line of cocaine each, discussed the virtues of Manet versus Monet, and passed a pleasant fifteen minutes or so before deciding they should get a move on, what with the sun expected to rise at dawn and all.

The replacement painting, nailed gently into a pale pine box, had been lowered over the wall some twenty-four hours earlier into what they hoped was the thickest part of the woods. That delivery also included a tightly wrapped self-inflating raft and a bag of thieving supplies such as a crowbar, hammer, nails, and whatever else Percy had thought they might need. The lot was found exactly where they had left it, and the pair set off through the woods at some distance from the house. They made fast progress to the one side of the palace that sat in darkness, all moat right to the wall, nowhere to walk or slip except into the water.

With the wrench of a string, the raft inflated, accompanied by a hideously loud wheeze that kept both Percy and Joe frozen and appallingly anxious for a good twenty seconds after it was complete.

"I think we're good." Percy shoved it into the water, and jumped aboard, almost sinking the flimsy thing rather than get his shoes wet. With little more than a resigned scowl, Joe set his own steadying boot into the shallow water to pass the wooden crate across. The crate was only about forty inches either way, perhaps four inches thick, but it was unwieldy, with sharp, unworked corners, so Percy sank down low, holding it on his knees to keep it from ripping the raft. Joe piled in behind him, plunging the boat dangerously low in the water, and together they made slow progress to the stone wall of the mansion, using the smallest, feeblest plastic paddles they were able to pack.

With an unsettling tearing sound, the raft eventually swept against the rough stone of the palace wall, but it held. All was going brilliantly, until Percy lifted his chin to Joe and said, "Pass me your whip."

"What?" Joe glanced down at that whip, marvellously adorning his manly thigh. "It's not a real whip, Percy."

"Of course it's a real whip," said Percy, losing patience and wrenching the thing, which resulted in Joe and the painting very nearly being flung overboard, saved only by a hard thump against the wall.

"Percy!"

"Now hold this."

Joe took the painting, begrudgingly, and settled down into the boat to let Percy do whatever ridiculous thing was about to land them first in the water, then in prison.

But Percy flung his cape back, locked eyes on an iron flourish overhead, and twirled his whip with a slight sway of his hips that took all Joe's self-control to not reach for him. The whip was set free, and landed, first try, with a tight grip on its target. Percy wrenched it back sharply.

Joe could control himself no longer. Running a hand over Percy's shapely calves, "That first bedroom. If you get us in there unscathed, we'll take a ten-minute break."

With one hot glance at Joe, "Deal."

Strong fingers twisted in the whip as it dangled between Percy's tight legs, and before Joe knew it, Percy was off the boat and scaling the wall.

"You're incredible," said Joe.

"Nothing to it, handsome." Percy raised his leg a little further than he really needed to, posing magnificently, but putting some unexpected strain on his weakening fingers in doing so.

"I can't believe you're mine," Joe marvelled.

"You like that?" Percy subtly flexed his biceps as best he could.

"I do," Joe sighed.

It was, all things considered, stupid to think he could make it across the expanse of the window unseen, and a more measured man would simply have ascended to the stonework above the window to make the crossing, then enjoyed his filthy, delicious reward. But Percy thrived on Joe's adoration, and therefore, he took the risk.

With an impressive twist, and a sideways run up, clutching the whip tight, he leapt from one side of the window towards the other. But it was a mansion, after all, and the window was wide. Wider somehow than his slightly drunk, somewhat high, love-addled brain had calculated. And therefore, Percy smashed straight through the old glass window, and slammed down hard on the wooden drugs table to a dramatic puff of white powder and scream of alarm from all those in attendance.

He quickly got his bearings, jumped to his feet and flung the whip back out the window, hoping no one had noticed it. And to further that scheme, Percy announced loudly, "I've come to create a diversion!"

"Fuck," Joe muttered to himself, steadying the whip against the dark wall. He pulled some rope from their bag to strap the painting to his back, and wondered how much easier this job might have been if Percy either didn't steal the drugs, or just took off his rubies.

"Dracula!" came a shout from inside.

Percy's sharp eyes shot across to the furious, much-higher-than-he-was, lurid figure of Philippe Dubois, who pointed an angry finger at him. "You owe me six thousand francs worth of cocaine."

Joe groaned internally as he heard Percy reply, "Fuck you, Dubois. I snorted the lot."

"Then…" Here Dubois pulled a large knife from god knew where, and levelled it at Percy. "I'll take one finger for each grand you owe me."

Joe didn't need to be inside to know what would happen next.

Percy's eyes lit, and a wide smile broke across his handsome face, pearlescent fangs and blood-red jewels sparkling keenly. "Let's dance."

CHAPTER FIVE
PERCY LEADS

It would take a lot of cocaine for almost anyone to feel confident in their ability to take Percy Ashdown on when he was spoiling for a fight. He was tall, muscular, always with a touch of madness about his compelling eyes, but he was very rarely standing atop the central table of a room towering over everyone else dressed extravagantly in the garb of a well-known killer.

Dubois may have been arrogant to a fault, but he was also rich to the point of moral ruination, therefore he yelled, "Security!"

He needn't have. The two men in black uniforms, who were already wishing they'd taken that other job, moved from the base of the stairs to either side of Percy. The guests backed up a little to enjoy the drama, hoping they had enough distance to avoid being hurt in the crossfire.

In a very tired voice, one of the guards said, "Kom alsjeblieft daar vandaan."

"I don't speak Flemish," Percy replied. "But 'no'".

The men, however, understood his refusal perfectly well. They threw a few pointed glances across at one another, while

Percy stood very still, waiting to see who would make a move first. It may have been nothing more than a nervous twitch, but whatever it was, the one on the right copped Percy's shoe on his chin for the offence of a sudden gesture. His head flipped up and back and smashed into the stone wall. Percy twisted around and brought the back of his heel across the other man's cheek. That man was large, and didn't move except for a recoverable snap of his neck, so Percy rebalanced himself and gave him a jumping front kick to the nose instead.

Blood. Blood was always good because it unsettled the opponent triple-fold. The guard looked at the red just long enough for Percy to smack a palm into his chin, and he was down.

The first guy had recovered to the point of unsteady standing, but he wasn't the target any more than the man with blood streaming down his face was, and Percy had no real interest in crippling either of them that night. He jumped down from the table and closed the distance between himself and Dubois in four short steps. Dubois's face remained defiant, as falsely smug as it could be in that situation, and Percy was determined to correct it.

He snapped Dubois's wrist back, and his knife clattered to the floor. Percy got one good punch in, his fist striking Dubois's cheekbone hard enough to break it, but within a half second of contact he was wrenched backwards and thrown to the floor. He felt the boot of a new security guard on his chest and locked an arm around the back of the man's supporting leg. He rammed hard into it, the leg gave at the knee, Percy twisted over and smashed a hand down on his kneecap, felling him into a screaming mess.

Percy was aware of Dubois in his peripheral vision, baying for his blood as he pretended to protest against being dragged from the room by even more security, but Percy was unable to follow because of the strong arm that tightened around his neck and jerked him backwards. Percy threw a sharp elbow into the man's ribs three times and met nothing but solid muscle.

It was a cheap shot, but Percy knew Joe might, by that time, be in a room alone with a deadly painting, so he flicked his wrist, releasing his dagger from its holster, and dug the blade into the man's thigh. He aimed for the edge, trying to avoid any major arteries as best he could, but the man inadvertently flinched and Percy took a larger slice than he had intended to.

"Fuck! Sorry." He turned, smashed the man's head down hard onto his knee and let him drop, unconscious and not in excruciating pain. For now.

The other guests had been forced out of the room with Dubois. There were four large men writhing on the ground, and Percy was just about to make a break for it when he heard the click.

He paused, back to the gun, blood dripping from his dagger.

"Zet het neer," said the shaky voice.

Percy guessed he was being asked to put the knife down. So he had a decision to make. Do that and risk a fist fight against a gun? Risk being hauled off to jail over this and leave Joe to deal with everything by himself? Or drop, aim, and fling the dagger into the man's neck, killing him in one clean blow. Because if Percy let him live, if Joe couldn't do it all by himself, how many more people would Dubois kill with the painting?

And above all, was this stranger's life worth risking Joe's?

With that final reflection, the man's fate was as good as sealed.

CHAPTER SIX
A LESSON IN MURDER

Percy slowly, very slowly, lowered himself towards the floor. He could hear the laboured breathing of the man behind him. He could all but feel the gun on his back.

He would have to be fast. A very quick roll to the left, a half turn, and fling the knife at the neck. Failure to murder would invite a fatal response, so a clean death was the only option.

Percy played the moment over in his mind. He would get one brief glance only. It had to be exact.

The muscles of his abdomen, his thighs, his right biceps tightened as a steel-cold calm settled.

But then, "Percy, don't!" came a familiar whisper from the shadows.

Joe, who had silently descended the stairs from a bedroom above, knew that look on Percy's face.

Percy scowled into the darkness. He could hardly get involved in an argument right now. He could hardly slow his slow descent any more than he already had. But he'd also had his concentration thrown off. And it had been a nice night so far, and he didn't want to piss Joe off by killing an innocent in front of him.

Then, in a flash, his troubles turned to humour with a slice of brown leather, and Joe's ridiculous idea that he could wrest the gun from the hands holding it with a flick of his whip.

He did manage to get the whip out into the room, but unfortunately it clipped his own shoulder first, resulting in some loud swearing, the redirection of the gun, a bullet slimly missing Joe as he slipped down the stairs, and the flop of misused weaponry onto the floor.

With a pleased chuckle, Percy did his roll, but took a little more care with his bewildered target, throwing the dagger into his right arm instead of his neck. He had weighed his chances that would be his good arm, and either way, the gun fell to the floor. Percy lunged forward and slid it back to Joe, then leapt up and smacked an elbow into the man's face. "What the hell was that?" Percy laughed.

Joe's eyes went to the flaccid whip. "You made it look easy."

"It is easy," said Percy. "It's all in the wrist." He winked suggestively at Joe as the man attempted to stumble to his feet.

"Could you please not sexualise my whip?" said Joe.

Percy looked him over with smouldering eyes. "You sexualised it the second you touched it." Then he turned back and broke the man's nose with a thoroughly disorienting headbutt.

"Percy, no." Joe winced. "Don't hurt yourself."

Percy, immaculately, confoundingly unhurt, took the man in a headlock and hauled him across the room. He shoved him against the sill of the broken window, picked up his legs, and tossed him into the moat.

Joe was at Percy's side in a second. "What did you just do?" Searching frantically, he pointlessly repeated, "What did you just do?"

"Come, Ignatius. We have a painting to steal." And he made for the stairs, but hearing no footsteps behind him, he sighed heavily, forced to turn back to Joe, half hanging out the window.

"Where is he? What if he can't swim?"

"Then the problem's solved," said Percy. "But there will be more of them soon, and I don't want to die tonight, so better him than us. Let's go."

Joe, eyes still on the water, began unbuttoning his vest. "He could be anyone. He's not a henchman, you know, he's in uniform. He's just a hired guard. What if he's got kids? A partner? What will his parents say?"

Percy placed a firm hand on Joe's shoulder. "You are not going in there."

Joe shoved him off. "Yes, I am." He threw down the vest and mounted the window.

"Joe!" Percy's strong arm threw him back to the floor just as gently as Percy could manage, which was understandably still quite rough. "Behave yourself! We came to do a job."

"Exactly!" Joe bounded up irritatingly fast.

"Look, I'll…" And with a remembrance of his nice corset, Percy stopped abruptly before volunteering to go in. He did, nevertheless, have the wherewithal to take up Joe's whip and search for the man. "Look. Over there. Flailing." He indicated towards some splashing close by. "He's fine."

Joe put a hand on Percy's biceps to look past his handsome frame. "I don't think flailing is 'fine' in a lake."

"It's just a moat," Percy argued. "It's probably not even very deep."

"The literal purpose of a moat is to be inaccessible," Joe said, all too sensibly.

"Then we're living proof this moat is bullshit." Percy arrested another of Joe's attempts to jump into the water before groaning loudly. "Fine. I'll save him. But if that painting kills more people because I'm busy doing this, every one of those deaths is on your head."

Joe watched open-mouthed as Percy aimed the whip. "Percy, that's an awful thing to say!"

"Sorry. It was, a bit." He flung the whip out to the man. "It will, in fact, be his fault for not having the decency to just drown."

After a few attempts, the rudely un-drowned man caught hold of the whip, and Percy pulled him back to the relative safety of the château with a great deal of huffing and grumbling, and quiet, steadily rising adoration from Joe.

Once the guard was helped back through the window, Percy ascertained that he did indeed understand English, and explained that he could choose to remain silent in a locked bedroom for the period of one hour, or he could have his throat slit there on the floor by Percy's hand.

The man, wet and wounded as he was, chose the former, and was soon escorted up the turret to the first floor room where Joe had kicked the window in and stashed the fake painting, along with their bag of burglar's goods. Percy suggested they tie the man up and shove him in the wardrobe, but Joe only gave the man the quilt from the bed to keep warm and asked him politely to please stay quiet.

It made Percy's job a little harder, but he determined to use the situation as a learning experience.

He took the opportunity to disable the bedroom door as they left, but they had only just reached their destination, third floor murder room, when the shout went out from the window below that the offenders were in the turret.

Joe quietly suffered through one of Percy's more withering looks for all of ten seconds, before he blurted out, "I'm sorry, okay?"

All too smugly, Percy leaned his shoulder against the heavy

door. "Never mind. If Dubois knows we're in here, and if he has any sense at all, he'll simply leave us to our gruesome deaths."

"And if he doesn't?" asked Joe.

Percy only offered an unhelpful, "We'll worry about that later. First, let's try not to die by ghost."

CHAPTER SEVEN
PERCY AND JOE TRY NOT TO DIE BY GHOST

Percy dropped to his knees and pulled a lock pick from his pocket.

Joe tried the door.

It was locked.

Percy frowned at him, then passed the pick into the keyhole. "Now, when we get inside," he said, working slowly and carefully, as though they weren't about to be caught by a eurotrash killer, "you need to keep your eyes on the painting. I'll take it off the wall and loosen it from the frame, but you need to watch both mother and child carefully and constantly and let me know if either one moves."

"Do you think…" Joe felt faintly ridiculous asking the question, but it was what it was, so he pushed on. "Do you think she crawls out of it like a living person? Or do you think the spirit just escapes? Are you sure it will be visible?"

"I'm not remotely sure," Percy said, pushing a second lock pick in. "And to tell you the truth, if she's invisible, we're completely fucked."

"Oh. Well, that's good to know. Thanks for that, Percy."

The lock clicked open, and Percy looked up with a grin. "You wouldn't be here if you weren't enjoying the danger."

True enough, but all that changed as Percy passed quickly into the room, as Joe stumbled in after him, and as Joe's eyes settled on the horrifying object. Percy moved deftly around him, jamming the door shut with a chair, cracking the wooden case open, getting everything ready, but Joe's gaze was locked on. His heart rate doubled, a tingle of sweat and a punch of adrenaline screaming at him that this was the time to flee.

The painting was undoubtedly an object of evil. It wreaked evil. It seethed death and hatred and despair, and he didn't let his eyes leave for a second as his entire body revolted. He refused even to blink.

It was down from the wall. Percy leaned it against the bedhead and took his dagger to the back of it. With the excruciating care of an art historian, combined with the smooth reflexes of a cat burglar, he set to work. Although he was intent, he called to Joe, "Are we all right?"

"I think so." But had the mother's head shifted ever so slightly? He studied her. No. Maybe? Had the little girl's expression changed? It was still harrowed, heartbroken, yet now… Was that a hint of consciousness? "Can't you go faster?"

Joe couldn't see Percy's face. He only heard the scraping and chipping behind the giant frame. "There's some very shoddy work back here. I just want to be careful."

Her hand. The little girl's hand. Was it a little lower on her face? "We're burning it anyway," Joe insisted, a little more urgently. "Just rip it out."

"It's a work of art—"

"Oh, fuck!" Footsteps sounded loud on the stone stairs outside. Joe's eyes were drawn irresistibly to the shaking door handle.

"I really hope you're watching the painting," came a calm reminder from behind the frame.

Panicked eyes flung back to the canvas. "Sorry. Sorry, she's…" The sheet. The sheet had fallen from the bed. The mother lay out long and still in her nightgown. "Oh shit. Percy, I think it's the mother," said Joe. "She's moved. I think she's coming."

"Stay calm." There was another loud snap. "Don't take your eyes off her."

But it made no difference where Joe looked now. Her sallow head turned slowly, slowly, unstoppably, as the dark dead eyes rolled their watery gaze onto Joe. "Percy, she's coming."

Percy worked faster, but just as determined, just as carefully, extricating the painting, a touch of sweat about his brow.

"Open!" came the shout from the door. Banging, shouting in Flemish, the handle being wrenched uselessly.

The woman began to rise. She made her way, if such a thing can be imagined, just like a painting. Her movements were a sort of fluid, but a sort that defied the laws of physics. Her body sat straight up in the bed, but her unseeing face that stared and flopped and sagged was pulled along behind her, relentlessly locked onto Joe, watching emptily from black slits as one utterly untenanted. As a corpse from which any soul has flown, only more wrong somehow.

Joe took an involuntary step back from the impossible thing. It was a ghost. A plain and ordinary ghost, and Joe should have been fine with that. He'd fought ghosts before. But after his possession, which had happened well before he took up with Percy, his duty and his bravery had taken a beating and what he felt more than both those things was fear. Fear that came with the knowledge of what that creature might do to him, not if it reached his body, but if it got inside.

"Percy," he whispered.

The reply came back just as though Percy understood his

every thought. "I'm here, handsome. If she gets out, we'll take care of her."

The pounding on the door reached the same deafening crescendo as the pounding of Joe's pulse in his ears, but he watched the mother so intently in her foul movement that it was too late when he realised.

The little girl. She had sunk down. And down. And the moment he finally understood was the moment he saw her grim little fingers curling around the frame. Joe ripped a dagger from his belt. "Percy, it's both of them."

There was a loud crack as Percy broke something apart. There was a sickening flopping sound as the mother fell to the floor in the picture. He heard the echoing count to three outside the door as the guards organised themselves to kick it in. Joe tightened his damp hand on the knife. And then a hiss. A hiss escaped the painting as the little girl's face pushed over the edge, pulled into the reality of his world, full of malevolent intent, boiling hatred, the unmistakable craving to spill blood, and all of it directed at Joe.

She dropped onto the bed.

The door banged open.

Everything went black.

CHAPTER EIGHT
SOMETHING UNEXPECTED

"Give me your belt." Percy had already unbuckled it and was pulling it free. Joe couldn't see a thing in the dark, but Percy slid the metal buckle over the handle of what must have been the walk-in wardrobe's door and looped the belt tightly, so tightly around a rail that the door was effectively locked.

Percy placed a protective hand on Joe's stomach, pushing him back a little behind him, as he took a step away from the door, waiting for someone—or something—to try it.

They stood, motionless, for what felt like an eternity of hot, tense silence, hearing nothing but their strained breath in the dark.

Finally, Joe felt Percy turn, felt his hands, warm, soft, but so full of safety, one on each cheek, and his head was guided gently down onto Percy's shoulder, a strong arm enveloping him. Joe fell into Percy, where Percy kissed his hair and whispered, "We're safe."

Joe's heartbeat, and Percy's heartbeat against his, and calming breaths, and not another sound besides.

It might have been the comfort. It might have been the fear. Or the cocaine, champagne, or the nerve-shaking jolt of adrenaline, but before he knew what he was about, Joe had grasped Percy and brought his mouth down against his own.

Whatever madness it was, Percy reacted in kind, with one kiss, then another. The taste of him, the scent of him, and all Joe knew was that he craved more. He moved an arm beneath Percy's, sliding his fingers over his silk-clad, muscular back. Percy's hands took a strong hold of Joe's waist, and turned him, shoved his back against the door. For the second time that night, he felt Percy's thigh push between his own, only this time it was calculated to grind against his hardening cock. And Christ, it felt good.

The handle at Joe's side shook, sending a jolt of panic through him. His head turned automatically towards the sound, but was wrenched back sharply by Percy's hand, and held there with a kiss. A thud against the door slammed into his back, once and again, and, "Shhhh," Percy whispered in his ear.

Well, no shit, Percy, thought Joe. It clearly wasn't the ideal time to make a lot of noise, on the off-chance anyone or anything in that room hadn't noticed them slipping into the wardrobe. But, one delicious second later, Joe understood Percy's instruction in full.

Percy sank his teeth—his sharp vampire teeth—deep into Joe's neck at the exact same moment he somehow managed to take Joe's dick out of his trousers and into his experienced grasp. Joe's lips opened in a silent exclamation of ecstatic shock, profound stupefaction, and he didn't know what else. It was pain, sharp pain that drew real blood, and it was pleasure. And when Percy licked his neck, when he slid his thumb across Joe's slit, massaging a circle around the head of his cock, it was all very close to overwhelming. Every one of Joe's senses was on high alert as the door banged behind him, as the handle rattled against his hip, as Percy's tongue violently found his own, then as Percy dropped to his knees.

"What are you doing!"

"Shhh!"

Joe's every nerve was a frazzled mess. Should he stop him? Very probably. Whatever was waiting just outside the door, whether it was security or ghosts, was bad. Very bad, but this was—

"Teeth!" Joe whisper-shouted at the first touch, which got a snicker from Percy, who removed the tips of his teeth in a flash.

He should very definitely stop him, but—

Percy's mouth slid over Joe's cock, and the warmth of him took over his entire body. There was nothing, nothing in that first beautiful moment, nothing but the all-encompassing, glorious, thick heat of delight. And Percy. Beautiful, perfect Percy, with his gorgeous mouth that was so perfectly fuckable.

A bang hit the door again, pulling Joe back to their sick reality, but even as he flinched, he felt the vibration of Percy's soft moan along the base of his cock. How his tongue could manage to take in every ridge and mound as though it was his personal mission to lick every millimetre in full, all while applying the perfect pressure, was beyond Joe's understanding. Percy's mastery of cock was as thorough as his understanding of fine art. Indeed, he raised the act to an art, and just as one may fall into rapture, become overwhelmed in the presence of aesthetic genius, so it was when Percy took Joe's dick between his lips.

He didn't go fast. His movements were long and slow, wet and hot, and pleasantly torturous. Even when Joe's head fell back against the door, even when Percy had to hold him in place with a hand on his abs, even when he breathed a plea for more, Percy never changed or relented the teasing, building rhythm.

The slick heat of Percy's mouth on Joe's dick became the

entire world. His only thought was pleasure, and with every whisper of desperation it crowded in on him, became his singular obsession. All faded into Percy and Percy's unrelenting, unforgiving mastery of Joe. His complete control.

Percy didn't seem to think about or even notice the handle. He didn't seem to care in the least about the banging door or whatever was going on out there. His only thought was Joe, and that in itself was mesmerising, and it pulled Joe into the same beautiful moment that was just the two of them. Where there was nothing stark and terrifying. Where it was only that untouchable, impenetrable, invincible something that it was to be loved by Percy.

He let himself sink into it, and before long, it could have been the apocalypse for all he cared. They could have been alone in the centre of Hell, but he had Percy. And so he took Percy's thick hair by the roots and sank his dick deep into Percy's abiding mouth. And he fucked him. Really fucked him, and in the heat and the bliss, there in that devastatingly beautiful suspension of existence, he took back the piece of himself so precariously misplaced by fear. Percy yielded to him, complied with every thrust, told him with his tongue and his provocative groans and his grip on Joe's thighs that he would do anything for him.

Powerful, untouchable Percy, on his knees and begging to be fucked in the mouth.

He used Percy exactly as he wanted to, and he thrust faster and more thoroughly, pulling Percy tighter against him, needing him, desperate for him until the dark and the perfume and the heat and the freedom and ecstasy reached its peak. He couldn't stifle the cry of euphoria that slipped from him as his entire body gave in and he came hard. Percy stayed right there, drank him down, adored him, worshipped him, and let Joe be the one, finally, to break free, to drop to his knees, and to kiss Percy.

"I love you," Joe whispered.

"I love you more," Percy whispered back.

Joe felt the smile against his cheek as he slipped his arms around Percy, and the two fell back onto the richly carpeted floor of the walk-in wardrobe together. Joe trailed a hand along Percy's corset, down and down, until his fingers found the firm bulge he was searching for. Sadly, he got only one stroke, before Percy pulled his hand back to his lips and delivered an authoritative kiss. "I'm saving that for later."

With an exasperated but satisfied sigh, Joe relented and let himself be held by Percy for some blissful time, until the endorphins began to settle, and their precarious position came back into view.

That was when Joe realised the door was silent. The handle was still. Not a sound rattled the wood or the atmosphere.

He sat bolt upright, though Percy remained so relaxed he wondered if he'd fallen asleep. Joe tapped his thigh.

"Hmm? What?"

He had fallen asleep.

"Ghosts, Percy," Joe whispered harshly. "It's suspiciously quiet out there, don't you think?"

Percy pushed himself up regretfully. "It can only be a good thing if they've left us alone."

"I'm not so sure." With his newfound sense of bravery, Joe silently approached the door, reached up and undid his belt from the knot into which Percy had tied it. He felt Percy close behind him again, a kiss on his neck, a reassuring hand on the small of his back, so he pushed down the handle just as unobtrusively as he could manage.

The door did not move.

A little harder, he pushed it. "Percy, it's stuck."

Percy came around to his side and applied a shoulder to the door. The virulent strength of the two made short work, the door refusing at first, as if trying to do them a favour, before eventually giving up in one sharp burst. Percy and Joe tripped and fell over a body, slipped in a puddle of blood, and found themselves in a scene of horror such as neither had experienced before. And that's saying something.

CHAPTER NINE
THE SCENE OF HORROR

There were more security guards than either of them had expected. Percy had guessed four might be after them. Six, Joe thought, a little more cautiously. But in that room were twelve dead men and women, contorted in a most heinous manner.

The first victim their eyes fell upon was the one whose blood was, primarily, now soaking Percy's very nice pants. Not Joe's, what with him wearing sexy Van Helsing leather, which he was finally content with. It is said the human body can hold ten pints of blood, and therefore, it quickly became apparent that the huge and gaping slash in that man's throat was not the sole source of their scarlet bath.

Joe's hand flinched away from the head it had inadvertently settled next to, eye sockets steadily leaking crimson, but he was quickly distracted by Percy's, "That's not good…" Joe followed his line of sight to the ceiling fan over his shoulder, grinding with a sickly whirring noise, under the weight of entrails. He wanted to say the entrails of one, knowing how long and heavy human entrails are rumoured to be, but he could not in good faith believe that. It hung lopsided and low and with a heft no one person could carry around daily. It still spun, and with that, dropped a pitter-patter of red rain along its path.

Percy and Joe both conjectured that although that mechanism was decorating a significant portion of the room, the stolid movement prevented it from accounting for the colour of the walls. Walls which ran and dripped red, the ghoulish pattern enhanced here and there by a handprint, by the scraping of fingernails clawing in their last-ditch attempt at life, from the very base and all the way to the top, and then out and across the ceiling.

"How is that even possible?" Joe whispered.

"I don't want to know." Percy was on his feet, pulling Joe up beside him, with his dagger out long, pointed at the painting.

There it sat, serenely, without a speck of blood even on the frame. Mother and daughter were back in position and, with one quick flip, Percy dropped it face-down on the bed. "Get the box."

Joe tried to ignore the squelching sound his boots made, the gaping eyes looking up at him from the few faces that still had eyes. When he stepped on a tongue, he very nearly retched, but instead he doubled his pace, and with the kind of brute strength that would have made Percy take him back to the wardrobe had he seen it, Joe lifted the box from under two especially broken corpses, and wrenched it over to the bed. He thrust back the lid to reveal the fake painting, which was a different sort of gut punch on first sight.

He felt it.

Or more precisely, he *didn't* feel it.

Percy had often talked of the magic of being in the presence of a painting by a true master. That the painting became not just paint on a canvas, but an entity. That the author's soul remained in the work, and, he said, you would always know by feel—before you examined the paint strokes or the preparation or the style—you would recognise a masterpiece by its soul. And this one had no soul. And for that, Joe was eternally thankful.

Percy's strong fingers split the real painting from the last poorly installed fastening that held it to its gilt frame while Joe pulled the fake out and lined up the box.

"Now, please be very careful," Percy began.

"No," Joe replied tartly. "Get them in the box."

Percy looked up, an unusual, if still stern, plea in his eyes. "Do me this one favour."

"What if they slip out the bottom?" said Joe. "Do you see this room? I don't want to end up smeared down the wall."

Percy's voice remained calm. "I see it, and that's why I'm asking you to be careful."

Joe narrowed his eyes at him.

"In a roundabout sort of way," Percy explained. "Don't upset them. We only need to lift it that little bit higher to avoid bumping it. And please, let's not scrape the paint if we can help it."

"We're going to burn it," Joe seethed.

The movement of Percy's delectable lower lip veered dangerously towards a pout. "What if the paint flecks are haunted?"

"What?" Joe snapped.

"I mean…" He tsked as though he simply couldn't be bothered anymore, and finished with an irritated, "You never know. Just please do this for me."

Haunted paint flecks. What next? Still, Joe couldn't be sure there wasn't something in the idea, what with having just seen actual paint come to life and crawl out of its canvas on a murderous rampage. Accordingly, he wrapped his fingers gingerly around the edge of the picture, seeing over and over in his mind's eye the little girl's teeth biting them off as he did so.

On Percy's nod, they lifted swiftly, clearing the edge of the box by a good inch. Percy barely pulled his fingers free before Joe slammed the lid down. Percy ripped a packet of nails from a pocket while Joe fished the hammer out of their bag. They made fast work sealing the box and had just set about getting the fake into the frame when they heard the unsettling but familiar sound of a bullet sliding into the chamber of a gun.

CHAPTER TEN

EUROTRASH PSYCHOPATH

Joe, with his back to the door, watched Percy raise his arms and announce, "Dubois."

"So you came for the painting," said the voice from the doorway.

Joe's stomach sank as Percy replied, "You're smarter than you look."

But, "Thank you," said Philippe Dubois as he advanced into the room. He paused at the foot of the bed, taking Joe in, eyeing Percy. "Who sent you?"

"I came for it because I want it," Percy replied.

"And who the fuck are you?" With a flick of his gun, "Mask off."

Percy pushed down the smirk, but Joe knew it was there, so he was doubly compelled when Percy pulled the string to set his eye mask free. He dropped it with a slight flourish, and it fell silkily onto the box in which the haunted painting was waiting to be stolen. An expectant silence settled.

"Well, who are you?" Dubois repeated, only more loudly this time.

Percy frowned towards Joe, as if Dubois had just proven a

55

point Percy had recently made, then he rolled his eyes and gave a bored, "Percy Ashdown."

Joe might have reprimanded him for saying his real name had he not known him so well. As things stood, he saw the admission for what it was: Philippe Dubois's death sentence. Nevertheless, he did not expect what came next.

Dubois's head tilted, and a hazy recognition came into his narcotic eyes. "Have you come to take it back to the gallery?"

Joe's gaze shot across to Percy, who drawled, "Judging by the state of this room, that may be a rash course of action."

Dubois kicked a bit of liver away from his shoe as if agreeing, yet he kept the gun trained on the pair. "So you know my secret. Who told you?"

"I'm an art historian," said Percy. "It's my business to know which paintings are haunted and which are not. And though we may be unable to display it publicly at this time, it's still an important work of art, and I don't appreciate the humidity in this room."

It took him a few seconds, then, "What?" said Dubois.

Percy dropped his arms and spun around to fix Joe with an expectant smile. "Show him, Ignatius."

Joe wasn't sure if he was more annoyed by the name or by Percy turning his back on the gun so fast he expected it to go off, but he was somewhat soothed when Percy thrust the fake painting upright and nodded at him.

"It's… uh…" Joe started. Percy waited. Dubois waited. "The paint. Here." Joe ran a finger close by a perfectly perfect swath of fresh paint, racking his brain for what to say. "You can see where it's… um… not… not like it should be."

"Your canvas is expanding and shrinking with the change in humidity," Percy supplied. "That causes cracks." He trailed his own finger over the place Joe's had been before flinging it in the direction of the window. "I know the sunlight is coming through there every afternoon, and hitting this painting head on. You're damaging the pigment. Do you think a century-old work can stand up to the heat of your stinking Belgian summer? I don't see an air-conditioning unit in here." He spoke faster the more irate he became, and he was clearly, genuinely pissed off, especially when Dubois cut into his lengthy reprimand.

"The fuck do I care?"

Percy's aspect darkened considerably, scaring Joe while also turning him on, a schism that he realised somewhere deep inside had probably ruined him for other men. His heart quickened as he heard Percy say softly, "What do you think happens when you make a ghost's home uninhabitable?"

Dubois whitened appropriately at the thought, and he looked a little harder at the painting.

Percy went on, pointing at the mother and daughter, "They may be blood-sated now——"

"Or they may not be," Joe put in.

"Good point, Ignatius," replied Percy, to some very tight lips, "and therefore we should end this conversation, and fast. What matters is this: if they can't go back into the painting, they're out. For good. You, everyone else in this palace, and then all of Bruges is fucked if you don't start to take better care of the thing. Look." Percy motioned him over. "You can see the portal to the netherworld beginning to close right here."

Dubois made his way closer, warily, but with eyes locked onto the painting. "Netherworld?" He repeated, leaning past Percy for a closer look.

"Netherworld?" Joe mouthed over the top of him.

Percy shrugged cheerily and cracked double elbows down on Dubois's back. He took his head in his hands and prepared to sever the spinal cord with a twist.

But, of course, Joe placed a hand on his, and dropped the infuriating words, "Do you have to break his neck?"

Percy stomped in a pool of blood just like a child and

yelled, "He's a goddamn killer! If there's anyone I should be able to kill, it's this bastard!"

"I agree," said Joe, "in principle. But… this just feels a little cold-blooded, you know?"

"Do you want to talk about blood?" Percy smashed a knee down on Dubois's struggling back to hold him in place and thrust a finger towards the still-spinning entrails. "Not one of those people will be going home tonight because of him." Percy closed a hand over Dubois's mouth and nose, wrapping his other hand tight around his throat.

"Are you suffocating him?" Joe gasped out.

"Shhhht!" Percy threw back, fuming, but wondering all the while how Joe managed to get him in a similar chokehold every time. Always with the not killing people. Unless he had a 'good' reason. He knew he never should have taken up with a priest. Even if he was sweet. And gorgeous. Even if he had a beautiful soul. Even if he was, all things considered, the best man Percy had ever met. And even if his dick was the most spectacular thing he had ever—

A sickening gurgling snapped him out of his increasingly delicious thoughts, so he squeezed a little tighter.

"Percy!"

"Just…" Percy let out a long breath. "We'll talk when he's unconscious."

"Oh. Okay, then." So Joe waited for Percy to semi-strangle Dubois. Which took longer than he thought it would, were he given to thinking about such things. "Do you think that might give him brain damage?"

"It would be an improvement," Percy gritted out.

Joe shrugged a half agreement, and a few seconds later, Dubois was dropped to the floor with his face in a puddle of blood. Percy, loyally, kicked him over so he could breathe, pulled out a cigarette and lit it. He threw the case and lighter across to Joe, who did the same. Percy shoved the smoke into the corner of his mouth and pulled the real painting, in its box, off the bed, saying, "We need to go right now. If we're lucky, he'll think we left him the painting and he'll become no more than another player in our gallery of villains. But you must understand the risk in us doing this. He has my name. And he's not some neo-Nazi thug. He's a billionaire. He could have either of us killed on a whim tomorrow."

"Sorry." Joe paled, but still grabbed their bag and pulled the door wide open for Percy. "I forgot. Just for a second. It just seemed so brutal to do it like that."

Percy shuffled halfway through the door, side stepping Joe. "That's generally how murder works. I don't want to be too blunt, but if you're going to be in the business, you may need to toughen up just a little."

"If?" Joe placed two stalling hands on the box, pulling Percy back. "I thought this was our thing now? Partners in crime."

"Handsome," said Percy, bemused by the combination of worry, disappointment, hopefulness, and downright irrefusable expectancy in Joe's gorgeous features, "to be partners in crime, you occasionally have to do crime."

Joe ripped the painting out of his hands. "I'm doing crime. Watch me steal this painting."

Percy pulled the painting back, and Joe along with it. "Kiss me first."

Joe raised a coy chin. "And we'll be partners?"

"Forever."

It was just as well Percy had asked for the kiss, because when Joe leaned forward, Dubois's bullet missed his skull by millimetres.

"The fuck!" yelled Joe.

"Dracula!" screamed Dubois.

"Shit," muttered Percy. He and Joe tumbled out into the stairway, with Percy just managing to hook the door handle and pull it closed before they tripped over one another. Both grabbed the painting, Percy ran up, Joe ran down, and the violent division sent them both crashing back to the ground.

"Are you insane?" Joe whispered, picking himself back up. "This way!"

Percy yanked the painting back. "That's exactly what he'll expect. Let's make for the roof and wait until he thinks we've escaped."

Percy almost fell over again with the energy Joe used to pull the painting back. "Rule number one of horror movies is don't run upstairs."

"Rules are for other people." Percy leaned close over the painting, his eyes burning into Joe with knee-melting authority. "That way is people. That way is discovery. That way is death. I've done this before. Now do you trust me or don't you?"

"Percy…" Joe sighed, yet before he knew it, one foot then another was ascending the stairs in pursuit. The staircase turned around and around, thinner, dizzying, until it took a final narrow twist towards a worryingly small and apparently disused door.

Without showing a speck of his apprehension that the door wouldn't open, Percy pulled the clasp back, and they were hit full force by a sharp snap of wind.

"Tell me this isn't the roof," Joe muttered.

"Dracula!" came the shout from below, accompanied by a bullet breaking a chunk of stone off the wall by Percy's arm.

"Shit!" Percy said again, and ushered Joe ahead of him, slamming the door shut behind them.

The calm and balmy spring evening had whipped itself into a frenzy of storm clouds, a moon dancing chaotically in fast, fleeting flashes, and a punishing wind that snapped the letters of the gothic weathervane to and fro on its sharply pointed axis.

Then it began to rain.

"Fuck! The painting!" cried Percy.

"Yes!" Joe called back, searching for something to block the door. "Fuck that painting! If we'd just burned it, we wouldn't be in this mess."

"No, I said— Oh, never mind." He ripped off his cape to wrap the wooden box.

"Now he takes off his disguise," Joe grumbled under his breath, pulling at a terracotta tile that wouldn't give.

"It's a very important work of ar—"

"Argh!" Joe yelled, arms flailing about the place in frustration. "Stop saying that! We are going to burn it!"

The door flung open, and the very first shot, let off with no direction but chance, knocked Percy straight to the ground. In a series of stills that blended together so fast Joe could never quite rearrange them properly in his mind again, Philippe Dubois, of all people, got the drop on Percy Ashdown.

One ugly shoe in front of another, he trod directly over the darkening ochre rooftop, the steam from the warm day greeting them with the scent and heaviness of ozone, a flash of lightning behind his black silhouette. He stopped, he turned the gun downward, and Joe lunged.

The second bullet found Percy's chest just as Joe wrenched Dubois back by the neck. The sound of the shot hitting Percy, his cry of pain, propelled Joe. He simultaneously clamped a hand down on Dubois's pelvis, slammed the other down on his chest, and brought his knee up hard. He smashed Dubois's spine in half with one enormous burst of anger and fear and grief. The scream echoed deep into the night, throughout the party, throughout the woods, and came to a halt with stomach-churning efficacy when Joe picked him up, and impaled him, gut first, on the sharp spear of the weathervane. A foul vermilion foam choked the sound out of him, spilling disgustingly down the five-hundred-year-old walls of the château as its most recent owner commenced his slow, torturous death.

Joe saw none of it.

He was on the tiles in a second, pulling Percy into him, though Percy had already been half way up without his help.

"Nice murder, darling." Percy grinned, with a nod at the twitching Belgian.

"Percy, you're…" Joe brushed a hand over Percy's chest, feeling the two small breaks in his corset. He looked up at Percy in shock, then slapped a hand down on him. "Percy! You're fine!"

"Ouch!" Percy yelled. "No, I'm not fine. It hurts getting shot."

"How did you not tell me you had a bullet-proof corset?"

"Well, that was obvious, wasn't it?"

"No, that wasn't obvious!"

"I mean, if you're going to have a corset made—"

"That was *not* obvious!"

"Have we even met? Do you even know me at all—"

His speech was cut short by a long, punishing kiss. Joe kissed Percy with every ounce of anger, terror, and relief that was wound up tight in his chest and his soul until the fervent, vital flesh and blood that met him with equal ardour convinced him Percy was viscerally alive. He fell, still catching his breath, into Percy's arms, to be held and loved in the warm, stormy night air, on the windy roof of the ancient palace.

Percy stroked Joe's hair in the moonlight, watching Dubois's body twitch, and thinking on the best way to broach the subject.

As illogical as it all was, Joe's actions made perfect sense to Percy. Joe didn't routinely kill people, and Percy could only guess at the worries now undoubtedly running around his mind as he hid his face against Percy's shoulder. Percy tried to cast his mind back to a time he didn't routinely kill people, but it's difficult for a grown man with so much life experience to remember the thoughts and feelings of his fifteen-year-old self. He probably felt bad.

No.

He had felt bad.

He had felt bad, then he had locked it away in the vault with all the other horrors. But that was very long ago, and now this oozing corpse in blue sequins only roused revulsion in him, both for what he had made Joe feel and for what he wore.

Percy would kill him again happily. Twice if he could.

Dropping another kiss on Joe's temple, Percy said softly, "I don't know if you realise, but that second bullet would have been it for me."

Joe tilted his face up towards Percy, who was an unusual, unsettling shade of serious.

"He had it aimed right at my skull. You saved my life."

Joe tightened his fingertips on Percy's collar and pulled him a little closer, moving his gaze down to the wet ochre tiles. "I'm sorry. I almost got you killed."

Percy took his hand and kissed it. "No. I almost got me killed. He almost got me killed. I completely underestimated him."

"If I'd just let you kill him earlier—"

"That's not you." Before he could say another word, Percy caught Joe's chin with strong fingers and a gentle thumb across his lips. "And it doesn't need to be." He kissed Joe, three long, soft pecks. He ran a hand over his back and pulled him against his chest, sinking into his warmth, settling him against his neck. "If it hasn't been too awful, I'd really like it if you'd keep doing crimes with me."

He felt Joe's laugh deep in his chest. "I did all right, then?"

"Mostly." Percy turned his head languidly to assess Dubois. "Though, as he was about to kill me, I'm not sure that counts as murder. Which is a shame, because it would have been a good one."

"What are you talking about?" Successfully provoked, Joe shoved him off and climbed to his feet. "That's a fantastic murder." A shot of lightning ripped through the sky, illuminating the grisly sight theatrically. Joe flung an arm out to illustrate his point. Unfortunately for him, Dubois's body flinched at the sound of the thunder that followed.

"Dracula!" he screamed.

"Why does he keep blaming me?" Percy let Joe pull him to his feet, before directing his voice at the dying man. "Ignatius did it."

Joe slapped his sore chest. "Stop calling me that!"

"Ouch!"

"Dracula!" Dubois screamed louder still.

"Joe." Percy turned to Joe, so Joe turned to Percy, and Percy said, "I believe it might fall within your code of ethics for me to put him out of his misery right about now before he attracts anyone else up to the roof."

"But…" Joe assessed Dubois, writhing on his metal skewer. "You know, maybe we should call an ambulance or something?"

"Handsome…" But with one look at Joe's conflicted face, Percy knew it was a lost cause. He decided to save them both the trouble. He started forward, flipped Dubois's legs up, wrenched him off the weathervane and onto his shoulder, screaming all the while. After a quick look below to make sure it was clear, Percy flung his body off the side of the building, where it splatted down onto the stone pavement, breaking the head apart, ripping a leg off, and generally leaving more of Dubois on the outside of his body than on the inside.

"What did you do!" Joe rasped out, already by his side and surveying the grisly mess.

Percy shrugged. "It was an accident." Then to the furious scowl, "I was aiming for the pool." Joe, he knew, was about to unleash a volley of reprimand, so Percy yelled, "Ignatius, come!" and dashed away into the dark stairwell.

With a great deal of swearing, Joe followed, and from there it was short work (relatively speaking), for the two to find a first-floor bedroom, lower the painting, then themselves, down to their waiting boat on the dark side of the mansion, and row their way back to the woods. A rope was fastened to the painting and hurled over the wall. Percy affixed his cape and his mask and the two wandered back through what was left of the party, out the front door, and, pausing only to pull their prize over the wall, they were away.

Had it been anyone but Percy, Joe might have considered it odd that he had chosen, in advance, such a location to burn the painting. Joe would have just destroyed it first chance he got. But considering how dangerous the entities were, the precautions made sense. Sense to do it in an abandoned shed on a lonely farm. Sense to put the painting aside for a second, outside, while he and Percy went in and lit the candles. Most of them. Percy disappeared for longer than expected to retrieve the painting, which, had it not been so dark, Joe might have noticed was in a box that appeared to have suffered surprisingly little from such an ordeal.

It made perfect sense too for Percy to tip the thing out face down, and Joe was relieved he didn't have to look at it then, or ever again.

In the flickering light, as the new day dawned, they splashed holy water on the back of the canvas. "Exorcizamus hanc bestiam in Nomine Patris, et Filii, et Spiritus Sancti." They threw salt onto the surface. "Quaesumus, Sancte. Protege adversus spiritus nequitiam et tyrannidem diaboli." They gave the lot a heavy spritz with lighter fluid. "Vade infernales invasores, putrescentiae mentis et omnes legiones diabolicae." And Percy dropped the cigarette from his lips onto the painting, watching the lot go up in flames. "Expellimus te a nobis immundum spiritum. Pessima bestia, te ad Infernus projicio."

Odd, the way nothing came out of there. No screams of the damned, no last-ditch attempts to murder them. But then, Joe had never exorcised a haunted painting before, and unlike Percy, he hadn't known what to expect.

CHAPTER ELEVEN
ALL IN THE WRIST

"And that"—the whip cracked across Percy's bare back, his muscles quivering as a carnal groan broke free—"is for lying about the corset."

Percy might ordinarily have responded that an omission isn't the same as a lie, but the gag shoved deep in his mouth and bound tight in his hair prevented any such response. Not that Joe was interested in Percy's excuses.

"And if you ever call me Ignatius again…" Another hot snap of leather on firm flesh, another cock-twitching moan, and Joe dropped the whip onto the bed.

He took up his champagne, surveying his beloved. What a glorious sight he was. His arms reached wide, biceps, triceps, tendons, everything straining against the ropes that fastened him to the bedposts. His muscular back was a patchwork of Joe's bruising punishment, and his ankles were shackled at the base of the bed, tight, waiting for Joe to do whatever he wanted with him.

And Joe intended to take full advantage.

He cast his shirt to the floor, down to only his oversized

crucifix and leather pants, which his dick strained hard against. He wasn't ready to set it free. Yet.

He ran a finger slowly down Percy's spine, right to the top of his perfect ass, listening for Percy's hitching breath. He paused there. He pulled a small package from his pocket and tapped a line of cocaine out onto the firm cheek, then inhaled the lot in one go. He kissed where the powder had been, over the rise and fall, to the top of Percy's leg, gently, then he wrenched Percy wide and licked up and over his tight hole.

Percy sucked in a gasp of air at the sensation, straining hard against his binds as Joe did it again, and again. He would have begged for satisfaction were he able to speak. Then Joe began the slow, galling circles, around and around, bringing a frantic shiver of sweat to his brow and back. Joe revelled in Percy's desperate need to shift his dick against the sheets, to find any relief from the excess of pleasure, and his accompanying frustration at his complete physical suspension.

Percy's thighs, calves, contracted in his yearning, his fingers curling tight against the wrought iron, and when Joe was satisfied Percy was really suffering, he stiffened his tongue and pushed inside.

Percy groaned, louder still, so Joe slid a finger over Percy's taint, squeezed his ass as his body shook with the intensity of the cruel delight. "Don't you dare come yet," Joe whispered. And he savoured the delicious shudder that was Percy fighting with everything he had to obey the command.

Joe didn't relent, licked him, teased him, held Percy in an agony of ecstasy, until Joe couldn't take it anymore. He snapped the binds from Percy's ankles and drove his knees up hard with his own. He ran a hand over the curve of Percy's firm ass, down the back of his thigh, and back up the inside, grazing his balls softly.

The sheets were wet with sweat, Percy's dick dripped with

his urgency for Joe, and Joe did consider stopping there, leaving him right on that torturous line as a fitting discipline…

But Joe was a man of ethics after all. More or less. And it may be noted that where Percy was concerned, he had a considerable weakness.

He slathered his dick with lubricant, and pushed a finger into Percy, carrying him closer to the beautiful edge. "Percy…" Joe leaned his body out long across Percy's back, wrenched his head back by his hair, and rasped against his ear, "Will you please try to behave yourself in the future?"

The response was instantaneous: "Like fuck I will."

Of course, Joe couldn't understand his garbled words at all, and therefore he obliged them both by taking Percy's gigantic, throbbing, utterly glorious dick in hand, and fucking him into the next day.

In the morning, Percy sat on the bed in the hotel room, rubbing his sore back, with the phone in the crook of his neck. It wasn't long before a voice down the line answered, "Pronto?"

"Luca, it's me. Everything's fine."

Luca made a vague grunt in recognition of Percy's achievement of stealing the painting, inasmuch to say the money would be in his account shortly, but Percy stopped him from getting off the line immediately by saying, "Listen, I think I might take some time away. From anything too… arduous."

"Ah," said Luca, a knowing warmth to his tone. "Your fiancé?"

With a smile at his lips, "Giordano told you?"

"He did. Congratulations."

At that moment the door smashed open and Joe stumbled in, arms laden with little brown paper bags full of pastries he hadn't been able to decide between, two coffees spilling out the tops of their cups, and a too-adorable blush on his cheeks at having interrupted.

Breaking into Percy's enamoured silence, Luca said, "Let me know if you change your mind."

Percy's eyes were all but devouring Joe when he replied, "I really don't think I will." He hung up the phone.

Joe dumped his goods on the table and passed Percy a coffee. "Who was that?"

"Luca. We'll have the money soon."

Joe raised his chin and eyebrows, calling Percy over to the table. "Great. That was fun. When can we do it again?"

Percy huffed a laugh and kissed his cheek, Joe's stubble and the heat of his skin a comfort he'd sorely missed in the last ten minutes since Joe had left. He ran a hand around his waist, searching for the small of his back as he brought him closer. "Maybe after Scotland."

"Yeah," said Joe, tilting his head to enjoy another kiss. "I guess we should get back to that evil princess situation that we haven't mentioned once this whole trip."

Percy, agreeably segueing into the next chapter while peeking into Joe's bags, asked, "Have you ever had krappin an' stap?"

Joe's fine eyes cut across sharply. "Is that a trick question?"

Percy watched him, awaiting his reaction as he revealed, "It's offal, mixed with suet and oats, stuffed into fish heads, then they boil the lot in seawater."

More abhorred than he was at seeing Dubois's exploded body, or a room full of dying neo-Nazis, or even when they were almost suffocated by soul-eaters, Joe gasped out, "They serve them just like that? Eyes and all?"

"Aye, eyes and all. A plate full of them. Staring up at you. Awaiting their fate."

"Percy, that's disgusting." Then on the same breath, "Do you know, I think there's something very wrong with people's fetishisation of peasant food. What is this self-degradation that drives people to such extremes?"

"Clearly they need God," Percy suggested.

"I'm not eating that," Joe declared, ignoring the slight slight. "I can just eat potatoes, can't I? I'll eat potatoes every day while we're there."

"Mmm," agreed Percy. "We'll set you up with a nice bowl of clapshot."

Joe scowled. "What now?"

"Maybe a festy cock?"

"Are you going to be like this the whole time we're in Scotland?"

Percy grinned. "Or maybe you'd prefer some rumbledethumps."

"You said we were going to Lerwick," Joe grumbled. "Not Hell."

"Only a culinary hell, darling."

"It's the same thing."

"But obviously," Percy said, letting out a heavy breath and becoming a little more serious with it, "all that pales in comparison to what's probably waiting for us at Cleo's mansion, Barmiston Hall."

Joe fell into a quiet, trepidatious reflection at the mention of the place.

"Are you sure you're in?" asked Percy. "Althea could use a steady friend in London if you'd rather go visit her. Because whatever's waiting there in Scotland... From what Althea told us, it wants blood. And it's probably desperately hungry by now. This is undoubtedly going to be a harrowing experience."

Joe pulled Percy's arm back around his waist. "And then there's the crapping to deal with."

"Krappin," Percy corrected, manoeuvring Joe in front of him and taking his hands. "Insult to injury, to be sure. So this is your out."

"Are you kidding? You and me, a dangerous supernatural killer, and a haunted inn in the middle of nowhere, Scotland? As though I'd miss that."

Percy narrowed his eyes. "What makes you think it's haunted?"

Joe held his gaze. "Isn't it?"

Percy's lips slipped to the side in a resigned sort of gesture, and he said, "I haven't got the full details from Leo yet."

"Better call him then." He kissed Percy's cheek. "Don't worry. We can take it. Whatever it is. So long as we're together."

"Always," Percy replied, heart warming with Joe's ever-growing confidence in the two of them.

And so they ate and packed, and Percy did call Leo, and Percy did decide to save the full details regarding their accommodation for discussion at a later time.

They left the hotel to catch their flight, and before long, they'd arrived in Aberdeen, ready to board the ferry to Lerwick, both of them hoping, after their last adventure, it would be smooth sailing.

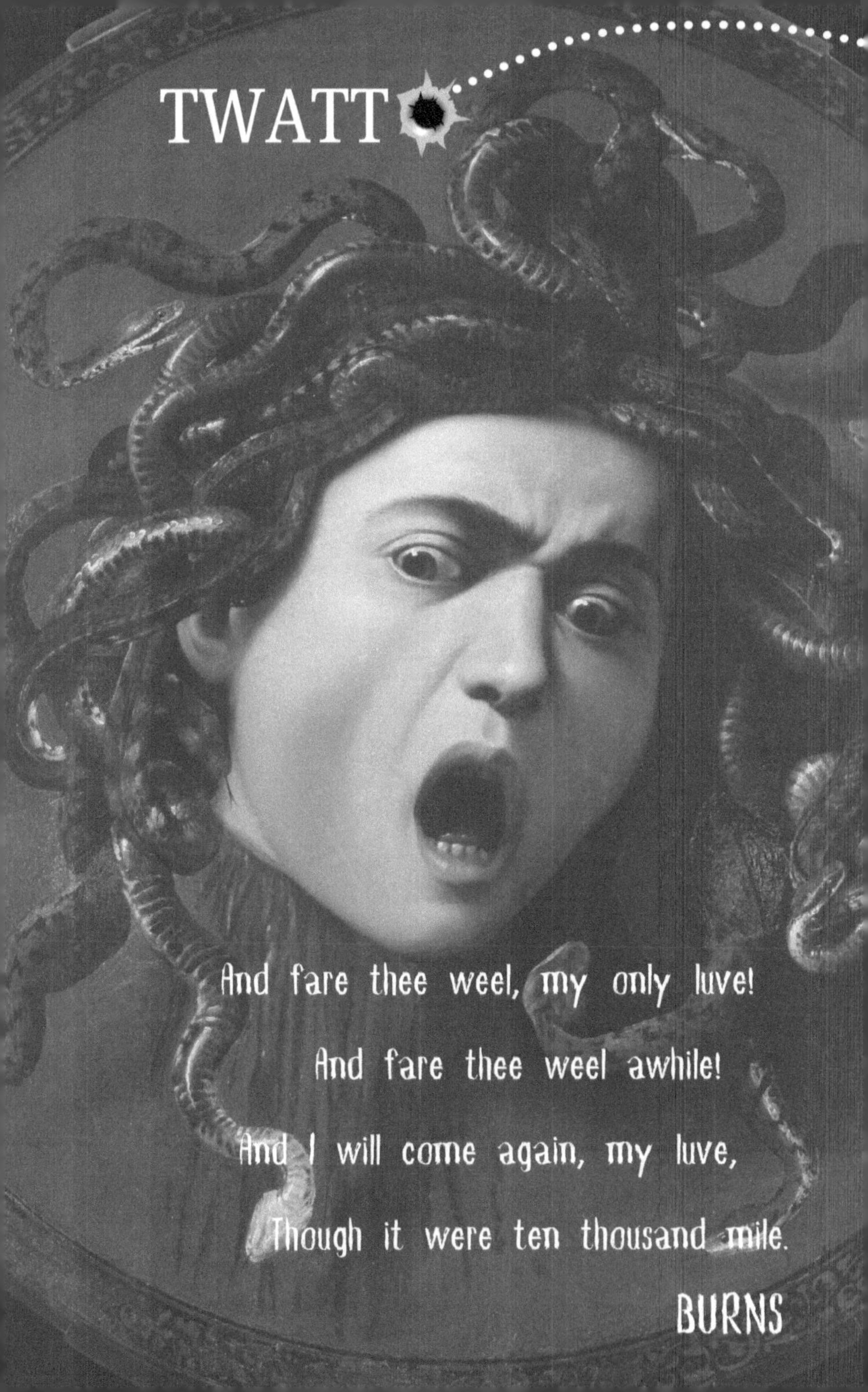

TWATT

And fare thee weel, my only luve!

And fare thee weel awhile!

And I will come again, my luve,

Though it were ten thousand mile.

BURNS

CHAPTER TWELVE

THE DEMON-SHAPED ELEPHANT IN THE ROOM

"Milk?" asked the waitress.

"No," Percy replied. "I like my coffee like I like my men. Bitter and acidic."

The unfortunate woman quickly disappeared with her little silver jug, leaving Joe and Percy at the small wooden table, staring daggers at one another.

A rough, altogether nauseating thirteen-hour crossing from Aberdeen to Lerwick might put anyone in a bad mood, so, Percy conjectured, perhaps that was why Joe was so foul-spirited that grey and foggy morning in the little cafe on the seaside in the small town at the north of nowhere. After all, Percy had only said that if Joe happened to become possessed by a ghost, demon, or similarly evil entity in the near future—which was unlikely at best—Percy would pull out all the stops to get him back.

All the stops being, Joe knew, a long and brutal exorcism. And that was generally a romantic notion, because Joe and Percy both understood the toll, mental and physical, that befalls an exorcist. It should have been charming that Percy would go through that for Joe without a second thought. And it

75

was, until Joe had said, "I don't know if I could withstand another exorcism."

To which Percy had replied, flippantly, "It's not as though you'd have a choice."

To which Joe had replied, a little testily, "I'm still traumatised by the last one."

To which Percy had scoffed, "Fuck your trauma. If your body isn't yours, then it's as good as mine, and I'll be damned if I'll let some demon take it."

Joe flared, surprising Percy with a vehement, "I'm not a piece of meat."

So Percy flared in equal measure, stating bluntly, "In fact, yes, if your body is inhabited by a demon, that's all you are to me or it or anyone else. You think the Church won't do worse with you than I would? Do you have any idea what a demon would do to you if it had you for any stretch of time? Hang yourself when I'm done if you like, but I've got dibs on that body."

"Hang myself?" Joe spat.

Percy softened, ever so slightly, with an eye roll. "Only rhetorically."

That was around the time the bad Scottish coffee was set down on their table. Percy took a sip, glowered out at the grey water, and shuddered.

He should have added milk. Spiteful bastard that he was.

He choked it down and waited for Joe, who was occupied fighting his need to vomit at the harsh smell of bacon and lard so early in the day.

Nevertheless, Joe remained angry, and he leaned across the table to drive the point home. "I have every reason to be bitter. Your brother killed me the last time I was possessed. I wouldn't even be here if the demon hadn't resurrected my body. And what Anna did to me——"

How infuriating it was the way Percy cut him off to jump

to her defence. "You know as well as I do, you would have skinned Evelyn alive in front of her if they hadn't killed you. And it's not as though she didn't slit my throat."

Joe gave a disgusted laugh. "Don't pretend it's the same thing."

"It's not," Percy replied darkly. "I murdered my brother."

"And I murdered a man who was like a father to me," Joe snapped. He quickly caught himself with a look around the half-empty cafe, returning to a furious whisper. "The difference is that you got Evelyn back. And you weren't tortured for hours after you did it. Do you know what it's like being in your body while someone exorcises you? While someone tries to rip a soul out of you? They cling, Percy. Demon souls fight. You can feel them tearing at your insides. When Anna cut me, when she poured salt in my wounds, when she burned my insides—"

Percy turned his face away, visceral pain at the very thought of it showing in a dark grimace. "Stop it, Joe."

"That's nothing," he seethed. "You feel everything, just as much as you would any other day, but it's nothing compared to what it does in your head—in your soul. The things you hear, the things you see—it turns you black, just as black and dark as the creature inside because you're all mixed up together until it's gone. And then you don't have the driving force anymore— the evil—you just have the memory of being so, so… wrong. And broken. In every sense of the word. And you try to get better, and be better, because you know how bad you became, but it's still there. It's always there. And there's the memory of what you did—what you *really* did—what your hands and your body did. And it gets so bad sometimes that you don't know what you were before." Shaking fingers reached for his coffee, and he wiped his eyes with the palm of his other hand.

Percy moved to stand, to go to Joe's side, but was hemmed in by their waitress placing down two metal trays of potatoes and sausages.

"Milk, please," said Percy.

As she walked away, Joe stared intently at Percy, his right ring finger tapping, tapping on the table. "Is that what it's been like for you?"

"No," Percy replied. "No, I have only the memory of beating and murdering Evelyn, of what I did to the others, of what it wanted me to do to them next, but then it was gone. It left by choice, and but for those memories, it left me untouched."

It was a generous admission. Joe knew from what Percy had told him that his brother's death, at Percy's possessed hands, had been cruel and sickening. He knew that what followed that death and resurrection was heinous. Joe wasn't there to see the fallout, but it lasted months, and drove Anna from the arms of her beloved Evelyn, straight into Percy's. And she loved Percy's brother with a dangerous, all-consuming obsession that scared Joe at times, so he knew whatever happened must have been beyond horrifying. Percy didn't talk about it, and Joe rarely asked, yet he knew Percy's use of the word 'untouched' was kindly meant but misleading.

Percy reached across the table and took Joe's hand. "We're not ready to talk about this."

"We won't ever be," said Joe, covering Percy's fingers with his own. "But it's something we need to figure out. Whatever we find at Barmiston Hall, after all that stress with the painting, when we go back home where horrible things just unaccountably never stop happening... I'm beginning to think things won't ever stop coming for us. So I need to know. If something takes you, do I bring you back?"

Percy didn't blink. "Yes. You?"

"No."

"Joe—"

Shaking salt over his potatoes, "No. Take my head or something."

"I'm not going to cut your head off."

"Then have someone else do it."

"There is no one else. And I'm not convinced that would stop a demon from resurrecting you, anyway."

"Percy," Joe squeezed his hand tight, the ghastliness of every haunting memory gathering in the back of his eyes as he fixed Percy with his desperate gaze, "I know you would do the right thing." He dropped his eyes, pulled his hand away, and took to pushing the food around his plate with a fork. "It's not like it matters. It was the same demon that took us both. I've performed dozens of exorcisms and it's never been that bad before. It was probably just a one-off. One bad demon."

There was no point in Percy telling Joe that he would literally go to Hell and slit the devil's throat with his own hands before he would let a thing touch Joe's beautiful neck, so he nodded, poured some newly delivered milk into his coffee, and added some sugar. "I'm sorry I said what I said. I didn't understand."

"Not many people do," Joe replied, before he began eating as an end to the discussion.

It was a moot conversation, and they both knew it deep down. Both of them were warded against demon possession. Both, coincidentally, by Anna. She had carved the symbol into Joe's chest herself (rather brilliantly, Percy thought—Joe disagreed) in a successful attempt to make Joe's body uninhabitable to the demon that was possessing him at the time. Percy's... Well, after he murdered her boyfriend, Anna marched right over to his house, the first opportunity she got, shoved him to the floor and pulled a knife on him. Damn sexy it was, too. Not that he'd ever tell Joe that. Joe was salty enough about the situation.

Every time their shirts were off, there the marks were. Percy loved it, that they had that same link that bound them in a way no other couple was bound. Also, that it protected them from demons, of course. But for Joe, the mark on Percy's chest was a daily reminder of the time before him. A time with Anna, whatever that entailed, and more than once, he'd wondered if Percy would let him carve a new one. If he'd consider laser surgery, or a skin graft of some sort to delete all traces of Anna's hands on his skin. Understandably, he hadn't suggested it, what with the proposition likely to put him on the wrong side of possessive, but it was a recurring idea.

Either way, everything had been fine between them until the topic of possession came up that morning. If they didn't talk about it, then they would undoubtedly be fine again. With that interest at heart, Joe asked lightly, "How do we get to the inn?"

"We'll get a taxi," said Percy, in a voice equally convivial to Joe's. "It's not a long drive. Though it is a bit of a walk on the other side. It's one of those lonely, windswept inns that sits all alone with only a few houses for miles around."

Joe chuckled. "One of those?"

"You know the sort. One room above a pub, and even the publicans lock up and go away at night. So it will be you and me, all alone, in the middle of nowhere."

"No surprise exes this time?" Joe joked.

Christ, I hope not, thought Percy, but he said, "Definitely not." After all, Lerwick's population sat below seven thousand, so there were only about… perhaps thirty people who might fit the bill. Give or take a few. Percy lowered his head and ate a little faster. "Should we go soon?"

"We should," said Joe. "You know, I'm actually kind of excited about this. Not whatever horrors we're going to find inside Barmiston Hall, obviously, but the two of us, the inn, the countryside. It should be a nice getaway."

"We'll make sure it is. The room sounds beautiful, from what Leo told me. All it's missing is you."

"And you." Joe smiled across at him, looking almost as

serene as he had some twenty-four hours earlier when they set out from Bruges. "I think that's all we need. Some time alone together."

Percy, still silently reeling inside from Joe's harrowing admissions, forced a wide smile. "It'll be an absolute dream. You'll see."

CHAPTER THIRTEEN
UNWELCOME TO TWATT

The tiny, windswept hamlet of Twatt is a small and forgettable conglomeration of roughly five farms and their assorted out-buildings. The slight rise the habitations are settled upon looks out over a few gently rolling hills and a deceptively deep and cold lake.

Percy and Joe's destination was beyond this lake and over one of these hills, and while Percy had mentioned it might be 'a bit of a walk', he had not prepared Joe for the likelihood the taxi driver would screech the car to a halt in the centre of Twatt and announce fearfully, "There's no way in hell I'm going down there."

Joe scanned the dull yet pleasant landscape and saw nothing worth worrying about. He saw nothing much at all beyond a few lonely sheep and short, windswept grass.

"I'll double the fare." Percy pulled his wallet out in readiness.

"I won't do it," said the stout taxi driver.

"Triple," Percy responded, splaying out a thick wad of large banknotes.

The driver eyed the money in the rearview mirror, but all

the show seemed to do was piss him off. He pulled a lever, clicked the boot open, and, mumbling about the wife and three children he had waiting for him at home, yanked their suitcases out and into the dust before either could catch up with him.

Joe shot Percy a bewildered look, while Percy shoved a cigarette in his mouth and took up the unwieldy cardboard box of 'essential supplies' he had composed before they left Lerwick. He dropped a few paces back from the road to avoid the spray of dirt and gravel that went up with the departure of the taxi, then sighed out, "Every time."

Joe remained where he was, in the middle of the road, head tilted at Percy in rather a cynical manner, Percy thought.

"What haven't you told me this time?"

"What?" Percy's handsome brow furrowed. "Nothing at all. You know Barmiston Hall's a dangerous place. It's hardly news."

Joe wrenched his and Percy's suitcases to the edge of the road, holding a handle out for Percy to take. "You didn't tell me it terrifies burly Scottish men."

"In the interest of searing honesty, you should know that Barmiston Hall terrifies burly Scottish women, too. Smoke." He plumped his lips a little to draw attention to the unavoidable cigarette that was hanging out of his mouth.

With a particularly angry click of his thumb, Joe lit the cigarette for him, then, a second time, thrust the handle of a suitcase towards Percy. Percy's reply was a shrug and consequent jingle of the bottles of brandy, wine, and whatever else he'd decided he needed to last a few days above a pub. He turned and commenced a leisurely descent down the hill, so Joe, with a clack of his tongue and a roll of his eyes, took a suitcase in each hand and followed, allowing Percy to commence his story. "Barmiston Hall is a place steeped in legend and myth for some eight hundred years now."

"I didn't realise it was that old."

"It's not. Not in its entirety. A good portion of the estate was built in the late-seventeenth century, with extensive additions in the eighteenth. Nevertheless, the land it sits on bears the marks of bronze-age inhabitants, and god knows what it's seen through the years. It probably picked up its most grisly rumours sometime during the eighteenth century. Bodies, dozens, at least, have been discovered in and around the premises over the years, in various states of mortal disarray."

Joe jogged a few steps to keep up with Percy's increasing pace down the hill. "Mortal disarray?"

"Well, all the usual signs of murder—heads smashed in and all that—but some… One woman was found in a remarkable state of preservation. They dated her death to some time around 1770, but she looks like she died yesterday. She was found with a brick between her teeth, hands and feet tied, inside a coffin bound with a locked metal cage."

"Fuck," said Joe.

"Quite right," agreed Percy. "She's in the museum if you'd like to see her?"

"Um… Maybe. But what else?"

"Witches' wards, cats and dogs with stab wounds. Strange scrawls have all been found within the walls. A few babies under the stones at the entrances." They reached the bottom of the slope, and Percy took a sharp left onto a gravel path, shoes crunching merrily as a light fog rolled off the lake and around their ankles. "Sacrifices, one imagines, and enchantments to keep something at bay."

"Something ancient?" suggested Joe.

"Possibly," said Percy. "The place was known for the slaughter of a local family in 1605, but when the same thing happened in eerily similar circumstances in 1855, well, people began to talk even more than usual. All the murders from all the years were conflated in the minds of the locals, and the place was abandoned. The blood from that last massacre wasn't even touched. The bodies were given a Christian burial, of course, but that was the last time anyone could bear to set foot inside. So for over a hundred years, it remained a grim, gore-ridden time capsule. Until the bolts that were nailed into the doorframe to keep people out rusted and fell free of their rotting wood. That's when some local teenagers did the usual thing and dared each other to stay the night."

Joe, sadly, said, "And they ended up brutally murdered too?"

"Quite the contrary." Percy grinned. "One of those teenagers was my good friend Cleo." Joe gave Percy one of his particular scowls, which Percy knew he would do, so Percy looked out across the lake instead of at Joe, and continued, "They spent the night. She adored the place. She left the next morning, back to Jordan, but she told me, even though she didn't set eyes on the estate for another five years, she never forgot about it. She said it had a sad romance that she found so compelling she would dream of it almost every night." Now he did survey Joe, who, he was pleased to see, seemed appropriately thoughtful.

Percy transferred his cardboard box to one hip, and took a suitcase from Joe in order to help him pass through a narrow divide between two hills—a passage that was paved underfoot and to twelve feet above with grey stone slabs. "Cleo wasn't all bad. In fact, there was very little bad about her when I first knew her. She was…" Percy trailed off there, aware of Joe's jealousy, and of the awful things that Cleo had since done that deserved no defence on his part. He shut off his fond feelings, explaining flatly, "Cleo, when she returned five years later, was even more in love with Barmiston Hall. She had been, by that time, married off to a rich husband, a prince, who she wanted to avoid at all costs, so she bought the place as a renovation project. Just as far away from the world as she could get, she said. It became both a refuge and an obsession. She rebuilt the thing, mostly with her own hands, and she saved every original part she could. You'll feel it when you go in. She's in the walls."

Joe's stomach spun out a queasy lurch with this latest statement, but before he could get a handle on what was a knee-jerk reaction to Percy's admission of his closeness to a villainess (who, as far as Joe was concerned, was an ex-girlfriend of his), and what was a reasonable aversion to the increasingly unsettling story, Percy pulled up, extended his arm out long, and announced, "There it is."

Across the lake, far off in the distance, mostly hidden by swirling mists and fog, arose the black and forbidding shape of a tall and terrifying mansion. Joe could see at first glance that what Percy had said of the age, of the architectural styles cobbled together over the years, must have been true. Here the roof rose smooth and slanted; there it was a jagged jumble of stone. On this side a tall, square turret; across the battlements, two small, squat round ones. The ailing sunlight, not helped by the darkening skies, weakly illuminated a patchwork of stone. Beige, grey, black, red brick, tiles… The place was a mess, but it was a beauty. It was all the wrong things compiled and shoved together disparately until they were exactly the right things. Scary but homely. Austere but cosy. A shelter, but one that screamed at Joe, viscerally, to stay the hell away. Yet he couldn't quite say why.

He didn't want to identify with Cleo—he refused to on every possible level. But something about the place grabbed him by the throat, just as it must have done to her. There was a pull, even as it repulsed him. It sparked a certain empathy in him that he immediately yearned to deny, so he was thankful when a curious Percy finished his silent assessment of Joe's unspoken reaction, and said only, "The pub's this way."

Percy continued around the bend of the hill, then turned right to circumnavigate another. Just as the rise of that hillside fell from view, so a single building, sitting in a wide, desolate green field, surrounded on all sides by the undulations of ancient land, revealed itself. There was green, more green, and white sheep grazing about the place, and the inn in which they were to stay. No other sign of life was visible in that small valley, bar a church at the very top of a distant rise, nothing more than a white speck encumbered by a giant black cross that loomed bleakly over the otherwise rustic landscape.

But the inn…

From the inn drifted music and light and laughter, and Joe couldn't imagine where all the patrons had come from to fill the place with such mirth.

Percy was already halfway across the lawn, and Joe hurried to keep up, feeling himself physically relax at the thought of a warm pub with ales and potatoes (because he staunchly refused to eat anything fish-head-related) but he slowed his pace on approach to the bright red door.

Above it, displayed proudly on a golden rod, was the name of the place, accompanied by a grotesque illustration. A woman's head, her mouth hanging open in a ghastly scream, her eyes staring in hatred and horror, a man's hand in her tangle of stringy black hair, stared back at them in violent reproach. From her neck dangled the strings and sinew of the life-carrying matter that had once attached her head to her body, and from that sign, from the mess of her painted decapitated head, dripped red. Real red, which splished and splashed down into a blood-red puddle at their feet.

Speechless, Joe turned his nauseated face to Percy for explanation.

"Welcome to The Witch's Head Inn," he said brightly. "I completely forgot to mention it, but this blood just reminded me. Turns out, our accommodation is quite cursed."

CHAPTER FOURTEEN
THE WITCH'S HEAD INN

Percy flung the door of the pub wide, ushered a reluctant Joe in ahead of him, and within the space of thirty-six seconds, the following events occurred in this order:

A woman behind the bar yelled, "That's not Percy Ashdown!"

"Percy Ashdown?" called a man from a nearby table. "It can't be!"

"Did you say Per— It couldn't be Percy!" exclaimed a woman sitting at the table with the man.

A blood-curdling scream shot out from god only knew where, every lightbulb in the room exploded, the music stopped, and the landlady smashed a full pint all over the stone flags of the floor.

The room fell dark and silent for the subsequent four seconds, until the landlady muttered, "Yep, that's Percy, all right."

A hideously loud sob broke out in the back somewhere, accompanied by the shout, "Fuck you, Percy!"

A man's voice followed. "That's the fucker, is it?"

The sobbing woman rammed into Joe's shoulder as she fled out the door, Percy calling as she went, "I said I'm sorry!"

"Debbie! Debbie, wait!" yelled the man, pausing only to shake a threatening finger in Percy's face, before sploshing through the dubious red puddle in pursuit.

And from there, the first minute of their arrival completed itself with the landlady plonking two pints of ale down on the counter and flashing an expectant smile, which allowed Percy to skip out on Joe's fuming non-verbal reprimand.

"What's all this Thomas Archer business?" she began as Percy settled his box on the bar. "Is that your boy there?"

"No," he replied with an encouraging raise of his chin at Joe, who pulled the suitcases up beside Percy and made himself smile politely. "This is Joe. My fiancé. Spectacular, isn't he?"

"My, yes, he is." The good woman moved her hands to her hips to thoroughly assess a now-pink Joe, then, "*Fiancé*! Don't tell me you're settling down!" Percy gave a handsome, slightly bashful chuckle, but before he could answer, he was cut off by, "George! George! Percy Ashdown's here, and he's got a *fiancé*!"

"Percy's never got a *fiancé*!" A short, nearly bald, but moustachioed man appeared from a doorway behind the bar carrying a box full of lightbulbs.

"George," Percy said cheerily by way of greeting.

George dumped the lightbulbs down, threw his arm around his wife, and with a happy nod at Joe, said, "Who's this, then?"

"That's Joe," his wife replied, adding scandalously, "Percy's *fiancé*."

"Isn't he beautiful?" said Percy, over a sip of ale.

"Ah, he's a looker all right." George extended a hand to Joe, who took it by instinct, too thrown to begin to get his bearings. "I'm George," he said. With a tilt of his head to the attractive sixty-something blonde by his side, "And this is Maisie."

"Hi," Joe mumbled, sinking to the stool beside Percy.

"What's all this Thomas Archer business?" said George.

"If we knew it was you coming, we'd have done something special," Maisie added.

"My assistant seems to have booked me under the wrong name," replied Percy. "What are you both doing here, anyway?"

"The Witch's Head is ours. We bought it. We own all three pubs in town now." Maisie cast her gaze long and loving over Percy's shoulder, prompting he and Joe to follow her lead.

It was a pub anyone would be pleased to own. Even before the lights blew, the wide, plentifully stuffed stone fireplace provided the primary source of illumination, and all the varnished wood that made the ceiling beams, the many low and intimate table and chair settings, the smooth and well-used bar, sat rich and welcoming beside its flames. Yellow and red stained glass augmented the little bar and the windows with a charming golden glow, and the glistening copper pots and polished viking shields that decorated every spare inch of space sparkled with all the pride of their adoring owners.

"Marvellous." Percy swished out the flame of the match that lit his cigarette, opened his mouth to speak again, and was cut off by another terrifying scream that made Joe spill his beer before he could take his first sip.

"She's rowdy today." Maisie sent a glare through an open doorway. "Haven't heard a peep out of her in months, and now with the lightbulbs again…"

"I'm on it." George picked up his box and wandered off.

With a knowing sparkle in her eye and an air of adventure, Maisie asked, "Would you like me to bring her out?"

"Yes, please," Percy responded at once.

Maisie gave a nod and disappeared.

"Bring who out?" Joe rasped.

"The skull," Percy replied.

"The what?"

"The *screaming* skull," Percy elucidated.

"Here she is," said Maisie, setting down a lacquered wooden block with a gold plaque and a perfectly preserved, fully toothed, bleached-white skull on top. "Isn't she a beauty?"

Another ghastly scream racked out of the thing the second it was placed before them.

"Hello, darling," said Percy, cigarette lazing at the corner of his lips, his fine fingers tilting the skull up to meet his eyes.

"Heeeeeeeee..." the skull wheezed.

"Hmm," said Maisie, eyebrows raised and hands back on hips. "She likes you."

"I like her too," Percy mused, leaning his head back to examine the remains that continued to sigh out the unearthly moan.

Joe shifted a little closer with an inquisitive gaze. "How's she making that sound?"

"I haven't a clue." Percy turned the skull, searching for some trick or other that would explain the noise, but it was nothing more than some old bone stuck on a plank of wood.

Joe manoeuvred the base in order to read the little plaque. "Molly Tulloch."

"That's right." Maisie leaned in close, the flames of the fireplace lighting a pair of watery grey eyes and scarlet lips eerily as she whispered, "Molly Tulloch. Also known as... The Headless Witch of Twatt."

Percy choked a laugh in the back of his throat, but Joe was already too caught up in the mystery of the thing to break into more than a smile. "She's the woman on the sign outside?"

"That's her," said Maisie, clearly impressed with Joe already.

Joe took the cigarette from Percy's mouth, along with the skull that was handed across. It was in supernaturally good condition, and no wonder, being a supernatural object. It was small, sleek, and it had exactly the same presence an occupied head would usually have. Joe placed it down carefully, keeping it close on the bar in front of him. "Why did they do it?"

"She's a witch. Isn't that enough?" came a booming voice by Joe's left arm.

"Not really, no," Joe responded on a sharp exhalation of smoke.

That stumped the man, who frowned at Joe briefly, until Percy said, "Hello, Charlie."

"Percy." The tall man, with white beard and hair, wearing a rustic woollen blue sweater, tipped his head to Percy. "When were you going to come say hi to the Mrs?"

"Oh, leave him be." 'The Mrs,' another sexagenarian, though a small and grey one, slipped her slender fingers around Percy's biceps.

For that, she got a kiss on her cheek from Percy, which made her shoulders curl delightedly and her hands grip his arm that much tighter.

"Vaila, have you met my fiancé?" Percy said. "His name's Joe, and he's beautiful."

Joe, again, blushed at his introduction, particularly when both Vaila and Charlie agreed loudly that he was indeed 'a very fine specimen of manhood'.

"Fiancé, is it?" asked Charlie. "Well, we'll need some scotch to celebrate, then."

"You always need some scotch." Maisie gave an eye roll, but immediately pulled a bottle from the top shelf and commenced the arrangement of six glasses on the bar. In doing so, she must have decided the skull was in the way. She placed her hands on the cranium to move it, at which contact it let out an ear-shattering scream, so loud it slipped from her fingers with the shock.

"Looks like she wants to stay," Percy said.

Maisie dusted her fingers as though they were tarnished by

the touch of the unwilling witch. "I've never seen anything like it. We've been here three years now, and hardly a peep out of her, except for that incident shortly after we took over. She screamed non-stop, didn't she, George?"

"That she did, Maisie," George called back from across the room.

"Non-stop," said Maisie. "We thought we'd made a terrible mistake buying the place, but she calmed down after a while. We hadn't heard a peep from her for months until the very minute you two walked in the door."

"Then a scotch for Molly, too, please, Maisie. I'll get the first round." Joe easily endeared himself to the small group with the offer, while sparking a small note of curiosity in Percy. George soon returned from fixing lights and cleaning up broken glass, and the six drank and smoked and chatted, while Joe in particular watched the skull, which remained quiet with a scotch in front of her, and the occasional cigarette shoved in the gap that served as a mouth. After roughly two hours of this merriment, Joe asked casually, "So, why did they murder her?"

"Murder?" repeated Charlie, a touch of derision in his good-humoured voice. "Looks like old Molly's bewitched your fiancé already, Percy."

Percy sent his bony rival a stern narrowing of the eyes. "She'll have to fight me for him."

Maisie laughed, but stayed on topic, addressing Joe. "You heard her screaming. That proves she was a witch. Now, I won't say all those other women should have been burned, but this one—"

"They burned her?" asked Joe. "The sign shows she was beheaded."

"They burned her *first*," said George.

"No, strangled," Vaila corrected.

"Strangled," George agreed. "As was the way up here.

Strangle them, *then* burn them, which I think was a good measure kinder than down south."

Maisie brought them back on track. "But, when they tried to strangle her, she simply would not die. Just kept screaming."

"So they tried to burn her," Charlie put in, "as you do."

"But she would not burn," said George.

"Just kept screaming," said Maisie.

"So they had to chop off her head," said Vaila.

"And she just kept screaming," said Maisie. "And she's been here ever since. They buried the rest of her Lord knows where, because of course it was unmarked. Her pale skin and snaky black curls rotted away through the years, all over this pub floor, and now here she is, enjoying a glass of scotch with the likes of you."

There was a clinking of glasses that Joe sat out as he took the smoking cigarette from beneath the skull's teeth and placed it between his own lips. Crossing his arms on the bench, resting his chin on his wrists, Joe leaned in close to look Molly in the eye cavities. He thought he heard her give one of her long wheezes, but the small group was loud and tipsy and talkative by that time, and he couldn't be sure. He cut into their conversation. "What were her crimes?"

"Oh, she was a wicked one, Molly," said Maisie. "What did she do? There was the— Was it a porpoise, George?"

"That it was, Maisie."

"That's right. A porpoise. She turned herself into a porpoise, went out to sea, and drowned a lad who'd been rude to her on land."

Joe's mouth set itself on a displeased slant.

"And she was a sea monster that other time," George offered.

"That's right." Vaila, on the Chartreuse by now, tapped her glass down on the bar and pushed it forward for a refill. "She turned herself into a kraken and smashed a whole ship to pieces. Killed six men! But they knew it was her who'd done it because one of them managed to snare the beast's tentacle during the attack, and sure enough, the very next day, Molly was limping." She moved her little head up and down, slowly, meaningfully, as though this were undeniable proof of the woman's guilt.

Joe kept his eyes on the skull, and Percy kept his on Joe's quiet face.

"And not only that." Maisie slid the green liquid that brought a distinct sneer across Percy's face back to Vaila. "She was known for making healing potions."

"The bitch," Percy threw off sarcastically.

"And then there was the old..." Charlie tilted his head downwards with an odd blinking of his left eye.

"Erectile dysfunction," Vaila whispered over her drink. "One man said, after he slept with her, he never could get it up again."

"And that was her fault too, was it?" Joe muttered.

"Well, that's what happens when a woman lays with the devil," Charlie replied, failing to hide the touch of irritation he was developing for Joe's evident distaste of the island's sordid history. "She's no use to any man once she lays with the devil. And a man should know what he's getting into before he goes in that."

"That?" Joe flared, sitting up straight.

Percy reached for his hand, drawing it down off the bench and onto his knee. "Shall we go see our room?"

"No." Joe withdrew his hand and snapped open Percy's golden cigarette case, lighting another smoke. He forced a smile that fooled everyone but Percy. "It's a fun ghost story. I want to hear more. How did they get her to confess?"

A communal sigh wafted around the little group.

"They did get a confession, didn't they?" Joe pushed.

"Of course," said George. "But Molly put up a fight."

"They asked her nicely at first," said Vaila. "As they always do. But when she lied to them, well, they had to start with the cashielawes…"

"What's that?" asked Percy.

"It's an iron cage." Joe spoke through the same smile, but his golden brown eyes were downcast and far away. "They put it tight around the legs of the accused, and heat it until it sears the flesh off the body." He said it as matter-of-factly as if he was reading the bus timetable, giving everyone except Percy the idea it was fine to carry on with the vile conversation.

"Two days, she lasted on that," said George, with a slow shake of his head.

"Because of her supernatural powers," Maisie added.

"All the skin burned off her legs, it was," George went on. "She would pass out from the pain, so they'd have to revive her to go again. She wouldn't give them a thing but her screams, so they were forced to turn to her family."

"They placed stones on the husband right there in front of her until they almost squashed him flat," said Maisie. "She didn't give an inch."

"Brought her little boy in and smashed his feet to pieces with a hammer," said Charlie. "And not a word."

"But it was the little girl that eventually broke her," said Vaila, shaking her head sadly.

Maisie took up the story with a softening of her voice and a glistening of her eyes. "For all the terrible things she'd done, she must have had a heart in there somewhere. They put that little girl's fingers in the pilliwinks, and crushed them right in front of Molly's eyes until Molly cried out that she truly was the Devil's own bride."

Joe, by this time, had fallen into silence, an unmistakably sickened pallor having taken over the usually bright cheeks. Percy gently drew his hand back, wrapping it in the nook of his elbow, where Joe let it remain this time.

"It was a dreadful business," Vaila said quietly.

"But it *was* four hundred years ago," George added.

Maisie cast her eyes over Joe, over Percy's watchful gaze on him, and said gently, "This little skull couldn't scream like it does if it weren't true that she was a witch. I can't agree with what they did to get the confession out of her, but she was *evil*."

Joe remained still, reflective, then stubbed his half-smoked cigarette out with a sudden and decisive jab at the heavily laden copper ashtray. "How much?"

Maisie looked back over her shoulder at the rows of bottles on their little wooden ledges. "How much for what?"

"For Molly," he said. "I'll give you a thousand pounds."

Vaila laughed in surprise, Charlie laughed along with her, George's mouth dropped open, and Maisie chided, "Don't be ridiculous."

"Two thousand," said Joe, his knee beginning to tap as his mind went to work trying to figure out where he was going to get his hands on that sort of money.

"She's not for sale," Maisie laughed out, but in an unsure and defensive sort of way.

"Four," Joe tried.

"No—"

"Five."

"I told you—"

"Fifty thousand," said Percy. The group fell silent, Joe set panicked eyes on Percy, and Percy lifted Joe's fingers to his lips, dropping a quieting peck on them. "That would probably buy half this place. You'll have your next pub in no time."

Maisie stood a little taller, looking as though he'd just told her she smelled like old turnips. "Absolutely not. Molly is *not* for sale. Now, if you'll excuse me, I'll get your room key."

Molly's skull screamed the second Maisie's fingers touched her, and it didn't stop. Maisie disappeared around the corner with her. They heard her shouting at the skull, the skull screaming back, then still more screaming but muffled, with the slamming of what sounded like a fridge door.

"You're mad. The pair of you," muttered George. Then to Joe, "I can see why he likes you so much."

"I do like him," said Percy, leaning a little closer and lowering his voice. "And I want that skull. As a wedding gift. Can you talk her around?"

"Percy," Joe whispered, trying to halt him, but with that sinking, nerve-racking, utterly adoring feeling he'd accidentally set a boulder in motion that wasn't going to stop for anything.

George let out a sharp laugh. "Maisie? The Devil himself couldn't talk her around. But it's not up to her anyway. It's the curse, you see. Molly can't ever leave this building. If she goes, the whole place goes up in flames. Or so the story says. We're not about to put it to the test."

Without missing a beat, Percy asked, "Would you consider selling me the pub?"

Maisie slammed a key down on the counter top. "Up those stairs, first door on the left. You'll be here by yourself from ten tonight until twelve tomorrow. Lock up the front door if you go out, and Don't. Touch. Molly."

"But couldn't she come up to our room just for tonight?" This request Joe paired with an artless flutter of his eyelashes so flooring that Percy thought it must be case-closed, irresistible as he obviously was.

Unfortunately for them, Maisie was made of sterner stuff. "Goodnight," she said sharply.

Too well-mannered to not follow direction, Percy tugged at Joe's unwilling arm, said their goodnights, and they made their way upstairs.

CHAPTER FIFTEEN

JOE'S MANY AND HARRIED THOUGHTS ABOUT THAT SKULL

"She's not a witch, she's a vengeful spirit!" Joe railed, pacing back and forth across what would have been a surprisingly grand room had he stopped to consider it. "Four hundred years— Did you hear that? Four hundred years trapped in that skull!"

Percy stretched out a little longer on the gigantic mahogany four-poster bed. "If Cleo's killed as many girls as Althea suggests, then it shouldn't be too hard to find a replacement skull over there. It's awfully white though, isn't it? We might have to go back into Lerwick to get some peroxide to bleach one."

Joe didn't relent his furious striding beneath the low carved-wood ceiling. "Their families are bound to want their skulls back if we find their bodies."

"A graveyard, then?"

"Yes!" Joe spun around with a finger waggling at Percy. "That's exactly what we need. Someone dead for long enough that no one will be personally upset about us digging them up —if they find out—but fresh enough that we won't damage the skull too badly when we boil it."

"I know the perfect one. It's about two hundred years old, and has been out of use for the last sixty. We should be able to find some shovels somewhere around the place. We'll dig up a head tomorrow night."

"That's perfect." Joe came to a satisfied halt in front of the small, cosy, twisting-iron fireplace, decorated with maroon glazed tiles, the flames snapping and cracking heartily in front of him, and finally he noticed it. And he noticed the deep red wallpaper, the thick carpet beneath his feet, the dark red drapes, and the gorgeously polished wood that comprised the ceiling and walls. He saw the adorable window seat, the cute casement windows, the sheep grazing on the grass outside, and the fields beyond dotted with more sheep, and nothing else but that church on the hill. And he noticed, when he eventually turned around, Percy, lying on one arm, his coat and shoes discarded, waiting for him.

"Do you like it, darling?"

Embarrassment, but the nice kind that comes with being very well loved, swept over Joe. His cheeks were pink again, and he took refuge in Percy's arms, climbing up onto the bed in front of him, resting his head in the nook of Percy's shoulder. "Sorry. I got carried away."

Percy dropped a kiss on his cheek with an indulgent smile. "Catholic guilt playing up again?"

"No!" Joe immediately snapped, but then, seeing Percy was only half joking, admitted, "Yes. A bit. But the Protestants were just as bad, obviously."

"They certainly were," Percy said in an attempt to mollify Joe, doing the quick mathematical calculations in his head at the same time, and coming up with only more and more dead on either side.

"And it was a long time ago," Joe meandered.

"It was," Percy soothed.

"But..." Joe leaned on his arm, a mirror to Percy, who kept

the same kind and patient expression. "I know you think it's weird that I'm a priest."

The same kind and patient expression.

"You can say it."

"I hardly need to, since you just said it."

Joe chuckled, softening enough to open up a little more. "I know there are a lot of assholes in the Church. A lot of them. But it's… It can be a very powerful position to be in, you know?" He fiddled distractedly with Percy's shirt buttons. "You're in these towns, and within a day of arrival, everyone sees you as the voice of reason. Everywhere you go, you have the ability to fit in. They see the outfit, and whether it's good or bad, it sends a message. And that's…" He raised his eyes to meet Percy's. "That's a kind of magic. That's gotten my foot in so many doors through the years. Places I could never have made a difference if I didn't do this. Have you ever seen a severely traumatised autistic kid being exorcised?"

"No," Percy replied. "And I can't say I'm sorry to have missed it."

"I can stop it," said Joe. "I walk in, I say one word, and the whole thing stops on my direction. There's no way I could do that without the collar. And it works the other way around equally well. I can get to a possessed kid before he ever gets the chance to murder his family. Whatever issues people have with the Church, they trust us to deal with demons, and they always come straight to us first. Even atheists do."

Percy's silence worked effectively as the kind designed to draw people out, like therapists use. The sort that makes a person feel safe but also vulnerable enough to feel the need to keep talking. It wasn't deliberately that kind, though. Percy didn't believe in God, but if he did, he hated him. Those were always and resolutely the only two options for him to relate to a Christian faith. Joe knew that. He sensed it as much as he remembered Percy stating it, and that meant this conversation was routinely off the table. Until now. So Percy simply kept his mouth shut lest he plug the flow of Joe's words.

Sensing the opportunity, Joe rushed out a long, winding, and slightly guarded explanation of his concerns. "But for all that, there's a weight that comes with the cloth. I know it well because… Well, you know I've associated with terrible people in this organisation. Awful, awful people. But those people, they need to be taken down from the inside, one way or another. And the people who are good, the decent, kind people who are just trying to make a difference using this… *framework* the Church has provided… they're doing their best. Like me. The sheath, for example—I really think we did the right thing by stealing it, but if I wasn't in the Church, we never could have done it. But then if the Church wasn't sometimes evil we wouldn't have needed to steal it… But then it keeps it out of the hands of someone like Cleo… But, then, other times…" He gave a long sigh, and got to the meat of the matter. "There are things like Molly. Molly, and how many other women did they burn? Men too, but mostly women. It makes me sick to even think about it. And I know I'm part of that. Even if Protestants did it here, I know the Church did it elsewhere, and that history becomes my history. And it makes me absolutely sick."

It was on Percy's lips to ask Joe to leave the Church. To keep doing crimes, and the pair would split all their ill-gotten gains straight down the middle. Because, after all, they hadn't yet discussed what life would look like when they got home. When Joe would be expected to shove stupid wafers down people's throats and spew bullshit at them from his pulpit every weekend. When Percy would still, likely, be jetting off to steal things, traffic things, give the occasional lecture at an elite university. When they would no longer be joined at the hip, inseparable, and so perfectly happy together.

But Joe's admissions quietened him. There was purpose

and meaning in the life, for Joe, that Percy had never quite realised the extent of before. As far as he was concerned, Joe could have done just as much good and more by letting the blood of his enemies then profiting from their fall… But Joe's way was gentler. Subtler. Possibly smarter. For certain things. And to Joe, it was the right thing. Which made it harder for Percy to say what he wanted to say, though it didn't do a thing to drown out the idea. "You could just steal the outfit."

Joe's laugh warmed Percy's chest from the inside out. "You're as ridiculous as you are beautiful."

"I'm not *that* ridiculous," Percy protested.

"No." The tip of Joe's finger, feather-light, touched the pronounced dip of Percy's upper lip, and slid down, parting his mouth, slowly, compellingly. "No one's *that* ridiculous."

Percy caught Joe by the wrist, kissing his knuckles one by one, staring deep into his eyes. "Leave the Church."

"No." The smile remained in Joe's gaze, in perfect synergy with the one on his lips, but both had a touch of melancholy about them now.

"Then listen to me." Percy placed a final kiss on Joe's fingers, then pressed those fingers against his own heart. "You're the best man on earth. I haven't doubted that for a second since the day I met you. You're not responsible for, or tarnished by, anything they've done. We all have an inheritance from parents and past lives, and it's rarely golden for any of us. The main thing is that you're going to make it right. You're going to *continue* to make it right. And I'll help you."

Joe's heart swelled with his words. "You didn't think twice, did you? About stealing that skull."

"What is there to think about?"

Joe shifted forward, his hips against Percy's, and kissed his beautiful fiancé. "Don't buy a pub over it."

Percy pulled back with a good-humoured frown. "I think I'd like to own a pub. We haven't discussed retirement yet."

"I am not retiring to Twatt."

"Why not?" Percy brushed a curl of Joe's thick hazelnut hair back from his too-beautiful brown eyes, a single strand threading itself through his long black lashes, allowing him a moment longer to linger on the gorgeous vision as he righted it. "You and me and the sheep? I'll cook and you'll be the bar wench."

Joe chuckled. "I can see it now. You half naked out the back, swearing at your pots and pans, a cigarette hanging out of your mouth the whole time." Joe kissed him again. "Come to think of it, for all I've heard about your cooking prowess, I'm yet to see any evidence of it."

"You will. When the pub closes tonight, come downstairs, and I'll take over the kitchen. I'll make you something you'll never forget."

Joe groaned softly, seeing the excitement on Percy's face, but starving after several whiskies and ales and nothing to eat since Lerwick. "I don't know how I'm going to wait that long."

"I'll find a way to keep you busy." Percy's thumb and forefinger were already working Joe's belt loose from its clasp. "But it will almost definitely involve me half naked, and a whole lot of swearing…"

CHAPTER SIXTEEN

DINNER WITH A WITCH('S HEAD)

Some time later, Percy stood in the pub kitchen, half naked, with a cigarette hanging out of his mouth. "Fuck you!" he shouted at the pan as his delivery of cognac resulted in a much larger flame than he had anticipated.

Joe, also half naked, sitting atop a bench, took a sip from the bottle of exceptional wine Percy had brought with them, adjusted his grip on Molly, who was tucked under his spare arm, and reflected that perhaps pub life would suit him after all. There didn't seem to be much of anything but horror in the world outside, while inside it was warm, Percy's stupidly thick, aged, expertly cut (supposedly) steaks that he'd bought from 'the best butcher in Scotland' smelled spectacular, and after an evening of incredible sex, Joe was very close to perfectly content.

For all the cursing and sparks, Percy had no trouble keeping several pans boiling, with the oven crisping dangerously thick chips all the while. When it was time, he plated the food as beautifully as a chef might, nodded for Joe to follow, and carrying two heavily laden dishes, settled them atop a table in front of the fire he'd been feeding throughout the entire process, until it lit the empty pub with a roaring warmth. He filled their wine glasses, then paused. "Should we put shirts on? This feels undignified."

Joe placed Molly in the centre of the table and dropped into his chair. The steak and wine and firelight said formal, but the line of Percy's adonis belt rising up behind the table, his abs and chest being licked by cosy orange light, screamed to Joe that formality was wildly overrated. "Sit."

It wasn't only the ungodly beauty of Percy that allowed Joe to reach the decision so quickly. The fact was, this first home-cooked meal felt right. It felt like this moment was the natural order of things. It held a promise of mornings in their kitchen together, after waking up together, after years together. Joe didn't want another night of starched shirts and expensive restaurants. He wanted a life with Percy—just Percy—and that was the moment Joe began to think he might be close to ready to go home.

Joe had agreed to marry Percy at least partially because he was caught up in the moment when Percy asked him to. And because he wanted Percy to be happy. And, well, who wouldn't want Percy for a husband? Only mad people, surely. But getting married had never, ever, been on his radar before. It wasn't even legal, so there had been no point in thinking about it, as far as Joe was concerned.

But there was Percy, fussing, adorably, about the amount of garlic in the sauce, the seasonality of the asparagus, something about the grain of the beef, and Joe wanted a gold band on his finger that would flash in firelight just like this for the rest of their lives. A million meals explained in excruciating detail until they were old and grey and just as in love as they were now.

Percy gave an apprehensive nod, so he must have finished his explanations around the time Joe finished his reflections, and accordingly, Joe sank his knife into the steak. Percy had cooked it exceptionally rare, and pale blood and oil mingled with the creamy sauce in a swirl that looked as delicious as it smelled. Joe bit into it, Percy watched on tenterhooks, and Joe, eventually, said, "When are we moving in together?"

Percy's face lit. "Really? It's good?"

"Good?" said Joe, trying to maintain the power of speech as the meat melted on his tongue, which he didn't know until that moment beef could do. He shoved more in, only this time doused in the perfectly garlicked sauce, mumbling around it, "This is the best thing that's ever happened to me."

And that comment, coincidentally, was perhaps the best thing that had ever happened to Percy, because he had wanted more than anything, as usual, to impress Joe. "Move into my place. I can do breakfast too."

Joe shook his head over a sip of wine. "I'm supposed to live in the rectory. Come live with me."

The rectory where Joe, when possessed, had cut the priest's head off and left it sitting in the centre of the dining table... Percy wasn't especially squeamish, but that mental image might enhance the dining experience there for some time to come. "My kitchen's brand new. State-of-the-art. I can do amazing things for you there."

"We'll get a new kitchen put in," Joe pushed. "Anything you like."

"But I have a dungeon at my place."

A good point. Joe had no dungeon. "But have you seen my courtyard? I've got grapes. And the cottage is adorable. Can you imagine brunch out there in the summer?"

Yes, Joe's place was all doilies and china and very old-fashioned everything. Quaint. In the extreme. Fine for a holiday. "I just don't see where I could keep my weapons. And I'm not sure the art would go with the rest of... it..."

Another convincing argument. Goya's Disasters of War

etchings would look a little out of place next to the tacky 'art' Joe's predecessor loved, that Joe now refused to part with, all kittens and rosy-cheeked children. And it was probably cruel to inflict that on Percy full time. And, to be fair, Percy's place, a refurbished church, was custom designed for Percy. Every inch of it, he had chosen himself, from the rugs to the 'borrowed' paintings to the antique chandeliers. His golden bathtub was something to behold.

Percy watched Joe quietly mulling everything over, and said, as casually as one might ask someone to pass the salt, "You know, if you quit the Church, you wouldn't owe them a thing, and you could live wherever you wanted. *With* whoever you wanted."

Joe relaxed his cutlery, a warning settling over his eyes. "That's the second time tonight you've asked me. The answer's the same."

"It was worth a shot." Percy threw back some wine with a deliberately calming smile and refocused. "Where would you keep Molly? Would she get her own special doily?"

He easily pulled a laugh from Joe. "I wasn't planning to keep her."

"Hrrrrrr," said Molly.

Joe and Percy locked eyes across the table, and a second later, she was in Percy's hands, his rich baritone speaking smoothly to her. "Would you like to come and live with me, darling?"

Molly kept her silence.

Percy turned her around to look at Joe. "Or do you think we should live with him instead?"

Joe rolled his eyes, and again, Molly didn't make a sound.

"Odd," said Percy.

"You're odd," Joe responded helpfully. He went back to his meal, though he kept half an eye on Molly as he ate. "I can't believe they wouldn't take fifty thousand for her. And I can't believe you offered it."

Percy shrugged. "We got a lot of money for stealing that Edvard Munch."

"You think the buyer will be satisfied?"

"I do. You saw. My artist's fake is just as good as the real one."

Perhaps Joe shouldn't have been surprised, by that time, that Percy had a regular professional forger on hand, but he still was. "You always have an artist for this sort of thing?"

Percy put his glass down excitedly. "Lakshmi. She's absolutely gorgeous. She's a proper criminal, and there isn't a thing she can't do. I'm in awe of her, truth be told. I could tell you of half a dozen paintings on display in prominent galleries right now that are hers. She's never dropped the ball on me once. Absolutely trustworthy, and a complete gem." He went back to his steak, a pleased gleam in his eyes.

"Hm." Joe ate. Joe drank. Joe couldn't bite his tongue. "And she's just a professional associate? Nothing more?"

Percy looked up brightly. "She is."

"A 'gorgeous' professional associate?"

"Well… I don't mean…" Five fingers tapped across the table. "I meant it in a—a gorgeous personality sort of way."

Joe studied him. Too carefully. "But *is* she gorgeous?"

"Gorgeous on the inside." Percy smiled. He wasn't giving an inch.

"And that woman tonight? Debbie, was it?"

The pleased gleam in Percy's eyes morphed into tired patience. "That was a one time only thing. And she knew that before we got into anything, so she really has no right to be upset with me."

Joe's cheek ticked with irritation. "Must have been memorable."

Percy let the comment go.

Joe did not let Percy's silence go. "You did say we were done with secrets."

"Are you sure you want that?" Percy sliced the meat slowly, and he kept his eyes on the glistening incision. "It's irrelevant to what we have now, and you're a very jealous person."

"I'm not a jealous person!" No response from Percy again, so Joe, a little more softly, prodded, "Was she… special?"

Percy's lips gave a little grimace. He let out a sigh, put down his cutlery, and said, "It wasn't remotely memorable for me. Not until the next day when she told me I was her first. And how was I to know? The woman was twenty-seven years old. She'd been chasing me for weeks, in that dull, stand-offish way some people do. I noticed, but I wasn't particularly interested. Then, my last night here, she threw herself at me. I told her before we hooked up that I had to leave the next day, and she still wanted to, so…" He twisted the stem of his wine glass. "It was something to do. Nothing more, nothing less. She played it off like it meant nothing, and I went with it. But in the morning she told me she loved me, begged me to stay, told me she'd given me her 'gift'. I suppose she thought telling me that would make me change my mind, but in all honesty, I couldn't get out of there fast enough. I did try to keep in touch and be chivalrous about the whole debacle, but she just kept crying every time she called, begging me to come back, as though we'd had anything to begin with. So I eventually stopped answering."

Percy expected to be reprimanded for just about any part of the confession other than the bit that Joe actually latched onto. "She chased you for *weeks*? I didn't know you'd stayed here for weeks."

Recommencing dinner, "I was here for three solid months."
Joe very nearly spat his wine. "Here? With Cleo?"
"Hrrrrrrr!" said the skull.

Percy scowled at the skull for the interruption. "Not *with* Cleo."

"Hrrrr!"

A little louder to drown out the unearthly rasps the bony mouth made, Percy continued, "She came and went while I was here, but I needed a place to get away to, so she let me stay at the Hall. I spent a good deal of my time in Lerwick, or travelling around Shetland. Between both of our comings and goings, not that much of it was spent with Cleo."

"Hrrrr!"

Joe turned the skull's face to the fire, his stomach doing that thing it always did when he thought of Percy with anyone else. "Were you two much closer than you've told me?"

"No. Maybe." The glass twisted a little faster and Percy's knee began to tap beneath the table, but he pushed on with the truth, just as he'd promised Joe he would. "I told you she was my friend. I told you we had a history, and I told you I wouldn't have thought her capable of the things she's accused of had I not witnessed the change in her myself. I got to know her very well over the years. We were close, but she was never my girlfriend. She was married before I ever knew her, and yes, I was her affair partner when the opportunity presented itself. Her husband's a bastard who will sleep with anyone in sight, so fair's fair. The marriage was a farce from day one. And everything that happened between us happened before I met you." Percy gave a little click of his tongue and glanced away with a small sigh. "I'm honestly still very fond of her. I miss her. And I still want proof of what she's supposed to have done. It's not that I don't believe Althea, because of course I do, but Cleo—"

"Heeeeee!" squealed the skull.

"I can see why they keep her in the fridge," Percy muttered, placing Molly's skull on the floor. "Cleo, as I was saying, was a nice person. She was sweet, and she was dreamy, occasionally caustic—often caustic, in fact—and I genuinely liked her. And that's all there was to it. I never fell in love with her, I never imagined a future with her, and I certainly never asked her to marry me."

Succinct.

Painfully succinct.

The last comment took the bitter edge off the pill, just as Percy had intended, but then Percy kept talking. "Oh, and I slept with Charlie and Vaila, too."

"What!" Joe actually did spit his wine this time, just a little.

Percy, mildly miffed, watched the trickle of red swirl into his carefully crafted garlic sauce, yet he held himself together admirably. "Would you like to swap plates?"

"Both?" Joe blustered. "At the same time? What are they, sixty?"

With an infuriatingly judgemental head tilt, "Ageism? I expected better from you, Joe."

"But—"

"And don't slut-shame me either. I can't entirely trust that they won't mention it, because Vaila looked like she wanted to invite you over, so I thought I should probably tell you before they do."

"But…" Joe's mouth did a silent wobble, before, "Charlie *and* Vaila? As in… From this afternoon?"

Percy shrugged. "Three months is a long time in Twatt." Joe was lost for words, so Percy helped him out. "Is all this honesty making you happy, darling? I'm doing my best. I could go on if you'd like more details?"

"No." Joe swallowed. Joe frowned. "I think… I think maybe we'll… We might stop doing that. With the honesty. To that extent, at least."

Percy smiled back proudly. "Just tell me anything you want to know. I'll give you all the details you like. I'm an open book now."

"Yes. You are. And I appreciate it." It was on the tip of his tongue to ask Percy exactly how many people he had slept with, but Joe was smarter than that. It was one thing to be forced to imagine gorgeous Percy with gorgeous Giordano, particularly if Joe was in the middle, but… No. He would let his mind wander no further than that. Ever again, if he could help it. "Maybe from now on, you just judge if it's pertinent for me to know something. And I'll trust you to make the decision whether to tell me about it or not."

Percy nodded, perfectly unsure which of the things he'd told Joe he should or should not have said.

"So, back to Cleo's place," Joe redirected.

"Herrrrrrrr," Molly moaned.

Joe glanced down at her. "Maybe we should give her a cigarette or something?"

"No smoking until after steak. What about Cleo's place?"

"Herrrrr!" said Molly.

"How terrifying is it?"

"Utterly. For a normal person. It was always clearly haunted. Lots of banging, creaking, things going missing. In truth, I never liked being there alone, though I felt safe enough to do it. But there's definitely a very dark feel in a few spots. One in particular. Cleo always talked about knocking through a sealed fireplace, restoring it."

Here the skull received a soft tap from Percy's shoe for an especially loud interruption, and he and Joe resolved silently to ignore her from there on out. "That fireplace, as I was saying, was sealed long after it was built. You could see the bricks were newer in that spot. Still old, though. I told her no, don't knock it through. Everything felt all wrong in that part of the house, but particularly there in that spot. Funnily enough, she'd always had the same feeling there, which is why she asked me and other guests about it. Everyone sensed it."

He bit the tip off an asparagus spear in a meditative sort of way, appearing to be sorting through hazy memories for anything else of significance. He hit on, "Oh, and there's a girl that wanders outside at night. A ghost of some sort. She weaves around between the graves. I watched her from the window, but she didn't notice me. Seems harmless enough."

"Graves?" Joe gasped out. "There are graves now?"

"Oh, yes. That's where we'll steal our replacement skull from." Percy dragged the long, green stem back through his sauce, explaining, "The place was abandoned, as you know, and I guess at some point another local cemetery filled up, so they needed a new one. The ground there doesn't freeze in winter due to some sort of microclimate around the lake, so it's a sensible option. There were already some dead buried there, anyway. They simply added some more."

"Ah. Good," said Joe. "So we're going to go to the haunted house you have a bad feeling in, to investigate murder, where there's a ghost wandering around the graveyard, where we're going to dig up a grave in that graveyard to steal a skull?"

"Mmm, and maybe more than one. Because if what Althea said is true, and Cleo's killed a bunch of teenagers, well…" He snapped a crisp chip in half and assessed Joe. "What would you do with the bodies?"

As though Percy needed a reminder as to why he adored Joe so desperately, Joe immediately responded, "I'd definitely bury them in the old graves."

Percy stifled the burst of butterflies in his stomach. "So we may have some rather grisly finds out there if we don't find the remains in the house. They should be relatively well-preserved from the cool of winter, depending what she did to them before they died. If she drained their blood first, I'd imagine there are fewer gases to build up in the bodies, so they——"

"Can we talk details after dinner?" asked Joe, also moving for a crunchily salted thick-cut chip in preference to what was left of his very red steak. He cracked it open and a veritable cloud of pillowy potato burst free.

"Sorry. Dreadful manners." Percy topped up Joe's wine and took another chip for himself.

Buying the exorbitantly priced, flaked sea salt had caused a minor argument at the shop, but as it crunched between Joe's teeth, he had to admit to himself, yet again, Percy had been exactly right to buy it. "The real question is, what did she want their blood for? If it was a spell, why did she need so much? And if she was feeding something… It's either very dead or very hungry by now."

"A worrying thought. And why only girls?"

"They're much easier to kidnap and overpower," Joe suggested. "And much less likely to be taken seriously by police if they look a certain way."

"Like Althea," Percy agreed. He softened the sentiment with a defeated chuckle. "My god, she has ghastly taste."

Joe laughed, too. "You're very good to buy her all the hideous things." Once he had accepted that Percy would spoil Althea and there wasn't a thing Joe could do to stop him, it had become its own entertainment to watch Percy's reactions to her choices. The yellow bikini in Sicily had very nearly pushed him over the edge, and it was just as well a bottle of wine arrived to keep him occupied about three minutes after she unveiled it at the beach. In front of Leo, of course, who didn't look half as disgusted as Percy had. Quite the opposite. Swallowing down a mouthful at the memory, Joe said, "Tell Leo to stay away from her, won't you."

Not that it was a question, but Percy supplied an assenting nod, topped with the news, "I told him I'd fire him if he makes a move within the next six months."

Subduing the eye-roll that came naturally, "I'm sure he's terrified."

Percy spoke in that rather soft and charming way he did on occasion where Leo and Althea were concerned. "He's a good kid. And when I'm done with him, he'll be the most eligible bachelor she's likely to meet. She'd be wise to throw her lot in with someone like that. But he knows he needs to let her get herself together first."

Joe raised an eyebrow. "He knows that, or you told him?"

"Both," said Percy. "But do give the boy some credit. There's a reason I made him my assistant." Joe took a breath to delve a little deeper into that mystery, but Percy was back to the last thing. "I think you're right about Althea's selection. On paper, she's a perfect victim."

"Interviewing her as a potential nanny would have allowed Cleo to ask more personal questions than any other job, I'm guessing. She would have known Althea was alone overseas and unlikely to be missed. That she had no family nearby."

"All true." Percy, finished his meal, pushed his cutlery together, and leaned back in his chair with his wine. "You're smart and pretty."

A perfectly unsophisticated giggle was carefully controlled by a deep-voiced, "Thank you."

Percy watched him a little longer, then decided aloud, "Let's do the first month at your place." It was worth it just to see the way Joe's eyes brightened.

"What? You'll move in with me?"

"We'll trial a month, if that suits you. Then, if we haven't been caught living in sin by your parishioners, we'll reassess the situation. Does that sound okay?"

Percy was a dream. An absolute dream. To have been a priest, with no hope of love for so long, and now to have a man who cooked like this, who was willing to make a sacrifice like that, who looked the way Percy did, who adored him and would do anything for him, who was about to go dig up bodies with him for no reason other than basic altruism—it was beyond logic. Beyond luck. Almost beyond reality. "That sounds more than okay. If you think you can put up with the décor."

Percy's eyes dipped over his exquisite fiancé. "There's only one thing I'm going to be looking at. If I'm with you, I don't care about the rest of it."

Joe squeezed Percy's hand across the table. "Explain to me how I got so lucky."

"Not everyone would call it luck to have a madman obsessed with them." Percy lit three cigarettes, passed one to Joe, and place another beneath Molly's white teeth, after he planted her back in the centre of the table.

Joe breathed in Percy's dangerous gorgeousness along with the toxic smoke. Blue eyes he would die for one thousand times over. His one true love. "I wouldn't change a thing."

True to his word, Percy could, and did, also make breakfast. Joe awoke in their four-poster bed to eggs and bacon and tea and toast and Percy. Half-naked Percy, crawling back into the sheets with a kiss, his skin cool from the morning air, flush against Joe's cozy body. Kisses fresh and beautiful, and the delightful energy of the man, rested and ready for an adventure, and so happy. Joe didn't think he'd ever seen Percy that happy, despite the screams of the cursed skull that had kept them both awake half the night.

He knew Percy must have, somewhere in the back of his mind, the horror of the day ahead, but he didn't say a word about it. It was, after all, par for the course. Pleasure where he could take it, appalling hideousness and death, then pleasure again and twice as frenzied. Back and forth, back and forth, like a pendulum.

It was strange for Joe to observe, but it was an honour to be the person—the *only* person—who got to be there for both extremes. And maybe, it occurred to Joe, maybe that was why Joe was the one. Percy's one and only true love. He was the one person who could face the darkness, then revel in the light with him.

They ate, they laughed, they talked about anything but the awful day that awaited them, then Percy finally climbed out of bed to address the pile of mail Leo had forwarded from his Paris office, which had sat waiting on a side table for a good twenty-four hours before Percy had bothered to look at it.

With the teacup and saucer balanced gracefully in one hand, Percy began sorting through the tower of letters. He made a quick assessment of business and personal, throwing the former to the side in a messy heap, then, one by one, he commenced scanning hand-written return addresses in the 'personal' pile. "From Aubrey," he began.

Joe smiled. Aubrey was a lovely woman, and one of Percy's most recent, though closest, friends. A woman firmly attached to, and in a relationship with, Percy's brother's god-sister. She didn't have a crush on Percy at all. Joe liked her a lot.

Percy threw down another letter. "Aubrey again."

Joe knit his brow slightly.

"Aubrey," said Percy with the third, adding a smug smirk.

"Is something wrong?" It had only been a month or two since last they'd met. Not long for such an accumulation of correspondence.

"She wants my soup recipe," Percy drawled. "And I'm not going to give it to her."

"She's written you three letters in as many weeks about soup?"

Percy nodded sharply. "She thinks I'm being unreasonable, but she wants to cook soupe à l'oignon in spring." He scoffed loudly at the thought.

Joe squinted. "And you won't let her… because?"

With an even harsher squint directed right back at him, "It's a winter soup. That's disgusting, Joe."

"Isn't it up to her when she eats soup?"

"Aubrey," Percy narrated as the next letter fell into the pile. "Not if it's my soup."

"Just give it to her—" Joe sighed out, only to be cut off by a loud exclamation.

"Aha! Look, one from Evelyn." Percy ripped open his brother's letter, an envelope stuffed full of several pages fully covered in elegant handwriting, then, "Oh."

"Mmm?" Joe raised his handsome eyebrows.

He received lightly pursed lips and a side-eye in response. "It's mostly for you."

With a smile spreading across his face that he was hopeless to hide, "Really?"

"Mmm. Really." There was a slightly joking but slightly miffed grimace as Percy threw the letter down on Joe's excessively beautiful abdomen, stretched back in the bed with the sheet barely covering him as he was. Percy leaned down and kissed him. He kissed him again. He kissed him once more and went back to his letters.

One last envelope remained, which Percy flipped over to read the return address on. His face fell, and he shoved the letter into his pocket without a word. Catching Joe's eyes on him, there was an attempt at a smile, quickly shut down by a mixture of whatever was going on in his head and slight embarrassment.

"Who's that one from?" asked Joe.

"Only…" The slightest pause, as though he considered saying something else. "Only Anna."

"Ah."

Percy's tea was placed down and forgotten. He turned his back on Joe, and he crammed himself secretively into the window seat without another word.

Joe hated the immediate physical reaction he had, but his heart already beat a little harder in his chest, and his stomach felt as though he'd just eaten six bricks for brunch. In his discomfort, he pulled the sheet higher and placed his own tea down, but Percy turned his head to look back within a few seconds.

"Did you want to come?" He waited there, slightly anxious-looking. "To the window seat?"

"No," Joe lied.

"Mmm." Percy returned to his letter.

It was none of Joe's business. None of his business at all. Whatever was between Percy and Anna was between them, and it was complicated. Very complicated. And Percy had a right to his secrets and his old relationships. Even if she was someone he had probably been in love with. Even if he was with Joe now…

What was the protocol for that sort of thing? Joe hadn't a clue. Was he allowed to ask where the two of them stood with each other? Or was that needy and possessive? But Anna was Joe's friend too, wasn't she? Not like she was Percy's 'friend'. She hadn't written Joe a letter. A letter like the one Percy needed to smuggle away to read alone.

Joe lay in bed and stared off into space, thinking the same thoughts over and around until he was stunned out of his reverie by papers falling onto his stomach.

"Read it." Percy wandered back across the room to take up his teacup. "Something's wrong."

Without another word, and with a good deal of surprise, Joe took up the letter from Anna and read. No flirting. No cute private jokes. Not much of anything. A rundown of how things had been, some thoughts on the books she'd been reading, the usual reflections on what someone might be up to on holiday, and some requests for book recommendations from Percy.

Joe was relieved to find it all so impersonal. It could have been addressed to him or to anyone else. "I don't see anything wrong."

"It's not what she says, it's what she doesn't say," Percy responded, tying the knot back up tight in Joe's stomach.

He threw the letter down on the bed with an irritated half-laugh. "What did you want her to say?"

"I don't know," said Percy, pacing. "Something of substance? That's the kind of letter you write when you're trying to not say something."

Well, that was true. No flirting. No cute private jokes. Not what Joe had expected, either. But the last thing he needed was Percy reading between Anna's lines. "She's clearly fine."

"What does Evelyn say?"

"I haven't read it yet."

Percy gave a directive nod towards the hefty letter, so Joe sighed and took it up. The letter was long, meandering, written over several days. It was warm and funny and very much like Evelyn. Percy offered an occasional scowl at Joe's various smiles and laughs and intermittent blushes until he finally set the letter down. "It's maybe a little guarded, but he seems fine, too."

"A little guarded." Percy waved his finger at the letter. "That's not like Eve."

"It's just a letter. He's got a lot on—"

"Anna," Percy interrupted. "What does it say about Anna?"

The colour this time was not a blush, but a flush of anger. "Nothing. Hardly anything."

"From Eve? There you have it. Something is wrong. We have to go back." Percy put on his watch, began gathering his mail, making as though he were about to leave for the airport right then and there.

Joe sat up in disbelief. "Over that? Over two letters that say nothing at all?"

"Yes," Percy said simply.

"Percy…" Joe watched him scan the room for anything

that might belong to them, though they'd had no time to unpack much. "Percy, stop."

Full of distraction, Percy spared him half a glance. "What is it?"

"What do you mean 'what'? We're here for a reason. We've got dead teenagers to investigate, a ghost trapped in a skull, zombies, Cleo murdering people—"

He was at the wardrobe, throwing his clothes into a suitcase. "Don't worry. We'll take the skull with us. If we go now, we have a few hours before they'll discover—"

"Percy!" Joe's furious tone finally halted Percy's movements. He looked across, but in a vexed way, like he'd just heard the worrisome whining of a mosquito. "Is this an Anna thing? Because…" Joe hadn't once wanted to ask it, because he was terrified of the answer he might get, but the question slipped out. "Do you love her?"

Lightning fast, Percy turned away, eyes searching the room again, but this time seeming to see very little of it. "They're our family. If they need us, they come first."

"Eve's your family, not Anna."

The words flew out of Percy's mouth, fast and sharp. "Can we not make this about your petty jealousy, just this once? You're becoming a bore."

Percy had always had a tongue like a viper, but he didn't turn it on Joe. Not once. Until then. And Joe crumbled on contact. He fell silent, and the look on his face was worse for Percy than the blow had been for Joe, but Joe couldn't have known that.

Percy was on the bedside in a heartbeat, even as Joe was trying to extricate himself from the sheets. "Stay. Please."

Joe, feet on the floor, sitting on the edge of the bed with his back to Percy, waited, unsure, the unprecedented nature of the thing sending him into a spin. He felt the weight of Percy as he leaned across, but he refused to look back at the sound of Percy's carefully gentle voice.

"I'm sorry. I'm very worried about both of them. If they don't have each other, then they'll fall apart, and… That's something I know too well…" On a long exhalation, without reaching for Joe, he finished with, "He cannot cope without her."

"And I'm sure you wouldn't mind being there in time to pick up the pieces." It was a bitter jibe that drew equal vehemence from Percy.

"How can you say that to me?"

"Do you love her?"

The response, this time, was fast and firm. "I love you and only you."

But in quick succession, "You would say that."

Percy's fury was barely repressed as he shot back, "Of course I'd say that, it's true. I can imagine how this looks to you—"

"It looks exactly like you want to be the rebound when they break up."

Finally it boiled over. "What the fuck is that?" Percy snapped. "She's my friend and I'm worried about her, and that should be okay. I should be able to talk to you about this. But if it's not Anna, then it's Cleo, or Giordano, or goddamned Debbie. I'm trying—really, I am—but sometimes it feels like no matter what I do, I'm never going to be good enough for you."

Joe turned back, his eyes flaring in anger equal to Percy's, but with a jab of guilt in his gut. "That's not true."

Percy's immaculate chin lifted in challenge. "It is, though, isn't it? I'm sorry I have a past. I'm sorry that didn't involve you, but had you not been quite so faithful to your God, had you put me first like I wanted to put you first, then nothing ever would have happened with Anna. If you would have chosen me, I would have chosen you, and we would have been together from the start."

"Like how Anna was with your brother?" The words Joe spoke shocked him into silence, and he badly wished he could cram them back in. It wasn't remotely fair, and he knew it, but he was too angry to give an inch by apologising, despite Percy's silent, withdrawn face.

He did the only thing he could think to do, and he fled the scene. He gathered some clothes and disappeared into the ensuite, slamming the door and leaving Percy to sit alone in the room to contemplate the many mistakes he'd made. Or hadn't made. Because they both knew Percy's brother was as good as dead when Percy took up with Anna, in whatever way he did. In whatever way had made him just as obsessed with her back then as he claimed to be with Joe now.

Joe wrenched the shower on and tried to get a grip of himself. Yes, he was jealous. Insanely jealous. But he had been doing so well. So well with all Percy's admissions and love affairs, and even if it drove him up the wall to think of Percy with all those people, he believed Percy when he said it meant nothing. He could see the way he fit with Percy so perfectly, in the way no one else could.

Almost no one else.

Because there Anna was and would always be. That little bit darker than Joe. That little bit more dangerous and probably more exciting for it. Forbidden. Off limits. The one person Percy couldn't have. Someone with breasts and hips and female lips that Joe wondered if Percy missed. Someone who was an atheist, and who, in so many ways, would compliment Percy…

By the time Joe was dressed, fixing his hair, he was calm enough to see how unreasonable he may have acted, but not nearly calm enough to control it. He had no doubt that once he walked through that door, he'd find Percy packed, fully dressed, ready to run back to Anna.

Joe refused. He wouldn't go with him. He was never going to be Percy's second choice. He would send a message that he didn't even need Percy, untrue as it was. But he wanted Percy to believe it. To know that if Anna threw Percy over, there would be nothing to come back to. That Joe would be somewhere in Europe for what was left of his vacation leave, and he would be… doing something. Anything. Anything that didn't involve Percy.

Joe, head held high, thrust the door open, expecting to see their suitcases in the doorway, but no. He saw only Percy, still half-undressed, watch off and set down beside him, writing at the desk.

Joe was both relieved and perplexed. "What are you doing?"

He didn't look up. "I'm sending Aubrey the recipe. Like you said. It's really up to her when she wants to make it. Even if I think it's a travesty."

He scrawled at his paper, while Joe felt perfectly undecided about what to do. Poke the beast? Give in to the anger? Let him get away with it as though he hadn't done a thing wrong? "I'll see you later."

In one quick shift, Percy's eyes fell on Joe's clothes. Black. With his white collar. Dressed for church. He sent a glower towards the cross on the hill. "I thought it was important to you that we work this morning."

"You seemed to have other things on your mind."

Percy's gaze darkened as he settled it back on Joe. "I have you on my mind. And nothing else. And now you're going to run out on me for that bullshit?"

"That bullshit?"

"We have things to discuss. I'm here, putting you first, and as usual, I'm way down your list."

"Way down my list? I have all of two things in my life."

"And there you go again, running off after this crap." He threw a hand towards the cross, his voice returning to the same incandescence it held before Joe had left him to cool down. "It makes you feel awful, you won't live in my house because of it, it took you forever to even look at me, and now one argument and you go running back to God. You throw your jealousy at me like I've done anything wrong, but I'm never your first choice, nor have I ever been. Not like you are mine, every single time. If anyone has a right to be jealous, it's me."

"You? Jealous?" Joe laughed bitterly. "Percy Ashdown, jealous. The man who simply reaches out and takes everything he wants in this life, without regret or consequences, imagines he has any idea what it's like to be jealous. Please."

Joe was on the other side of the bedroom door within seconds, ignoring Molly's wheezes as he walked out of the pub, splashing through the puddle of her blood, to make the miles-long walk to the distant cross on the hill, to prove some stupid point to Percy that he was no longer sure he wanted to prove at all.

CHAPTER EIGHTEEN
GOD'S FUCKBOY

Percy watched Joe from his window. Ever more distant. Smaller and smaller. And gone.

And just as lovely as ever.

He opened a bottle of brandy and paced the large room for some time.

He'd never, never meant to speak to Joe like that. Not ever. The ridiculous question had thrown him was all.

He wasn't *in* love with Anna. He loved her, certainly. Adored her. But he was absolutely not *in* love with her. It just so happened that the exact second Joe had asked him, Percy was experiencing the vile and irrepressible memory of being possessed and slamming his fist into her stomach so hard he'd knocked all the air out of her. And the thought of that— anyone or anything doing that to her again… He'd felt he might vomit. He had momentarily felt incredibly ill, and panicked, because he couldn't trust that she would call him if she needed him. If *they* needed him. Not after everything. Not with his brother and Joe involved, and all their feelings on the line.

Then, right in the middle of that memory, that galling question.

He'd reacted with his habitual defensiveness that invariably took the form of attack, and now the damage was done.

And Joe, who accused Percy of harbouring secret feelings that Percy didn't remotely harbour, had run off to be with that bastard, God.

It was incensing, to say the least. Percy here, left alone, with no choice but to drink this very good brandy by himself and ruminate on unpleasant feelings. And Joe, over there, probably sharing his feelings with that prick. Talking about what an asshole Percy was. Wearing that nice outfit that he knew Percy liked so much…

But Percy would set it right soon enough.

He dropped into the seat by the desk and doubled his effort writing the letter Joe had asked him to write to Aubrey.

He didn't write one to Evelyn or Anna. He would ask Joe to write those instead.

When he finished his letter, he set to pacing some more.

It took hours.

Whatever was keeping Joe so long with his stupid religion was taking forever.

That stupid bearded bastard… What were they even talking about?

Percy searched the inn and failed to find shovels to dig graves. He did find a nifty crowbar, though, and this he took up to their room to present to Joe later.

He sharpened his knife.

He tried to think up something extravagant to make for dinner.

Finally, he caught a flash of Joe through the window and readied himself as best he could.

Upon Joe's return, the first thing he saw was Percy reclining in a high-backed red-velvet chair, long legs crossed and thrown to one side, arms languid on darkly varnished mahogany supports, except the one lazy hand, upturned, with Percy's good brandy in the correct glass, warming and unfolding in the heat of his palm.

He was just about dressed. Pressed grey trousers down to his beautiful bare feet, his leather belt pulled tight, cinching in his white shirt. The tie, he had forgone, and the shirt folded open three-buttons down, giving just the right sort of glimpse of skin. His cuffs were undone, loosely rolled past his elegant wrists, which would have felt so nice pressed against Joe's instantly desirous lips.

Desirous, but wary.

Joe threw his key down on the side table, leaned his shoulder against the door to shut it, and slid his hands into his pockets to await Percy's welcome.

The voice came bitter and acidic, like a bad Scottish coffee. "You've been with *Him* again, haven't you?"

Joe burst out laughing then leaned his head back against the door.

Percy swished the brandy around in faux irritation. "What's He got that I haven't?"

"I don't know." Joe shrugged. "Magical powers?"

Percy's sulky reply swept over a handsome pout. "I've got magical powers."

"Billions of followers?"

Percy rolled his blue eyes up to the ornate ceiling. "Sycophants, the lot of them."

"Mostly true," Joe conceded.

Percy dipped his head to the side, thick dark hair tumbling across his left cheekbone as he settled his gaze on Joe. "Is He as good looking at me?"

Joe's delectable lips drew into a smile. "Not according to any depiction I've ever seen."

"What if I grew a beard?"

"Don't you dare."

Percy's smile mellowed to penitent adoration. "I'm sorry."

Joe's eyes softened to their usual state of ardour. "Me too."

"Come here."

Joe kicked his shoes off, Percy placed his brandy down on a nearby table, and lifted his arms in time to catch Joe's hips as Joe leaned over and placed a long, absolving kiss on his lips. Percy held him there with one hand drifting up to caress his cheek, his sincere blue eyes searching Joe's. "I love you. And I won't be difficult if you want to go to church again."

Joe kissed him, then let his head rock back to make way for Percy's lips on his neck. "It's kind of messed up, you know. Being jealous of God."

Percy uncrossed his long legs and wrapped them around Joe's thigh, pulling him in a little closer. "Can you blame me?" His heated words whispered over Joe's ear. "He's the only other man you'll get on your knees for." Percy sank his teeth into Joe's earlobe, and his hand moved to Joe's belt.

"Percy," Joe whispered, on a smitten, resigned, ecstatic, defeated breath. His fingers slipped under his white collar to pull it loose, but Percy's hand closed over them the very same second.

"Leave it."

Percy's other hand was on his dick now, already leaking pre-cum against the inside of his black vestments. He closed his fingers around the thick length and ran a too-light stroke all the way up. Joe pressed into him, greedy for more, and Percy shifted his hand softly, that little bit too distant. Percy found his mouth, dragging the tip of his tongue across Joe's lower lip, the same so-close-but-too-far temptation driving Joe mad from both directions.

He wrenched Percy's belt open, refusing Percy's control of the game. He fell to his knees and broke Percy's enticingly erect cock free of his just-applied trousers. His first kiss fell right at the base of his dick, and from there he kissed a line, slow and gentle, up one side.

Percy ripped his own shirt over his head and settled a little deeper into his chair to get a better view. He knew how beautiful he was. He positively revelled in it. The only thing that could have enhanced that image of his firm and undulating muscles in the glow of firelight, of that glorious, pulsing, full erection, was the long dark eyelashes of his lover, closed in their enjoyment of his dick. The lips that were too pink for decency. The deep brown eyes drunk with lust that looked up at him when he reached the crown of his cock, and said, "On my knees like this?"

Gently, gently, he kissed Percy's dick, his lips hot and wet and begging to be filled to the brim with Percy's cum. "Very nearly," Percy breathed, fully expecting Joe to follow what was closer to a direction than a hint, and slip that beautiful mouth over the tip of his cock. Instead, Joe grinned, then dipped his head to the other side, beginning another teasing, torturous, incensing climb of Percy's long shaft.

That sensual, glorious, completely delicious bastard. Percy had a good mind to take him in hand, but after all, a priest on his knees kissing your dick in an ancient lodge on a stormy Shetland day is something that should be savoured. In theory. If you can stand it long enough.

Joe's kisses moved all the way to the tip again, then that smile—that delectable, vicious smile as he sank back down, sending Percy close to apoplectic. "Stand up," he said sharply, fully prepared to take Joe's dick in his own mouth and show him how it's done.

"Nah, I'm good down here." And he kissed a little higher, along the centre, just as provokingly.

Percy's dick throbbed against his nose. "You're a troublemaker."

Joe's lascivious eyes rose over the gorgeous cock. "I learned from the best."

The hotter than hot—volcanically hot—perfectly wet mouth took Percy deep. "Fuck," he sighed out. Joe was wonderful. So wonderful. The best fiancé a man could ever ask for. The best fiancé whose fingers needed to explore Percy's sculpted abs even as his flat and firm tongue traversed Percy's length. The best fiancé who it was impossible to stay mad at or argue with for more than five minutes because he was too, too sweet and entirely too beautiful.

Then why this niggling doubt in the back of Percy's mind? Why this something, even now, when he was halfway down Joe's throat, that seemed to sit between them?

That something, he knew, was the relentless and harrowing question that would not budge from his mind: what would God's dick be like? Would it be longer, or wider, or more glorious than his? He wondered if Joe would make that satisfied rumble in the back of his throat if God was fucking his mouth. He wondered if God would have half the self restraint he had to let Joe take his time and wind him up to the point of explosive insanity, or if God would take a grip of Joe's hair and plunge his cock so deep Joe would have trouble deciding whether dick or air was more essential for survival.

The thought of it, of God fucking Joe, drove Percy mad. Madder than usual. Which is saying something, because Percy, an atheist, should have been above such speculation, but that day, he discovered he was not.

Joe's lips were tighter around his dick, his movement was swifter and even more exquisite, and under normal circumstances he would have had Percy on a hair trigger by now.

But what did God's cum taste like? Better than his?

He couldn't stand it anymore.

"Darling." He lifted Joe from his dick, his bewildered, slightly panicked eyes at having been thus torn away from the object of his desire, adding a spark of regret to Percy's uncontrollable jealousy. He soon extinguished it by leaning forward to meet the lips he turned up. "How much do you love me?"

Brief enamoured confusion swept over the handsome brow. "More than anything."

"That's what I thought." Percy stood, Joe's chin still in hand, pulling him to standing with him. He slid a palm behind Joe's belt and grabbed a hold of his dick, just as Joe took his in hand. Percy worked at the belt with his other hand, their lips pressed together, then Percy turned Joe, who backed away easily enough towards the bed, which was not at all where Percy wanted him.

A quick shift in a new direction, and Joe found himself spun around, tripping with one shove from Percy to land in the soft, cool confines of the window seat. His back was against the glass with a firm press of Percy's hand, and Percy had Joe's dick in his mouth a second later. Immediate, scalding, fast, it was enough to make him come within seconds, but Percy pulled back when he felt the familiar sensation of Joe's orgasm on the way, and Joe caught himself, right on the edge, in unprecedented confusion. "What are you doing?"

Percy's mouth again, deliberate and fast and hot for perhaps a minute, and Joe so close, and then gone again. "Percy!"

Percy was up, Joe was up, and Joe was turned and thrown against the glass, smooth and icy against his burning hands and cheek. Percy, always prepared somehow, had lube from god only knew where, kisses on Joe's shoulder, and a hand on Joe's cock. Joe's cock, wild and erect, displayed for anyone who should happen to walk past the inn at that moment, being worked by Percy's devilish hands as his ass was invaded by the most divine dick known to man.

"We can't do this here," Joe managed to whisper as he felt the first welcome inch of Percy.

"Why not?" Percy sighed against his ear. "Are you worried someone's going to see?" Because there was no one. The pub wouldn't open for hours. They were surrounded by wild nothingness, only sheep and green hills and all the low grey sky and Joe being fucked up against the vaulted window of his sumptuous bedroom. No people there to witness the way Joe's hips bucked back against Percy, the way his body pleaded for more, the smooth strokes that Joe loved and indulged in and tried to deny, so he, maybe, could return the favour for Percy. No people to comment on or notice the compelling sight of a naked adonis defiling a priest in the window.

But Percy wasn't looking for people.

His dark, cool, jealous eyes fell on the huge black cross of the church across the way—the only building in sight—the only witness, other than Joe, of his physical and spiritual supremacy. "Who do you love?"

"You, Percy," Joe gasped out as Percy drove into him, fingers deep in his hair, teeth in the skin of his neck, that hand running over his dick as if it were his own.

"Me, and who else?"

"Nobody," Joe groaned, half in perplexity, half in ecstasy. "Only you."

Percy held Joe's hand to the glass, fingers entwined with his, his other forearm guiding the movement of Joe's hips, fucking him harder and harder, and always, always those relentless fingers fucking his dick at the same time.

"I'm not going to last much longer," Joe rasped.

He needn't have. Percy knew it for a fact because he knew Joe's orgasms as well as he knew his own. He knew exactly how desperate he was, how needy he was, and how much power he had over Joe when he stopped, halted the movement of his fingers, his thumb pressing on Joe's slit, the very tip of his own dick hard up against Joe's sweet spot, when he said, "Then who's your god now?"

"What?" A flooring clarity hit Joe as he turned his head, and saw Percy's molten gaze aimed straight out and across the barren landscape, directed with burning hatred at the church on the hill. "Percy—"

Percy took a firm hand to Joe's shoulder and slammed his dick in hard. "Who?"

Wrong.

Wrong. Wrong. Wrong.

So wrong.

But fuck, it was hot.

Percy's jealousy, Percy's love for him, Percy swiping his thumb across the top of Joe's cum-laden dick and doubling down on the cruel bliss of his command over Joe's pleasure. "Percy—"

"Say it," he hissed against the shell of Joe's ear.

Joe's head was wrenched back against Percy's shoulder, a bruising kiss delivered to his parched lips, and a dick shoved so deep into him he fleetingly decided that reports of the torturous nature of death by impaling had been grossly over-stated. He could no longer hold back the flow of desperately loving words that broke free. "It's you. Percy, it's you."

Percy pulled back and sank his dick deep again. "Who?"

"Percy, it's you," Joe all but begged, the unrelenting beat of Percy's hand almost choking his pulsing cock. "It's you. I love you so much. You're my god now. It's you Percy. Percy—" A silent scream of pleasure cut the words from his mouth. Long ribbons of cum painted the window, obliterated the church from view, drew a whimper from Joe and doubled him over until he could barely support himself with the intensity of his full body orgasm. Percy, meanwhile, redirected the stream of Joe's cock, coating his religious garments in his own spunk, which Percy ran his hand through, smearing it all over his shirt, his collar, his neck, then, satisfied, he really let loose. He took a hold of both hips and fucked Joe just as hard as his pride demanded, his heart aglow at being the chosen one—at being *everything* to Joe.

Joe's dick was so sensitive, so tender from its thorough use, that a short time later he flinched pleasantly at the gentle hand that found his balls. "Percy, I can't."

"I know you can." And Percy fucked him. And he didn't stop fucking him until he'd wrung a second, miraculous, celestial, exultant orgasm from Joe, before his hazy, sex-drunk brain could allow him a moment to think. Only then did Percy let go, with the air of a victor, convinced of his permanent place in Joe's heart and mind—convinced that even God couldn't fuck Joe half as well as he just had. He indulged fully in his pleasure, anointing Joe's skin with cum, confident the last boundary between the two of them had been obliterated, as he fell shaking against Joe's back.

Beautifully spent, he kissed Joe's cheek, pulled out, slapped Joe's firm ass, and went to clean up, perfectly satisfied with the way the morning had eventually gone.

Joe, meanwhile, watched his cum drip and thin and evolve into a milky, misty vision of the church. He was assailed by a mingled shock of shame and self-reproach, augmented by the all-too-familiar sensation of not really knowing why he felt that way. His hand went to his wet collar, and in half a second, he had wrenched his trousers back up over his hips. "What did you do?"

"What's wrong, handsome?" Percy virtually sang from the bathroom.

Joe was in the doorway, eyes aflame, lips tight. "Did you deliberately fuck me in front of the church?"

Percy's eyes cut from his handsome reflection over to Joe. "Yes. I wanted Him to see." He skipped past Joe and picked his crumpled trousers up from the floor, inspecting the creases regretfully.

"I'm sorry, what? Who? *God?* You wanted *God* to see you fuck me in the window?"

That grin was straight back on his happy face. "Yes." He threw the trousers down and moved to the wardrobe for a fresh pair.

"You don't even believe in God!" Joe yelled.

"Technically, no, I don't," said Percy, sliding his legs into the immaculately pressed trousers, ripping a new shirt off its hanger. "But just in case, I want to be sure. We're probably both destined for Hell, but should I end up in purgatory, you're coming to keep me company. Best He knows now, so He doesn't get any ideas about keeping you as his fuckboy." He dropped a swift kiss on Joe's lips, retaining his grip on Joe's chin, his eyes loving, authoritative, hypnotic, as he said, "I'm yours and you're mine. There's no one else. Ever again. Don't you agree?"

Joe, heart in his throat, whispered a bewildered, "Yes."

"Then let's get ready and go investigate these dead teenagers." And off he wandered, like a happy, sexy, bouncy golden retriever puppy, to swill brandy and clean windows and do it all, seemingly, without a care in the world.

Joe would have been appalled—more appalled—if not for that last flippantly made comment.

Percy's heart, deep, deep down, below the layers of possessiveness and thoughtlessness and impulsivity, beat good and true and strong. Joe knew the turmoil that was, and would always be, just beneath the surface.

And Joe loved every ludicrous inch of him.

And Joe, despite what he thought he should feel at having been thus manipulated into renouncing God in favour of Percy Ashdown, was, in fact, all aglow inside.

It was a nasty emotion, jealousy. Yet the taste of Percy's filled him with a reassurance not quite as good as, but on the way to as good as, that gold band that he had begun to dream of.

What did it matter if Percy needed to know he was Joe's most loved before he stepped into the waiting horror? If, before he put himself on the line, again, to do the best he could to make the world slightly less shit, he needed Joe completely?

It may have been all manner of wrong, in theory. Yet somehow Percy always found a way, no matter what, to make even the worst things feel exactly right.

And what god wouldn't understand that?

Not one Joe could ever put his faith in.

PERCY'S SOUPE À L'OIGNON

Dearest Aubriest,

How to begin? I know I haven't written for a long time, so I'll start with my apology. Please know I received every one of your letters and please don't stop writing simply because I'm a terrible correspondent. In truth, Joe and I have been far busier than either of us thought possible, but that's no excuse.

Speaking of Joe, things are going remarkably well. I'll read him all the parts of your letters fit for public consumption (which, don't worry, isn't much) and he misses you terribly too, though not as much as I do. He's annoyingly insistent we come and see you all again soon, however, as you will soon see, this letter will be stamped from Lerwick in the Shetland Isles, which makes it rather difficult to get to Endymion College. In fact, even Lerwick is located a considerable distance from where we're actually staying, but the journey to town is a pleasant one and worth it to bring you your salvation.

Here we come to the point of this letter. I have, as you will no doubt have seen by now, enclosed the document you requested. I told you already, never to do this in spring or summer, only winter or late autumn at a push, but as you sounded desperate, and as I hear it is unseasonably cold there, I will allow it just this once.

I provide one final warning and I hope you will take my words seriously: if you do this on a warm day, you will regret it. Not only will you never forgive yourself, no one else will forgive you. People have longer memories than you think for this sort of thing. Don't fuck it up.

Now, we've discussed stock at length, and I know you're on the same page here. (I'm sure you appreciate the joke as I am writing at the time.) (That probably didn't need pointing out, but I'm not getting a fresh sheet of paper now.) Your stock is going to be beef stock, and of course you will be making it yourself. Don't skimp on this step (I know you won't).

I will pause briefly here to add one more word on the stock. I notice you didn't mention who your guests are, and whether this is due to delicacy (and you should know you need not be delicate with me—we'll have it all out when I get back) or because you know I'm unlikely to care who your friends are, but if you are inviting Evelyn, you may, this time only, use a good vegetarian beef stock. You know, I say 'good' and I know what you're thinking, but it's Eve and we must make allowances for his sensitive nature, and these things have come on in leaps and bounds over the years.

I know. Believe me, I know.

You're only going to use brown onions. DO NOT think you can add an expression of artistic intrigue here. Brown onions or nothing. If you use red onions, shallots (god forbid), any mixture of onions, you are going to sink the thing before you even start. Brown onions only. Yes, I know, you call them yellow onions. I'm not going to fight with you about this again.

You will fry your brown onions in butter and olive oil, and I swear, Aubrey, if a pinch of sugar so much as approaches that pot, I will know, and I will never give you my risi e bisi recipe. It goes without saying that I got it from the best and wisest of all Venetian nonnas (yet here I am saying it) and I will not betray her trust to a person who puts sugar in her onions.

Your sweetness, of course, will come from an appropriate cooking time. Slowly, slowly, in butter, oil and salt, you will fry your onions for at least six hours. Eight is better. Don't you dare tell me you have more important things to do. This is not a soup you can rush and if you turn it off one minute too soon, I will know. The veil is very thin here in Scotland, so don't think I won't smell it.

Watch your onions religiously, adjust the heat appropriately, scrape the pot over and over. This makes your soup rich in flavour and colour. This is the key. If you fail to give your soup the appropriate care during this time, it will be an embarrassing failure no one will ever forget. No one worth mentioning, anyway.

When AT LEAST five hours have elapsed (and I know you're watching the heat carefully), you're going to add some garlic. Here is a small flourish of your choice. I like to slice them lengthways, paper thin, but you do as you see fit.

Yes, I know, but fuck the purists. Those bastards would have the leeches on you trying to suck the impurity from your soul. It clearly didn't work on me, because here I am telling you to put garlic in the soup. Everyone will say, what is it that sets your soup apart, Aubrey? Flavour, Aubrey.

When you add your garlic, you will also add a few sprigs of thyme. I know you want to put a bay leaf in, but this isn't fucking cottage pie. Constrain yourself.

You will cook it for AT LEAST another hour. Then (and here is the most important thing) add your Armagnac. No, not wine, not even beer, not anything else. Believe me, I have tested every possible ingredient myself, and this is the final word. DO NOT cut corners here. Make sure you get a good Armagnac. If you wouldn't serve it to me, then don't put it in your soup. And don't use a thimble-full either; you're entertaining. Use a good glug and completely clean the pan with it. Make sure every speck of brown that was coating your pan is incorporated seamlessly into your onions.

By now it should be looking rich, glistening, sticky—all the things a good onion soup should be. Now you may add your hot stock, stir, and walk away while it simmers, knowing you have done a good thing.

When you return an hour later, longer if you like, you can finish the soup. Take it off the heat and add another glug of Armagnac. Just do it. A big one.

I know you bought that baguette the day before and it's a little stale. You're still going to toast it. Make your slices thick and slice them on a bias. After you toast them, add butter and yes, rub more garlic over the top. It's fine.

Grate the cheese. Comté or go home. Buy three times as much as you think you will need and then grate it all. Don't think about it, don't look back. No one is going to tell you there's too much cheese, and if they do, ~~you have my permission to stab them in the eye~~ you won't be inviting them back.

Then everything can sit and wait until you're almost ready to serve. This is a good time to shower. No one wants you to smell of onions.

Reheat the soup. Cover the top with your toasted baguette slices, then cover those in Comté. I don't want to see even a hint of bread or soup through the cheese. Just pile it on there. Then the whole thing goes in the oven. Keep the lid off, and I know you will know when it's ready. Golden! Completely melted! Bubbling. You must get it to the table exactly like this, with the brown liquid forcing its way up through the few tiny holes you didn't realise you left in the molten cheese.

You can thank me later.

It's been impossible to sleep here as the inn is quite cursed and the screaming skull... Well, it's exactly as one would imagine, so I am sleep deprived and if I've forgotten anything, I apologise in advance. Give the recipe and the method a good study and see what you think, but I've done this a thousand times and I'm quite sure that's everything.

~~Say hello to Candide for me, and~~

I'm going to ask you to keep this letter to yourself just for now. If that would be all right with you. It's rare I would let you claim the glory for a soup such as this, but consider that my gift to you. You may not be able to keep the truth of my having made contact from Candide, but I trust her to let that lie. The fact is, other than a postcard here and there, I haven't written to Eve or Anna at all, as I promised I would, and you know things are ~~a little complicated~~ ~~difficult right now~~ ~~somewhat touchy~~ not in need of any explanation. Let's just make this our little secret, seeing as you owe me for saving your dinner party.

We might have a lot of killing to do this evening, so I best be getting on. If nothing horrifying pops up between tonight and next week, Joe and I are planning a small break, at which time I will sit down and write you a real letter. There is so much to tell from the last few weeks I could make a novel of it. Or a series of short stories, at the very least.

As I said above, please do not stop writing. Your letters sometimes take a while to reach me, but I will make sure this gets to you in time.

I miss you. I honestly don't know when I'll be back. I do want to see you all again soon.

Enjoy your dinner party. I know you'll be amazing because you always are.

Percy.

Percy and Joe kept to the pebbly edge of the long lake, boots crunching, water lapping, as Barmiston Hall menaced larger and larger against the granite morning sky.

Joe wondered if Percy felt half as nervous as he did. Quiet by his side, the shoulders of his black coat paling with the fine mist of fog sweeping over the lake, he looked the same as he always did. Bold, confident, alert, aware, and in control. Ready for anything.

The first grave appeared on their left. A small, old, oval-shaped stone, fallen face-down in a tuft of tough grass. Another, a little further along, overgrown except for a few blackening and illegible letters etched at the top. Then more and more, dotted here and there, unvisited and unloved. Forgotten dead, mouldering damp in the ground.

Percy's path meandered to the left and away from the lake. Joe followed him up a green incline, hard by a wall, until they rounded the corner into the closest thing the island had to woods. Small but dense, a folly of sorts, Percy wandered, sure-footed, over roots, fallen branches, and a carpet of bluebells which he crushed underfoot, until somewhere around the centre of the plantation he held back the drooping, ponderous branches of a great willow tree.

Joe entered the green arbour and watched as Percy circled the thick trunk, then ripped away some old bark and leaves, before thrusting his fingers into a hollow.

Joe slapped his arm back from the tree. "Were you never told to not stick your hands into dark holes?"

Percy shrugged him off, held him at bay with one hand, and groped deeper in, up to his biceps. "It's Shetland. There's nothing venomous here."

Joe watched on with a small tremble to his lips. "Black widow spiders are everywhere now. It's a fact. London's crawling with them."

Percy winced with the effort of his grasping fingers. "Are you frightened of spiders?"

"I'm a rational human." Joe took an involuntary step back from Percy and the seemingly bottomless hole. "So yes."

"I hear a black widow bite is like holding a burning match to your skin for twenty straight minutes," Percy replied, screwing up his face and stretching his arm further still.

With the delivery of Percy's informative comment, a small panic overtook Joe at the thought of what must lie unseen in there, and he lunged for Percy. "Fuck! Could you—Spiders!—fucking—stop it—"

While Joe blustered out random words, he yanked at Percy, Percy fought him off with his spare hand, and a small one-armed scuffle broke out between them, until, "Got it!" Percy withdrew, unfurled his clenched fingers, and revealed his rusty prize. A key. Long unused and about as forgotten as the dead out in the lawn. With a proud smile, he said, "I want to point out that I didn't pretend to be bitten by a spider just then."

Joe let go of him, shoving his frazzled locks back, assuming an air of dignified self-control. "You're very mature. Thank you. I appreciate it."

Percy, naturally, had only one response. "Kiss me."

Putty-Joe placed a gentle kiss on Percy's lips and felt himself calm at the soft press that met them.

Percy cast a glance over his shoulder towards the thicker side of the woods, where a great wall surrounding the estate blocked what little sunlight was available that cloudy day. "The easiest way in will be via these trees."

"Over the wall?" Joe assessed the dense boundary ahead of them.

"Mmmm. There's broken glass on top to keep intruders out. Be careful."

Percy boosted Joe into the tree, where, lying on a thick branch, Joe pulled Percy up next to him. It was a relatively simple matter from there for the pair to traverse the jigsaw of abundant and untouched growth and make their way to the top of the wall. There they perched to examine a discordant scene. Behind them, lush woods, flowers, endless green. Inside the walls of the property, the ground was devoid of all life. No plants. No insects. Some grass had tried and failed, evidenced by a few yellowy-brown clumps here and there between wide cracks in the bare earth, but that was the sum of all nature in the place.

With two dizzying and ill-advised leaps, both landed on hard, compacted dirt.

Joe's eyes swept across the cold, unfeeling expanse, and to the face of the house. Iron bars clung to every window, bolted on the outside, making the place utterly inescapable once trapped within. It was a dwelling, he knew, that a new guest, once arrived, would not have expected to leave any time soon. "Poor Althea."

Percy commenced a slow walk to the entrance, offering only, "The bars are new."

The castle, because that's what it was to Joe's eyes, loomed three stories high, stark and uneasy, as though the black stones might topple over and swallow them up at any time. If Percy had said the place was held together and fed with the congealed blood of a thousand victims of barbaric murder, Joe would have believed it. There was an atmosphere. Not like any other haunted Scottish residence on a dark and forbidding day. It was unique, and Joe had never felt anything quite like it.

Percy, his boot on the first step, evidently shared Joe's foreboding. "I've got a very bad feeling."

Joe's fast pulse doubled its speed. Percy pulled his dagger free, and Joe readied the nice crowbar Percy had gifted him an hour prior. Both forced one foot in front of the other up the stairs and across the aching porch.

Percy pushed the old key into the keyhole, began to turn it, and Joe said, "Do you think it's odd she'd leave a key to get in when the place is otherwise so impenetrable?"

Percy's dark eyes cut across to Joe's. "Yes. I do think it's odd. Be on your guard."

It took some work, but the key turned roughly, the lock clicked jarringly, and the door groaned open, echoing throughout the enormous hall, two stories high, and made of stone that stared blankly back at them with all the sympathy of an executioner.

A musty scent hit them in the face.

Musty, with an undercurrent of putrid rot.

"That's dead," said Percy.

Joe nodded.

"Old dead," Percy clarified. "Not freshly dead."

Joe passed the tip of his tongue swiftly over dry lips. "Thanks."

The floor held a thick layer of dust, recording each footprint as they stepped into the towering room. The walls were decorated with tapestries, paintings, everything old and antique and too much of all of it, mismatched and matched so that it should have been welcoming. The look was right, but every inch held a creeping dread, as though the décor itself breathed and desired their cruel demise.

Three interior doors came off the entranceway, and Percy led them directly forward and into a grand lounge. Everything, again, was thoroughly covered in that thick dust. "How long ago did Althea say they left?"

"Six months," Joe supplied. "Seven now, since she's been with us."

Percy, in the centre of the room, turned sharply. "It can't be. This dust— It's on everything. And it's undisturbed. How could that build up in seven months?" He ran a finger along the length of a picture frame, examining the brown powder that coated his fingertips. "It's very fine."

Joe dropped down, the floor creaking as he passed his hand across the smooth wooden boards. "This doesn't feel like dust." He ran his thumb over the soft, yielding brown. "And it's dark. Too dark. It feels like—"

"Ash," Percy finished. His eyes went to the grand fireplace, black and gaunt and towering over them. Perfectly unused. The fresh logs that awaited burning were covered in just as thick a mess as all the rest of it. The lounge, the cushions, expensive ornaments Percy had seen Cleo buy at auction— every speck was covered in an even film. "What the hell's happened here?"

Joe watched as Percy turned his attention to the ceiling— the floorboards of the level above. Anticipating Joe's question, he supplied, "It's carpeted. Whatever might be up there... It can't explain this..."

A vase flew across the room and hit the wall with a loud smash, narrowly missing Joe's head as it went. The vibration, the thump against that wall, set loose a chain reaction along the floorboards above, and a slow, thin shower of dust fell over their arms, hands, shoulders, all through their hair. Percy slowly turned his hand over, watching the almost weightless particles settle there.

He was shaken, to say the least. Shaken by the change and the tone of a place he knew well. Shaken by the rising fear that he had no idea what any of it meant. Child sacrifice was awful, routinely, yet he had steeled himself for that inevitability. This was something different. The house that seemed alive all around them. The death that seemed to have invaded the very ground upon which the house stood. The betrayal, if it was that, by his friend…

The first solid shards of doubt slid into his gut and hardened there with every speck of dust that settled over him.

This had to be larger than Cleo—larger than anything she could have done—because Percy had his suspicions about what that ashy substance was, as it touched their lips, landed on their eyelashes, as they breathed it deep into their lungs. And despite everything he had seen and heard, Cleo, doing what she would need to have done to make this—it was too incongruent.

It must have been something else.

Something much, much worse.

"We should do a search." Joe was careful to hide his fear and disgust when he spoke, because Percy had never looked quite like he did at that moment. Not in front of Joe. They had a job to do, and there was no chance Percy would walk out on it, therefore Joe offered what little protection he could by taking control. "A methodical search. We'll start on the left side of the house and work our way through. We'll do the downstairs first, then we'll go up. Stick together, make two clear sets of footprints, and we'll check the dust for anyone else's tracks as we go."

The tight line of Percy's jaw shifted ever so slightly. "Ghosts don't leave footprints, handsome."

With a glance at the broken vase, "If it's only ghosts we're dealing with, we'll be fine. It's not like we haven't done it before."

Percy's shoulders softened, and his eyes mellowed a little, from confused and verging on desperate, to warm, with a touch of melancholy. "I'm glad you're here. It gets very old doing this sort of thing alone. And it's nice that it's you."

The infernal terror pounding at his every fibre was the only thing that prevented Joe from melting into a useless heap. It was one of those moments he felt like Percy's only one. It brought his heart very close to bursting to be needed like that, the rare time Percy showed that soft shade of vulnerability.

Joe held his hand out, and Percy gladly took it.

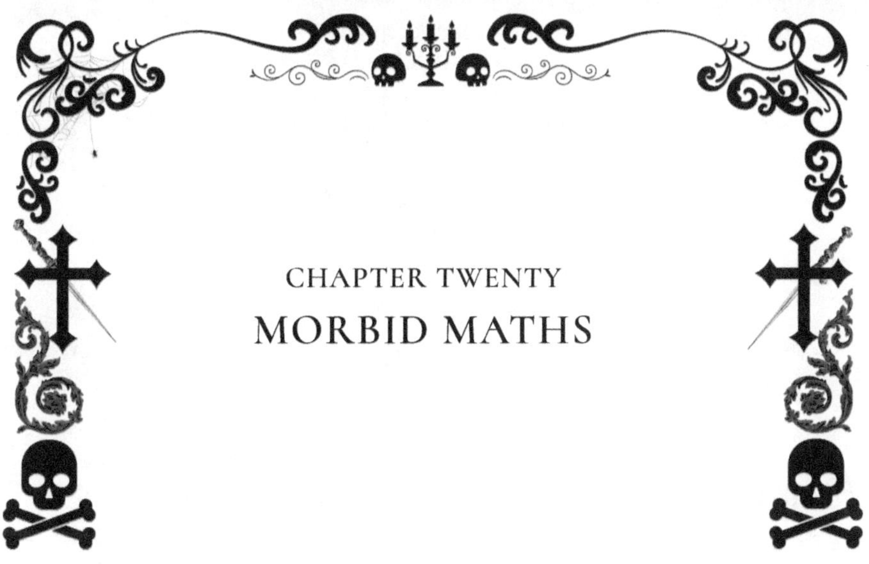

CHAPTER TWENTY

MORBID MATHS

The two were in firm agreement that enabling a fast escape from the haunted house was probably a wise idea. They took the coffee table and a chair from the lounge to the same part of the wall they'd climbed over, and erected a sketchy platform.

This being done, they reentered Cleo's home, and threaded their way through the wide and ever-changing lower floor. It was, just as Percy had said it would be, a strange time capsule. Items extravagant or intimate that had belonged to the many previous inhabitants were strewn here and there. Pieces raided from antique shops and opportunity stores. All of it curated with a loving eye.

For the second time in as many days, Joe got the unwelcome feeling of a vague… 'fondness' wasn't the word, because he was set to despise Cleo from day one, but… He felt the presence of a whole and full person who must have had a sensitive temperament at times. He couldn't help but imagine her placing that broken milk jug on the mantelpiece. Worthless, Percy said, but, to Joe, it was still pleasing. Something of a past

159

and a home. Families sharing meals. The conjuring of the eye of the person who found it in a shop long ago and fell in love with it on the spot. That first honest and simple burst of love— an expression of the little hopes—the great hopes—people sometimes pin on inanimate objects.

Percy was quiet, but he filled the occasional too-long silence with guarded comments on certain items. Guarded, Joe knew, because it might upset him to hear too much about the way Cleo and Percy, together, related to those items. How many had he steered her towards? How many had he delighted in the discovery of? How often had he admired her taste and wealth?

Not where the John Constable painting was concerned, at least, Joe knew. Percy had once described Constable's work as 'cloying and dull all at once, with an offensive knowingness'. Joe got a small, pleased kick out of the hate-filled glare Percy sent the thing when he laid eyes on it a moment after Joe had. He couldn't help but wonder what it was doing there. Did she love it? Was it an investment?

At about the midpoint of their reconnaissance, Joe paused at a small doorway leading through to a low hall, the floor of which was the only place they had discovered thus far that was free of the clinging dust. He stared warily down the passage for a time, and the longer he stood there, the less inclined he felt to explore it. The house was already disturbing, even for one as well versed in the supernatural as Joe was, but that passage… A kind of vertigo began to overtake him, and while the logical side of his mind told him his very purpose in being there was to explore such strange and forbidding areas, there was an accompanying nausea, a clawing dread, that prevented him taking a step closer.

Percy appeared at his side, his voice making Joe jump at the sudden reminder of life. "You feel it too."

"The bricked-up fireplace?" asked Joe, eyes deep in the void.

"Just at the end of the hall. Hopefully, we can avoid it."

Their attention was called away by a rumble behind them. Two handsome faces flicked to the mantelpiece to see a large, heavy candelabra, shaking, more and more violently, until it was rocking side to side, edging closer.

Both hearts pumped fresh blood in readiness to dodge an assault, but the thing simply slipped to the floor with a sharp clang, and rolled to still in the dust.

"It is quite heavy, I suppose," said Joe.

Percy laughed, threw an arm around Joe's neck, and brought them back on track.

Every remaining room was much the same, in that each was completely different from the last. The same homely, chaotic, orderly disorder, over and over. Parlours, the library, the kitchen and bathroom, the occasional guest room. But wherever the building meandered, if it ran beneath those upper floorboards, the dust coated every surface, and remained totally undisturbed until they passed through. When they finally wound their way back to where they began, and to the base of a thin and uneven staircase by the living room, they felt marginally more confident that they were alone.

Until the top step creaked.

Percy's foot was on the bottom stair, blade at the ready, eyes locked on.

Joe's hand was on his arm. "It's a ghost. It has to be. Unless there's another way in upstairs?"

"No." Percy gave a nod and slowed his movement. "You're right."

"So just… keep an eye out for flying objects. We'll be fine."

"Yes. Though…" Percy commenced the ascent, thinking out loud, "There wasn't a poltergeist here before. There were —obviously it's haunted, but never anything physical like the vase and the candelabra. That suggests it's a new ghost and, well, you know what that means."

"A trauma haunting." Joe took Percy's little finger into his hand, drawing his worried gaze. "We knew this was going to happen. Or that it was likely. That's why we're here."

"It's the ash, though. If it's what I think it is…" He trailed off, not ready yet to reveal his full, grotesque thoughts to Joe. "What if it's not ghosts?"

The floorboards above shifted, and a shimmer of powder fell between them.

"If it's not a ghost, then what the hell is it?"

Percy shook his head in response.

Joe released Percy's hand and let him be just as alert and ready for a fight as he needed to be.

The top of the stairs intersected with a thin hall leading away to the left and right. Carpeted, just as Percy said it would be, a deep and rich blue, with barely a hint of dust.

Percy checked both directions and led them off to the right. The hall continued, thinly, clad in faded cream and gold floral wallpaper to a barred window at the end. A painting shuffled, flew off the wall and smashed into the wall opposite. "This is different," said Percy, ignoring the painting. He quickened his pace to the nearest door and stopped dead, bracing himself against the frame.

Inside was a spartan room. One bed, metal frame, bars on the window. He quickly moved on to the next. One bed, metal frame, bars on the window. Then again, then again, until he strode past Joe back up the hall to find exactly the same on the other side. "She's turned it into a prison."

There was, above, a third floor yet to investigate, but Percy moved around the stairs and to the base of this next flight, then dropped to the floor. He dug his dagger deep into the blue carpet and ripped it apart. He tore two long lines, parallel, then slit a path between them, flipping the carpet back to reveal the floorboards.

Dusty beneath that carpet.

He dug the knife between two planks and levered it back and forth until his dagger was like to snap.

"Let me." Percy moved back, and Joe brought the crowbar crashing down on the old wood. He hit it three times, hard, gaining enough purchase on the splintering wood to slide the crowbar in. His hands and his wrists shook with the effort, until finally, the board snapped in two.

Percy moved strong fingers around the broken plank and wrenched it back with a loud crack.

Dust and more dust lay beneath the floorboard. Thick dust. Disturbingly thick.

Percy straightened his hand and pushed it in. Down and down his fingers sank, touching a solid surface only once he was in to the wrist. "That's a lot of dust." Percy's harrowed gaze passed towards the expanse of the hall, his mind calculating just how many metres square that floor was, because it leaked the dust over every inch beneath. He ran his hand through the mess, searching, saying, "You're a priest. Just how much ash do you think a cremated body makes?"

Joe had, for some time, been thinking the same awful thought. It only made things worse to know Percy had already come to that conclusion. "About three litres."

"And less for a teenage girl, I'll wager." His hard eyes met Joe's. "So, how many do you think it would take to fill this space?"

Joe wanted the foul suggestion away from both of them as quickly as possible. "You don't know that's what this is…"

His words drifted away as Percy's search halted, and as he held up a small, blackened object. Small and round. Unmistakably bone. "Vertebra?"

The enormity of it washed over Joe in one sick wave. So sick that he felt his mouth water, the bile at the back of his throat, his stomach churning as he stood, staggered to the bannister of the staircase to support himself.

Percy's hand was on his back, travelling softly to his shoulder, where he gave a gentle squeeze, then snapped Joe out of the swoon with his thickly spoken words. "Save it. We haven't figured out where that smell's coming from yet. Things are about to get a whole lot worse."

CHAPTER TWENTY-ONE

ANOTHER HORRIFYING DISCOVERY IN THE HOUSE OF DEATH

The third and final floor was eerily similar to its predecessor. Smaller, thinner, but what space there was had also been converted into cells. One bed, metal frame, bars on the windows.

Percy peered through the grimy glass and down at the dead, brown earth far below. Every inch, right up to the wall, lifeless, then flourishing beyond that stone barrier.

He assessed the makeshift graveyard. It was probably a pointless exercise, as Cleo had locked the place up so long ago, but he couldn't help but observe, with a touch of relief, that the graves looked undisturbed. Something heinous awaited them within the house. He could sense it in the walls, and he could smell it on the musty air. The last thing either of them needed, in addition to that, was the unveiling of an eight-month-old corpse at the bottom of a long dig.

"Althea said there was a secret compartment somewhere in the house."

Percy turned to look at Joe. He was holding it together remarkably well. Perhaps better than Percy was. Even as he made the assessment, Percy's hands gripped his dagger tighter than usual because his fingers shook, and he was trying very hard to hide that fact from Joe. Maybe to make Joe believe he was more capable than he really was.

What Percy wanted was to flee. To tell the police, pass the buck, and pat himself on the back for a job well done. Cleo would, in theory, be found, arrested, and that would be the end of that grisly saga. But two considerations halted him.

First, the house was alive and bad. Police might, eventually, get everything they needed. But Percy expected at least a few would die in the process, maybe more, if he and Joe didn't fix the place first. It was a death trap, set and waiting. He didn't know how, or where the spring was, but he was determined to loosen it before anyone else set foot in the place.

The second, and more pressing, consideration—the thought that had begun to nag at him incessantly as they searched the house—was the increasingly certain belief that Cleo wasn't to blame. At least, not for all of it.

Althea knew her. Recognised her. Told them she did it. Percy saw Cleo, saw the change in her, saw the supernatural creatures she presumably had some sort of control over. One thing and another all pointed straight at her…

But not these walls. Not the forethought and the cold calculation. Not the time it must have taken to build these cells. And if she needed blood for some reason, maybe the undertaking made sense at an extreme stretch… But there were so many dead beneath his feet. So many girls burned to obliteration and scattered into one careless, thoughtless mess.

Cleo, he was sure, didn't have it in her to do it.

He knew her.

She didn't do it.

But what could have happened there in that forgotten mansion, on that small and lonely island, to set such a cascade of gruesome events in motion?

His eyes flicked to Joe's patient face. "Follow me."

Down the first flight of stairs, reluctantly, Percy dropped one foot before another.

The dark, suffocating feeling the entire house and the very land had taken on, he now recognised as the same foreboding he'd felt in front of her bricked-up fireplace, only amplified one hundred fold.

She must have knocked it through.

Dust flew up around Percy's ankles as he reached the ground floor and quickened his pace across the long hallway, darker, lower, more claustrophobic, where floorboards gave way to slate, until they arrived in that small, miserable little room at the end. A huge eighteenth-century bookcase that sat bereft of books was taken in four strong hands, and on Percy's lead, was hurled to the floor. The entire wall behind was smooth and seemingly untouched, out of the ordinary only because it was the one ordinary spot in the old, cold remains of the original twelfth-century dwelling, where a ramshackle fireplace had once stood.

"Smash it."

At Percy's word, Joe rammed the crowbar into the plaster, looking at Percy with a mixture of impressed and fearful when it went straight through so easily he almost lost his grip.

"Stand back." Percy took his place in front of the wall and kicked an enormous hole in it.

Just as quickly, that smell—that dead and rotting, thick and malevolent, humid and clinging smell—flooded the room, and sent both Joe and Percy into a fit of retching so extreme they were forced to stumble back to the passage, leaning on one another for support.

"What the fuck-blurrrrh," gagged Joe.

"I don't kn-uuuurrrh," gurgled Percy.

"Is it—is that—dearrrgh," Joe tried.

"Not dead," uttered Percy, bracing himself against the wall

and heaving great breaths into his lungs. "Not *just* dead. What-ever that is, that's worse."

"Okay." Hands on hips, gaining control of his stomach spasms, "Are we going in?"

"I don't think we have a choice. Are you ready?"

"Yes. Deep breath."

As though it would help at all, each took in a lungful of comparatively fresh air, and strode full speed back towards the hole in the wall. They attacked it, kicking it through with arms over their mouths and noses. Once the gaping hole was big enough for an easy escape, Percy took out a torch to illuminate the gloom.

It was a black staircase, glistening wet with slime, all enshrouded in curious, unexplainable white mists that made it impossible to see beyond the distance of a metre.

"I feel like this is a very bad idea," said Joe.

"I agree." And Percy stepped through.

The air was the sort of humid one expects in an area of mass decomposition. Like a dumpster. Or a body bag, occu-pied and left in the sun for three weeks. Immediately their hair was wet against their faces, and the warm mist mingled with the sweat that broke out on contact with heat and fear.

The stairs were wide, short, and uneven. They were old, clearly, crumbling here and there, but not worn. This staircase, it occurred to Percy, had always been kept out of the way. By design, it, and by association, this entire space, was meant to be seen by very few people.

The further they descended, the more the mist thinned, and they found themselves in a sort of antechamber. The stairs covering the full width, wall to wall, came to the ground about three feet from a narrow, arched stone doorway. Inside, a long, low-ceilinged, granite-walled room presented itself. The floor, when their boots finally touched it, was slate, wet and trickling with the inexplicable, malodorous heat of the chamber. There was no light—no fire to warm the atmosphere—but the ground, the walls, the very air, all thrummed with a sweltering and unpleasant energy.

On approach to the doorway, Percy lowered the light of his torch towards the ground, and found there the enormous pentagram Althea had spoken of, carved into the floor. The edges glistened black and green under his illumination, which traced the unmistakable lines, coming to rest on metal restraints at the top, then the bottom, held fast to the slate with screws driven deep into the rock.

Percy looked to Joe, who had pressed the backs of his fingers to his pale lips, and whose eyes stared at the horrifying evidence of immense suffering with a slightly disparate vacancy to them. Percy could virtually see him attempting to compartmentalise the day's atrocities. Trying to shove this into the 'movies I wish I'd never seen' category, and out of the 'images that will haunt me every waking hour for the rest of my life' category.

Percy wondered at his instinct to keep silent in the obviously empty space, but Joe responded to a wordless nod from him with his own equally noiseless gesture. Each took an opposite side of the room, which was perhaps thirty feet long, maybe twenty wide, so neither was ever so far from the other that it wouldn't be a simple matter to dash to the other's assistance should it be needed. Even if it meant dashing over that dismal, deeply cut pentagram.

Joe's search along the left wall discovered chains and handcuffs, grim and stiff, but all-too-usable. Percy's wall was bare and blank, from the top, all the way to the bottom, except where a thin slit, maybe two inches tall, six wide, sat at the base of the stone. It lay there in such a way as made it apparent the slit was no accident. The ancient wall was built around it, the stones beneath and above of the same uniform size and age, designed with the clear intention of keeping that slit open.

Strange, but lent an especially unsettling air when coupled with the fact that this slit was the final destination of the sharp ridges of the pentagram, slashed here, slashed there into the slate, and leading down the slightest of inclines, straight to this hole.

Percy heard Joe's footstep by the back wall, and turned to see him supporting himself against a table, taking in a long, shaky breath. Percy's raised torchlight revealed a flicker of reflection from the items he had found there. Items which came into harrowing recognition on approach, rusted as they were. It was sparse, what was left, but the two short, sharp paring knives, a cluster of rusty razor blades spilling out of their little box, and a cleaver, told a story neither was quite prepared for.

Percy took an arm around Joe, who attempted a stoic silence, but Percy felt his watering eyes against his neck when he pulled him in, felt the trembling in his chest, and held him closer still.

He thought only of the stone and the structure, of the age of the buildings, of topics and ideas as bland as his mind could manage to think of, because otherwise it would break all apart.

Joe whispered, low and barely audible, "I can't stand the thought…"

He couldn't finish, and he needn't have. It was Althea who had told them about the place. Althea, who was seventeen years old, who was kept a prisoner in this house for months, since she was only sixteen. Althea, who had shown Joe the scars she received when she was strapped to the rusty restraints on the floor, when Cleo had cut her all over and let her blood drip and drain into the pentagram, to be funnelled into that slit in the wall. To whatever was in there.

A good, healthy flush of anger propelled Percy's quick steps away from Joe, across the wet brown-red dust at the bottom of the carved floor, and onto his knees by the wall. He aimed his torch through, evoking an immediate screeching howl—ear piercing, abrupt, and unearthly. Percy reeled back at the shock, and straight into Joe's arms.

Joe's only response was a meeting of the eyes, then an eager nod.

Percy repositioned himself, and, a little more gingerly this time, aimed his torch into the black.

A growl, a fierce growl right at the wall, and deep huffs of ferocious hot breath snuffled at the light.

Percy lowered his head, down and down, and almost against the putrid floor, then leapt up, pulling Joe with him at the flicker of pink. A flicker at first, then a long, encroaching, thick slit tongue poking and lapping at the carved stone.

"What the fuck is that?" Joe took a few steps closer, then was arrested by Percy's hand on his arm.

"It's got a long, forked tongue, and it drinks blood. We don't need to know what it is. We just need to burn it."

"Agreed." Joe wrenched his gaze away from the slithering tongue and back to Percy. "Where can we get a whole lot of gasoline?"

"Lerwick. We'll have to go in immediately—"

"We can't." Joe turned, casting disgusted eyes over the pentagram, the chains, and the shackles. "How many girls? She's filled the roof with them. She needs to pay for this. And — Percy, you said, that smell…." Joe searched the silent walls. "Where are the rest of the bodies?"

He was right. Just like he always was. Percy absolutely would burn the place to the ground, but to delete all the evidence of the horror… Joe was, unfortunately, completely right. "Maybe we can poison it."

"We can." The pair thought for a time. "It can't be too hard to get blood from a butcher—"

"I'm not convinced it likes blood from a butcher."

"No." Joe wrinkled his nose and mouth at the slobbering

pink mass, still searching over the floor, the growl behind it blowing gusts of bad air over their boots. "No, I'm not convinced it does either."

"We'll figure something out." Percy accompanied the words with a scrunch of his fist that flexed the fine veins in his beautiful wrists, that drew Joe's eyes, and gave him an inkling of what he was thinking.

Joe grabbed his hand. "Not your blood. Not ever." And he retained the hand against his chest as he led Percy back to the door of the room. "I think we have two options. This chamber needs to be sealed again, for obvious reasons, unless we can take care of this whole mess before anyone else comes. So we can search the entire mansion and try to find another way into that compartment with that—" He glared across the room. "With that beast, whatever it is. And see if we can find these bodies, which, I don't know, are they in there with it? Or are they somewhere else? And *that*—searching for this scent of dead—that is going to take a long time, because we still haven't found any clues in this entire house, but..." He tightened his grip on Percy's hand. "Percy, I think there's one way we can be sure, quickly, where the bodies are."

Percy trusted and valued Joe's common sense and intelligence immeasurably, so of course he asked, "And that is?"

Percy was therefore horrified and flabbergasted when Joe replied, "A séance."

Staring at his beloved with humour in his eyes, for it must have been a bad joke, "Have you gone completely mad?"

With a slight jut of his lower lip, "I don't think so."

Percy's intonation switched to clipped with the realisation that Joe was perfectly serious. "I'm sorry, but I had assumed you wanted to survive the night."

"One might say that's a little melodramatic—"

"The house of death," Percy announced through gritted teeth. "The house that was boarded up for one hundred and thirty years because of the evil here. The house of the massacres. The house where a ghost has been throwing things at us since we walked in the door—"

"Yes, exactly!" Joe shouted so loud he drew a howl from the beast, and both he and Percy took an involuntary step away from the thing. "Exactly," he stage-whispered. "Something—some*one*—wants to communicate with us. It might be one of the girls."

"It might be dozens of the girls, mad from months of imprisonment and torture, all at once, wanting to break through and take their revenge on the first person they come across. Or it might be some evil lord from three hundred years ago who brought this beast here in the first place. Is that really who you want to have a sit down with?"

Joe gave a small shrug. "It's worth a shot, isn't it?"

"No, it's not."

Percy broke from the conversation and was halfway up the stairs before Joe caught him, placing a stalling hand on his arm. "It's not like we haven't done this before. It's just a séance."

Percy spun around, furious. "Need I remind you of the mess you got into when Eve and Anna did their little séance and you ended up possessed?"

"Eve and Anna," Joe waggled a finger at him for emphasis, "are shit at doing séances. Not like you and me."

"You've never done a séance with me in your life," Percy rebuffed, feeling a touch of pride that he refused to let show at Joe's implied compliment. Damn right he was better at séances than his handsome brother.

Joe stepped up level with Percy, intertwining their fingers. "But I know you'd be great at it. We can do this. We can find the bodies, kill that thing, and end this. Today. There will be a warrant out for her arrest by breakfast tomorrow, and she won't touch anyone else."

"She won't anyway," Percy argued, a little petulantly. "She's living in hotels. Leo updates me every time she moves. We're keeping tabs on her."

"For how long? For all you know, she might be planning to come back here tomorrow. To feed that—that whatever it is, with more victims. And then what does she intend to do with it?" Upon Joe voicing that worrying notion, both looked back at the long tongue still lapping at the dried blood of dead teenagers. As though he needed to add a little more to drive his point home, "It's clearly supernatural, or it would be dead by now. We're the only people who can fix this. We need to finish it. Right now."

"Fine." Percy took a step closer to Joe, their lips almost touching. "But at the first sign of trouble, we pull out. Promise me."

Joe's gleeful smile did not quell Percy's concerns. "Yes!" He slapped a kiss on Percy's lips, bounded up the stairs, and disappeared through the hole in the wall.

Percy sighed just as heavily as his feet hit the filthy stairs, and he called, "I never picked you for a séance-lover."

Joe poked his head back around the corner. "What could go wrong? They're just kids." And he was gone to search for candles or something.

"Mmm," Percy grunted, making his way out of the wall. "Just kids…"

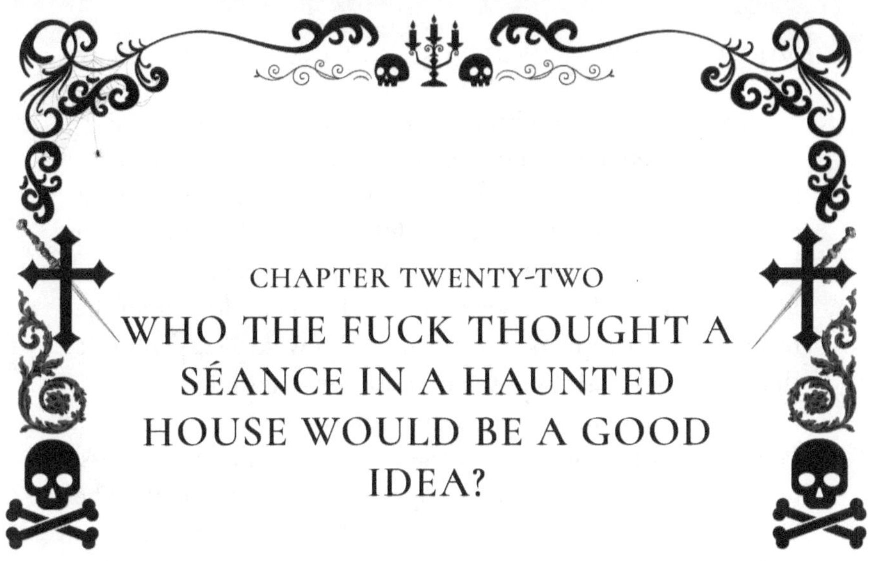

CHAPTER TWENTY-TWO
WHO THE FUCK THOUGHT A SÉANCE IN A HAUNTED HOUSE WOULD BE A GOOD IDEA?

Joe was successful in his search for candles. So many candles in such bright abundance that one might think he was enjoying the affair. Joe was an experienced ghost-chatterer, though. And Percy imagined ghosts probably made a nice change from the usual demon possessions that priests were wont to deal with.

Thankfully, there was no sign of a demon in the house. The occasional religious artefact sat upright and undisturbed. The dust, as Percy had pointed out, kept no prints. Movements in the house cast no shadows, and more damning still, as bad as the whole place stank, there wasn't a hint of sulphur. Every interference with their exploration since arrival had been perfectly poltergeist-like.

Filling himself up with every such fact and reassurance he could conjure, Percy ripped his knife out of the floorboards, having carved the well-known characters, digits and words of a ouija board straight into the wood. For this, he received a loud tsk, and was forced to reiterate to his betrothed that the house would be ashes before long.

Sad as that was.

It was a piece of history, after all. A gorgeous one. But a cruel and relentlessly murderous one. Even the art historian in him was resolved: houses that repeatedly kill have to go, aesthetics be damned. And if the John Constable painting went up with it? It was simply the price they had to pay.

Of course, a few choice and non-cloying antique items had been quietly wrapped in a nearby throw for easy removal, should a quick dash from the premises be required.

While these and more preparations were being seen to by Percy, Joe had, in addition to the candles, found several glasses in the kitchen and lined them up in a row on the floor. When he dropped down next to Percy, their knees touching, a frisson of barely repressible excitement bubbled behind Joe's pathetically hidden smile, and they both felt the nostalgic thrill of that first stupid teenage séance.

More or less.

Percy, by the time he was sweet on that one particular girl who didn't have the faintest idea about how to truly pull a séance off, was too-thoroughly versed in supernatural evil to be very concerned when she suggested the idea at a slumber party. He logically knew the thing wouldn't work, and it didn't, but until it was over, there was that background, 'what if?' A touch of fear that Mandy might murder them all that night, just like his older brother had murdered his nanny that one time. It was a different trepidation to the kind the other participants felt, but there was that similar something simmering away. Fear, but only a controlled touch of it, which quickly dissipated.

Mandy had used Scrabble letters for the board, and it quickly became apparent she and her friend had planned and rigged the game with no other purpose than to have the 'spirit' find out if Percy liked her too.

Joe's first séance experience was nothing alike, yet totally alike. The village graveyard had always been rumoured to be haunted, and happy to be anywhere but at home, Joe had snuck out of his bedroom window after dark, as he often did, to smoke cigarettes with other kids who also hated to be at home. They were an ill-matched group drawn together mostly out of loneliness and agreement about what they didn't like rather than any shared interests, but it was company and relative peace.

Out of sheer boredom, they had gone to the graveyard, set up a makeshift board in the caretaker's shed, and the séance *worked*. It worked like magic, which it really was, to Joe and to the rest of them.

First contact with the other side.

The first real proof of life after death.

Joe returned again and again, sometimes alone, sometimes with the others. Good things came through, bad things came through, but things came through, and from that very first séance, Joe's life was changed and set, irrevocably, on the path that found him in Scotland that afternoon, next to the love of his life, about to do something that had always, to him, been a positive experience, even when it wasn't.

Percy and Joe, both of them, were physically warded against demon possession. Ghosts don't possess people—not without their permission anyway—so they weren't worried about that. Thus, both were lulled into a sadly misplaced sense of confidence.

Joe's index finger touched the glass. Percy's index finger touched the glass.

"Are there any spirits with us today?" Joe commenced. He received a lightly contemptuous glower from Percy for the effort. "What?"

"We know there are spirits here. They've been throwing things at us since we arrived."

"Yes, but—"

"They're going to think you don't know how to do a séance and you'll lose all credibility."

"Oh, sorry, I didn't realise the desperate murdered undead were quite so judgemental."

"They've probably had a lot of time to think this sort of thing over."

The glass had, by this time, meandered unnoticed to YES.

Joe let out a sigh so heavy it disturbed the surrounding dust. "Are there any spirits with us today *who would like to communicate with us* via this incredibly professionally made spirit board my smug associate has so skilfully erected?"

With a shove of his shoulder into Joe's, "There's no need to be snarky about it."

Joe fixed Percy with a cool eye, which Percy met with an amused challenge, and neither noticed the movement of the glass away from and back to YES. "You want to talk about snarky?"

"I want to kiss you." And Percy leaned across before Joe could argue, both adoring the other's smile they felt beneath their lips. Meanwhile, the glass slipped from under their fingers, went flying across the room, and smashed against the wall, raining a thousand tiny shards into a puff of cremated dead.

"Homophobic ghosts?" asked Percy, watching the brown cloud settle.

"You are such a shit," Joe mumbled. He grabbed the next glass and plonked it down, putting his séance voice back on. "Is there anyone in the room right now who would like to communicate with us via this here spirit board?"

The glass slid to YES.

Joe smiled, Percy watched him with a healthy touch of anxiety, and Joe asked, "Who are you?"

The glass scuffed along the old floor, scraping over the carved letters.

H E L P

Shifting forward a little, Joe spoke again. "We will. That's why we're here. Where are you?"

HOUSE

"Helpful," Percy muttered.

Joe spared him a scowl, then said, "What's your name?"

HELP

"I can. Listen to me. I need to know where your… uh…" He broke off, unsure how to break the news of having been dismembered to the spirit.

Percy offered, "It knows, Joe."

"Right." Joe nodded, licked his lips, then pushed on as gently as possible. "If you're talking to me through this board, you must know… you're…"

"Dead, darling."

"Hmm. Yes." He cleared his throat. "You must know you're dead. And I need to find your body to help you."

HELP

"Do you know where your body is?"

HOUSE

"Is it in the ceiling?"

HELP

Percy leaned in close to the glass, and spoke louder than he had so far, addressing the spirit. "Who killed you?"

The glass moved smoothing and unerringly.

CLEO

That same unsettling feeling—that same something that Percy had felt earlier that afternoon—raised itself in a tingle about his shoulders and the back of his neck. "Cleo, and who else?"

"What?" Joe whispered, but the glass slid back across the floor.

CLEO

"This isn't right," said Percy.

But all the while, the letters were being touched by the glass, splitting Joe's attention between Percy's mumbled words and the board.

HELPME

"We will," said Joe. "Your body. Where can we find it? Are there others?"

COMING

The anxious tingle quickly transitioned to a hammering of adrenaline in Percy's veins, and he announced. "It's time to go. End it."

As if by design, the entire upper level of the house gave an almighty crack, tumbling a shower of ash over everything beneath.

HELPME

"Goodbye." Percy tightened his fingers to move the glass to 'Goodbye', only to find Joe's grip fighting him. "We have to go. What are you doing?"

Joe shook his head. "Let her talk."

Percy relaxed his hold as requested, allowing the increasingly swift trail of the makeshift planchette to pick out its letters, but he said softly, "It's lying."

"What do you mean, she's lying?" Joe replied, eyes hard at work, reading. "You can't know that. She's just a girl."

"And you can't know it's just a girl."

COMINGPLEASE

Another great shudder from above and a splintering of wood at the top of the staircase.

Percy's wary eyes went to the lower portion of stairs, visible from their position.

HURTSMEHELP

A series of bangs flew across the walls of the room and a scream shot out from nowhere. A scream in the voice of a teenage girl.

"Fuck," Joe whispered, then louder, "What's coming? Where is it?"

BEAST

Percy pulled Joe's arm, hard, but Joe's fingers were white with their chill grip, his eyes dark and intent, his brow deeply lined in troubled thought.

Taking a hand to his cheek, Percy tried to break Joe's insistence. "Darling, listen to me. I don't think Cleo did this. Not alone anyway. Whatever you're talking to—"

Another crash sounded on the stairs, drowning out Percy's words. Another shower of dust hit the floor, only this accompanied by an ungodly howl from the creature below.

PLEASE

Joe's eyes remained on the floor, and he said, "We have to get her out."

Another crash on the stairs, the sound of the bookcase shifting by the hole in the wall, the glass scraping.

HELPHELPMEHELP

Percy's eyes swept the empty hall, then fell on Joe's far too stricken face, watching the frantic movement around the board, reading, always reading. "Move the glass to goodbye now, or I'll drag you out of here without closing this séance."

"Percy." Finally Joe's eyes met Percy's. His spare hand fell on Percy's arm and squeezed. "I'm taking her out."

The faintest narrowing of Percy's eyes signalled his too-slow understanding, which only hit when Joe dropped the briefest of kisses on his cheek, his slightly shaky voice saying, "Whatever happens, I trust you."

Like lightning, Percy's flat hand shot out and slammed against the glass, flinging it free of Joe's grasp a millisecond after Joe uttered the fatal words: "Take me."

Before Percy's horrified eyes, Joe's head flung back, eyes rolled up so far only the whites showed beneath the open, fluttering eyelids.

Percy took Joe's face in his hands, desperately trying to calm the movement of his spasming body. "Please don't do this. Fight it. Get it out!" Hopelessly, he slapped his hand against the unresponsive cheek. "Joe! Wake up!"

Joe stilled, eyes closed. Calm, deathly immobile, frozen in place despite the banging and the howling and the screeching of furniture and the groaning of the very walls all about them.

"Joe!" Percy shouted.

His eyes snapped open. "It's coming."

Percy's strong hand took Joe by the throat and slammed him down on the floor, the furious growl from his lips hot on Joe's. "Get out of him, or I'll kill you with my bare hands."

The bookcase flung into a wall in the other room. The echo of wood cracking rang down the hall. With an enormous crash, the staircase fell in, as though a giant invisible foot had rammed down hard in the centre.

But all Percy saw was Joe's face that now, he knew, was no longer Joe's face. The expression was entirely wrong. The body, the movement, the very breath, all wrong and not Joe. And worse than all of it was the foul threat that slipped out of Joe's beautiful mouth, completely unperturbed. "Kill him, then. I could use the company around here."

Whatever the thing was—and Percy didn't believe for a second it was the ghost of a teenage girl—it had defeated him in ten well-chosen words.

Percy's pale and trembling hand released its lethal grip, and he turned his gaze to the moving shadows in the hall. His hand reached for Joe's and pulled him to his feet. "Run." But he didn't quite trust the thing to do it, so with his dagger in one hand and his other arm linked through Joe's, he ran, and he pulled Joe's body with him. Through the lounge, through the entranceway, through the door and down the stairs, then through the barren and parched yard to the wall, where he shoved Joe ahead of him. "Climb. Get out of here, then leave his body."

Without a word of argument, without even a look, the thing clambered over the table and chair and into the tree, just as nimbly as Joe would have. Percy followed close on his heels, but as he breached the wall, Joe's feet hit the ground. He took off out of the woods, Percy's boot slipped on a carpet of moss in his pursuit, and he fell hard on his shoulder. "Fuck!" Springing to his feet, he chased after him as he made for the lake. He sprinted in a single-minded hunt, faster than he ever had before, closer, closer, and with his whole being intent on catching up, he flung himself against Joe's back, knocking the body to the muddy, pebbly bank in one violent collision. He wrenched Joe's shoulder over, slammed his back to the ground, and straddled his strong torso, pinning his arms down. "You're out. You're free. Leave him now, or I swear I'll find a way to make you regret it."

Joe's brown eyes studied Percy. They stared in the way one does when one's gathering intelligence. Expressionless. Deep. Too deep. So deep into Percy and his soul that Percy was sure it could see how hopelessly terrified he was. How easily and completely conquered he was. He put on a good show but in truth he hadn't the vaguest idea what he might do. He didn't even know what he was up against. He was all alone on a lakeside by a haunted mansion with no one to help and the love of his life beneath his hands, real and tangible, and so far away from him he may as well have been dead already.

The crushing realisation brought Percy near to collapse, the fight the only thing holding him up.

Then the air was almost completely knocked out of him when the thing said, "Very well."

"What?" he whispered.

Joe's body went limp, and he sank a little deeper into the mud.

"Joe? Joe!" Percy's knees crunched down into the wet gravel. He wrapped his arms around Joe, and pulled him to his chest, cradling him on the bank. "Joe? Wake up. Please."

A soft groan. A soft groan and a sign of life that Percy felt through the tender flesh of his arms into the depth of his heart. "Joe?"

With a thick, gravelly voice, "Percy?"

Percy placed gentle fingers on his cool, clammy cheek. "Oh, my love, is it you? Are you there?"

"What..." Joe's bewildered hand settled at his temple, and

his cloudy gaze focused on Percy. He dropped his arms to the ground and sat up, taking in his surroundings. "How did we get out here?"

"You don't remember?"

"No. There was…" He glanced back towards the black mansion. "We were doing the séance, and I…" His pretty mouth fell open, his eyes widened, and, "Oh."

"You absolute bastard!" Percy shoved him off and climbed to his feet, making furiously for the inn.

"But— Percy! Wait!" Joe was after him, but in a half second Percy spun around.

"You fucking shit! 'Take my head!' That's what you said. You said I should take your head if you ever got possessed again, and you went and fucking did it without so much as a word of discussion. You fucking— Fuck!" Joe stumbled back with the violent kiss Percy pressed against him, then Percy was gone again, wrenching a cigarette out of his pocket, lighting it, and snapping in a whirlwind of smoke, "If you ever pull that shit again, you're dumped. I'll break up with you on the spot. I'll dump you, and I'll leave you to your fate, and—"

Joe's hand caught his and wrenched him back around and into another kiss. Percy's eyes remained tight shut through it, and tight shut after, the cold wind of the lake and the taste of Joe and the feeling of being all-consumingly bereft not washing away with any of it.

"I'm sorry," said Joe.

Percy looked at him. At the living, guilty, hopeful eyes that he adored with every fibre of his being. "You're too good. You can't be trusted, and I'm never working with you again."

"Okay," said Joe. "That's fair. But will you make me another steak?"

"No," Percy grumbled, turning his back again, trudging in a slightly more sedate, if still incandescent manner, as he puffed on his cigarette. "You can have the bad Scottish food from now on. Because that's what you deserve. Fish heads for every meal until we leave. Which will be tomorrow, as it goes. And I'm never doing crimes with you again. Judas."

Joe chuckled in his warm way as he linked his fingers with Percy's. Percy, of course, yanked his free, dramatically, but Joe only captured his hand again and touched it to his smiling lips.

CHAPTER TWENTY-THREE
FISH HEADS, FISH HEADS...

The pub was lit and warm and full of noise when they returned. The door was flung open, "Percy!" called Maisie, a brain-cleaving scream broke from the skull, and every lightbulb in the place smashed.

Only this time, the screaming didn't stop.

Great, sorrowful, heartrending screams that didn't relent until Molly was stuck back in the fridge.

"Thank god for that," muttered Joe.

"Sorry?" Percy's sharp eyes shot across to the placid face. "You've changed your tune."

"And she's changed hers too," he threw back. To the searching visage, he added, "It's been a long day."

"Too long," Percy agreed with that curl of his lip he rarely used on Joe. He made his way across to the bar and made an apology for being unable to stay for a drink. He cited Joe's falling into the lake as the reason, being a perfectly believable lie, what with the both of them still wet and unkempt and covered in mud. Maisie was all warmth and compassionate understanding, and she readily took their orders for dinner.

Which, for Joe, was meat. And more meat. And any meat, apparently, because he ordered the steak 'rare and bloody as it comes', the mutton pie, which made Percy wince, and to top it off, krappin an' stap. Fish heads.

Maisie's eyes lit, and she decided then and there that Joe was a keeper. Percy, meanwhile, waited and smiled, and wondered who or what exactly was standing next to him.

He led the way calmly up the stairs, held the door to the room open, and shrugged his coat over his shoulders as Joe did the same. Joe slid his boots off, just as Percy did, then Percy gripped Joe's trusty bottle of holy water and dumped the entire thing over his head in one enormous splash.

Joe slid a hand down his face and flicked the cold water to the floor. "I'm not possessed."

"Bullshit," Percy growled. "Joe wouldn't eat fish heads."

"Percy, we're in Twatt." Joe wrapped his hand around Percy's little finger, just as he had so often done before. "It's a thing people eat. And I'm starving."

"I suppose that makes sense," said Percy, wandering across the room to take a seat on the bed. He slid the top drawer of the bedside table open, saying casually, "It's always good to try new things, and we did— Catch!" He hurled Gideon's Bible straight at Joe's chest.

With his usual fast reflexes, Joe caught the huge book in his powerful hand and held it high for Percy to see. "I swear to God—I swear on my soul—I am not possessed. I'm just hungry. Please stop throwing things at me."

Percy kept his gaze on the fingers wrapped around the holy book and waited. And Joe held it just as long as he needed to, still dripping with holy water, to prove it wouldn't burn or maim him in any way to do so. Eventually, his shiver from the cold snapped Percy back to his senses. "Sorry. You have the first shower."

Joe gave a weary smile and a nod, and made his way to the ensuite. There, in the doorway, he turned back. "Do you want to come?"

He was so beautiful. So beautiful, and his smile was so sweet, and his tone hotly provocative… But Percy… didn't want to… And he didn't know why. So all he said was, "I should let Maisie in when she comes up."

"I guess." Joe laughed with that nice blush of his. "It might be a little awkward."

Percy laughed too, in a shallow way, and Joe disappeared into the bathroom, the pipes of the heated water soon screeching almost as loudly as the skull had.

Percy busied himself laying out fresh clothes, tending the fire Maisie had set, lighting a candle, picking a bottle of wine from the carton he'd brought. All the while, the same sparring thoughts shuffled back and forth.

Joe was fine. Nothing like when he was briefly possessed in the house. He was Joe now, in every word and mannerism. Percy could see it.

But the fish heads. And his comment about the skull. Not Joe. Not Joe, who wanted to pay five thousand pounds for Molly the night before. Who planned to steal her because he felt so sorry for her. Not Joe, who turned a sickly green when Percy told him about the cooking process of krappin.

But he was fine. Beautiful and funny and sexy and very much Joe.

But also not quite Joe.

"Your turn?" Joe in the doorway. Joe in a towel. Joe in a towel with his rippling abs and the steam rising off of him.

And Percy side-stepping him with a light peck on his cheek, and shutting himself behind a locked door for reasons he couldn't explain.

Tired.

They were tired.

Exhausted. Stressed. It had been a horrible day, and Percy had yet to ditch Joe and go back to burn the Hall down. So he would shower. He would eat. He would rest. He would burn the Hall early the following morning, and he would run back home with Joe. Away from everything, and all better, and together, like they should be.

Forcing himself to believe everything was perfectly okay, or soon would be, Percy dressed and returned to the room to find Joe, gorgeous and smiling, lit by the fire and one slim candle, utterly resplendent, with two glasses of wine poured, waiting for him.

Percy took his place opposite, and Joe raised his glass. "Thank you for putting up with me. If you'll keep being my fiancé, I promise I'll never do anything that stupid ever again."

A genuine smile broke across Percy's face, and he felt ridiculous. That glow that had been in his heart since the first night he'd spent with Joe grew and grew, and the tink of glasses and the taste of wine somehow set everything right.

Joe cut into the steak, both rare and tough somehow. "You're right. I did something dangerous because I panicked, and I'll never do anything like that again. I promise."

"Forget about it. I'm just glad it wasn't anything more serious than a ghost." Percy meditated on some too skinny and greasy chips. "Did you get any insight? About where the body was, or what the thing wanted?"

"She just wanted out," said Joe. He looked at the fish heads, but hesitated. Undecided whether to take one, perhaps. Percy watched him carefully. Joe gave that shy smile Percy loved, and moved for the pie instead.

With hearty relief, Percy also took some pie, thick, claggy, and over seasoned. "I meant what I said about leaving tomorrow. I don't want you anywhere near that place."

Joe's hand fell on Percy's with a little squeeze, like he always gave. "I know I scared you."

Percy pressed shaky lips into a hard line until he could speak steadily. "Never again." Then the heartbreak that was right on the verge of escaping, the pent-up grief and anxiety from the lake, all of it about to spill over, transformed into sheer horror.

Joe took his fork and sank it deep into the gill of a fish head. He lifted the broiled pink thing, dripping and steaming, and rested it on his plate.

Percy watched on, aghast, and whispered, "This has gone far enough. Don't."

"What has?"

As though he didn't know.

Maybe he really didn't know.

He didn't know, because, almost in slow motion, Percy watched the sickening event unfold.

Joe lifted the fish head, the whole thing, the round and protruding mouth of the meal dropping open as it moved towards Joe's, the wobbling eyes staring dully at nothing as they approached the beautiful lips. The whole thing, eyes and mouth and the gelatinous insides, shoved in and filling Joe's incomparable lips to the brim with an accompanying, nauseating crunch.

Percy's chair slammed to the floor as he leapt up. He snatched the exorbitantly priced, flaked sea salt from the table, smashed the glass bottle down hard, broke the top clean off, and showered Joe in a snowy baptism of fresh salt. His face, his hands, all through his hair, all over the krappin, which was already ruined anyway by dint of existing.

But he didn't burn.

Joe, finally pushed over the edge by the unrelenting series of assaults, was up and shouting, while Percy stared only at Joe's skin, searching for a wisp of smoke, a whiff of sulphur—

anything at all. But still nothing, except a very angry fiancé who, after yelling at him with a great many curses, disappeared, slamming the bathroom door behind him.

Salt did nothing. Nor holy water. Nor the Bible. That was undeniable. There was nothing left to try. Joe was in the clear. He had to be.

Percy grasped the krappin, flung the window open, and hurled the full dish outside to a bleating of frightened sheep below. He swept the salt from the table and onto the floor, righted his fallen chair, sat back down, and smiled sweetly at Joe upon his eventual return. "You're never to kiss me again."

"Percy—"

"I threw the fish out the window."

Joe eyed him in total silence, until Percy smiled a little wider, to which Joe smiled a little, to which Percy laughed, and so Joe laughed too.

It was, for Percy, finally, relief. Proof that Joe was Joe, because he understood the absurdity of the mess with the humour Percy had come to expect and love from him.

Joe sat, and they ate badly cooked steak and mutton pie and drank the wine and let the talk meander over everything but the Hall and the awful events of the day. It suited Percy perfectly, because he wasn't about to tell Joe he was going to sneak out and burn the house without him, but then he'd also promised he wouldn't lie anymore. It's so much easier to sneak around if people just don't specifically ask you about things. And so it went well. He was surprised the topic of Molly's theft never came up, but Joe was likely not in the mood for ghost stories any more than he was.

The wine and the warmth and the food heavied their eyelids before long, and so they crawled into the gigantic bed. They lay facing one another, and Joe placed a gentle kiss on Percy's lips. Then another. Then another. Then his hand slid down, and Percy caught it. He brought it to his lips. "I'm exhausted." Joe's lovely eyes dulled, so he added, "Truly."

"But that's what we always do."

"Not always."

"Always." Joe rolled onto his back with a sigh.

Percy wrapped his arms around him and kissed his cheek, settling his head by his shoulder. "Tomorrow."

Joe looked across at him, eyes and voice cold. "Don't you trust me?"

"What kind of a question is that? Of course I trust you."

"Don't you love me?"

"Joe… Of course I love you. I can be tired one night and not have it mean anything."

Joe rolled over completely, turning his back on Percy.

Percy raised himself onto one supporting arm. "Seriously?"

"You still think I'm possessed, don't you?"

"No. Joe, no." Percy placed a hand on his arm and pulled him back, feeling a sick guilt at the sight of his dejected face.

"I thought you'd know me better, you know?" There was a tear at the edge of Joe's eye that he swept away with the bottom of his palm. "Like you'd be able to tell the difference between me, your fiancé, and the ghost of some Scottish manor."

"I do. I can." Percy touched a hand to Joe's cheek and leaned in close. "I promise you, I'm just tired. I know you, and I love you, and I'll make it up in spades first thing in the morning."

Joe's eyes and lips softened, so Percy dropped a kiss there, and slid an arm under Joe's neck for him to snuggle in like he always did. And he did. And Percy held him warm and safe, the weight and the movement and the smell of him the same as ever…

But he was right.

Percy still felt, in the pit of his gut, something was off.

He had no reason to think it. Joe had passed every test he could think of, and Percy felt awful that he couldn't switch it off, whatever alarm was buzzing away inside.

He was tired.

He was sure he would wake with it gone and back to normal in the morning.

That reassurance in mind, he switched out the lamp, and closed his eyes, and very shortly, he was sound asleep.

CHAPTER TWENTY-FOUR
WAKING NIGHTMARE

It might have been the cold or the absence of warmth that awoke Percy some time around two o'clock that frigid and unforgettable morning. Or it might have been the screech of agony that came from beneath the casement window. Percy was never able to remember too exactly, so great was the horror that intruded on his previously peaceful mind.

Comprehending only two ideas—that Joe was gone, and that someone was hurt—Percy dashed from the bed and to the window in a very few fast strides. There he dropped to the floor on sight of the terrifying exhibition playing out before his eyes.

Mistaken.

He must have been mistaken.

A cold sweat made him grip the ledge twice as tight for stability. His hammering heart allowed no sound but the rush of blood in his ears. The terror… Indescribable terror forced him to turn to every ounce of the cold distance that had carried him through his entire life just to make himself look a second time.

The sheep that had given that howl of a savage death trembled and twitched on the cold, wet grass. Steam rose from the great gash that ran from the creature's throat to the bottom of its belly, its quivering innards shining as they oozed out into the moonlight. To the shaking of its every dying nerve was added the gouging movement of cruel teeth hard at work, ripping and tearing the raw flesh apart. And there, deep in the blood and gore, was Joe, crouched on the ground like some sort of primitive animal, devouring the still-hot insides.

In his dizzying withdrawal past the windows and to the relative safety of the bed, Percy's eyes fell on two more of the once-white creatures, red and mutilated, splayed out in the nearby field, the rest of their kindred having fled to the hilltop by the church.

Percy, desolate and broken, had only one surety left in the world, and that was his dagger. Without any ability to plan or think beyond base instinct, he took it from his suitcase and carried it to the bed with him. He assumed the position he'd woken in, and lay down on the cold weapon, gripping the hilt tight, the blade warming beneath his hip, counting his breaths in and out, and willing his body to stop shaking.

So long he lay that way, waiting for more cries of death. He thought he heard the wet sloshing of the heinous meal. He wondered if Joe's body would return once the thing was done eating…

Then, finally, the door of the pub.

The slow step on the stairs, one after another, approaching…

Approaching…

He relaxed his eyes to closed, trying to block out the bloody vision that replayed itself endlessly before them.

He counted seven seconds of slow breath in, seven seconds of slow breath out.

The door opened. Joe's hands closed it gently. The soft sweep of bare feet on carpet came closer, closer, until the presence stood over him. Stood there. Watching. Studying. Waiting.

He heard the breath in and out of Joe's lungs, the presence so thick and malicious and watching.

Seven seconds in.

Seven seconds out.

"I know you're awake."

Seven seconds in.

Seven seconds out.

A pulse that raced so fast he felt he might faint, because if that thing went for his throat… Would he have the heart to do it? To drench those sheets in the blood of the man he loved? Or would he let it tear him apart?

Seven seconds in.

Seven seconds out.

If only the shaking would stop.

The bed shifted. The depression of a weight on the other side. The heat of Joe's body.

He dare not open his eyes.

Seven seconds in.

Seven seconds out.

He laid there for hours. What felt like endless hours that stretched on and on as if it were a lifetime. Just as long as he could stand it, too terrified to open his eyes, fully expecting the thing to be quietly watching him the entire time. Waiting.

But some time around five, Percy forced himself to flutter one eyelid, just a little.

The back of Joe. He was turned away.

The first hint of a hope of survival bloomed in Percy's heart, and softly, softly, he shifted onto his back and listened. Joe's breath was just as even as he had forced his own to be all those long, desperate hours.

He completed his move to the edge of the bed, and sat up, the blade hidden beneath the sheets, but totally unrestricted, free for him to wrench forth any second.

He barely felt the once-comforting carpet underfoot as he gradually shifted his weight from the mattress.

The springs gave a creak, and he froze.

Joe's breath hitched—paused… and recommenced just as regularly as before.

In the slow agony of fear, Percy made his way to the door. He traversed the doorway with the same hideous burden of care he'd used to survive thus far, and called on every last gasp of self restraint to not sprint down the stairs.

When he finally made it to the kitchen, he closed that door just as carefully as he'd opened the one above, then dashed for the phone.

He dialled for an operator, and sucked in the deepest breath he'd taken in hours. "The Grand Hotel, Euston, London." At the release of his words, a bone-shattering scream broke from the fridge. Blood curdling beneath his skin, he whispered a hopeless, "No… No…"

Another scream, and on the line a voice said, "Grand Hotel, London."

Another scream, and Percy was ready to throw himself on his own knife. He whispered desperately, "Hold. Please hold. It's vitally important."

Another scream, just as he wrenched the fridge open and fell to his knees. He took the skull in both hands and brought her close to his face, placing a finger over her bare teeth. "Please. Sshhh. Please, please, shh. Please."

"Eeeeee," the skull softly wheezed in response.

Cradling Molly in his arms, he jammed the phone back under his ear. "Kathryn Highsmith. I need you to connect me to her room immediately… Yes, of course I know what time it is… If you must know, her mother's about to take her dying breath in St Mary's, and she needs to get here immediately. And don't you dare tell her that. You put the call through right now."

"Heeeeee," Molly sighed.

A groggy voice came on the line, but before Althea had time to collect her wits, Percy commenced the urgent message.

"Althea, Joe and I are very close to dying, so do the following things right now, exactly as I tell you. Sit up. Turn on your lamp. Walk to your desk and pick up the pen… Done? Good. I'm going to give you Leo's number in Paris." He rattled off the digits and had her read them back. "Tell him to book me and Joe on the next three flights going from Sumburgh to Aberdeen… Yes, all three. And the corresponding second and third, and following three from Aberdeen to London… Got that? And tell him I want a room at the most dangerous and notorious hotel the city has… It doesn't matter why, just do it… Okay, stop talking and listen… Quiet… Tell him I need a sturdy chair, and a lot of rope… Not for any reason at all… Stop talking, Althea!… Good. Then tell him to be on the first flight from Paris to London. Now here's your task. You need sleeping pills… No, I don't care where or how you get them, get them. I want them dissolved in a bottle of water, waiting for me the second I get off that plane. You'll need enough to knock a man out, but not kill him… Well, do you want to work for me or not?… No, no, it's only Joe, but you can't let him see you or we might both die… Calm down… Althea, this is serious. I'm depending on you to not fuck this up… No, it's nothing to do with Cleo."

At that, the skull, relatively placid in his warm hold a second earlier, gave a strange squealing sound Percy hadn't heard before. It drew a touch of his attention, but then so did Althea's not unreasonably panicked voice on the line.

"Yes," he continued in his desperate whisper. "Okay, it is somewhat to do with Cleo—"

That squeal, only louder and more insistent.

"No, you're perfectly safe. Cleo isn't—"

His words were cut off by that squeal. And that third time,

something in him clicked. His eyes snapped down to the skull. He lifted her face level with his and repeated the word. "Cleo."

That squeal. That squeal that suddenly felt extremely deliberate.

No longer hearing Althea's pleas on the line for more information, he placed the skull on the metal kitchen bench and dropped to her level, studying the inanimate object with extreme scrutiny.

"Cleo?"

That squeal.

It could be considered proof of how very fit, strong, and well-schooled in a horror Percy was that he managed to keep his wits after the sort of day he'd had leading up to that moment. He swallowed hard, and asked, unwillingly, "Cleo… is that you?"

"Heeeeeeee!" she hissed back desperately.

He snatched her off the bench, pulling her up to eye level. "How the hell did you get in there?"

The door clicked, and in one lightning movement, Percy spun around, sweeping the skull behind his back and out of Joe's sight. Because there Joe stood. Just as lovely, just as loved, with a soft smile, and so much blood all over his beautiful lips —a sea of dry, sticky scarlet smothering his cheeks, his chin, his beautiful throat. "What are you doing?"

Percy's hand slowly replaced the phone on its receiver. "I had to call my mother. The time difference, you remember?"

Joe eyed the phone for several tense seconds, then his eyes focused back on Percy. "That's right."

Percy gave a nod and a tentative smile. "Yes, that's right, handsome."

"Handsome…" Joe's lips tilted up into the soft smile Percy knew so well. "He…" The thing paused, stared hard at Percy, then made Joe smile a little wider. "I love when you call me that. No one else ever called me that. It makes me so happy."

Inside—deep, deep inside—the first coil came undone. The first of the many parts of Percy that would soon fold and bend and snap and fall apart.

With his stomach like a lump of iron and so little oxygen reaching his fiery lungs that he could barely say the words, he choked back his grief, and uttered the one thing he still knew. "I love you, Joe."

The thing stepped forward, beautiful warm fingers entangling with Percy's cold and shaking ones, pulling his chest to Joe's. Joe's lips touched Percy's cheek, Percy closed his eyes against the tears, and his trembling lips were kissed by Joe. By the thing in Joe. But by Joe. And Percy kissed him back, to convince it he had no idea, to convince himself that Joe was still in there somewhere, and in the hope the thing would end his life right then and there, in the arms of the man he loved.

In that kiss he tasted Joe, and he tasted dead meat, and he tasted despair. Utter and complete despair, wrapped up in a warm embrace, and he didn't believe at all he had the strength, intelligence, or bravery to go through with what he was about to do.

But what choice did he have?

It was that or slash Joe's throat right there and let him bleed out on the kitchen floor.

An instinctive reaction took Percy's hand up and over Joe's chest, to his precious neck, which Percy touched softly with the tips of his fingers, before he pulled back, cold and calm, resolved.

He looked into the brown eyes he'd gazed into so lovingly weeks earlier, when he'd asked Joe to spend the rest of his life with him. When Joe had promised he would.

With a heart of ice and a voice like sunshine, he said, "Handsome, I have the most wonderful surprise for you."

Lie still, lie still, my breaking heart;

My silent heart, lie still and break:

Life, and the world, and mine own self, are changed

For a dream's sake.

ROSSETTI

LONDON

CHAPTER TWENTY-FIVE
DESCENT

It's never until a person really sits down to think about it that the myriad dangers of a short flight become apparent. At least, that was the case for Percy.

He was prepared for all the obvious. A smashed window depressurising the cabin. A cockpit stormed, a pilot murdered, and a plane downed. The nearest passenger's eyes gouged out by strong, statuesque thumbs before the victim ever saw it coming. All the usual sorts of airborne brutality. But knowing the beautiful man by his side could kill him easily and efficiently with barely a quickening of his pulse kept Percy especially wary.

He didn't know if the beast possessing Joe could tap into Joe's admirable intelligence. He didn't know how hungry it was —how many of those on board it might need to slay to slake its thirst for blood. Because Percy believed that's what it was out for. The rare steak, the rarer sheep's insides…

These facts put together with the details of the séance, which Percy had been over and over in his mind, had sparked in him a harrowing hypothesis: that the very thing possessing

Joe now was the same thing that had been desperately licking the floor of Cleo's basement the day before.

He'd heard the bookcase being shoved away from the hole in the wall, he'd seen the flash of a shadow, something moving down that dreary hallway, and ghosts did not cast shadows. But then it had stopped. The very moment he knew Joe was possessed, all noise from that hallway had stopped. And whatever was down there never did come after them.

But what the hell was it?

Percy's leg tapped in his tailored woollen trousers, and the long and frenetic release of adrenaline never let up. The newly boiled water for tea—would that be thrown in his face? Those little plastic forks; seemingly harmless, but not nice when the long, thin side is rammed deep into an ear canal. Strings on life jackets that were so handy for strangulation. The strong plastic of a life-saving oxygen mask tube, the perfect tool to garrote a man. And did the beast have supernatural powers? Percy hadn't seen any sign of them other than its uncanny ability to access Joe's memories and use them to crush Percy's spirit one word at a time.

The thing knew he was in love with Joe. It knew. How a creature with a forked tongue who drank children for snacks might know what love was, Percy couldn't begin to understand. But it understood, and it played him like a harp.

It was a little smile here. The press of Joe's hand there. That touch on his back when he walked past, and the off-beat jokes like Joe would make. Chip, chip, chip again, it scraped away at Percy's obsidian heart, breaking his resolve, breaking him, yet, unwittingly, giving him a slight advantage.

It was so painfully simple for Percy to react to each and every touch, look, and word with a natural expression of love. Tinged with sadness now, perhaps, but easy enough to be convincing. If the creature knew that Percy knew it had Joe's body, it didn't let on, and neither did Percy, and so the long, exacting, nerve-rattling game continued.

He shifted a brown leather Oxford against the bag between his feet, feeling the hard, reassuring press of Cleo in the silent skull. She hadn't made a sound since he'd asked her not to, and Joe was no wiser than Maisie and George that he'd made away with her at first light.

He couldn't be sure, but Percy had a sneaking suspicion that should the creature in Joe discover Cleo, it would smash the skull in a heartbeat. And then what would happen to whatever was left of her?

He glanced across at Joe, still, and for the last hour, poring over a world map in the back of an in-flight magazine. He seemed to be thoroughly engrossed tracing the thin red flight lines, resting his fingertip on some country or other, then starting again. It was odd, but whatever kept him occupied and not thinking about murder was good enough for Percy.

But then, why would the thing kill a plane full of people? That would hardly aid its survival.

An airport full of people, on the other hand…

He hoped Heathrow security, putting on a better display in London than the regional airports they'd just come through, would be some sort of deterrent, assuming the thing had any violent intentions beyond the destruction of several sheep.

Throughout the long taxi ride to Sumburgh, the creature had looked out the window and watched the scenery. It had boarded the first flight and sat patiently. It didn't complain at the sharp turnaround time at Aberdeen. It simply boarded the next plane to London as though it was a normal thing to do. As though it was Joe.

And now it sat there in Percy's partner's body, biding its time.

Until what?

The hope that it wanted something, anything at all—even blood—was enough to keep Percy going. He could work with whatever it was. He'd feed it every virgin child in the country if it meant getting Joe back. He'd bring back his powerful sheath and hand it over. He'd find the *Necronomicon* for it if it asked. He'd do whatever it took, just so long as it wanted anything that wasn't Joe.

Descent into London was announced, and Percy's pulse reached the sort of fast where he felt the icy calm begin to descend. That cold and lonely place he would always go, where he didn't have to think twice about what atrocities he might commit, because there he could access no regret, no mercy, in just the same way nothing could touch him.

CHAPTER TWENTY-SIX
HEATHROW

Joe's body leaned a warm, tired shoulder against Percy's. Percy swept a hand around Joe's waist, and the creature touched Joe's beautiful head to Percy's cheek, the softness and scent of his hair easing the tight fist that Percy's stomach had become.

No sign of Althea.

Percy wished a bomb would go off. Just detonate right there in the baggage claim and leave nothing of him or of Joe or of anything else.

It was good that there was no sign of her. But it was also very bad that there was no sign of her. No random water bottle sitting conspicuously out in the open like he'd hoped for. Just more and more people surrounding them, and Percy wondering how long he had until he'd have to risk giving Joe a concussion, or worse, if the thing tried to abscond.

The crowd shuffled, bunched, thinned, and bunched again.

Percy felt the press of something long, cool, and hard into his hand.

He made no move beyond carefully curling his fingers closed on the object. He slid it up his sleeve, moving his fingers down and down and down, recognising a plastic cylinder, tapering to a long, flimsy plastic lid.

He popped the cap.

There was an audible tap as it hit the floor.

"Did you drop something?" Joe leaned his head forward. Percy jabbed the syringe into his arm, squeezing the plunger until the chamber was empty.

The sweet head that had been on his shoulder a moment earlier snapped across fiercely. "What the fuck did you just do?"

Joe tried to fight Percy off as he hugged him tight to slow the fall, keeping his arms glued to his side, but whatever had been in the syringe was powerful, and it was now flowing through Joe's body and brain with unnerving immediacy. "It's all right, darling. You'll be all right."

Percy was on his knees, bracing Joe, whose eyes fluttered open and closed in a futile attempt to stay conscious. A shaking hand ran over Joe's heaving chest, and Percy whispered, "I've got you. You're safe."

A coat fell over Joe's body. Percy caught the glint of a metal band being slipped onto Joe's wrist. Leo had already climbed back to his feet to address the forming crowd by the time Percy recognised him. "Stand back! He's epileptic or some shit."

Percy flicked the bracelet around. Narcoleptic, it said, etched right there in shining silver next to a little caduceus.

Brilliant boy.

"Narcoleptic," Percy corrected, loudly enough for a size-able chunk of the crowd to hear.

"Narcoleptic!" Leo cried out in response. "Will he be okay?"

Percy was impressed, deeply, until Leo winked at him right there in front of everyone.

Ridiculous boy.

"He'll be fine," Percy said sharply. "Just— Could you help me take him to my car?"

"Certainly!" Leo was already pulling Joe to his feet, groaning under the weight that he really should have expected. Percy moved himself under an arm to take the majority of the heft he was used to handling, though, unconscious, laid out on his back across the floor of an airport, Joe presented more of a challenge than usual. They made it about three feet, Joe's lead-like legs dragging on the floor behind them, when they were set upon by no less than four airport officials with a medical kit, shoving everyone out of the way, and insisting Percy and Leo lay Joe back down.

"He's fine," Percy grunted. "Narcoleptic. It happens a lot."

"Does he have a medical bracelet or something?" Leo asked. "To prove that?"

Percy's cheek twitched with irritation, but he controlled himself. "He does, actually. Would you mind lifting his sleeve just there? The left one."

Leo wrenched it up accordingly, and Percy scanned the faces of the officials for the acceptance they soon showed. Until Leo's display of bobbing eyebrows set at least one of them on their guard. "And how can we be sure you know this gentleman?"

"His name's Joe Bruno," Percy supplied. "His passport's in his top left pocket."

Leo had the good sense to let the man reach in and find it for himself. He eyed the passport. He eyed Joe, Percy, Leo, and the passport again.

Percy's arm began to shake under the weight, the heat of his sweat making his grip slippery, his bag cutting into his shoulder, Cleo's skull knocking against his thigh. His mental resources were already wildly depleted, and he wondered how far he'd get if he knocked the man to the ground right there and made a break for it.

The man turned, made to say something to one of the others, but then, "Percy!" Althea's voice cut across the wide room. She was breathless at his side a second later. "He hasn't passed out again, has he?"

Percy could have kissed her. He mumbled something about it having been at least two weeks since his last collapse, but she spoke over him, addressing Leo. "Are you with Percy and Joe?"

"Who me?" he said as though he were the understudy of the worst actor in a sixth-grade play. "Why, no, I was here when he collapsed, and—"

"Thank you. I'll take it from here." Althea slipped her tiny self beneath Joe's arm, and Percy let out a grunt with the extra weight he was forced to take to prevent her from being crushed when Leo stepped away.

Leo did, at least, remember the passport. "He'll probably need that."

The man, hesitatingly, slipped it into Joe's pocket, and as his colleagues had already begun to disperse, he did the same. Althea yanked at Joe's arm to get them moving again, while Leo ran off in another direction.

"You didn't think of a wheelchair?" Percy huffed as soon as they were clear.

"You should be happy I'm here at all." She surprised him with her angry tone, but he was far too tired to take it much to heart. "What is this? What's going on with him?"

Percy staggered against a wall and paused there, dragging deep breaths in and out of his lungs until he felt a little recovered. He readjusted his grip on Joe and trudged on. "He's possessed. There's something in his body and it's not a demon, and it's not a ghost, and if he wakes up, we're probably all dead."

Althea made no reply, well aware by that time that supernatural forces, such as zombie hands, definitely did exist, but still living in the reality where normal people reside, where such a claim felt like it should have been ludicrous.

"Or maybe he won't kill us," Percy continued, pausing for an automatic glass door to slide open. "I don't know what it wants, but I do know it likes to drink blood. I might need you to visit a butcher for me. Where's Leo?"

"He said to wait there." She tilted her head down a long tunnel, full of exhaust fumes and housing a road jammed with cars and buses. "Taxi bay fifty-three."

"He's got a car, hasn't he? Because if he expects me to take my unconscious possessed boyfriend home in a fucking taxi—"

"He got a car," she rushed out. "A nice one, too. Not like that red one you rented, but—"

Percy let her waffle about the car and focused on the little yellow bay numbers painted on the asphalt as he dragged Joe along. He didn't have it in him to notice people staring, or to sidestep any smaller items of luggage that he could more easily kick onto the road. "What did you put in him, anyway?"

She stopped mid-sentence. "Leo knows. I tried to calculate with the pills, like you said, but the water didn't look clear when I dissolved them, and I couldn't find a bottle that didn't show the liquid, and I thought, how would you get it all into him? But I thought, what if he drinks too much, or not enough, or what if it tastes too bad, and how am I going to fix that?"

"You're right." Having found bay fifty-three, Percy leaned himself back against a dirty concrete pylon, settling Joe's chest against his own. He threaded his arms beneath Joe's, and he linked his hands behind his back, transferring the strain from his burning biceps to his wrists and forearms. "You did well."

The heat, the humidity, the car fumes added a special irritation to the layers of anger, fear, and grief that Percy was already trying to keep under wraps. He felt a trickle of sweat that he didn't have a spare hand to shift, tickling its way down his temple, so he closed his eyes, leaned his head back, and waited for Leo.

Interminable, that terminus. Buses, taxis, idiotic tourists with too many bags and no idea where they were going, shouting, gawping, existing. But in the black of his closed eyes, Percy saw only Joe. Covered in sheep's blood. Beautiful, beautiful Joe. He wondered if that would be his last memory of him. All of it, the whole beautiful, romantic adventure, over and done and boiled down to that one hideous night. And it would be his fault for bringing him along. And Joe and all memory of him would be gone, and Percy would be left with only blood and death. And no Joe. Ever again.

He tightened his arms and let his head drop forward, which only made things worse, because when his lips touched Joe, it felt so much like kissing a reheated corpse. His head smacked back into the concrete and "Fuck!" he shouted.

Althea stayed still and silent, like a shrewd person does when she's scared and trying to keep herself safe, and somewhere inside he felt like shit because he knew he was making her feel that way, but everything was too much for his regret to reach the surface.

Finally, Leo pulled up in a nondescript black hire car. Percy turned and backed himself and Joe towards the door Leo had opened for them, Leo taking Joe's legs to help ease him in. He slammed the door shut behind them, and Percy nestled a hand in Joe's hair, Joe's head on his knees, and he kept his own eyes open and staring at the dark road because he didn't want to see the blood in his mind's eye anymore.

After a quick discussion between Leo and Althea, that Percy couldn't hear a word of, Leo held the door for Althea to climb in, then moved around the car and took the wheel. "I've got you a place in Hackney," he said. "The whole building's derelict. It'll just be you. It's down the end of a lane, by an estate."

"I don't want anyone to hear the screams," Percy muttered.

Althea threw a panicked look back, and not receiving even a glance from Percy, she focused on Leo. "Screams?"

Leo, pretending to be concentrating hard on driving, carried on with his report. "It's not the kind of estate where anyone will care. The place next door looks like a hub for trafficking or drugs or something. I haven't had a chance to check it out properly yet, but I doubt they'll be calling the cops."

Percy gave a tired nod and let his head fall against the window.

A moment of tense silence passed between Althea and Leo in the front, then he said, "I got a chair. A big one. It's wooden, but it's incredibly sturdy. And it looks comfortable too, because I thought you might want that, since it's… him." Leo couldn't put his finger on why he didn't want to say Joe's name. Something in Percy's all-pervasive dark air. Leo had the sense that one wrong word could easily push him somewhere regrettable, so he kept talking to cover his near misstep. "I got ropes. A couple of different sizes. I got some tape, in case you need that. I got chains and padlocks, of course. But I can grab anything else you need. I've hired the car for a couple of days. So…"

No response from the back.

"So that's that…" And Leo drove on through the thick silence, while Althea stared hard out the window, stomach and fingers in knots.

Traffic was bad, and it took over an hour to reach their destination, during which time Percy listened for every change of Joe's breath, keeping a finger on his pulse for any sign of a quickening. Eventually the buildings got tighter, dirtier, and boards began appearing in windows. The yellowy bricks that define that part of London appeared in abundance, and roller doors that remained down and locked and covered in faded spray paint all the day long darkened the already grim streets.

Leo took a right into a cul-de-sac, and Percy saw at once

he'd picked the perfect location. A man's scream here would invite no more action than the locking of a deadbolt.

Crumbling, triple-level Victorian era habitations lined both sides of the street, half of them obviously abandoned, the other half in such a miserable state of disrepair that they could only have been the worst sort of squats.

Leo pulled up in front of a house at the end of the street. The right side should have had an identical building flush with its wall, but that had fallen down long ago, leaving nothing but a crumbling shell, augmented with curling wires and burned bricks, cordoned off by an ineffectual rusted metal fence.

At the top of the street was a vast expanse of questionable grass, leading to one of the widest, most densely packed council estates in England. The whole ramshackle conglomerate was covered in a sordid black mould, which also featured on the interiors of many of the windows—those that were not missing.

The house on the left of their temporary abode provoked a little more interest and a little more concern. The car they pulled up in wasn't luxury, but it was shiny and expensive, and it drew the immediate interest of a watchman who waited on the stairs. A tall, skinny, but wiry lad who looked like he'd given up any hope of a reprieve, and therefore had little to lose by pick-pocketing this lot. Or worse.

Leo's supposition about that house, Percy decided, was almost certainly correct. Just the fact they had a watchman in that part of London indicated something particularly nefarious. Who would they need to look out for besides other criminals? No police were going to be wandering down that block any time soon.

Percy had no reservations about dealing with him, should he have to, but it was trouble he didn't need, so although the man's eyes burned into him when he climbed out of the car, Percy spared him only one long glance, with something of an intimidating raise of his lip, before calling Leo out of the car to take half of Joe's weight.

Althea then climbed out. She slammed her door, looked up at the dilapidated house, but paused as her attention was drawn to the vacant lot next door. A scruff of ginger fur had caught her eye. That and the gentle step and green eyes of a small, dirty kitten clambering over the ruins.

The watchman ran his eyes over her bright purple track pants, her fluorescent yellow parka, and muttered, "Slut."

She instantly responded with a canned, "Go fuck yourself."

But Leo's eyes blazed and he very nearly dropped Joe's feet, which he only managed to keep a hold of as some pavlovian survival instinct sparked in the back of his brain. "What the fuck did you just say?"

"Leo!" Percy's furious tone snapped him back to his task, but his eyes barely left the scrawny redhead, who never stopped smirking back at him until the four had made their way up the uneven concrete stairs and were concealed inside. Althea slammed the door, Percy and Leo mounted the internal staircase at Leo's direction, and the cold, grim embrace of desolation wrapped around the lot of them.

Percy and Leo kept such addresses as these on file. 'Safe' houses in several major cities. It was clear though, by the musty smell and the damp that penetrated their very pores as with sickened fingers of unsavoury dew, no one had lived here for a very long time

Percy pulled Joe backwards over thin and threadbare royal-blue carpet. The stairs creaked and groaned every step of the way, and some part of him wondered just how rotten the wood beneath their feet was. The Victorian staircase was long and narrow, and when he finally mounted the summit, he stumbled back in exhaustion, tearing a hole in the sagging turquoise wallpaper as Joe's body slumped heavily onto him.

A low groan came from Joe, and, "Fuck!" hissed Percy. "Where?"

"Here." Leo nodded to Althea, who was, understandably, far, far quieter than usual. She skirted around Joe's feet to hold a bedroom door open. Leo grasped Joe's legs again, and both men redoubled their efforts, dragging him into the bedroom.

The carpet was a mean aquamarine-blue, burned and bare in places that revealed scuffed floorboards beneath. The room was one broken window beset with ivy, looking down upon an overgrown courtyard of nothing more than bare bricks and dead tree branches. It was an old bed with an iron frame and a filthy sagging mattress. It was chipped blue paint, cracks in the walls, likely a lot of asbestos leaking out of the gash in the ceiling, and it was fucking miserable.

The sturdy chair Percy had told Althea to tell Leo to buy was an oversized monstrosity from the seventies, but it looked as though it had been carved out of one giant tree trunk. It was thick, lacquered yellow, and padded, also in blue, on the base and the back.

Odd, the way Percy relished that small touch of comfort for Joe, given what he was about to do to him.

The chair had a twin, and, as much as he could manage to feel it, Percy was thankful to Leo for buying a pair, so he would have a place to rest his tired bones.

Leo steadied the first seat, Percy dropped Joe into it, and Althea pulled a black duffel bag out of a dark corner, emptying the contents onto the mattress.

A wide, long, and heavy chain was wrapped around Joe's body, across his midline twice, then looped over his shoulders, tight. This fastened him to the chair with the help of an enormous, brand-new padlock, the key of which swiftly disappeared into Percy's pocket. Leo had chosen the simplicity of packing tape for Joe's wrists. Around and around they wound it, then around his shins too. This being done, Percy leaned

Joe's drooping head against the back of the chair. He gave a long sigh, echoed by Leo, who, having missed the reveal before and having gone along blindly with Percy's plans, finally asked, "So what did he do?"

"Possessed," said Percy.

"Ah, shit," Leo replied. "Not a demon?"

"No."

"Because you've both got that warding—"

"Correct."

Percy remained where he was, watching Joe, and Leo tried, "Ghost?"

"No. Whatever it is, it's not affected by salt, holy water or the Bible."

"Fuck." Leo blew a long, low whistle over his lips. "How about a djinn?"

An outlandish suggestion in any other conversation, perhaps, but Percy responded with, "In Scotland?"

"Maybe?"

"Mmm. Maybe. Maybe not. Think harder. Get me some books or something. Can you…" Percy began to revive a little with the discussion, remembering that the reason he'd put himself and Joe through the entire ordeal of the morning was to get the two of them to a city big enough to access all the information and supplies that might be necessary. He commenced a short pace, thinking aloud, watching his shoes alternate blue carpet and brown floorboards. "I want you two to go to a good library and find out everything you can about anything that possesses. Every type of ghoul or sprite or spirit or faerie. Anything. I need to know every weak spot every one of them has. Make me a list, then we'll start systematic torture of the being to find out what's inside."

Althea, lost in a thousand visions of supernatural horror, snapped back into the room. "Sorry, what?"

"Done." Leo had perked up twice as much as Percy in

response to the latter's business-like change of mood, and was standing a foot taller, a tentative smile replacing the frown he'd worn for the last hour.

"He'll need something to eat," Percy continued. "I need you to visit… a butcher. I think…" He scanned Joe. "Get me raw meat. Good cuts, though. Something nice. And get some blood, too. I don't know how they sell it, or if they do. Just try to get some… I suppose sheep's blood would be good to drink."

A sick sound squelched in the back of Leo's throat. "Just jars of sheep's blood and good raw meat? Nothing else?"

"Pliers."

"Of course."

"Copper wire."

"Obviously."

Althea's scared eyes drifted between the two, while Percy's hand went to his coat pocket. "My knife. Fuck, my suitcases."

"In the car," Leo reported, adding a proud smile.

With no acknowledgement whatsoever of Leo's fore-thought and effort remembering his belongings, Percy instructed, "Get the suitcases from the car before someone steals them. Speaking of which, you'd best put the car in lockup and use the underground. I'll need you back here as soon as possible, so use the photocopier at the library, take notes, whatever you have to do to get every scrap of informa-tion back to me within two hours. Maximum."

"All right." Leo started towards the door, Althea running after him, centimetres behind. She consequently smacked into his back when he stopped suddenly to ask Percy, "What about you? Are you hungry?"

"No. Hurry. And find me a gun. Oh, and a blowtorch."

"A blowtorch?" Turning a distinct shade of green, Leo cast a glance towards Joe's sleeping body. "You're going to use it? On him?"

A spark of warning flared in Percy's tired eyes. "It's not as though I have much of a choice, is it?"

With a sharp nod, Leo was out and on his way, Althea following.

Alone, Percy stood still and took a few long and deep breaths. Then he pulled Cleo from her bag. He checked her skull for missing teeth, bumps or scrapes. He placed her down on the mattress. She was silent. He stroked the rough shell of her scalp and asked, "Do you know what's going on?"

A soft hiss escaped the gap between her teeth.

Percy said, "He's tied up. He can't hurt you."

From the skull came a little grunt, or something as close to a grunt as a thing with no lips and no tongue and no throat can make.

Percy glanced back at Joe's body, mute and unmoving, and he whispered, "Are you frightened of it?"

"Heeeee," she wheezed.

"I can't leave him right now, but I promise, you're next in line." Percy placed the skull at the head of the bed, out of Joe's sight, then slumped into the chair opposite him to await the coming interview.

CHAPTER TWENTY-SEVEN
INTERVIEW WITH THE BEAST

Joe's eyes opened slowly, hazily, and the first thing the beast saw was Percy.

Percy had remained there, quietly seated beside his beloved, for two straight hours. He watched intently, curious to see if the drugs had affected the being's thoughts along with Joe's body. "Do you know where you are?"

The eyes closed again, and Joe's body drifted back to sleep. Percy kicked his knee. On the side. Not too hard, but hard enough. The eyelids fluttered open.

"What do you want?" Percy asked in a crisp tone.

"Sleep," the thing mumbled.

"I'll tell you what." Percy leaned forward and gently slapped Joe's face. "Give my fiancé back, and you can sleep for as long as you like."

A little laugh crept up Joe's throat. "That's right," the thing said, smiling beneath closed eyes. "You're in love with him." Then its eyes opened wide, and it scanned the room. From one wall to another, the gaze ran, alarmed but intelligent, thinking. Focusing back on Percy, the thing said, "You know. How do you know?"

Percy let out his own soft laugh. "Eating sheep while they're still alive was a bit of a giveaway."

"Oh." It thought for a time. "He… 'Joe' doesn't do that?"

"No. Joe doesn't do that." Percy's eyes sharpened with the breadcrumb of information. "But if you can access his thoughts, you should know that already."

"Hmmm." The thing made no more response than that.

"What do you want?" Percy asked again, a little more forcefully.

The chains about Joe's chest clinked as he tried to stretch his arms out. "I'd like you to untie me."

"Let's think a bit bigger, shall we? Do you want blood?"

"Yes."

"I can get that. Do you want to…" Percy pressed his lips in pause. He was going to do whatever it wanted, anyway. Why hold back on the untoward offer? "Do you want to kill a lot of people?"

"Not particularly." Percy let go a small breath of relief, until it said, "Unless they taste good."

"Noted," said Percy. "That's easily solved. Get out of Joe, and I'll round you up as big a feast as you like. What do you need first? A new host?"

The thing laughed one of Joe's bemused, disbelieving laughs. "You'll kill me the second I'm out of him. Why do you think I haven't taken anyone else?"

"Bullshit. You could have jumped bodies at the airport and been away. I wouldn't have had a clue where you were. You need to be invited." It was a guess, but it was based on a wealth of supernatural knowledge, and the beast's silence made it as good as fact in Percy's mind. "I'll get you a new host once we agree to some terms. Someone willing. How about that?"

Joe's head shook slowly, side to side, but his eyes remained locked on. "You're a liar, Percy Ashdown. I know better than to trust you."

It wasn't Percy's first exorcism, if that's even what this was. He'd spent plenty of time around demons and other foul supernatural beasts, prone to targeted, personal attacks. But this was Joe, and Joe's lips saying his name—accusing him— and it felt like a belly full of razor wire. "Did Joe tell you that?"

Joe's head leaned back with as much nonchalance as a man chained to an ugly chair could muster. "I can see it all playing out in his mind. Anyone else I take, you follow them and kill them. He's thinking of all the methods you'd use to track them down. He's thinking of all the people he's seen you kill. He's thinking of all the secrets you've kept from him. He knows, and so I know, that you would never keep your word."

"Huh." Percy settled a little deeper into his seat, an oddly whimsical smile drawing across his face. "It's sweet, really, that Joe thinks I'd chase after you. That he imagines I've an ounce of altruism left in me." Percy's gaze remained on Joe, fond, distant, then dulling with every passing second as the smile disappeared. "The unfortunate fact is, Joe's never seen me really pissed off."

Percy stood, making his way around behind the beast. He took his dagger from beside Cleo, who remained as inarticulate as her skull should always have been. He settled back into the chair, his forearms resting on his thighs, fingers toying with the knife, and he leaned in close to the beast, talking softly. "That's what I love about him. He has a faith in things, and people—a faith in *me*—that makes me…" He searched for the word. "A little crazy, truth be told. So Joe doesn't actually know how far I'd go, because even I don't know how far I'd go. And that means you don't either. But I would do a lot of damage before I'd let you take him from me."

Joe's expression fell, a little glint of panic sparking sharp in the golden flecks of his irises. Percy was glad to see it there. Was it Joe's fear? Could the creature feel that?

Percy's ice-blue eyes stayed trained on Joe's. "Is he watching now? Can he see me?"

The creature assessed him for a time, then, tentatively, "He can."

"I'm sorry, darling." With a flick of his wrist, Percy's knife slashed clean across Joe's arm in one fleet, smooth, controlled move. The skin broke wide open, Joe's pale-blue shirt turned scarlet, and Joe's lips cried out in pain and shock.

"Aha!" shouted Percy, climbing to his feet. "So you feel pain? I can definitely work with this."

But he was soon shut up when the blade slipped from his fingers, exactly as though an invisible hand had yanked it clear. With a flash of steel, it twisted around in midair and lodged itself deep in Percy's shoulder.

"Fuck!" He fell back against the bed, cracking the small of his back on a protruding wooden slat, and he slipped to the floor with a splatter of blood. "Ah, fuck!" He wrapped his fingers around his dagger, took a few deep breaths to prepare himself, then wrenched it free, streaking a ribbon of blood across Joe's cheek with the volition of the release.

Joe watched on, breathing a little harder, a nasty smile marring his beautiful face.

"Telekinesis?" Percy grunted, blood seeping between the fingers he held to his wound.

"Among other things."

"Then why haven't you killed me?"

The creature eyed the blood. Joe's tongue passed hungrily over his lips. "I still might."

Percy followed the voracious gaze to his scarlet hand. "You want this? Are you hungry?" He shoved himself to standing, leaving bloody handprints on the filthy mattress. Joe watched his approach, until Percy's legs were between his own, a press of heat against his thighs, Joe's chest straining against the binds.

Percy glanced down at his bleeding shoulder. With a groan of pain that forced its way from somewhere deep in his gut, he dug his thumb into the great gash. Joe's breath came out with a rasp, and Percy held his arm out long, above the head of the beast. "Gently."

He lowered his hand steadily, eyes burning into Joe's, until his bloody fingers came to caress Joe's cheek. The thing waited, taking him in with wary eyes, while Percy's vermillion thumb came to rest at the corner of his lips. Joe's lips parted softly, and Percy ran a slow, thick trail of blood across his lower lip, to the midpoint, where he felt the warm, wet press of Joe's tongue. The lips closed and Percy let his thumb slide into the hot, wet mouth.

It could have been Joe, but for the red lips. The closed lashes and the feeling and the innate trust were all there, and Percy was on the verge of leaning over and kissing him. Yet the logical part of his brain pulsed on, behind an odd new hammering—a vague un-wellness that he put down to perma-hangover and tiredness. He said, "How about we get you someone to eat? As a show of good faith."

The delicious suction released, and Joe's head fell back. "I'm assuming you didn't manage to get me here all by your-self. Is that girl here? That little friend of yours? How about you go find her for me, then you slit her throat and let me drink her?"

Percy let out a heavy sigh. "Just when I thought we were getting somewhere." His next intention was to throw himself despondently into the chair, but a wave of nausea hit him full in the throat, and the room shifted sideways. He doubled over, grasping for the edge of the mattress, then collapsed onto it, heaving air in and out. Joe's face, surveying all with a knowing-ness that made Percy a little sicker, moved in and out of focus, while Percy swallowed down a flush of bile. He talked over it. "So either you need me, or you like me. I sincerely doubt it's the latter, but there must be a reason you didn't bite my thumb off just then."

Percy reached across to his bag, ripping the strap free from the tangle of encroaching ivy where it had fallen. Dead brown curling tendrils snapped, and a vague idea flared in the back of Percy's mind that it was odd the damp environment of the house should produce those barren little tendrils, or turn the edges of those leaves crisp. Had they been that way before? They must have been…

The thought died with the flick of his lighter and the very necessary pull of air through a cigarette.

"I don't want to hurt you," the creature replied. "I do want to drink you, though."

Percy laughed, crossing one leg over the other and leaning back. "Please, Christ, would someone tell me why that's still sexy when it comes out of Joe's mouth?"

"Probably because he feels the same way." The creature seemed to take a risk by adding, "It's been a long time since I was with a human." He looked down, and for the first time, Percy noticed the very noticeable bulge in Joe's pants.

He spoke only to Joe when he responded, "Thank god for that. I thought I was being weird with how hot that was just then. We'll store it away for another time."

"He'll watch you die before you get the chance," came the deadpan reply.

Percy tapped his ash to the floor. "You know, you flip from pleasant to miserable so fast it's hard to keep track. There's my dagger." He nodded towards the floor. "Why isn't it in my neck? It's just you and me here, and pretty soon I'm going to start torturing you. Which is something I've gotten pretty good at over the years."

Joe's eyes dulled and blinked, and Percy could virtually see the thing checking in with Joe. "He's very scared you will."

In perfect honesty, Percy replied, "That's because he's smart."

The creature let out one of Joe's laughs that rattled down Percy's back like a skeleton's finger tapping on each vertebra. "And you think I'll leave him? Because it hurts a bit?"

Seething over a cold smile, "It will hurt more than 'a bit'."

Their eye contact held, but Percy began to get the unpleasant feeling he was being studied more than he was managing to intimidate.

Another lurch of nausea poked at his chest, and he inhaled some smoke to spite it. What the fuck kind of time was this for a bout of food poisoning? He hadn't eaten a thing—not since the mutton pie.

He glared towards the window in frustration, and just as he did, a little curl of ivy let go of the wall, spurring a great shudder through the entire vine—the whole drooping, tired-looking, dark mass.

The whole *dying* plant…

Percy's eyes snapped back to meet Joe's, as a full grin broke across his face. Joe said, "Someone will eventually come and untie me. You might last a few more hours, maybe even overnight, but you'll give in to make the sickness stop, or you'll leave, or you'll die. That boy and that girl will do the same. And if none of you let me go, I'll wait right here with Joe. I'll wait right here in this little room, staring at that doorway. Maybe for months. Maybe for years. I'll wait here while he grows thin. While he feels every London winter through that smashed window. While the spiders crawl up his legs and nest in his hair and his skin. I'll wait and I'll wait, and one day, someone will come and untie me, and I'll be on my way."

"I wouldn't count on it," was all the reply Percy could manage over the screaming panic in his brain. Was it poison? Dark magic? Was the sweat prickling down his neck due to illness or stress?

"I've got him and I've got time," the creature continued. "Two things you don't have. So, by all means, you can torture him. Let his screams be the last memory you have of him. Let your abuse be all that he remembers of you. Or you can unchain me, and when I'm done with him, you might get him back. Eventually. I don't need him for too long."

Percy wasn't in the habit of believing beasts from the abyss (as presumably this thing was), yet he felt a traitorous spectre of hope at the being's words. "What do you need him for?"

The creature retreated into silence.

Percy assessed the ivy. It was wilting fast. He knew nothing about plants beyond his enviable culinary skills, but he didn't imagine he'd long withstand whatever force was so effectively draining the life out of the vine. The same force, he surmised, that must have left the grounds of Barmiston Hall parched, expired, devoid of all earthly life. He dropped the cigarette to the floor and stamped it out. "I think I'll start with the fingers. A hot wire inserted beneath the nail usually does the trick."

The thing raised Joe's eyebrows. "Does it need to be hot?"

"Purely for show," said Percy. "Something about the sound of the sizzle when the metal hits the moisture of the nail bed. The scent of burning nail and skin, the way the steam rises off it. People tend to do what I want on the first nail. A few make me go two nails deep. But I've never had to stretch to three."

"And you would do this to him? A person you claim to love?" A new chuckle sounded in Joe's chest, but there was an edge of nervousness to it.

Percy smiled a wan smile. "I'll break every bone in his body if I have to. You might want him now, but we'll see how much use he is to you when he can't walk anymore." He glanced one last time at the terminal ivy. "I'd say I need an hour to get the job done. Two at the most."

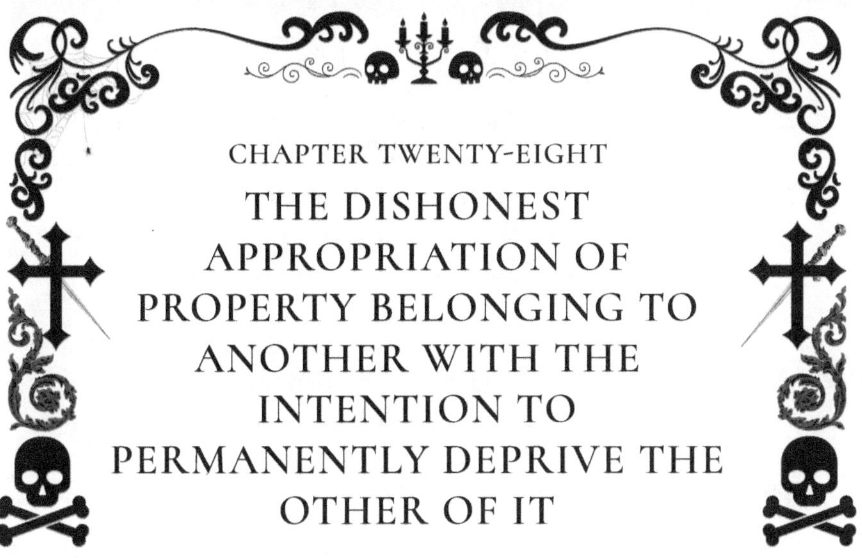

Althea stretched and shook her aching fingers. She checked the enormous clock on the wall. They had ten more minutes before they had to dash for the tube back to Percy and Joe.

She copied down the text in front of her in a frenzied, mechanical haze of thoughts. There was no way she'd get it all finished in time. And how was she supposed to smuggle a book that size, that old, out of the British Library? She'd checked it for security tags and failed to find any, but that didn't mean there wasn't something hidden somewhere in there, waiting to set off a sensor if she tried to escape with it. And she wasn't about to go to jail over something she didn't even understand. Like possession.

She'd heard stories growing up—seen with her own eyes men who claimed to be possessed, eating shards of glass and stabbing themselves to prove it during religious ceremonies. But somehow the distance of London and all the years of trauma had pushed that childhood terror into the background, where she could ignore it—believe it was myth or trickery. But here it was, back with an undeniable vengeance.

Or was it? All she'd seen from across the airport was Joe, leaning into Percy, just as sweet and desperately misguided in his choice of boyfriend as he'd always seemed to be. And then he dropped. Joe on the floor, at Percy's hand. The rest happened so fast, and Percy was too scary to challenge about any of it.

She felt she owed him. He said she didn't; he acted as though she didn't—as though she was barely an acquaintance, since they'd met at the airport. She wasn't worried about any repercussions if she didn't follow through with whatever he requested, but… she was terrified of him. Without a doubt. He switched hot and cold, with no rhyme or reason she could figure. She'd seen him crush five men with a car just for scratching his boyfriend's cheek. He was right to do it, because in hindsight they were most likely zombies, but it's not as though he knew that at the time.

Life was cheap to Percy. Any and all life except Joe's was Althea's supposition, and she didn't want to put herself in the crossfire of a weapon like that.

Yet here she was, scrawling desperately lest she disappoint him, while she knew she should probably be at the police station reporting him instead.

This, she figured, must be how Leo felt. Under the thumb, too scared to fuck up, living on a perpetual knife edge of anxiety. And how had he got Leo under his control like that?

A pile of papers settled noiselessly on the table beside her, followed by Leo settling into a chair. He threw back that dark curl of hair that hung perpetually over his gorgeous cheekbones, and Althea's heart sprang like a mousetrap. "All done?"

"Yeah." He glanced nervously at the clock, just the way she had. After leaving Percy, Leo had dropped her at the library, then gone directly to get Percy's 'tools' and meat. By the time he got back, she had swaths of supernatural-related discourse for him to photocopy. He'd done three loads, but there was more and more again to be assessed and copied and brought back to Percy. "We'd better get going soon."

She licked her lips, turning a few pages forward. Long and large pages full of dense, small text. "It's all about possessions. And there's also those ones I've marked there." She indicated two tall piles of books, ripped Post-it notes sticking out to mark the important places.

As though reading her mind, Leo said, "We'll never get it done in time." He reached across, brushing Althea's shoulder, allowing her a scent of him. He smelled exciting, like travel. He smelled like a hint of Paris and train stations, then fresh country air and adventure and coffee. He pulled her book down onto his knees beneath the table, cast a furtive glance around the room, then reached into his pocket and pulled out a flick knife.

She audibly gasped. "You can't do that!"

He wrapped the knife in his fist, rammed the blade into the paper, and slashed a line down the book. He cut far more than he needed, only asking afterwards, "Where does it end?"

Her quick fingers searched the edges of the pages beneath the desk. "I think it's—"

"They've seen us."

Althea jumped, in full panic, eyes darting around the room.

"Joking." Leo's smile was too close and too, too cheeky. It was the sort of smile that suggested he would, regularly, go too far with any and all hijinks. And that it would always be fun. His eyes rested on her with an expectant sparkle.

Althea was hopeless at hiding her feelings around Leo. Pink and smiling wide, she whispered, "Stop it. You scared the shit out of me."

She soon separated the pages they needed, and Leo slammed the book shut the second her fingers were free. "Cover me."

"Wha—"

He lifted his shirt and pulled out the waistband of his jeans, and Althea got a full and compelling view of his abs and the top of his underwear. A new madness of confusion swept over her, and she didn't know whether to keep looking down his pants, which was what 99% of her wanted to do, or whether she should do as he asked and cover him somehow. The one percent of intelligence remaining grasped her yellow puffy parka from the table and swept it over his lap, pulling several books with her as she went. The lot crashed to the wooden floor with a deafening echo all around the room, and every single eye in the gigantic space settled on the pair of them. She looked around, mortified, then infuriated by the unnecessary "Shhh!" the man a desk over felt the need to level at them, as she froze there, arm wrapped around Leo, like a lizard playing dead.

A fluff of hair tickled her cheek as Leo tilted his head a little closer to whisper, "Stealthy."

She slipped straight to the floor to die of embarrassment. And to pick up the books she'd dropped.

Althea adored Leo with all the fanatic passion of a teenage girl, only multiplied roughly one million times by the bizarre circumstances in which they'd met. Her, running from an evil princess, being chased by zombies of all things, alone with two enormous, completely mad, dangerous and armed men. She'd spent half the trip wondering if she'd be better off back with the princess. But then there was Leo. A touch of normal. So handsome. Refusing to stick her in the baggage hold like Percy had told him to. Leo on the line first thing when she woke up in a new country in a strange hotel room. Leo talking her down from running away, promising her that Percy could be trusted. Then Leo, by her side in the fanciest restaurant she'd ever set foot in, quietly showing her which cutlery to use. And then he kissed her there in the middle of the night. Then nothing.

Nothing but a friendly phone call to 'check in,' when he

had stayed on the line until it got awkward, then hung up. Nothing until she phoned him in a panic after Percy's call, and then it was all business. All business until just now, when she wanted to believe he hadn't kissed her that night just because he was drunk.

She heard the soft rustle of papers beneath the loud rustle of her parka as Leo finished secreting the information, and just as she got her fallen books in order, he leaned down to take them from her. She held them, the two paused there, and she whispered, "There must be a better place to do this." She climbed to standing, then pulled the books into her arms, as though they might serve as a shield against her embarrassment. "Come on."

She took off somewhere, anywhere, imagining there must be some private space to be found. She soon heard Leo behind her, carrying her noisy parka, and the noisy bags of things he'd bought for Percy. She walked and walked, but it was all brightly lit tables. More tables and more, full of people and lamps and sunshine streaming in, and she decided it was a stupid library —not at all like libraries should be. Until she saw the restroom sign.

She spun around, perfectly flustered to almost crash into Leo for the second time that day, then squeaked, "Wait here." She dashed into the restroom, not stopping to think twice, checked the cubicles, and finding the room empty, she reached back around the corner for Leo and yanked him in. The two tumbled into a tiny stall, his shoulder smacking the door back against the wall so it rebounded twice as hard into them, knocking Leo against the other side, where her puffy parka just about pushed her over, and she almost fell onto the tampon bin until he caught her and pulled her up. She slammed the lid of the toilet down, climbed up on it, taking a seat on the cistern, leaving Leo lost as to where to dump his armful of everything.

"Don't you dare let my parka touch that floor," she said, eying him carefully.

"I wasn't," he mumbled, trying to turn and hitting two walls. "Is this really better?"

"Better than you cutting books up in front of everyone, yeah. Give me your knife."

"I—" He twisted his hips sharply to the left, as though he could pull the thing out of his pocket with an elbow.

"Let me." She slid the books onto a high windowsill, all dust and dead flies, then, resting a hand on his shoulder for stability, climbed down into the small space between the toilet and the wall. "Which pocket?"

"It's, uh—the—uh—left." She reached around him, breasts against his back, squeezing her hand around his ass, before he could bluster out, "Front—front left—it's not…"

"Oh, okay. Just let me…" She felt her way across, beneath her parka, fingers searching along his belly, down over his belt.

He flinched back as her hand trailed lower. "If you could just hold my meat…"

"Hold your…" Eyes inches from his, hand over his zipper, she froze.

His mouth dropped open. "My—no!—Not that meat—not —I mean—Ah!— Could you hold Joe's meat? P-Percy's meat? Someone's meat! But not *my* meat!"

Althea burst into an uncontrollable fit of giggles, and lunged for his knife as his head slammed back against the door in mortification. She turned her back on him, climbing up onto the toilet seat, and reaching the first of her books down, unable to stop herself, saying, "You don't want me to touch your meat?"

"That's not—" he blustered. "I didn't say *that*—"

She found her place and slid his knife down the page. "So, you *do* want me to touch your meat?" She couldn't help a glance back at his red face, his eyes shut tight.

"Al—no—I mean. Uh—"

"Is there someone else that's…" She balanced the freed pages on top of his bulky load. She had been feeling confident enough to say it, until he looked up, and she saw his eyes were bright and full on hers, expectant but worried. She felt a wave of bashfulness, and she moved for another book.

A silence followed, broken only by the ruffling of pages, the slit of the knife, and the rustling of her parka as Leo shifted awkwardly. After a time, he said, "There's no one else."

Her fingers shook slightly as she added to his paper pile. Why would he tell her that if he didn't want her—specifically *her*—to know that?

Probably because she'd asked…

But he would have lied if he wasn't interested. Wouldn't he? That's what she'd—

"Are you?" came his tentative voice. "Seeing… anyone?"

She flipped open another book. "No." She threw a nervous glance over her shoulder at Leo, and Leo smiled. He smiled a smile that looked relieved and hopeful. Althea's heart grew so big on the spot that it threatened to blow out her eardrums. "Is that… Um…"

Another silence. A tense and full one

Althea slipped the next excerpt under her arm and pushed another book against the wall in readiness. It was huge and heavy and hard to balance.

"Al…" The small sound sat there. She wasn't sure if she'd like it if anyone else called her that, but she liked it from him. "You know, I've been getting your new passport organised. Your real one. And I saw that your birthday's coming up."

Another dangerous flutter of her heart. "Tomorrow."

"Yeah. And, before this happened, I thought…" Long silence. "I was going to check with Percy, but I thought…" More silence. "I thought maybe I'd catch the train over and, um, depending what your plans were…" She turned around to look at him, so he dropped his gaze to the floor.

"That would have been fun."

His eyes lightened and flitted back to hers, briefly, before lingering somewhere on the wall. "I thought I could get you your first official drink. Or something."

Althea slammed the final book closed and clambered down to the floor. "I thought you weren't supposed to drink."

"I can. If I want to." There was a rebellious anxiety in his features, mingled with what looked like irritation.

She took the teetering pile from him, impressed he hadn't spilled it already. "Actually, there's this place that does cheese toasties. And they use really fancy cheese. I think even Percy would approve. It's got onions and… I don't know, they put butter all over it, and garlic, and it all kind of crisps up and the cheese is all melted on the outside and inside at the same time and… Could we do that?"

"We could!" he virtually shouted.

Leo glowed. Positively glowed. He nodded, and Althea knew that one smile would keep her running for a good six weeks. "Okay. Let's get this back so we can—"

"Yeah."

The wad of papers was, by this time, as heavy and as thick as her small hands could hold. As thick as stealing one of the larger books would have been. And Althea needed to stash it fast. "I don't think this will fit down your jeans."

"I could put some in these bags." He shuffled them a little, smacking the meat dankly into the wall.

"Actually…" Althea disentangled the handles of the first bag, steadily cutting a red line into Leo's fingers, and shoved it up onto the cistern. The meat sagged over the edges, but the containers of blood held it steady. Next, she took his other bag, which gave a metallic jangle. "This is heavy. What's in it?" She dumped it on the closed toilet lid.

"Just tools," Leo mumbled, turning his relieved wrists around

"Well, let's see how much we can fit." She pressed Leo's arm to turn him, then lifted his shirt. He complied, and she went about shoving papers against his back, trying to keep the thing some sort of professional. Trying not to think too hard about how beautiful his slim, naked back was. Trying not to think too hard about that kiss. Trying not to wonder if he might turn back and kiss her now. If she should just kiss him. If he was half as turned on as she was thinking about kissing his neck. "Leo?"

He swivelled back around, pulling his shirt down over the stash with one hand, trying not to let the gigantic parka touch anything with the other. "How much is left?"

She pressed the remaining papers against his chest, he caught them by instinct, and perhaps having taken temporary leave of her senses due to the closeness of Leo in the toilet cubicle in the British Library during the theft of bookish goods, she ripped her shirt off, having remembered she was wearing her favourite purple bra, which she hoped would pull Leo a step closer to the kind of intimacy they'd shared in Italy. "Can you help me?"

Leo's face turned blank, his cheeks turned pale, and he took several seconds to recover himself, which was both amusing and endearing to Althea. She pressed a hip towards him, but when he secured the papers, it wasn't with the careful, smooth, moulding movements her hands had traced over Leo's form. He arranged the papers brusquely, quickly. He blushed, but the sweet embarrassment was gone, and his eyebrows knit tightly. The documents being thus stored, he handed over her shirt, rough and unin-terested.

Horrifying, the way she felt the need to turn away to put it back on. She slipped it down over the stolen pages, then felt the press of her parka against her elbow. She pulled it over the top of everything and zipped it right up to her chin.

When she faced him again, he had gathered his bags, and his hand was on the latch. There he paused with averted eyes just long enough to say, "As friends. Us going out, I mean."

"Yeah," she whispered, the hot press of humiliation burning against the back of her eyes. "I know. I didn't think it was… something else."

He gave a nod and opened the door, keeping about five paces ahead of her all the way to the station, where they boarded the train, then stood opposite one another, saying nothing all the way back to the safe house.

CHAPTER TWENTY-NINE

INSTRUMENTS OF TORTURE

Percy thunk, thunk, thunked the flat side of his blade against his thigh while he thought his plan through.

How best to cut Joe so it would heal more easily? Where best to hurt him that would leave fewer noticeable scars? Exactly how far away was the nearest hospital? Was it a decent one? How long would they have to wait in the ER? How much blood is too much blood?

Any.

Any blood is too much blood

He hadn't been able to stop himself from binding Joe's cut arm with a clean handkerchief. He'd made some stupid comment to the creature that he was just getting started, but in truth, he couldn't stand to see the fresh wound there, seeping and clotting.

He thought about the upcoming weeks of bones knitting, the sting and stink of disinfectant, feeding Joe soup through a straw into a wired-up jaw.

And Joe hating him all the while, wishing they'd never met.

'Take my head or something…'

Not an option. No option but to torture Joe until he got the thing out of him. Then he would deal with the fallout, just like he always did.

The creature spoke. "Do you know, right now, you make him think of his father?"

A well-aimed stab at the gut that hit its mark. "You have no right to tell me that."

"He would sit right in front of Joe's bedroom door, blocking it, just like you—"

"Shut up."

"And he'd watch Joe. Watch him trying to pretend he wasn't frightened. Watch him crying. For hours, he'd sit there drinking, watching, all day in that little room—"

"Shut up or I'll gag you."

Joe's lips laughed out a warm, cruel chuckle. "Do you think that's why he stays with you? Because he's searching for the approval he never got? Trying to win the love of someone incapable of caring for him, always locked in the same old trauma, in that same mud-floored bedroom?"

That jab twisted, turned, and redirected itself sharply into Percy's heart. He held steady, fingers tightening on the chair, refusing to take part in the vicious entertainment, but pulled so taut on the inside he was ready to snap.

The creature watched for the effect of its words, and seeing nothing, it probed a little deeper. "Or is it just that he doesn't know any better?"

Percy dropped his foot to the floor, leaning forward. "He's with me because he knows I'd cut his father's throat as soon as look at him."

The amused eyes sparkled a shade brighter, the brilliant glimmer of white teeth grew a little wider, and he said, "Too bad Joe already did that."

White-hot fury fought with horror, and a nerve moved a flash of ready violence down Percy's arm, restrained only by the memory of kissing those cheekbones so lovingly twenty-four hours earlier.

The door opened behind Percy and a coffee was shoved in his face. A paper bag, translucent with grease, was dropped in his lap. The morale-shattering clank of instruments of torture rattled his insides as Leo dumped everything out onto the bed.

"I got your pliers," Leo commenced, adding with a double-raised eyebrow, "needle nosed." He shook a little box. "Razor blades. I had to go to a different shop for those, but it's fine. Here's your copper wire, hammers—I got a big one and a little one because I wasn't sure how much you wanted to—" he glanced at Joe "—well, you choose. Tweezers, cheese grater, vegetable peeler, and of course…" He lifted the star item. "Your blowtorch."

Percy flinched at the hiss as Leo clicked the flame to life.

"That'll do," Percy said weakly. "And what did you learn?"

Leo raised his chin. "Al?"

Althea, eyes glued the implements on the bed, stepped forward until her knees hit the mattress, where she unzipped her parka. "Leviathans, banshees, wendigo, hyenas—"

"What?" Percy asked.

"Uh…" She glanced at Leo, who gave her an encouraging nod. "Some people believe hyenas can possess people.

"Let's keep it to Scotland, shall we?"

Althea let loose the papers from beneath her shirt, nervous fingers trying to arrange them into some order as Leo added his pages to the mess. She rattled out, "Djinns, Dybbuks, ghosts of course, and then demons."

"It's not a demon. I've tested it."

"I know, but…" Althea sucked in a small but fortifying breath of air. "This really all felt very, um… Well, in Indonesia, we might try different things to anything I found here. Like salt-fish. Nails under his pillow. Or cats, for example. Some spirits are scared of cats, you know? And there's one next door, so it wouldn't be hard to… um…" Percy's dead-eyed gaze quietened her. "Just some ideas… I had…"

He stood with a queasy lurch and shoved the greasy sandwich bag at Leo, who accepted it with a fallen face that Percy failed to notice. He grabbed his bag, turned it up, spilled its contents onto the papers and torture devices, then made his way to the head of the bed, where he smuggled Molly Tulloch's skull into the bag before throwing it over his shoulder. "Out."

Leo made his way to the door on command, but Althea remained where she was.

A sick clawing inside Percy's gut made him even less tolerant than he ordinarily would have been, allowing him only the rough utterance, "Now".

Yet she remained, sneaking a sidelong glance at Joe. "What happens next?"

"He's going to torture me," said Joe, just as calm and easy as if he were discussing the weather. "Because that's how Percy Ashdown treats the people he says he loves."

Althea, caught between Joe's blasé response and Percy's returned glower, said, "He won't." But the brand new metals on the bed shone bright and evil in the dull light. "Percy, you won't, will you?"

"Out," he repeated.

"No."

Joe said, "What do you think, Althea? If you love someone, you don't hurt them. You do what you can to make them happy, right?"

Raising her hands to her hips and her chin in defiance, "That's exactly right."

"But the funny thing is, he won't let me drink you." The creature watched the boldness fade from her face, while Joe's expression kept the same sardonic grin. "How long do you think it will be until he cracks?" He glanced pointedly down at his bandaged arm. "How many holes and slits do you think Percy will put into this body before he serves you up on a platter to save Joe?"

Althea jumped at the touch of Leo's hand on hers, pulling her gently towards the door. "We should go."

"You should run fast and far, Althea," the beast agreed. "I wouldn't trust Percy. And you know you shouldn't either."

Percy's stomach rose and squelched with a whiff of the lunch Leo still held in his hand. He staggered after the pair as Althea fled and Leo retreated, scowling at Joe all the while. He turned the corner with them, pulled the bedroom door shut, and leaned a shoulder into it for support.

Leo, taking in Percy's damp, sallow skin, stated the obvious. "You don't look well."

Percy twisted to let his back take his weight against the wall, closing his eyes to fight off the nausea. "He's poisoning me. And he's going to poison you too unless you get away from him."

"Then you need to leave with us." Leo attempted to take Percy's arm, and was immediately shrugged off.

Percy reached into his bag, saying, "I'm sorry I don't have time to make this any less traumatic for you, Althea, but meet Cleo." He pulled the skull out and held it up to Althea's horrified face.

"What is that?"

"I told you, that's Cleo. I need you to take her downstairs—out of the house, if you start to feel sick at all—and see what you can get out of her. Anything about Barmiston Hall, Molly Tulloch, The Witch's Head Inn, just how the fuck she ended up in that skull, and what the hell she's been keeping in her basement."

Leo, knowing he should be the one to diffuse Percy's madness, being the more experienced of the two, could muster up only, "What?"

On a gasping breath of sickness, "And don't let him see her. Bring her directly back to me, in this bag, and don't let him know you have her. You'll have to do it all in yes or no questions, and you've got ten minutes." He shoved Cleo towards Althea. "Take."

With tentative fingers, Althea held her first human skull. Studying the lifeless object, she whispered, "Cleo?"

"Herrrrrrrrr," the skull breathed.

Althea squealed and dropped the bone, which was caught in Percy's long fingers. "And if you don't get her back to me, intact, within ten minutes, I'm feeding you to Joe."

Leo slapped his arm. "That's not necessary."

"It was a joke."

Leo shook his head. "I don't think you realise how scary you are right now."

With a sickly smile, looking like a man who'd been inhaling shoe polish for three days straight, Percy slurred out, "Althea doesn't think I'm scary."

"You're terrifying," she said.

"Am I?" Percy let out a tired laugh. "That's good. Because I've got a lot of torturing to do. Wish me luck."

He disappeared into the decrepit room before either of them could stop him, had they had the wherewithal to think how to do so in the first place.

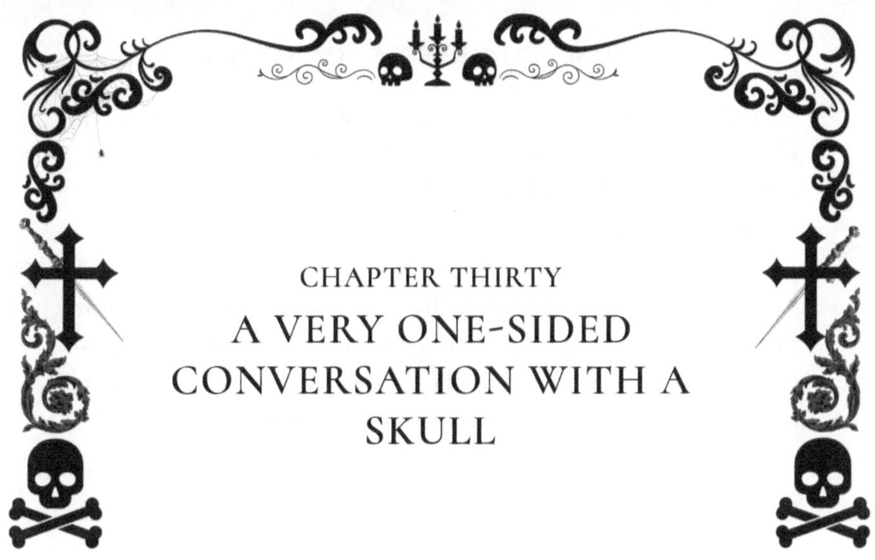

CHAPTER THIRTY
A VERY ONE-SIDED CONVERSATION WITH A SKULL

Leo pulled out a notebook and clicked his pen into action, drawing Althea's, "How are you this organised?"

"I'm a P.A. It's what I do." She continued to look askance at him as he straightened the skull to symmetrical with his own and ignored the un-ignorable curtain of curls that covered half an eye as he leaned forward. "Are you called Cleo?"

"Herrrrr," Cleo hissed.

Leo let out an excited laugh at the new amusement.

Althea wrenched the skull away from him and spat, "Why did you bleed me like that?"

To which Cleo made no reply at all.

"Yes or no, Al," Leo reminded her softly, not attempting to remove the skull from her furious grip.

"Um. Did…" She stared hard at the skull, her voice weakening. "Did you torture me?"

Two grunts ground out in response.

"She's clever," Leo observed. "We didn't even need to explain the system."

Althea kept her attention on the old bone, irritated as she was. "Well, if you didn't torture me, then who did?"

"Yes or no…" Leo whispered.

"Ugh!" She shoved the skull back at Leo. "If you're so smart, you get some answers out of her then."

Leo, used to dealing with the whims of someone far more temperamental than either Althea or Cleo, accepted the challenge with reassuring grace. He looked into Cleo's eye-holes, and in quick-shot, fired off, "Do you know what's inside Joe?"

"Herr."

"Will it hurt Percy?"

"Herr."

"Can we get it out?"

"Herr."

"Did it come from your basement in Barmiston Hall?"

"Herr."

"And are you the same Cleo I've met before?"

"Herr."

"So, something trapped you in there?"

"Herr."

"And you know what it was?"

"Herr."

"I'm going to name every supernatural being I can think of, and you make a noise when I get to the right one, okay?"

Althea sat back in astonishment, less bewildered perhaps by the supernatural nature of the event than by her companion's unexpected skills, which made that ever-burning flame in her heart flare a little brighter.

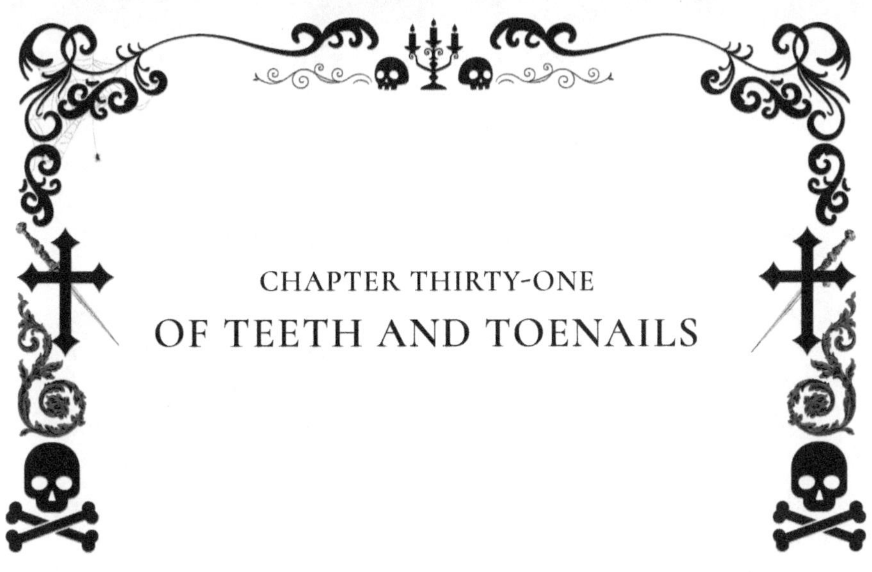

CHAPTER THIRTY-ONE
OF TEETH AND TOENAILS

Percy turned the needle-nose pliers over in his hand, glanced (with his most malevolent smile) in Joe's direction, then threw them down and took up a larger pair, contemplating them in the most obtrusive manner possible.

A tooth extraction hurts. It's not only the pain of having bone ripped from flesh and nerve, but the psychological horror of it all. If you do it just right, the victim can hear the thing crack, and they know there's no going back then. They wonder how many more you'll pull. They wonder about infection. They wonder if they'll ever eat solids again. And it's invasive. You're inside their body. They can't see what you're doing—they're trapped in their mind with the imagery and the agony.

But the fact was, he'd only take one. One from the back. And they could get Joe a nice white replacement. They'd go see the best Harley Street doctor and have it fixed by the same time tomorrow.

Percy turned to his victim—his fiancé—and his eyes fell on Joe's beautiful lips. On Joe's beautiful smile. And he thought of Joe remembering him plucking a tooth from his mouth every time he ate for the rest of his life.

He threw the pliers down.

Back to the needle-nose pliers.

He could pull a toenail off. He wouldn't even have to look at Joe's face when he did it. And Joe would barely see the damage. He could simply put some socks on afterwards. Percy would buy him a nice pair. Cashmere. The nail would grow back within six months to a year. But today, at the very peak of suffering, he'd tell the beast the lot were coming off…

Percy dropped to the floor and unlaced Joe's leather shoe. The feel of Joe's heel in the palm of his hand as he slid the shoe off tapped at his resolve, but he stayed firm this time. He looped a fingertip over the elastic of Joe's sock and pulled it downwards, trying to disregard every precious hair, trying not to think about the graceful curves and dips of Joe's ankle, where Percy had pressed his lips so many times. Trying not to think about the length of his beautiful foot, as exquisite as any Michelangelo. Trying not to think about his toes.

Percy grabbed hold of the other shoe, then repeated the process.

Those toes.

Those toes drenched in sunlight, hot Sicilian sand clinging to them. Those toes poking up out of a steaming bath. Resting against his chest.

He took the pliers up, and he felt the creature's gaze on him. There wasn't the slightest flinch or attempt to pull the limb from his strong fingers. It was almost as though it was willing him to do it.

We'll see how long that lasts.

Percy clenched Joe's calf beneath his arm, brought the pliers to Joe's big toe, opened them millimetres wide, touched the steel against Joe's skin, and in his most gruff and threatening voice, said, "Leave him, or you'll regret it."

"He'll heal. Probably."

"I mean it. This hurts more than you can imagine. The

intensity of pain, once I start, cannot be overestimated. If I were you, I'd definitely—"

"Are you going to do it or not?"

"Fuck!" The pliers went flying across the room, where the sharp tip stuck in a crumbling wall. Percy stalked over to the bed, lit a cigarette, and began another furious pace of the small enclosure.

Weak.

Too weak to be of any use, and not at all the man Joe needed. A disaster since the day they met. Never strong enough, never kind enough, never once what Joe needed. And now was he going to let this thing have Joe's body?

'Take my head or something…'

"Leo!" he shouted. He stalked to the hall, slamming the door behind him. "Leo, up here now!"

Two stairs at a time, the quick footsteps pounded up to him. "You won't believe what we got, Percy. You're going to be so impressed. Cleo never did any of that stuff to Althea."

Althea, one step behind him, nodded, adding breathlessly, "She's been trapped in this skull by a witch called Molly Tulloch, born fifteen-eighty-six. It's her skull, from when she was burned and beheaded in sixteen-sixteen, accused of witchcraft."

Leo shot her an excited smile and took over. "Molly did some kind of body swap with Cleo at the Witch's Head Inn. She's been in Cleo's body for years. She killed all those girls—Cleo didn't even know that happened."

"That's right!" Althea jumped in. "Because Molly Tulloch is the former owner of Barmiston Hall!"

The two fell silent, awaiting Percy's approval, but all he said was, "And?"

"An-and," Leo stuttered. "And that's about it. Which is a lot, for ten minutes of yes or no—"

"Jesus Christ, I know all that," Percy spat. "Isn't it obvious? Haven't you been paying attention at all?"

"If she's been stuck in a pub the whole time," Althea protested, "what did you think she'd know?"

Percy's eyes were like two pools of molten iron when he ground out, "I want to know why she opened her stupid basement when I told her not to, and why she's terrified of whatever's inside Joe."

"Well, you might have asked us to ask that, then," Althea snapped.

"It's not my job to ask, it's your job to anticipate," Percy shot.

Althea opened her mouth and took a very deep breath, but Leo hurriedly cut her off. "I don't know why Cleo opened up her weird basement, but obviously she did, and when she went down there, this thing, whatever's got Joe, took over her. It marched her over to the pub, and swapped Molly into Cleo's body on the spot. It—it and Molly—were waiting that whole time for someone to open that wall. It willingly returned to the basement once it got Molly out of the skull. It's in league with her. That's why Cleo's scared of it."

Percy grasped his face with both hands and smacked a kiss against his cheek. "You beautiful boy!" Leo coloured to the tips of his ears, his boyish smile spreading clear across his face, while Percy went on excitedly, "I can work with this. Where's my gun?"

"Right here." Leo, Althea saw, had been keeping the firearm in his pocket for some time. At the library? On the tube?

He handed it over to Percy, who checked it was loaded in an easy, familiar movement, before saying, "I want you both out on the street with me. Keep a watch and let me know if you see anyone coming."

It was around two o'clock in the afternoon, and with

another hour or so before children would start trickling home from school, the dangerous street was deserted. All except for the lookout at the house next door, leaning back on a crumbling stone balustrade, who noticed the three spill out, and who mostly kept his leering gaze stuck to Althea. "Slut."

Percy raised his weapon with the kind of steady arm that let the watchman know he'd used a gun before. "Make a sound and you're dead." He tilted his head towards their own door. "I want you to shift something for me. I'll tell you all the details once we're inside."

"Nah, man—"

"Did he just say something?" Percy asked. "Because that's the kind of thing that gets you shot."

Leo chuckled. "Pretty sure he did."

Althea, who hadn't been expecting to kidnap anyone, asshole or not, stayed quiet, wondering what would happen next.

"In," Percy directed.

With his best swagger, and another one-over of Althea, the man trod down the stairs and into the building.

"Upstairs." Percy kept a sensible distance, jogging a little closer at the top to stop him getting the jump when they rounded the corner. "Open that door."

For most people, discovering a bound man in a derelict building is an unnerving vision. For the red-haired criminal, it was a relief, plain and simple. He changed from wary prey to salesman on sight. "Alive like this? I'll do it for a hundred quid. If you want me to work him over first, throw in another fifty."

"Sit down," said Percy, kicking the bedroom door closed in Leo's and Althea's faces.

The man pulled the chair back, threw himself into it, and assessed Joe. "If it's just the body, same price. If you want me to kill him for you, that's gonna cost you five hundred."

"Five hundred for a hit?" Percy asked, shock mingling with exasperation in his tone.

The watchman offered a displeased wrinkle of his scabbed lips. "I could do four hundred. But I'm not going any lower than that. Not unless you've got a pair."

Percy tsked his beautiful tongue. "Is it any wonder the rest of us can't make a decent living with you lot undercutting the competition?"

"The fuck?"

Percy aimed his gun at the man's head, and he said to the beast, "I know you're working with Molly Tulloch. And do you know what? I don't care. You go to her, you kill people with her, you do what you like, but you do it without Joe. This here," he shoved his gun towards the silenced and bewildered man, "is your golden ticket. He won't be missed. Walk him out of here and I'll give you money to get you where you want to go. I'll give you directions. I'll buy you a fucking flight. This is it. Out of Joe."

Joe's body gave one slight shrug of the chained shoulders, and a bored, "No."

A strangled gasp of frustration ground out of Percy as he pressed the cold length of the gun's barrel to his own temple, shouting, "What do you want? You want a body? A host? Here's a body! It can be any body, surely. Why do you need Joe's body?"

"He's nice," the thing responded.

"Of course he's fucking nice," Percy yelled. "That's why I'm marrying him! Get the fuck out of him now. Right now, or I blow this fucker's brains out! And this is the only body I'm bringing you!" Taking one fist full of the greasy, wiry hair, Percy glued the watchman's head to the muzzle of his gun and directed, "Tell him you let him in."

"What?" The watchman's legs shook as he descended into

panic, eyes closed tight and wet with tears. "I don't even know what you want. What the fuck is going on?"

Percy wrenched his head back by the hair, yelling, "Look him in the eyes and tell him he can have your body. Do it now!"

"I don't—"

"Three…"

"Stop, dude. Please. I—"

"Two…"

"Please—I—you…" Terrified eyes searched for Joe's, and he yelled, "You can have me!"

"Your body," Percy shouted. "Tell him you let him in."

"Okay! Okay!" He raised shaking hands in the air, begging Joe with desperate eyes. "I let you in. You can have my body. Okay?"

Percy stared into Joe's face for a reaction that never came.

"One…"

Joe said, "Do it."

A deafening shot shook the ceiling. Blood and brains painted the bed, the aquamarine carpet, the blue walls, the browning ivy, the shards of glass clinging to the window panes, as the deafening sound echoed around the courtyard. The ringing stayed in his ears and the sickness escalated, the panic and the hopelessness and the anger, and Percy wrenched the bedroom door open, took five fast steps across the landing to a broken-down bathroom, and vomited in the sink. He retched out his nausea, his bile, the three sips he'd taken of the coffee Leo brought him, and it felt good. The pain in his lurching insides, the constriction in his chest and neck, the tears that were only physical, hot on his eyes and his cheeks as he purged it all, gripping the cracked and blackened porcelain until he was even emptier than he had been. He staggered back against the wall, gasping in shaky air, then kicked off the tiles, crashing into Leo's arms. "I think you need to sit down."

"I need to kill him," Percy said.

"What the fuck?" Althea shouted, stealing her eyes away from the splattered remains all over the bedroom. "No. I won't let you." She fronted up to Percy, despite the hot gun swinging on his index finger, despite the sweaty slick of hair and the deranged, bloodshot eyes.

"I'll do it for you," said Leo. He reached for the firearm, which Percy pulled back sharply.

"You won't touch him." Percy's mind was slower now, ticking through a thick fog of disparate ideas, crushing illness, the need for sleep, a nightmare that seemed to be rising up out of his darkest thoughts and all around him. "I need to *almost* kill him," he corrected. "I need to make him uninhabitable. A friend of mine did that once, and it worked."

"Not Anna again," Leo whined, long and wearied.

"That was a demon," Percy continued, "but it's the same principle, isn't it?"

"Yeah," Leo conceded. "That sounds right."

"Leo!" Althea snapped. "We're not killing Joe."

"He said, *almost*, Al."

Percy glared towards the bedroom door. "It's not giving that body up. And I can't... Fuck, Leo, I can't even torture him."

"What?" Leo stared back at Percy, for the first time in his life, as though Percy was actually mad. "I'll torture him then. Easy."

"No one touches Joe except me," Percy said. "I want something that leaves no trace, something with an antidote. Now think, the pair of you. Think poisons."

"This is ridiculous," Althea blustered. "Do you think you're James Bond or something?"

"Ian Fleming's a hack. Think Agatha Christie. Poisons. Quickly."

Althea threw a panicked look at Leo, but he was already deep in thought.

"Uh… Arsenic?" she tried.

"With an antidote, I said," Percy muttered.

"Um… Mercury?"

"Mercury? Why the fuck would I give him mercury?"

"Well, I don't know," she shouted. "Cyanide, death cap mushrooms, puffer fish?"

"You're terrible at this," he shouted back. "Why did I hire you?"

"Sorry, am I hired? Is this me being hired?"

"Not with that attitude."

Leo, all the while quietly withdrawn, said, "Heroin." Eyes on the floor, voice thin, "You can start slow, and just add more until he starts showing signs of an overdose, then we hit him with the Narcan. That'll fix him. And it's a one-time thing. It won't leave a trace."

Althea searched their serious faces for any sign of jest. "You're mad. You can't give him heroin."

Percy addressed only Leo. "Will he know he's dying?"

"Yeah," Leo mumbled. "He'll know."

"Right. Heroin and Narcan. Have it to me within the hour." Percy moved for the bedroom door, but felt his arm caught in Leo's hand.

Leo retracted it the moment he turned, asking softly, "Could you? I don't think it's good… for me…"

Percy touched a hand to his shoulder, keeping him both physically and emotionally at arm's length. "If the neighbours come looking for their man, I need to be here. You understand that?"

"Yeah, it's just—"

"One hour and it's done." Percy tilted his head towards the stairs. "Go. Quickly."

Leo didn't speak to or glance at Percy again. He hunched

his shoulders against the cold, pulled his collar up around his cheeks, and left.

Althea wasn't so withdrawn. She brought her face to within an inch of Percy's, cutting into him with unflinching eyes. "You're a real prick, you know that?"

Percy watched her bolt after Leo, heard the door slam, and muttered, "So everyone keeps telling me."

He staggered down the stairs behind them, carpet seeming to shift beneath his feet, walls swaying with sickness, keeping a safe distance. When he got outside, Althea was disappearing around the corner at the bottom of the street.

He turned his back on her and made for the vacant lot next door.

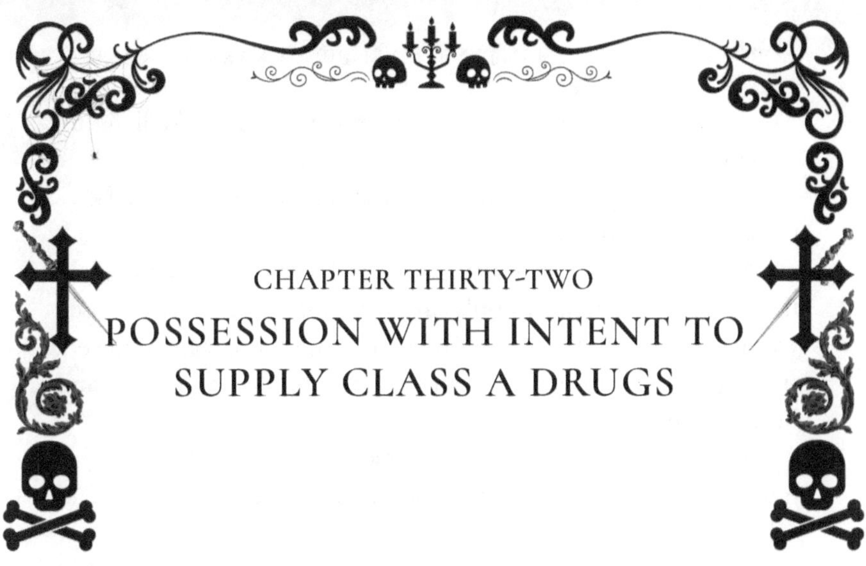

CHAPTER THIRTY-TWO

POSSESSION WITH INTENT TO SUPPLY CLASS A DRUGS

By the time Althea caught up with Leo, his cheeks were wet, his eyes were red, and she had to grab his coat to pull herself onto the almost-empty train before the doors closed on her. "Where are we going?"

He had thought he was alone. At the sound of her voice, he wiped his face over with the sleeve of his sweater and coughed some firmness into his tone. "'We' aren't going anywhere. Stay on until St. John's Wood, and I'll come meet you later."

Althea let out a sharp huff of incredulity. "I'm not going to let you do this by yourself."

"Al…" He shook his head, staring into the black of a tunnel. "It's not a big deal."

"Yes, it is. He's such an asshole."

A tic of anger clocked across Leo's jaw. "Don't talk about him like that."

"Are you joking? He treats you like shit. He treats everyone like shit, and I've had enough of him. As soon as we fix Joe, I'm out." She pressed her arm against his, softening her tone.

"And I want you to leave, too. Come with me. We'll figure something out."

Touched, but unrelenting, a small laugh sounded in Leo's throat, "You don't get it."

"I think I do." She grasped his hand, eyes locked with his in their dark reflection. "I don't care if you used in the past." Leo wrenched his hand away and moved for the door. She followed, staying close by his side. "That's it, isn't it? He knows that and he sent you to buy it anyway."

The doors opened, and he paused on the threshold to give her one final instruction. "Stay out of it. I'll meet you at Crocker's Folly in St. John's Wood."

She shoved him through the doorway and tripped out after him. "I'm buying it. Give me some money."

She attempted to slide her hands into his pocket, but he dodged back out of her reach. "No! Get back on the train."

"Fuck off, Leo. I'll do it by myself." Althea strode towards an underpass, and the thought of her alone in there scared Leo twenty times more than the slim possibility of her being arrested for buying drugs. Thus kicked into gear, he ran after her, which she must have been expecting because she continued ranting, "He doesn't care about anyone but himself. I mean, even Joe. Have you seen the way he talks to him?"

Leo scoffed so loud it echoed in the dripping black. "Are you joking? All he does is fuss over Joe. It's embarrassing." He put on his poshest voice, which turned out to be a very good approximation of Percy. "'Has he got his champagne? Did you dry clean his shirts? Can you book us another romantic dinner? Have you got his Halloween costume organised? Extra tight across the crotch. You'll figure it out.' And what does Joe contribute? Fuck all."

Althea splashed in a dubious puddle in her haste to turn on Leo. "He has him chained to a chair, about to shoot his veins full of heroin until he's dying."

"And whose fault is that?" Leo threw back. "Joe's incalculably stupid. If I'm in a haunted house, literally the last thing I would ever do is invite a spirit into my body."

"He's kind!"

"He's dumb! And he makes Percy weak, and he makes Percy do stupid things, and he's going to get Percy killed one of these days. And if anything happens to him, that prick will wish Percy hadn't given him the Narcan we're about to steal."

He stomped off towards the light, and with Althea three grumpy steps behind, they came out into a dirty intersection, all pigeon droppings and filthy tatters of wet newspaper. Leo kept his momentum into the roughest-looking burger chain restaurant in London, then whirled back on Althea, saying, "Sit here. Don't move."

He was out the door. She glanced down at the closest table, sticky with cola, cold clumps of lettuce, stray chips, and mayonnaise-laden chunks of tomato scattered about. She chose to stand and watch him through the window.

Leo relaxed his shoulders, shoved his hands in his pockets, and began a slow strut of the pavement. He looked about, making brief eye contact with any unsavoury character in sight, and she had to hand it to him, he did look shifty. It was maybe sixty seconds until someone wandered up to him. A quick discussion was had, each nodded, and the interloper disappeared. Leo paced. And paced. A couple of minutes later, the man was back. He pressed his hand against Leo's right there in the street, the exchange was made, and Leo wandered back inside.

Althea thrust her hand straight into his pocket and was successful in plucking out the little plastic package.

"Hey!" Leo shouted.

But she was gone, halfway across the street already. "Narcan?" she called over her shoulder, hearing his shoes on the road behind her.

"Give it back!" he yelled.

"Make me!" She ran down the stairs and broke into a sprint the second her feet hit flat ground.

"Al!" Leo was taller, leaner, faster, but she still made it to the other side of the underpass before he caught up with her, grabbed her arm and spun her around, to find her irritation had given way to amusement. She looked as fresh and excited as she had on the beach in Sicily, and she side-stepped him and twisted away, where he caught her with a hand on each hip and walked her back into the red-brick arch of a wall, her hands shifting behind her back, fists clenching tight around the drug. "Give it to me."

Leo's voice was low and firm, his mouth an inch from hers, and his eyes just about as gorgeous as she'd ever seen them. She simply raised her chin and kissed him. One quick peck that she'd been dreaming of giving him for weeks.

Leo's face went blank. He froze as though she were Medusa and it was the first good look he'd ever had of her. His lips parted and a small flash of alarm leapt to his eyes. Althea took his hand from her hip, and slid beneath his arm, setting a more sedate speed towards the train. "Narcan?"

"I'm still thinking about it," he mumbled, shoving his hands back in his pockets, sinking into the collar of his coat, studying the asphalt beneath his feet as he wandered after her. "A hospital, I guess?"

"You don't think a paramedic would be a better bet?"

"I guess."

"You guess." She rolled her eyes. "We'll definitely have to go to a nicer suburb for that if we want them there within the hour."

He flicked his wrist over to check his watch. "We've got forty minutes."

"St. John's Wood, then?"

Leo said nothing, which she took as agreement, and they stood on the edge of the platform, a blast of hot air from the tunnel making their outsides almost as much of a mess as their insides were.

CHAPTER THIRTY-THREE
PERCY'S SECRET WEAPON

Percy's shoulder smashed against the doorframe in his haste to return to Joe. A black bruise began to form under his skin on impact, but he held his precious cargo safe in the palm of his hand, stumbling forward in a dizzy tumult of queasiness, only to shove an orange fist-full of fur in Joe's face. "Are you terrified?"

Whiskers tickled Joe's nose as both he and the stray kitten attempted to pull back from the close contact that was foisted upon them. "No. Should I be?"

"Not a Pontianak, then… I didn't think so." Percy let his arm drop, kitten still spilling over either side of his palm, tail swishing with annoyance. "Worth a try." He plopped the kitten onto the bed, kicked the dripping corpse out of his chair, and took his place once again. He focused on Joe's eyes, clear and deep, and using every ounce of energy in his ailing body, commenced, "Exorcizamus hanc bestiam in Nomine Patris, et Filii, et Spiritus Sancti…"

"You're going to exorcise me?" Joe's quizzical smile deepened.

"Quaesumus, Sancte, corpus hoc ab insidiis diaboli

defende. Protege adversus spiritus nequitiam et tyrannidem diaboli…"

"But you know I'm not a demon."

"Vade Satana, infernales invasores, putrescentiae mentis et omnes legiones diabolicae. His verbis Satanam sub pedibus nostris opprimimus, ligamus et proicimus in foveam profundam…"

"And you should know, your boyfriend doesn't like being exorcised. It doesn't bother me, though."

"Expellimus te a nobis immundum spiritum! Pessima bestia, te ad Infernus projicio."

On completion of the incantation, Joe's inhabitant's reaction was exactly as Percy had expected it would be, which was no reaction at all. Nevertheless, it ratcheted Percy's anger up a notch, and with no other plan in mind, he repeated the words with twice the vehemence, and exactly the same result.

All the while the kitten pawed its way over the mattress, toying with a coil of copper wire, smacking the razor blade box to see what it could get out, then, once it caught the scent, scratching at the plastic bag of meat and blood.

Percy made an absentminded sojourn to the foot of the bed, repeating the incantation he knew by heart, untying the bag, unwrapping the lamb, and pulling out a chunk of bloody meat for the kitten. It was snatched from his fingers greedily, sharp little teeth tearing it apart, the white scruff of fur on the cat's chin turning pink.

Percy took the greater part of the package back to his chair and held it before Joe. "Is he hungry?"

"I'm not going to let him eat."

The sound of the meat smacking into the wall made the kitten jump before it realised what had happened, then it fell on its unexpected feast with bestial fervour.

"I'll have you out soon," Percy said, to both himself and the thing. "As soon as they get back."

"You're going to torture him again?" the beast goaded. "Will you bring him a puppy next?"

It was Joe's sense of humour all over, and Percy winced. He wondered how Joe was coping inside his body. What it was like sharing with this creature.

His own possession, the one time it had happened, was horrifying. The things it had made him do were forever on display in a gallery of his worst nightmares, but it was the feeling—the exposure—that he still reviled. He couldn't hide from it. It was in him and it *was* him. It knew his thoughts, his memories, his emotions as well as if they were its own.

Joe, Percy knew, hadn't told him a thousand things. He'd lied about where he came from. He refused to say how he ended up with the Church. He never shared anything about his family, and if he'd truly murdered his father, Percy could understand that, because he'd murder his own father in a heartbeat if the opportunity presented itself. None of that bothered Percy in the least. What he really hated was the way, earlier, the thing had so flippantly hurled Joe's secret horror into the open. Not only for Percy to hear, but for Joe to see and relive. And now its brief foray into humour was another brutal reminder that it was still sifting, searching, flaying. Working its way through Joe. And Percy knew enough to know that whatever it might pull out next could be far worse for Joe.

So Percy said, "I was five years old the first time I met a demon. I was at my father's house with my older brother, Michael. My father had taken up with a new woman, a witch, literally, and since then he'd had very little time for me. Nor had my mother, having been left to raise two boys without his help. My brother though… He was ten, and he had all the time in the world for me."

Percy stretched his legs out onto the mattress, crossing them at the ankle. "You wouldn't think a child of that age would remember so well, but… I worshipped him. I loved him as much as I feared my father. Because every time my father raised a hand to me, Michael stepped in front of it. He meant the world to me."

Joe's eyes narrowed on Percy's relaxing frame. "Why are you telling me this?"

"I'm not," replied Percy. Yet he continued, "One night, I was in the playroom with Michael, and with our nanny. She was only nineteen, just an underpaid teenager trying to get some savings together." Percy felt a gentle tug at the base of his trousers, the tentative touch of the kitten's paws trying him out. He kept still. "I don't even remember what we were doing, but what I do remember is the way Michael, very suddenly, wasn't Michael anymore. It was before he'd even said a word, before his expression changed. There was an absence of him. It's like that feeling when you find a dead animal on the side of the road. And you know it's dead, even though it seems like it's only sleeping. It looks just the same, but there's something imperceptibly different. It was like that. Michael was simply gone from me and my life. And so subtly. So suddenly."

The kitten made its way across the bridge of Percy's legs, digging its claws in here and there for stability, making tiny pinpricks in the expensive wool. "When his expression did change, I was terrified. I knew the thing meant to hurt me. I remember I burst into tears and scrambled away from him. Our nanny, Estella, had no idea what was going on. She tried to calm me down, but I couldn't tell her what was wrong. I didn't know. I just wanted her to take me away from him."

The kitten's soft purr punctured the cold air, its claws pulling in and out of the fabric on Percy's thighs as it softened him. "Demons are strong. Even in a thin little boy's body, they're strong." He settled the kitten with the stroke of one hand, just as large as the feline was, encouraging her into a little ball, where she set about cleaning herself. "He dragged Estella across the room, quite deliberately, in hindsight, in front of the closed door. And he murdered her there. He did it slowly. And when he was done… she was barely recognisable as a human being, let alone as the young woman she had once been. Her screams…" Percy's brow contracted over closed eyes, and he lifted a finger a small way into the air. "I can hear it. I hear it when I'm sleeping. I see her still. And what makes me shudder even to this day is the way my father and my stepmother had to force what was left of her body out of the way to open the door. The dull thud of her skin, the squelch of her organs, the sound of them stepping in the puddle of her congealing blood."

The kitten raised its nose up to Percy's thumb, and he ran it over her forehead. "I believe it spared me because it knew that would be worse for me than dying would have been. I've never told a soul this, but when it was done, it stood there, in my brother's body, and it watched me. It watched me and it waited for them to come. Maybe it planned to kill them in front of me, too. Finish me off last. But I don't think so. I think it just enjoyed my sheer terror."

The kitten swatted at Percy's index finger. He let her take it between her teeth and chew on it playfully, his other hand stroking her scrawny back. "They got it out of the room, eventually. I don't think the demon could have known what a powerful witch my stepmother was. But they got it out, and there I was, alone with Estella. What was left of her. It took me so long to work up the courage to step over her. To push her out of the way. Because she was still very real to me. Like Michael had been. And all of it was gone, and they left me there. And then…" Percy breathed out a sigh, his eyes moving to his cigarettes, over on the bed, out of reach. He let the kitten nuzzle her face into his palm instead. "And then they told me the whole thing never happened. Well, my stepmother did. Any mention of it got a backhand across the face from my father. One word. But she, to her credit, sat me down and talked me through the lie. She said that I'd dreamed it. That my brother had gone walking off the property never to be seen again, and I'd made up the story to explain it to myself. A sick daydream. She stuck to that lie for decades."

Percy laughed a hollow sort of laugh. "Well, you know how that story ends, handsome. We found him and we exorcised him, and I began to fall in love with you as we did it. But you never knew the first half. I never told you how badly my mother fell apart, but it's exactly as you would expect. I never explained to you how she forgot to feed me. Couldn't do the washing or find clothes for me. How she could barely even look at me after that. She simply broke down. I was five, and I did my best, and so did she, but it was never enough… I couldn't tell her the truth, of course, because what would that have done to her? The damage was already more than enough. I felt so hopeless and alone all those years. And I never told you that…"

He wet his lips, staring out the broken window at the black and mossy brick wall, the purr vibrating up through his hand, the one and only touch of comfort in that isolated, miserable room. "I'm sorry if I'm a little brusque at times. There are things I worry about that I don't want to trouble you with. But what I've always worried about the most is that if I lose control again, if I drop that ball one more time, I'll find myself right back there in that room. At the mercy of something like that demon. And so I've tried to make myself… I've tried to be strong…"

The kitten had fallen into a cozy slumber, curled up in Percy's hand. Percy sat still, chewing on a thumbnail, while the sound of a door thumping into gore reverberated throughout his mind and down his spine. Joe's body sat just as quietly as Percy's, captivated successfully by the horrors of Percy's past.

The thing took a breath, and Percy intercepted with, "And did I ever tell you what I did to that older boy who took advantage of me at boarding school? Prepare to be horrified, darling…"

Percy talked on and on, swimming through his malignant sickness, which he felt crushing him on all sides, growing worse and worse, his own world growing darker and darker, borne on only by the faint flicker of hope that Joe would be waiting for him on the other side. That he would understand, and that he would forgive Percy, because those words and that horror were all the power he had to keep the thing safely away from Joe's hidden scars, whatever they might be.

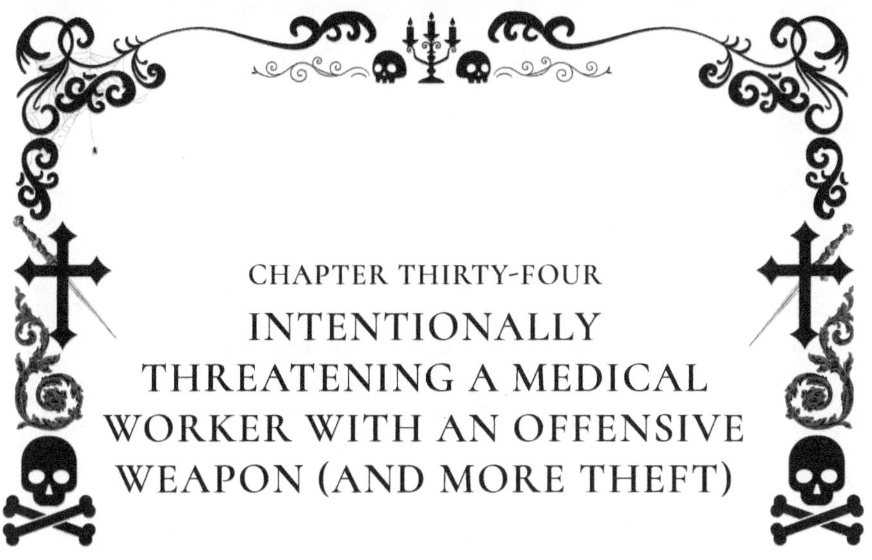

CHAPTER THIRTY-FOUR
INTENTIONALLY THREATENING A MEDICAL WORKER WITH AN OFFENSIVE WEAPON (AND MORE THEFT)

Leo and Althea rode the train in silence until Althea broke it with, "Sorry I did that."

Though he was looking away, she saw a flash of his smile, just at the corner of his handsome face. "Thanks for taking it." He followed that quickly with, "He's not doing well, you know? He would never ask me to do that. Not usually. He doesn't even let me drink."

She knew it probably wasn't wise, given his apologetic tone, but she said, "He puts you under too much pressure."

"No." There was such conviction in the word, such a forbidding frown, that Althea began to think it was a hopeless case. But Leo went on, "I need it. I need to stay busy. He knows that. And he told me. From day one, he said he'd never go easy on me." The grin returned, almost as wide as the last one. "But he does. Even if he doesn't realise it."

Relieved to have him smiling and talking, she asked, "How did you get involved with him?"

Leo glanced across at her, a furtive sort of glance, then he lowered his eyes to the train floor, and closed them, looking a lot like someone about to take a leap from a very great height.

His brow drew tight, and on a long breath, he commenced, "So, you're right. I was—*am*—a heroin addict. Because, like Percy says, it won't ever stop. I haven't touched it in years, but if all the elements were just right, it's an easy thing to slip back into. And feeling that little plastic bag in my hand, being around people like that, in this city… It's not a world I can be part of. Not without that temptation. So I live in Paris where I run his office. Sometimes he sends me off to Krakow to hide money and weapons. Sometimes he fills entire days with cigarette and shirt orders. Other days I need to fly last minute to Tunisia to smuggle some girl out of the country."

"Some girl," she muttered, adding a blush when he gave her a full dose of his playful smile.

"It's non-stop. He's into art theft, forgeries, but then also art preservation. He's got real work at real universities, and he's in constant demand there, but then he's off to deal with some weird supernatural thing, or find some enchanted item. And then there's the even shadier stuff. He has a lot of enemies. The death threats are constant. And it never gives me a second to stop and get mixed up in anything."

Althea laughed. "I'd say you're pretty mixed up."

"Yeah, but not…" Leo set about fiddling with the sleeve of his sweater as his smile faded. "I need to tell you that I was fifteen when I met Percy. And I was a call boy."

"Like…" Althea tried not to look shocked, but thought she must have misheard or misunderstood. "Do you mean like… Julia Roberts?"

"Yeah, but without the boots."

"Leo…" She gave him a shove, taking heart in the shoulder he pressed back against hers.

"I started a few years before that, and um… Home life wasn't good. So…" He trailed off, running a hand through his hair.

"A few years before? How young?"

"I don't remember. Twelve or thirteen?"

"That young?"

Leo provided a shrug for an answer and skipped over it. "So I was working this party. This guy who owned the place, he was a regular. I was just meant to look pretty and then wait and see what the host said to do later, with whoever. It was a thing he did. I'd done it before. But anyway, I was high, as usual, and I was looking at this painting on the wall in this guy's apartment. And then Percy's just there next to me, out of nowhere, like a ghost. He looked at the painting for a bit, and I was about to walk away, but then he asked me what I thought of it." Leo fell quiet, conjuring up the image in his mind's eye. "It was a picture of this… It's this dead lamb, lying on the snow. And blood's coming out of its mouth, a stream of red on white. And its mother's standing over it, protecting her dead baby. But she's surrounded by crows. Dozens of crows all around, and this blackening sky, like a storm's coming. And the mother, she's not ready to say goodbye to her baby, and she knows, the second she moves away, those crows are going to rip the little lamb to pieces and devour it. But she can't stay there forever."

"Fuck," whispered Althea, pulling Leo back to the present.

With a flush of pink about his cheeks, "That probably sounds stupid."

"It doesn't sound stupid at all. It sounds beautiful."

He breathed out the nervous spectre of a laugh. "Percy asked me what I thought of it. And, 'cause I was high, I guess, and because he was the only person who talked to me, I was honest. I said, 'I feel like the dead one. Like I don't care that they're coming for me, because I can't feel anything anymore, because I've already moved on. But then I feel so sad for her that she doesn't understand how hopeless it all is. That she hasn't given up yet. It breaks my heart that she's mourning for her baby and it's all so pointless. It breaks my heart that anyone has any fight left in them.' Percy didn't say a word. He just looked at me, and I hated the way he looked at me. And I think it was because it had been so long since anyone really looked at me, properly, and so I walked away, and he didn't come near me again. The night went on, and they gambled at cards while I served drinks, and Percy won some priceless artwork, which is what he'd come for in the first place." Leo laughed then, heartily, with a wide smile. "The guy who owned it was furious when he realised he'd been played. So Percy, cool as ever, says, 'I'll give you one last chance to win it back, then we'll both walk away, no hard feelings.' The guy screams at him that he has nothing left to bet. 'One last game, winner takes all,' Percy says, 'but you throw that boy in.'" Leo glanced at Althea, aglow with a mixture of pride and good humour. "You can imagine my face. Percy pointed at me, the host stared at me, I looked over my shoulder like there'd be someone else there. And the deal was done. No one asked me. Not a word. And can you guess what happened next?"

Althea chuckled. "I guess he won, and you both lived happily ever after."

"He lost," Leo said. "Percy lost, that guy opened his mouth to gloat, and Percy stuck his gun straight in it."

"Jesus." Althea covered her mouth with both hands, her shoulders shaking with laughter.

"He's got his gun in there, between this guy's teeth, and in the most polite voice ever he calls over to me, 'Grab that painting, would you?' Everybody in the place looks at me, and I'm frozen to the spot, so he adds, 'Or I could blow his brains out?'"

"So you did it?"

"Of course I did it! I took it, I shoved his money into my shirt, I opened the door for him, then we're in the hall. He pushes me onto the fire escape, and before I even know what's happening, we're in his car, speeding across town. He bundles me into his apartment, slams the door, takes the stolen painting and hangs it directly on the wall where it had a hook waiting, and he offers me a drink. Then he gave me the option: take all the money he'd just won and go, or stay and work for him, and get even more money in the long run."

"Fuck," she repeated.

"I know!" he agreed. "I was terrified of what 'work for him' meant. I mean, you've seen the size of his dick."

"Yeah, just that once." She shook her head slowly. "I don't know how Joe deals with that."

"Well, he's one giant asshole, so he should be able to handle—"

Althea slapped his arm. "Joe's lovely!"

"Anyway, long story short, Percy promised me a fresh start, and I agreed. I didn't expect him to nail the door shut and start weaning me off drugs that same night. He took over the whole thing. Fuck knows where he got the meds, but he did it. Then, when I recovered from that, he got to work having me tutored. Got me from reading like a third grader to now, where he makes me read two novels every week. He taught me French and Italian, though I'm still shit at Italian. He got me new clothes, specially made, never off the rack. New shoes, money, deportment and elocution lessons. He says I'm going to Cambridge in a few years. But that he won't pull any strings, so I need to be ready. He pretty much gave me his Paris apartment. He'll stay there too if he's in town, but he almost never is, anymore, so it's essentially mine."

The sadness that had been in Leo's voice at the start of the tale had given way to gushing excitement. "And this work I do for him, I love it. I can really do things to pay him back for all of it. Not that he sees it that way, because he says I don't owe him a thing, but it makes me feel like I can. And..." He shifted in his seat, facing her as much as he could, searching her eyes deeply as if to confirm she understood the importance of his words. "You only ever see him when he's stressed. You don't get to see the guy I know who did all of that for me. Who lived with me. Who, for a while, was like…" Leo grew embarrassed, glancing away again. "I'm not going to say like a dad or anything, but… he, um… I don't know. I don't know that much about his past, but I know it's fucked up. I think he's had a really hard life, even if he doesn't let on. And what I said to him that night, about the painting, it must have sparked something in him, because… I think he just wanted to bring me back from where I was. Like that dead lamb. And he did it. And now, it's nice that he pays me, really well. It's nice that he does all those other things, but I'd do anything for him without it. He's the only person who ever loved me, and I love him." He shuffled back to front-facing, letting the first hint of bitterness for some time slip into his tone. "And when he gets bored of Joe, things will settle down again."

Althea took several seconds to state what she thought, and she did so as gently as possible. "I hate to break it to you, but there's no way Percy's going to get bored of Joe."

The train slowed on approach to their station, and Leo stood with a grimace. "I don't even know what he sees in him."

"Besides the fact that he looks like a model?"

On a derisive snort, "He's had plenty of hot guys. Giordano's way better looking."

Althea rolled her eyes. "Giordano looks exactly the same."

"That's racist."

"You can't be racist against Italians."

"You just found a way."

Althea breathed out a silent laugh as she hopped off the train by Leo's side. "I think your bigger problem will be what happens when we get this thing out of Joe's body, and he dumps Percy's ass for treating us all so badly."

"Dump his meal ticket? Not likely."

"Is that really what you think of him?"

"Name one useful thing he's ever done."

"He saved my life."

"Percy did."

"Joe did," she corrected on a curt note. "Percy wouldn't have even noticed me that day. He would never have sat down next to me, asked me my name. Joe had no idea how bad things really were for me, and he had his own stuff going on, but he stopped everything just to listen to me. A complete stranger. Because that's who he is." She threw out a demonstrative hand. "Meanwhile, Percy goes in guns blazing, dick against the wall—"

"Dick against the wall?"

"You know what I mean."

"Not re—"

"And that's what everyone sees. The big show, the largesse. All the things he does for you, buys for you. But in Joe, I think I get what Percy likes. Because I got a taste of it. Joe is just a really good person who cares deeply about people. And I know it's probably hard for you to watch, but if I were as messed up as you make Percy sound, and if someone like Joe put his arms around me and told me it was all going to be okay, I'd never want to let him go. I'd probably chain him to a chair, too. I'd probably even think I was in love with him."

With a look of abhorrence such as she'd never seen on Leo's face, he interrupted, "Do you have a crush on that twat?"

"No, you idiot," she muttered. "I have a crush on you."

"Oh." He walked on a little further, then, "Good."

"Good?"

"He's a twat."

Althea rumbled out a long, low groan, then finished the thought that had been so rudely interrupted. "Joe's wonderful. And I think Percy's infatuated. But to give love—real love—you have to be capable of being loved. And I don't know if Percy is. I think he's fundamentally broken. He's all prickles and smashed glass all over. Don't get me wrong, I like him, mostly.

All the things he's done for me, and for you, by the sound of it. There's a real goodness in there, but that dark side of him… I just don't know if he can let someone in like that. Completely and forever. It's why he pushes you away, puts you in danger, leaves you all alone in Paris. It's why he talks to me the way he does, why he goes through lovers like they're disposable napkins. And that's what he'll do to Joe, only a thousand times worse."

"He's just tough. That's what keeps us safe. And you and Joe too."

"No, Leo. One of these days, he's going to go too far, and I just hope Joe comes to his senses before he gets hurt too badly. That's the only reason I'm still here. To try to prevent that and repay Joe for what he did for me." Althea pulled up at a phone box at the top of a leafy and expensive-looking street. "Now, do you want to pretend to be the overdose victim, or should I?"

It took Leo a moment, processing her words, to respond. "You call. I'll jump the paramedics with my knife when they try to help me."

Fingers already tapping out 999, she replied, "One dose of Narcan coming right up."

CHAPTER THIRTY-FIVE

TIL DEATH...

"And so I think that makes… Three? Yes, three priests I've killed now. Plus the bishop. And a lot of monks." Percy's eyes were open, but he may as well have been talking in his sleep. He shuffled the papers Althea and Leo had brought back, searching again for anything of use while he waffled on, but it was all old news. All of what they'd stolen, he already knew a hundred times over. Most anything could be defeated with the right combination of salt, stabbing, or Latin, but not this thing.

A bead of sweat that had been gathering momentum at his temple dripped onto the page, spreading out strands of printer ink like the tentacles of a kraken. The kitten lay purring by his fingers, sated by another belly full of good meat.

"How are you feeling?"

Percy shoved the papers to the side and let his head drop against the back of the chair. "Like the Devil shat in my mouth. How are you?"

"I'm great."

"That's nice. How's Joe?"

281

"He's doing well. He's worried about you. He knows you're going to die right here in this room."

"I'm going to have him out within the hour." A choking cough seized Percy's throat, his gut surging upwards, and he covered an empty retch with an unsteady hand.

Joe chuckled. "I don't think you've got an hour."

Percy dipped his forehead into his palms, and he drew long, even breaths in and out, trying to calm the nausea. The pulse of his blood ticked in his ears just as the seconds hand ticked its way around his watch, unerring, unrelenting. "You must want something. I don't understand why you don't just take me and go. You could get anything you want. Walk me out of here and be done with the whole mess."

"I waited four hundred years in a dark cellar, trapped in the body of a demon, thirsting for blood, and you don't think I can wait a little longer for you to expire?"

Percy's quick eyes examined the thing. "That was a demon's body?"

"That's not the point."

"But you're not a demon. You're not a demon and you want Joe, but you won't kill me to get him. And come to think of it, you haven't tried to kill Althea or Leo either. What's that about?" Percy tried and failed to stifle a groan at the sharp pain in his abdomen.

The creature smiled. "That should be your intestines. They'll start bleeding soon. Have you ever shat blood?"

"That's a bit personal, don't you think?"

"It'll come out everywhere. Your eyes, your ears, your mouth. It's going to be horrible for him to watch."

That was true enough. Percy could feel it. He could feel his mind and his strength ebbing away. And the gripping, maddening fever. The pain that had begun to throb in every nerve.

The idea that he could get a train, or simply walk away

from it, began to shadow every thought. That he could so easily leave the aching and the sickness behind.

'*Take my head…*'

What if it made Joe kill Althea? Made him devour her, like he'd done to the sheep? Made Joe watch that. Maybe that's why it was letting Percy die there. So Joe would have to live with his death. So Percy wouldn't be able to protect her when the time came. Because it's not as though it would want to eat him. He'd been marinating in scotch and cigarettes since he was at least fourteen. He'd taste terrible. He lit another smoke. "Your friend, Molly. I can find her." Silence reigned for a good ten seconds, broken only by the sound of the tailor-made cigarette pulling away from Percy's lips. "And I can kill her."

Percy took in the small muscle at the top of Joe's upper lip, flinching. "You see," he went on, "when you two did whatever you did, back in Scotland, she stole the body of a very good friend of mine. And I intend to get it back. But more than that, I intend to get revenge. For all of it. So if Joe's hungry right now, your friend Molly will be twice as hungry. That cut on his arm? She gets two."

Joe's smile was nervous, but spiteful. "You'll never make it in time."

"If I leave now, I'll get better, isn't that right?"

There was a gentle tapping of Joe's naked foot.

Percy pulled the chair up, knee to knee, with the man he adored. "Take me. Run to her. That's what you want, isn't it?"

There was a flitter of something in Joe's eyes. Understanding? A touch of hope? But behind it, he saw fear.

Percy had two choices. Talk to the thing, reason with it, like Joe might have. Or retreat into the cocoon of savagery that had protected him since he was a small child.

Percy, as was the wont of a lifetime, chose violence.

He leaned closer, nose almost touching Joe's, and in the most callous voice he could muster, he delivered the ultimatum.

"Take me now, or I'm going to burn her all over again. I'll make it slow. I'll put her in the body of someone I really don't like, and believe me, I'll make it last. I hear they can burn, wide awake, for ten solid hours if the kindling is sparse. But you know what? I think I'll try for twenty."

A fire ignited in the golden eyes and Joe's head smashed forward, splitting Percy's eyebrow right at the scar. "Fuck!" Hot blood gushed over Percy's eye, turning the room red, dripping down his cheek as he whirled back and away from Joe, away from the thing that had brought his hand into a fist, quickly and better aimed at the wall than at what used to be his lover.

A searing relief of pain shot through him as the wall gave way with a crack and a puff of ancient plaster, then another, then another, huge chunks falling to the floor at his feet as he smashed great gashes into the side of the room. He kicked at it, kicked more and more worthless holes, then he flung himself back on Joe, hands on the arms of his chair, taut with packing tape, close enough to see his own blood on Joe's forehead, close enough see the bruise spreading fast there, close enough for the creature to feel his spit on Joe's cheek when he growled, "That was it. That was your last chance. Whatever happens now, you'll pay. You'll pay with Molly Tulloch's blood."

Percy tore himself from the room, nothing but blinding, throbbing pain in his head and abdomen, offset only by the anger that overwhelmed the screaming of both. He fled downstairs, out the front door, and paced a circle in the empty street. A new lookout watched him, and he thought he might shoot him too, just for the intrusion into his own private nightmare. He set an incandescent stride up the road to avoid doing it, but it wasn't as though he could leave. Leave Joe there, alone. Which he had already done. Even if it was only for that breath of desperately needed air. He ran back to the door and braced himself against the entrance as a new wave of sickness smacked him dead in the face.

The blues, the hideous aquas and turquoise and sapphire and every horrendous shade of blue and blue and blue. The house made him sick. Being near Joe made him sick. And he made himself sick.

He paced up the street in the same frenetic fury, then, seeing a group of children at the top of the road returning home from school, staring at the sweating, filthy, bloody corpse of a man that he was, he veered off course, into the scrapheap that used to be someone's home, that sat forgotten and as broken down as he was, flush up against what was supposed to be a safe house.

The first rotting beam of wood he saw, he cracked a foot down upon and split the thing in two. He picked it up and smashed it into a wall, breaking it into a dozen splintered shards, but the damp thud wasn't nearly satisfying enough. Sheets of metal were ripped up and hurled across the yard with a deafening clatter. A metal pole rolled into his boot. He grasped it, strong and defiant in his hands, and smashed it into a wall of bricks, one hundred years old and not yet fallen, until the day it met Percy. The tired concrete gave way to his anger, and the lot toppled to the ground. He smashed the pole into corrugated iron. He found an unbroken shard of an old window and obliterated it. He wrenched old piping free, broke apart every recognisable thing, smashed and pulverised and destroyed every remnant that was left of what had once been a shelter until his exhausted body was too tired to go on.

He fell against the pile of broken-down bricks, the rubble slipping under his weight, gashing into his side, yet he lay there, in the miserable grey London afternoon, the sky and the walls just as dispassionate, unfeeling and stoic as they had ever been. A mass of clouds swirled low overhead, and a filthy drop of rain made a splash of pink in the blood on his cheek.

Percy sat forward.

It was Joe, and it was Joe, and it was Joe, all in a swirl of nausea and misery and aching everything.

Joe, who had ripped him out of a lifetime of sadness.

Joe, whose gentle fingertips he could feel even now caressing the hair at his temple.

Joe, who felt like the place on the pillow where the sun had kissed it moments earlier.

Joe, who'd never asked for anything, but that one simple request. To not let him live through that horror a second time. To not let him do those things that creatures of darkness would use his body for. To spare him. One simple request, that even now, even as he knew he was about to bleed out in front of Joe's eyes, he couldn't bring himself to fulfil. He would have bought him the earth, murdered every person in the street, pledged himself heart and soul for all eternity, but the simple act of slitting that one precious throat…

Leo would have done it for him.

But the thought of that gargle of blood, the red bubbles of air seeping at the slit…

The light going out of Joe's eyes forever…

Time was running out and he could feel it in every cell.

Percy picked up a broken half of a brick and hurled it at the building next door. It cracked in two with a puff of weak concrete, smashed down onto an old tin can, and sent the thing rolling, rolling, until it came to a halt right in front of Percy's shoe.

A movement inside caught his eye. He focused on the jarring twang of a silken strand. The twang of one long pincer plucking, pulling, righting.

Percy leaned a little closer.

Plucking, twanging, long and black… and deeply repulsive.

There she was. Shiny, black, leathery, and bulbous: a black widow spider.

The sight sent a shudder down Percy's back, but the reaction it would have drawn from Joe… He was utterly disgusted by the things. Terrified of them.

Even in the midst of dejection there was a heavier beat in Percy's chest with the memory of Joe, last time he had been Joe, so anxious to keep Percy's hand out of that hollow in Cleo's tree. But there were no black widow spiders in the Shetland Isles, as far as Percy knew. Not like London, which was riddled with the loathsome black beasts, according to Joe.

Percy turned the tin upside down, and with three hard taps, he knocked the spider to the ground. He watched the thing flip itself over, then it paused on its dagger-like legs, waiting to strike as soon as its assailant should make itself known.

Percy's hand reached a thin piece of wire towards the spider. It took a few steps back, but he pushed, and it grasped at the metal. Percy lifted it, entranced, watching it slip and curl and grasp, until it was upside down again, two small, sharp fangs, shiny and clear as day.

He wondered at the creature. The thought of those fangs piercing his skin. Of the drops of blood that would burst free at the injection site. The feeling of it. *Like holding a burning match to your skin for twenty straight minutes.'* Those tiny fangs and the delivery of such strong venom that it could kill a man.

It could kill Percy if he didn't get help in time.

It could kill Joe…

Percy's left hand searched frantically in his trousers pocket, pulling his golden cigarette case free. He clicked it open and half a dozen too-expensive cigarettes fluttered to the ground. He balanced the spider over the gleaming container, lowered it gently down, and clasped the lid closed. In a frenzy, he tore the ruins apart, searched under every cup and can and piece of old iron in the place, in every crack and crevice, turning the lot inside out until he'd collected every deadly black arachnid in that small slice of London.

Percy was halfway up the stairs before he knew what he was doing, two thoughts alone swirling around his nauseated head.

The thing felt Joe's pain.

The thing felt Joe's fear.

He rounded the top of the stairs, he thrust open the door, "You're back!" came the faux-delighted lilt of Joe's voice… But the words died on his lips.

Percy no longer looked scared, lost, or desperate.

He looked insane.

Utterly mad.

Far madder than usual, and he walked straight to Joe, took his dagger to his shirt, and ripped a slit in the cotton to halfway up his arm. "Handsome," he said, "this is going to hurt."

He clicked open the golden case and shook the spiders down onto Joe's skin. Joe's entire being reeled back on sight, as though the creature was just as horrified as Joe would have been, but before it could get a handle on what was happening, Percy's index finger pressed down hard on the leathery curve of a spider's back, and it slid two fangs deep into Joe's flesh.

A cry of pain shot from Joe's mouth, his hand squeezed into a fist, and all Percy thought about was how fast the blood would flow due to his panic, speeding the venom through every inch of his body, assailing the creature with the same sickness he'd felt since he walked in the door. He provoked another and another, a sea of black crawling over his beloved's skin. Tears of agony streamed down Joe's cheeks and he drew great breaths deep into his lungs.

Finding a semblance of control, the creature flung the spiders across the room where they landed with a tik-tak against the wall, only for Percy's shoe to crush the life out of them, one after another, seeing by the pools of blood on Joe's arm that they'd fulfilled his evil purpose.

The door burst open. "Percy!" came Leo's shout. "Percy, you'll be so impressed this time. I got your smack!"

Percy's wild eyes eviscerated him with one glare. "The fuck do I want smack for? It's antivenom I need!"

Althea's eyes went to the growing red welts on Joe's arm, and her voice barely made it to Percy's ears, weak as it was. "What the fuck did you do?"

"Black widows," he shouted, with an unnerving twitch of his bleeding eyebrow. "Maybe ten. Maybe fifteen. Who knows?"

"No…" The word slipped from Joe's beautiful lips, with an accompanying flash of regret at the utterance.

Percy laughed, dropping to his knees between Joe's legs. "I'm going to die? Then we'll die here together. Today. I told him from the start that I'd drag him down with me. Then here we go. You might outlast me, but you're not walking him out of here without me."

"Then so be it," the thing growled back at him, teeth clenching on its spiteful words. "He dies slow and horrible. Just like you."

Percy could see Joe's muscles begin to spasm beneath his skin, the venom already hard at work on its victim. A sweat broke about Joe's brow and every extremity began to tremble.

"Leo!" Percy screamed. "The antivenom now or Joe's death is on you!"

The drawn out and fading yell of "Fuuuuuck!" drifted down the stairs as Leo fled from the house.

But Althea didn't budge, her voice on a knife edge of dismay. "You've really done it this time. You've killed Joe."

"Go," Percy ground out. "But if I'm dead when you get back, don't give him the antivenom or you're next. Run."

"Percy—"

"Run!"

He heard Althea's footsteps fade behind Leo's. When the door slammed safely shut, he said, "That's it. It's done, and I've murdered you. There's no coming back unless you do what I say." For the first time in so long, Percy let his hands fall on Joe's chest. Joe's heart beat hard against the venom, his breath hitching beneath Percy's gentle touch. Percy looked deep into his eyes and begged, "Take me."

On quickening breaths, the beast rasped, "I'd rather see you dead."

"Why?" Percy screamed, climbing to his feet. "Why are you doing this? Can't you see I love him? Can't you see I'll do anything? Anything!"

"But you won't. You've chosen that girl over him again and again. You haven't offered me the boy once. You don't know what sacrifice is. You don't know what love is." Joe's gaze went to the corpse on the floor. "You give yourself readily because you have no respect for life. You don't understand love or beauty. Because humans don't. Because you're just the same as all the rest of them."

Percy glowered back at the thing. "I'm not like anyone else."

"Oh, but you are. You're all anger and violence, and when you don't get what you want, you smash it all to pieces. Look what you've done to him. This person you claim to love. You could have let him go. But you won't. Because you're just as pathetic and selfish as all the rest."

Pathetic and selfish. Percy knew it, believed it, with every inch of his soul, but he still attempted to argue, "Joe doesn't want that."

"And he doesn't want to be shot full of spider venom, either. Do you think this is how he wanted to die? Here in this stinking room next to a dead stranger watching the man he loves bleed to death?"

"No, I don't!" Percy shouted, yet all he could see was the red of Joe's arm, swollen and bitten, the newest, blackening bruise on the ridge of Joe's eyebrow, the blood from the cut he'd inflicted, and Joe's bare, beautiful feet on the filthy floor, and all of him chained and taped and shaking with the deathly delivery flowing through his veins.

This was no hero's death.

This was no lover's death.

This was no sort of death at all.

He dropped onto the mattress, at the foot of the bed, his hands paled to an eerie white as they rested on his thighs. His fingers tingled, as though he'd fallen asleep on them. He opened and closed them, the cuts on his knuckles smarting as he stretched the wounds. "We were supposed to grow old together. Just the two of us. We were supposed to…"

He drifted off, groping through the unrelenting malady, the impending death of his body, as all the memories he had left narrowed to one thin slit of Joe. "We never did make our plans. Go home, travel Europe, open a pub. Anything. I would have done any of it." Thinning, thinning, and blackening. "But it's over now, isn't it? Our beautiful dream. Or mine. My beautiful dream. My beautiful idea that someone like Joe could be for someone like me. In this life. In this world." He smiled sadly over at the beast. "Because you're right. It's all stinking shit, the whole lot of it. I've seen more horror in my time here than… Well, I suppose you know all of that now. And you know Joe, and you do know him, because he's in there somewhere."

His voice faded where memories took its place. "God, he's so beautiful. And I don't mean his eyes and his hair and his— his touch. Christ… I'm never going to feel that again, am I?" Tears started to Percy's eyes, and he pressed them against the palms of his hands. "He's so sweet. He has the most beautiful soul I've ever seen. And I never thought someone like that could be for someone like me. Because you're right. I'm not good enough for him. No one is. No one. This whole world… He's too good for it, all of it."

He looked again at Joe, but this time, he spoke only to Joe. "These last few months, this one tiny fragment of my whole life, I got to see what true beauty looks like. What love really is. And it's every time you look at me. It's every time you let me rest my head on your chest. It's every time you hold me and you kiss me…" He raised a trembling finger to his temple. "Right here. I can feel it now. Your lips, right here. And they're gone. And you're gone… This thing…" He shook his head, closing trembling lips to control his voice. "Handsome, it's not going to give you back to me. Not before I die. I thought I could do this. That I could destroy it, or cheat it…"

A single tear dropped from Joe's eye, running slow and silent down his cheek, his face so quiet and still, almost as though it was Joe.

"Then it's done." Percy reached for his dagger, which clanged emptily against the mess of metal and meat and useless research strewn all over the bed. "I'm sorry it had to be like this, my love. And I'm sorry for all the things I did to you today. I didn't want to let go. But I know better now."

Legs like lead, a head swimming in black, he staggered to Joe. His thighs straddling Joe's for stability, he placed his fingers on Joe's cheek, palm cupping his chin, and the creature raised Joe's face up to him. Those eyes, faithful and golden through the longest, darkest lashes, that Percy had adored since the second he first saw him. "I never meant for any of this to happen. If I could turn things back and make it that you never crossed my path…" A tear fell from Percy's eye onto Joe's skin, and that tear ran red with the haemorrhaging of Percy's blood, in one long, fatal streak down his cheek, and down his neck.

"If I could change that night you came to my house… The way I fell in love with you…"

He leaned down and kissed Joe, dying lips on dying lips, deathly cold against dangerously fevered, desperately loving and lonely and forever broken, against the promise of eternity. He pressed the icy blade to Joe's neck. "If I could change it all, I wouldn't trade a second. Because this thing is right. I'm selfish, and I love you. I love you desperately. Obsessively. Greedily. You're everything. And you always will be. So listen to me when I tell you, it doesn't end here." The blade sunk deeper, indenting Joe's flesh, though it did not break, while Percy's hand searched over Joe's cheek, storing away every last sense of Joe's living, breathing self beneath his touch. "If they take me to Hell, I'll murder the Devil to get to you. If they send us to purgatory, I'll find you. I'll burn the gates of Heaven to the ground and make God my slave if I have to. I will follow you to the end of existence and back again, and I won't ever stop. Don't forget me. Don't you ever forget me. There isn't a force in this universe that could keep us apart. You go first, darling, but I'm coming right after you. Your blood, then mine, on this knife. I promise you, I'm coming for you." His forehead dropped against Joe's, tears of blood running fast, scalding their two faces. He touched their lips together in one last soft kiss. "Goodbye, my love. But only for a time."

Percy pressed the dagger, Joe gasped an enormous breath of air, then screamed, "Percy, stop! Stop! Percy, it's me!"

A trickle of blood painted Joe's neck, reddening his collar. Percy's hand held the vicious blade there in his skin, stalled by something in the voice—something indefinable, unfathomable —something primal. But he didn't dare to hope. He remained, like a brutal statue, frozen in the act of murder. Void.

Almost void.

Almost empty, but for that one vibration of tenderness.

He knew the soul behind that voice.

The knife clattered to the floor. Percy threw his head against Joe's chest, red tears bathing his shirt through and through, and heaving sobs and arms wrapped around Joe's waist. Then Percy's hands on either side of Joe's face, searching desperately.

Joe, truly Joe, stared back at him, eyes wet with tears and as adoring as they'd ever been. "It's me. Percy…"

"Fuck. Fuck, fuck, fuck." Percy scrambled for the dagger, slitting the electrical tape.

Joe's arms were around him, kisses all over his hair, his temples and cheeks, anywhere he could plant one, strong arms pulling him close. "Baby, it's okay. It's okay now. You did it."

Percy shook his head in the heated darkness of Joe's embrace. "I almost slit your throat. Jesus Christ, what did I do?"

"Nothing. Nothing at all. You're so, so perfect. Percy, look at me." Percy flinched away, but Joe brought his chin up with loving fingers. "Your eyes. We need to get you out of here."

Like a wind-up toy, Percy acted on command, his every movement bereft of thought, the residual energy of a dying vessel. He found the key, he unlocked Joe, he unwound the chains, and Joe, shaking in every inch of his body, heart ramming a million miles an hour, gasps of breath fighting at the venom in his blood, took Percy's exhausted weight against his body, and they two trudged down the stairs. They braced themselves against the wall, slipping, but with Joe's red and swollen arm on the railing catching them every time. He dragged Percy out into the street and refused to let him fall onto the broken asphalt. He kept on, up and up, to the brown-green expanse of the council estate, where he finally let Percy sink into his lap, stroking his hair. "Rest here."

A fog of all-encompassing fatigue swept over Percy. Against the heat of Joe's body, the touch of his hands in his hair, the reassuring press of the breath in his body, Percy was ready to slip away. But he sunk his fingernails into the dirt to grope his way back up. "I need to kill it."

Joe forced him back down. "Shhh. It's gone. It's not there anymore."

"Gone? Gone where?" Percy muttered, face pushed into Joe's knee, eyelids fluttering closed. "How do you know that?"

A small mew sounded at Joe's hip.

Percy was up quicker than a shot. "Moxie! Thank Christ." He scooped the kitten up, taking her to his chest, then collapsed back onto Joe. "This makes no sense. It must have gone somewhere."

"Mew," said the kitten. Percy pulled her up against his cheek.

"You called it Moxie?" asked Joe, more than a hint of worry in his voice.

"Leave Moxie alone. She stays with me." As if in agreement, the kitten stretched a tiny paw across his bloody closed eye. "It's going to be after Althea next. We need to find her and get away from here. We'll go to Paris tonight."

Joe let slip a small laugh. "You're not going anywhere tonight, Percy. Or for some time. It's gone. And it didn't really want her anyway. It was just testing you."

Percy rolled onto his back to look at Joe. "Do you know what it was?"

"I do. But let's save that for another chapter because—"

"Fuck that, Joe. What is it, what did it want, and why did it give you back?"

Their attention was snatched away to the end of the street by the fast and untrustworthy movement of an ambulance. It hit the tight corner of a brick wall, grazing the side of the van with an ear-piercing scrape. It overcorrected and smashed the railing off someone's staircase. The accelerator propelled the thing too fast off the stairs it had mounted, and the vehicle screeched to a long and disturbing halt just past their safe house.

"Leo!" Joe shouted as soon as saw him jump out. "Althea!"

The pair bolted up the street to them, Althea just about knocking Joe over with her arms around his neck, and Leo on his knees in front of Percy.

"Are you all right?" Althea asked.

"I've been worse," Joe laughed out.

"Come here." Percy pulled Leo's head down to his shoulder, where Leo let out a little whimper, patted away by Percy's hand on his hair. "I'm so sorry."

Leo, refusing to leave the desperately needed embrace, spoke into Percy's shoulder, "I got your antivenom."

Percy broke a tired smile. "You're the best, Leo. I'd be lost without you. Truly. I'm really sorry."

A sniffle sounded, but Leo hid the rest of his emotion with a gruff, "I guess we'd better inject him, then."

"Ah, I might actually go to the hospital for that," Joe cut in, receiving the usual scowl from Leo. "I can drive myself."

"You're not leaving my sight," said Percy, wrapping his hand a little tighter around Joe's thigh.

"No, I'm not," Joe agreed. "You're coming with me. Come on."

Joe stood shakily, with Althea supporting him from under one arm. "Did you kill it?" she asked.

He shook his head. "No. But it's gone. Out of me, anyway. And not in Percy."

"But where to?" Percy wondered, still in a muddle on the grass. The kitten gave another little mew, so he pulled it onto his shoulder, where it purred against his cheek, then set about licking the blood from his face.

"You're planning on keeping that?" Joe asked, failing to hide an unaccustomed distaste that, had Percy had an inkling Joe felt for cats in general, would have scarpered any chance of a relationship from the start.

In a quick, defensive manoeuvre, Percy dropped the kitten into his shirt pocket and let Leo help him to his feet. He cut off Joe's next comment by saying, as he walked towards the ambulance, "I'll drive us to the hospital. Leo, would you mind terribly burning the house down?"

Leo's back was erect, head held high, smile returned in full. "Not at all. I'll make sure the body's burned first."

"Good lad. And could you get Cleo out?"

"Of course. I'll bring her to you right after."

"And then book us somewhere nice. You and Althea too."

"Ritz or Savoy? Or—or Claridges?"

"You decide. But could you organise some cat litter or something? And I don't know, shots or whatever it is Moxie needs?"

Joe and Althea staggered two steps behind in bewildered silence. Joe glanced over at her, managing a smile, despite feeling he was likely to drop dead any second. "Are you okay?"

Althea burst into a nervous bout of laughter. "Me? Yeah, I'm fine. No spiders or anything."

Joe laughed, and to Althea's delight, he soon showed he was still very much Joe. "It's been a day though, hasn't it? I didn't see that much, but I know you must have been through a lot."

She replied, "I saw my first murder, held up two sets of paramedics, stole an ambulance, bought heroin, destroyed some priceless books, and almost watched you die. Yeah, it's definitely been a day. But not a bad one. Not entirely."

"So… I'll see you at whichever expensive hotel we end up at?"

She stole a quick glance over at Leo, who was nodding earnestly to Percy's every instruction, and said, "Yeah. Yeah, I think you will."

"I had a feeling I might."

They embraced, then Joe climbed into the ambulance next to Percy, who hit the siren despite Joe's protests, and drove them to the closest private hospital with his usual careless grace.

CHAPTER THIRTY-SIX

THE MOXIE IN THE ROOM

There was no force in a private London hospital, or anywhere in all the world, for that matter, that could have kept Percy from Joe's side, as he was treated for numerous spider bites. Even if, as they were enlightened by the doctor, there were no black widow spiders in London, and they had both been the victims of the trickery of false widows. Joe swore up and down that he had in fact read reports of the deadly Latrodectus spiders invading the city, citing his symptoms as evidence of their presence. He was informed that his panic accounted for just about every physical symptom beyond the pain in his arm, and he and Percy were, therefore, a quiet combination of relief and embarrassment by the time they were left alone for several hours of surveillance, as it is rare one is bitten by fifteen false widows at once.

There, in the small room, Percy kept the same watch over Joe that he had since the appalling incident began, only now, he was by far the weaker of the two. The pain and the nausea had retreated the moment the creature did, but Percy, who hadn't eaten in two days, not even raw sheep, had also barely drunk a drop of anything, let alone water. He had punched walls, been

299

head-butted, thrown up, kicked things, fallen over, smacked into walls and doors, dragged Joe's unconscious body from one place to another, run upstairs and downstairs, expended more energy in worry and cursing and breaking things than was ever advisable, and had very nearly dropped dead from mass haemorrhaging that afternoon. Needless to say, he wasn't at his best. A drip had been forced into a shrivelled vein, but he still commandeered an uncomfortable chair rather than the bed he had been offered elsewhere in the building, away from Joe. His head leaned back against the wall, long lashes closed over bloodshot eyes, and Joe didn't move a muscle, in the hope he would fall asleep.

For Joe, the greater part of terror during the entire ordeal, besides the spiders, had come from the uncertainty of what it all meant for Percy. The being inside had swayed over whether to kill him, back and forth, a thousand times. Joe had watched Percy walk the tightrope, sickeningly high, unsteadily, and he'd never once been able to tell which footfalls were strategically placed, and which were blind luck. He knew the being's intentions regarding his own body, but he couldn't have gone on without Percy, any more than Percy would have gone on without him.

"Are you going to tell me what it was?" Percy's eyes remained closed, and he spoke in a thick, almost-asleep voice. "Or is it too terrible for me to know?"

Joe, who didn't want to rouse him any more than he had just roused himself, supplied a plain and succinct answer. "It was Molly's familiar."

Unfortunately, that did indeed rouse Percy, who studied him from beneath a deep frown. "Her familiar? Her evil magical friend?"

"In a nutshell."

Percy thought things over, concluding with a small nod, "That explains a lot. The demon form in the basement, why it wanted to get to her so badly... And what, its plan was to march you over to her for a grand reunion?"

"Basically. Had you let me go, that was the thing's intention. Only it doesn't—didn't—know how to find her. That's why it didn't kill you in the first place. It thought it could tag along, pretend to be me until it figured things out. But it's not all that good at pretending to be human."

"No. And certainly not at pretending to be you." Percy reached a hand out for Joe's. He held on, letting a moment of quiet fall between them, then asked softly, "Do you still love me? After all those terrible things I told you?"

"It's not possible for one person to love another more than I love you," said Joe. "I'll always love you. Nothing changes that."

Any tension disappeared with Percy's smile. "I'm glad I tried to murder you."

Joe laughed, retaining his beautiful fingers. "So am I. But now that's over. It won't try to hurt us again."

A little white paw stretched out of Percy's shirt pocket, requiring him to take his hand back to pat it. He did so with an intensely peaceful, sated sort of smile that made Joe pause the conversation there.

"She's smart, too, you know?" Percy mumbled sleepily, palm coming to rest on the small, purring mound. "They have no idea she's even here. It's almost as though she knows to keep quiet."

"Yeah," Joe agreed, trying his best to keep his tone light. "She's unusually smart."

"Isn't she?" Percy peeked down at the pink nose and white whiskers, and Moxie offered a little mew for his trouble. With a satisfied glow, he closed his eyes again and sank a little deeper into his chair. "Pretty too."

"Mmm," Joe offered, glaring at the vibrating shape on his

fiancé's chest, the paw that scrunched into his shirt to be covered and stroked by his fiancé's loving fingers.

He would tell Percy.

Any minute now.

Just as soon as the time was right.

The time wasn't right when Percy and Joe were hooked up to tubes at the hospital. A cab ride was hardly the place for a discussion like that. Upon a three a.m. check-in at Claridge's, when Percy saw the date and fell into a small fluster about how it was 'officially Althea's birthday', Joe was kept busy talking him out of swinging by her room with surprise champagne.

The art deco halls of the hotel, the gorgeous elevator, the well-appointed bathroom and the much-needed hot showers kept Joe's mouth closed. Then, when they finally climbed into their enormous bed, in their beautiful penthouse, a grossly luxurious contradiction to the room they'd spent the day in, all Joe wanted was to hold Percy in his arms and let him rest. So, despite the ginger kitten that nestled itself under their duvet, right in the crook of Percy's arm, where Joe wanted to be, Joe wrapped his arms around Percy's neck, kissed his temple, and leaned his forehead against his cheek for what little was left of the night.

Thick curtains kept the room in artificial twilight until the following afternoon when the pair awoke. Joe was the first to rouse. Cool air, warm bedding, and the smell of Percy. It was his forever place. His lips pursed to kiss the stubble of Percy's cheek, and he felt the movement of a smile as Percy woke into the same delightful reality. Percy's head tilted languidly, and their lips met. Joe's dick was already hard, and Percy's beautiful hand reaching across to caress his jaw only made matters more pressing.

Joe, having been strapped to a chair for most of the previous day, when all he'd wanted was to take Percy into his arms, was all over him in a flash. He rolled onto his front, locking a leg over Percy's thigh. He moved one hand to Percy's cheek, the other intertwining fingers with his and forcing his arm above his head, where he intended to keep it, to have Percy on full display while he showed him just how much he appreciated everything he'd done to keep them together. Joe's lips moved to Percy's neck, kissing him over and over, the smell and the taste of him never enough, ever again. His other fingers took those of Percy's he'd draped so artfully, allowing a hand to slide down the beautiful neck, his chest, over his pecs, his hard nipples, and down and down until a sudden and searing pain elicited a loud "Fuck!" from Joe, who flung the covers back to reveal Moxie, curled up on Percy's abs, with an unmistakable smirk on her furry little face.

"Get out!" Joe seethed, shaking his bitten finger at her.

Percy frowned across at him as though he'd gone totally mad. "Don't yell at Moxie." He then redirected his attention to the kitten using the most soothing of tones. "How did you get down there?" The kitten stretched innocently as her master's big hand lifted her up, placing her on the bedside table with a long stroke from her forehead to the tip of her tail. He rolled over to Joe, who was staring pure malevolence at the cat, and pulled him down with an arm around his neck. "Where were we?"

Joe kissed Percy, because how could he not? Percy was a

mass of sensual muscle, and Joe knew well he was beyond help. Percy took his hand and brought it down to his dick, and a too-loud groan of pleasure ripped from Joe's lips at the feel and the promise.

"I've missed you so much," Percy murmured between kisses.

"I wasn't sure we'd ever do this again," Joe whispered, grinding his dick against Percy's thigh.

Percy took a fistful of Joe's hair. "I'd never let anything come between us."

"Mew," said Moxie, pushing her twitching nose up to Percy's.

"Out!" Joe yelled. He scooped the kitten up, dashed off to the bathroom with her, and slammed the door behind them. Percy waited, hearing nothing but indecipherable mumblings from Joe, punctuated by the occasional meow. A few moments later, the door reopened, and Percy heard Joe's loud whisper, "He's *my* fiancé, and you will keep your paws off him!" The door was closed, with Moxie on the other side howling in protest.

Joe crossed the room in a furious temper, and wrenched open the curtains, where the small shock of an exquisite view over half of London distracted him enough to calm him slightly.

Percy watched him lean against the window, coveting the thick thighs, the shapely calves, the curve of his beautiful ass. "No morning sex?"

Joe shifted his weight, every gorgeous muscle flexing in the afternoon sunlight. "We need to talk. About Moxie."

"Can't it wait?"

Joe pulled his eyes from the scenery to argue that no, it was quite vital he tell Percy all details in full at once. But then Percy leaned an arm behind his head and kicked the blanket down. Reclining on the mass of pillows, one leg bent, every inch of him on display, there could never have been a more beautiful frame for the artwork that was Percy Ashdown's dick.

"We should talk…" Joe attempted.

"Then talk," said Percy, wrapping his fingers around his cock. He gave it such a compelling stroke, drinking Joe in as he did, that Joe found his conundrum was suddenly far less pressing. In fact, he was quite sure he could spare another hour. Or two. And after all, it's very hard for a man to talk when his mouth is that full…

CHAPTER THIRTY-SEVEN
THE UNAPPETISING TRUTH

Percy kept Joe busy until well into the evening, when the two were required to dress for dinner. Joe kept his good humour, forcefully, while the kitten followed Percy from room to room, sat on the vanity and stared at him as he showered and shaved, and purred against his legs with every other step he took. The thing ingratiated itself with a seemingly artless love that soothed every one of Percy's recently frayed nerves, and by the time he dropped her into his coat pocket to bring her along to dinner, Joe had developed serious regrets about having let the situation get so far.

He had eventually decided to gamble on the hope that the etiquette demands of an elegant and crowded restaurant would keep Percy's temper under wraps when he delivered the news. But then he knew Percy, and a light sweat prickled at the back of his neck at the thought of the coming conversation.

Leo and Althea arrived at the table shortly after Percy and Joe had. Leo was dressed in a grey suit jacket, navy shirt, black slacks, and looked every part the gentleman Percy had so care-fully curated. Althea wore an excruciatingly bright dress, too long and too wide, some kind of fuchsia and fire-engine red combination which, to Percy, was worse than the tears of blood he'd cried the day before. Joe kicked his foot when he saw 'the look' descend, and Percy said, "Happy birthday, Althea. You look gorgeous."

The ice between them was effectively broken, though Althea remained wary until he slid his chair across to hers and produced Moxie, secreting the kitten between them. Althea's loud gasps of adoration very nearly sunk the whole charade, but it wasn't long until Moxie was stowed under the table, happily devouring the tuna tartare Percy had ordered for her, sans garlic, onion, herbs, citrus, oil and vinegar.

After a time, all pleasantries having been dispatched, entrees being finished, mains just delivered, Joe lowered his voice, trying to avoid his words reaching the kitten's sharp ears while she ripped apart her 'rare as rare comes' steak. "We need to talk about what happened yesterday, and what happens next."

"Next?" asked Percy, the spark of battle flaring in his eyes. "You said it was gone."

Joe nodded, swift and reluctant. "Uh. I said… I think I said it won't be a problem anymore."

Percy's fingers wrapped tight around Joe's and his voice dropped to concerned intimacy. "Are you okay?"

"Yes. Yes. Very okay." He squeezed Percy's hand, though it did nothing to shift the line of worry he'd created. "Very, very much better. And we're safe now." His eyes sought Althea's. "All of us. I'm sure of it. And I need you to know that, while the—the thing that was in me was, and *is*, very dangerous, it won't hurt any of us."

"I've been thinking about this," said Percy. "It must have gone somewhere. Some poor bastard in London is almost certainly walking around possessed, and I think we need to start checking the papers for any leads."

Leo pulled out his little notebook and commenced scrawling. "Ritualistic murders, cannibalism, that sort of thing?"

"Precisely," said Percy. "The evil prick. There's no way I'm letting it get away with this." The kitten jumped back onto Percy's thighs, pink tongue lapping at her whiskers, and Percy stroked her coat. "When I get my hands on it, I'm going to strangle the life out of it." He then, caution to the wind, picked Moxie up and kissed her ear before setting her down on his legs and putting her paws on the table. "Look. She thinks she's people."

Althea and Leo made approving comments, but Joe's face remained flat. "Percy, I think you need to try to move past your anger with the being, as quickly as possible, because—"

"I'll murder it," he said, stroking Moxie's whiskers. "I'll force it into corporeal form, and when I do, I'll rip its head off with my bare hands." A small cheer went up around the table from all but Joe, while Moxie raised her chin to enjoy Percy's soft scratches.

For Althea and Leo's sake, Joe revealed, "It was—is—a familiar." He kept his gaze on the kitten, whose green eyes watched him with interest. "It's Molly Tulloch's familiar."

"What?" asked Althea. "Like a witch's cat?"

Joe's mouth pulled into a hard line. "Exactly like that."

"I didn't know familiars could jump bodies until yesterday," said Percy. "It explains the magic, though. And the sickness."

"And why it wanted to get back to Molly," Leo suggested.

"And why it was so pissed off when I said I was going to kill her," Percy muttered. "That has to be an intense bond."

"That's exactly it." Joe latched onto the shift in conversation. "I need to tell you... In this situation... It's a bit unusual..." He gave a small tilt of his head and a shrug. "It's in love with her."

No one made any response, least of all Percy, as they all let this latest intelligence mingle with their memories of the last few days.

Joe said, "The familiar, whose name, if it has one, I don't know, came to Molly, like familiars do, to help her with magic. She was a real witch, a powerful one, and they worked together. For years. And this familiar took human form, eventually, and it fell in love with her. And she with it. And, Percy…" Joe looked across at him with a sympathy that inexplicably put him on his guard. "They were so in love. Like we're in love. And when the witch hunters came for her, she locked her familiar away. She locked it away to protect it, in the basement, with magic of her own, and she went to meet her fate. Alone. But they were so intertwined by then. They'd shared everything, and what they did to her, her familiar felt it too. All of it. All of it from the torture, to her death, to her being trapped in that skull. They were only a short walk apart for hundreds of years, both of them imprisoned. In love. And despite its magic, because she'd bound it, to keep it safe, it couldn't do a thing to help her."

Percy wet his dry mouth with a sip of wine, then stated, "Well, that's fucking miserable. No wonder it was such a prick."

"Yeah, it really was," Joe muttered, with another glance at the quiet cat. "But that's also why it let us go. Sort of."

"Sort of?" asked Percy.

Joe coloured with a mixture of guilt and embarrassment, but trudged on. "We presented the second opportunity in hundreds of years that the familiar ever had for escape. Cleo was the first, but it sacrificed that chance for Molly. It gave her Cleo's body. It expected her to free it. But when Molly got strong enough, she left her familiar. After all they'd been through, she abandoned it there in the basement. And then when we came…" Joe watched Percy's face, his eyes dimming as images of that afternoon closed in on him. "Percy, I'm sorry I put you through all that—"

"You should be," Leo snapped.

"I am," Joe said softly. "Genuinely. I was trying to help."

Leo, nowhere close to accepting any apology from Joe, said, "It was fucking stupid."

"Leo." Percy's reprimand was quiet but firm. Leo sipped his coke and withdrew into angry silence.

"I know it seems stupid," said Joe, trying to catch Leo's averted gaze. "And I'm trying to apologise. It was a thing I did, thinking it was a ghost, thinking we had it under control. And had I known how out of hand things would get, I might not have done that. But even with that in mind, I believe, in hindsight, I did the right thing."

A loud tsk rolled off Leo's tongue, and Joe said, "I trusted you to handle it, Percy. And I know that was a lot to put on you, but I also believe, if it was anyone else but me, you'd agree it was right to try to help those girls."

Percy, easily convinced by the altruism he'd come to see at part and parcel of a life with Joe, cracked an adoring smile. "It was a good and noble thing to do."

Leo refused to make further sound or acknowledgement, as disgusted as he was, so Joe said, "I want to say thank you. To all of you. I know you went through a lot." Meeting Althea's eyes, "I never would have let you get involved like this if I could have stopped it."

"I know," she said. Adding, with a pointed look at Leo, "It wasn't all bad."

He allowed a light blush in response.

"Don't beat yourself up," Percy said. "It's done. It's over. We made it out unscathed. And by the sounds of it, you have some information that could help us locate this familiar."

"Mew," said the little kitten, with a piercing glance at Joe.

"I do," said Joe, returning her stare. "And I'm going to tell you. Now."

The kitten dropped its paws from the table and started a soft padding up Percy's stomach. "She's lovely, isn't she?" he said. "Do you think they'll really mind if I put her on my shoulder? She seems to like it there."

"I think they'll mind," said Althea.

Percy glanced around the restaurant, and seeing no eyes on them, lifted her to his cheek for a cuddle. She licked him, and he marvelled, "It was love at first sight, Moxie and I. I've never fallen so fast. No offence, Handsome."

Joe glowered at Percy and his cat. "None taken."

"Marvellous little thing." He rolled her onto her back and rubbed her tummy. "Sorry, what were you saying?"

"I was saying—" Joe attempted.

"See how she doesn't use her claws?" Indeed, the cat had Percy's hand wrapped in its front paws, back legs kicking his palm playfully, teeth so soft on his hand it was barely a tickle.

"I was saying—" Joe tried.

"She's awesome, Percy," Leo put in. "A much better side-kick, if you ask me."

"I was saying—" Joe endeavoured.

"She's got such a mischievous look about her, but she's just so cute," Althea fawned.

"I was saying—" Joe repeated.

"Look, I can lift her up." The kitten held tight to Percy, wriggling around with a joyful growl as he raised his arm.

"Percy, could you put the damn cat away?" Joe snapped.

Percy, Althea, and especially Leo, looked over at Joe, aghast. Percy apologised and slipped the kitten back into his shirt pocket.

"I was saying—"

"Look, she's still watching me." Percy nodded down at his pocket.

"I was saying," Joe reiterated ten times as loud, before dropping out a heavy sigh. "Don't you think it's weird how attached she is to you?"

"Moxie?" Percy held his finger over his pocket to be swatted. "Not really. We have a connection."

Lips drawn tight, "She's a cat. You've known her for a day."

Percy topped up Joe's wine, somewhere very close to the top, and said, "Handsome, I'm beginning to think we need to talk about your jealousy issues."

Already pushed to close to the limit of his patience, Joe verily seethed, "My what?"

Percy gave a placid, consoling, infuriating pat of Joe's hand. "I love you. Only you. But this is the point that I feel like it's tipping over into a you thing and not a me thing, you know?"

"What?" Joe very nearly shouted.

"Moxie's my forever girl. But you're my forever guy. And there's no need for you to feel threatened."

Joe's fist slammed down on the table so hard the glasses rattled and he jumped to his feet, shouting furiously, "It's Moxie! Can't you see it's Moxie?"

Percy, in perfect shock at the outburst, said softly, "What's Moxie?"

Joe, cowed by the scowls of the waiting staff, dropped back to his seat. He took a few deep breaths and tried a shift to the comforting nature he'd learned as a priest. Percy's feelings were on the line, so Joe explained as calmly as possible, "The familiar and Molly were in love. It watched her—*felt* her die, horribly. It lived her descent into madness. It's never stopped loving her and it... It didn't leave because you almost killed me."

Percy grew quiet, listening intently.

"After it possessed me, it took a long time to trust you. To trust us. Because it's traumatised, terrified by everything they went through. But when you said those things to me…" Joe moved his chair closer, taking Percy's hand. "Percy, when you said those beautiful, beautiful things to me, it was the most pure, most romantic moment of my entire life."

"So murder-suicide does it for you."

"Percy…" Joe fought back the chuckle, though his smile was irrepressible. "Percy, I'm so madly in love with you." His tone and face set a little more serious as he went on. "And those things you said, they were so loving, and that's when it understood. What we have, it's real. It's a love that will span all of eternity. It's a love that even death can't conquer. It's so rare, and so beautiful, and… And it didn't want to take that away from us. Because that's the kind of love it had with Molly. And…" Joe took a breath and squeezed Percy's hand a little tighter. "Percy, you're very handsome, and you're—you're very sexy—"

Both Althea and Leo groaned loudly.

Joe carried on, disregarding them both, "You're captivating. And enigmatic. And that familiar… it… it reacted to you like… most people do when you decide to be charming… Even if it was totally artless. Which made it that much more charming."

A quiver of worry shot its way through Percy. "I'm not sure I understand what you're getting at."

"The, um…" Something akin to the idea of gutting himself popped into Joe's mind, and he began to think that might be preferable. "The familiar likes you. A lot. You have to understand, you're the first man it's seen in centuries. And you're a very attractive man. And you did that sexy blood-play thumb thing…"

Percy grinned. "That was hot, wasn't it?"

"So hot," Joe agreed ardently.

"Why did they invite us?" Althea whispered.

"I don't know!" Leo snarled.

"So, all things being what they are," Joe sighed out, "I would go so far as to say… the familiar developed a small crush on you."

Percy's mind had not yet grasped the concept simply because his self-preservation instinct wouldn't allow it. Perhaps the familiar had liked him. What of it? What did any of it have to do with anything now? With finding and slaying the thing? It was irrelevant, so why was Joe harping on about it? Percy said, "I know you're not jealous of a beast from the abyss, Joe."

Joe wiped a tense hand across his wrinkled brow. "I'm not jealous, Percy."

"Because first it's Moxie, and now it's this. But I'm willing to try couples counselling if that might—"

Irritation boiling over, Joe snapped, "Would you shut up and listen to me? It adores you, Percy. You made it not only trust you, you made it fall for you. So when it left me, it took a form where it could stay close to you. Where it knew you would keep it safe." Joe's eyes moved to the ball of fur trying to clamber up Percy's chest. "Where it would get all the best of you, because it found a weak spot."

Percy's hand closed around the kitten as the understanding began to dawn on him. "You're being ridiculous—"

Joe raised his voice a little louder. "Where it can lick your face, and watch you shower—"

Percy spoke louder still, over the top of him, refusing to hear it. "This is complete nonsense. I won't have anything to do with—"

"And where it can bite your fiancé when he tries to touch your dick!" The restaurant fell quiet at these last, shouted words.

Percy turned a ghastly shade of grey. He scrunched the scruff of fur on the kitten's neck, and lifted her, slowly, to look into her bright green eyes. "Did you take Moxie?"

She reached out a be-socked paw and tapped him on the nose. "Mew."

Percy dropped the kitten onto his dinner plate. He stood, scraping his chair back, feeling over his pockets. "It's been a long week. Please accept my apologies." He pulled out a cigarette and shoved it in his mouth before flinging a credit card down on the table. "Put it on this."

"Percy," Joe tried, "it won't hurt anyone else."

Percy held up a silencing finger. "Get anything you like. No drinks, Leo. We'll talk tomorrow." And he stalked out of the restaurant.

Moxie pounced after him, but was caught mid-air by Joe. "You've caused enough trouble." He turned to Althea and Leo, the two of them perfectly mute. "Um. Happy birthday, Althea!" And Joe, too, sprinted out into the night.

Leo leaned across and said, "What if we just order every single dessert on the menu?"

Althea's eyes grew wide. "Can we do that?"

Leo raised a hand for the waiter. "I think we deserve it."

CHAPTER THIRTY-EIGHT
THE BREAKUP

Joe followed the scent of Percy's very particular tobacco blend. He didn't know London well, but when he'd run about two blocks, he came upon the Savoy and hedged his bets. There were three bars in the hotel, but it was in a quiet corner of the American Bar that Joe found Percy starting the last of the three cocktails he'd already ordered. "Three more of those, please," Joe instructed the barman, then he took a seat by Percy.

Percy glanced at him, downed the cocktail, and lifted a hand for another.

"Drunk is good," said Joe. "But it's not going to solve anything."

"That's where you're wrong. If I stay drunk forever, then I won't have any more problems."

"Percy—"

"Don't try to make it okay. That was it. That was my final straw. I'm done. You and me..." Percy's eyes flitted away to the dark recesses of the bar. "We're done."

Joe's heart skipped a beat when he heard the words, but his

voice was strong when he replied, "Do you remember what happened last time you tried that? I didn't listen then either."

"And look where that got us."

"It got us engaged."

Four more drinks were set down on the table, three empty glasses taken away. Percy took up the next to avoid speaking.

Joe said, "I had the best time with you in Sicily. And in Bruges. The best time in my whole life."

Percy countered with a maudlin, "I almost lost you yesterday. I thought I got away with it. I thought we could have that happy ending. And I let myself feel hopeful. I thought we might solve this mess. Together. But you know, there's always going to be that one last thing. That sting in the tail. It's this life. It's just the way it goes."

Joe pressed his knee against Percy's beneath the table. "What happened to eternity? Burning down the gates of Heaven?"

"That's when you were dead and I didn't have anything to lose. But now you're back—"

"So you'll throw me away before you lose me again?"

"Something like that."

Joe let a few empty beats fall between them before he asked, "And Cleo? Are you going to throw her away too?"

Percy's eyes closed slowly, and remained that way when he said, "It's not like that."

"Of course it's not." Joe pulled at Percy's hand until he drew his gaze back. "I know you and I know you're going after her next. I love that about you. I love that you could walk away right now, with me, which I know is what you want. And I love that you won't."

"Joe, it doesn't matter what you or I love. That's the rule of evil. It will always destroy what we have. It will come back again and again and chip away at this. If it's not Molly, then it will be some bishop with a basement full of soul eaters. If it's

not that, it will be a group of fucking Nazis with a nice painting. There will always be something. There's no escaping it."

"It's because you seek it out," Joe said softly. "If we'd
already moved to our nice pub, you wouldn't have a clue those
things were going on out there."

"The pub would inevitably be haunted. You know that as
well as I do."

"Probably." Joe chuckled. He sipped the blood-red drink,
which was, as always, wonderful. Percy's taste, everything about
him, always wonderful, in its bittersweet way. Joe ventured to
point out what Percy must already have known. "Molly will be
ready for us this time. You know she's powerful. Maybe even
more powerful than her familiar, and it almost killed us both so
easily. We've seen her raise the dead—god knows what else she
can do. And I'm willing to bet, the thought's already crossed
your mind that if you kill her body, Cleo's trapped in that skull
forever."

That idea, until then unspoken, had occurred to Percy, over
and over, but only as background noise. He'd been too busy to
let himself worry about it. "I'll figure it out."

"No. There's no way I'll let you do this on your own. I
know I'm not a hitman. Or much of an art thief. Or a traf-
ficker of fine arts and artefacts. But what I am is a man who's
in love with you. And it's time for you to take your foot off the
pedal, just for a little while. Let me help."

A sceptical smile cut into Percy's cheek, bereft of humour,
and he shook his head.

"I know." Joe lifted Percy's fingers and kissed his open
palm. He placed his hand on his chest and held it there. "It's
control. It's what you need. I understand that now. But I need
you to slow down and listen to me." Taking Percy's hand to the
table, he reached inside his coat, and produced Moxie, setting
her down by Percy's fingers.

The act elicited Percy's sharp, "Get that thing the fuck away from me."

Joe grasped the hand he withdrew. "This cat is the key to everything. It understands Molly. It can help us fix this. It *will* help us fix this."

Percy stood to leave, but Joe was up faster, locking an arm around his waist. "If you try to go without me, I'll come anyway. I know I let you down—"

"You didn't let me down." But even with that comment, thrown out so blithely, Percy remained avoidant, his chin pulled up and away, the distance palpable.

"Would you stop saying that? Even now you're trying to protect me, and I need you to stop. You've done enough."

"It was a good and noble thing—"

"It wasn't good and noble that got us out of that," Joe cried in exasperation. "It was your passion, and your violence, and your anger. It was your steadfastness." He wrapped his fingers around the opening in Percy's shirt, feeling the strong beat of his heart beneath the palm of his hand. "Percy, when you said those things, when you talked about tearing eternity apart, when you almost slashed my throat and yours, that's when I realised. You're never going to change." Percy withdrew a little further into himself, eyes to the carpet, words lost at his lips, and Joe put a hand to his cheek and moved closer, chest against chest. "And I have never felt so safe in my entire life."

Finally, Percy's eyes met Joe's, their lips an inch apart. "I thought, hoped, I was right when I agreed to marry you. I've been in love with you since our first week together. But when you put that knife to my throat, that's when I knew. You're the one true thing. We're forever, because *you're* forever. You make me feel so safe, and I won't give that up. I won't ever give you up, so stop talking like that. If that trust you had in me is broken, then let me prove myself. Please. I'm not going back to the emptiness I felt before I had you. Before you filled me up with your brutal, beautiful way of loving. With every ridiculous and perfect thing that you are." His chest heaved out a frustrated groan. "I love you. I love you to the end of existence and back, and I'm never leaving you. Not for all the world." Joe's two hands on Percy's cheeks pulled him in, and had Percy wanted to resist the soft lips that caressed his, it wouldn't have been possible.

It was over. They both knew it. But Percy tried a last ditch, "It's not safe."

"Fuck, Percy, nothing's been safe since the day I met you. You live in a constant storm. You are a storm. There's no escaping that because it's who you are. But I need you to understand, I want to be in that storm with you. You're all I want. You're all I've ever wanted. We're going to fix this. We'll get Cleo back in her body, Molly reunited with her familiar, and then we're going to get your kitten back to you, too."

"Percy!" the barman called across the almost empty room. "No cats in the bar!"

"I've had a long day, Ben," Percy shouted back. "Can't you see I'm breaking up with my fiancé?"

"No, he's not!" Joe called out.

Ben watched the two a moment, then rolled his eyes and said, "Drinks are on the house."

"Two more Devil's Cocktails," Percy responded.

On a double take, Joe asked, "Are they really called that?"

"I didn't name them. But they are very good."

"They are."

He let Joe take his hand and settle him back into his seat. Moxie had long since stretched out on her belly, and for a while, had been shuffling towards Percy. He ripped his hand away from the paw that reached for him. "Don't you ever touch me."

It was Joe who leaned over and scratched her behind the ear. "Don't forget, your kitten's in here too."

Percy watched Moxie twist her head up to enjoy Joe's pats, eyes half closed with the sensation, that constant purr he'd already grown to love rattling out of the tiny body. "I wonder what that must be like for her."

"Not bad, I think," said Joe. "She's warm and well fed." He snuck a glance up at Percy. "She's loved. I don't know what it's doing to her brain to be melded with a being like that, but the familiar isn't intrinsically evil. It's just an asshole."

"Mew," Moxie protested.

"You are," said Joe, rubbing her chin.

Percy still refused to touch the little beast, but Joe could see he wanted to. He picked her up and put her on Percy's shoulder, where she nuzzled against his neck. Percy tilted his head away, but as Joe expected, he let her stay there, albeit with the disgusted look of a man who'd just had a bird shit on his shoulder.

Joe hid a grin behind his drink. "So did you say we're off to Paris next?"

"Joe—"

"Shh! I'm going. And you'll see. I'm going to be a proper criminal, proper ghost hunter, proper witch, um, de-body-erer, and no fuck ups. Watch me. Because, Percy, I'd travel all the way to France for you."

Percy levelled a powerful glare at him. "You're going to be like that?"

"I'd walk over to that bar and back for you," Joe quipped.

Percy rolled his beautiful eyes. "Why did I bother to save you?"

Joe leaned close by Percy's ear and said, "I'd burn through every cigarette in that case, drink every drink in this hotel, then take you upstairs and fuck you senseless."

Finally, a full grin broke across Percy's face, and he was

Percy again, just as much as Joe was Joe again. And they two were as hopelessly in love as they both knew they would always be.

Moxie chose that moment to stick her purring nose in Percy's ear, and he reached up and stroked her back. "Fine. You can come to Paris. But no fucking around. And I won't go easy on you."

"I won't go easy on you."

"Stop flirting. I'm trying to be morose."

"I won't let you be morose. You'll see. Once we get through this next episode, there's a happy ending waiting for us. I promise."

"I hate to break it to you, Handsome. I don't think you and I are cut out for the happy ever after lifestyle."

Joe, with an arm around Percy's neck, his lips smacking against his cheek, said, "If I'm with you, no matter what happens, that's my happy ending."

"You should probably aim higher."

"It's not possible to aim higher. You're it. Will you marry me?"

Percy, by this time as pink and happy as a schoolboy deep in his first crush, replied, "It's nice to be asked."

"I'll take that as a yes." Joe wrapped his second arm around his fiancé and kissed him long and loving. "Come on. Let's forget the rest and go back to the hotel."

"Ben," Percy called out. "Get us a room upstairs, would you? And mind this cat for me."

Ben, ever the professional, was on the phone with barely a blink.

"It's a ten-minute cab ride," Joe protested. "To your penthouse. That costs a fortune."

Percy pulled Joe around the table, walking him backwards, kissing him over the words, "I can't wait that long." He dumped a grumpy but compliant Moxie on the bar, danced Joe past reception, and within minutes they were alone, just Percy and Joe, with all the cares and worries of their world shut outside that room, outside that bed, kept decadently at bay, until the hour came when they would have to open their door again, and let the horror back in.

The Devil's Cocktail

Combine the following ingredients over ice and stir:

Two shots of ruby port

One shot of dry vermouth

Half a teaspoon of fresh lemon juice*

Strain into a chilled martini glass.

Peel a slice of rind off a lemon, squeeze it over the

top of the drink to spritz with citrus oil, then throw

it away. Or just garnish it with a twist if you really

must...

*Always fresh lemon juice – we're not messing around

Serve as an aperiftif or offer several as a main course

if you're feeling particularly dejected about things like

your fiancé and your kitten being possessed...

"Those who
do not weep,
do not see."
HUGO
PARIS

Percy stood back from the enormous vault door as the bank assistant twisted the dial open. It dislodged with a gasp of temperature-controlled, hermetically sealed air.

Percy awaited the man's departure before he made a move.

A metal grill clanked closed behind him, then he switched the light on inside the vault, and a veritable museum appeared before his and Leo's eyes. Paintings, vases, antique tables and cupboards, weaponry, jugs, jars of things that looked decidedly sticky and unpleasant, some very good cheese, and a sizeable safe somewhere at the back of it all.

Percy made his way around, over, and through the priceless mess, then applied handsome fingers to the wheel of the safe. Left, right, left, right and left again, then a click. Inside sat half a dozen small lockboxes that had rested untouched for years.

A silver key, minuscule, was slid into one of those lockboxes, and a drawer snapped open.

Leo's voice drifted over Percy's shoulder, barely louder than the paintings that stood witness to his act. "Are you sure about this?"

Percy pulled out a petite, black velvet box. "Perfectly sure." The lid creaked on tiny hinges as he eased it back to reveal what he had come for.

A ring.

The gold was thick, a little crooked and dented, coarse and uneven. Centred in its unsure setting was an inlay of sapphire, delicately carved to depict the crossing of two hands. The jewel had been constructed some two thousand years prior, in Rome, for the very purpose Percy intended to use it today.

The promise of forever.

He released the ring from its satin enclosure, and stretching his hand open, slid it onto his ring finger.

It was that tiny bit loose. Not enough to slip over the knuckle by accident, but enough to slide freely. On Joe, it would be perfect.

Percy held it up, the sapphire glinting in the light. "Do you think he'll like it?"

"I think he'll love it." Leo was honest and open in the statement, as he always was with Percy, though he may have let a little too much honesty slip through when he then joked, "And if it doesn't work out, I'll break his finger and take it back."

Percy let the childish jibe go, well aware of Leo's jealousy, and determined to see it through to the other side as smoothly as possible. "Once you give an engagement ring, you can never ask for it back. You do it once and you do it right, or you don't do it at all. Remember that."

"But…" Leo paused over his words, while Percy tilted his hand back and forth, admiring the ancient adornment. "It's your favourite thing. It's irreplaceable. Priceless. It's—"

"Eternal," Percy finished for him. "Just like me and Joe."

CHAPTER FORTY

THE PARIS APARTMENT

The ring was Percy's main purpose for returning to Paris. That and to get away from all the trauma of London and Scotland. There was still no trace of Molly. Cleo had been reported missing by her husband some weeks back, but given he was a tyrant, friends, family, and police took the view she was more likely to have fled from him than to have come to any harm. A few media outlets dropped the suggestion that he may have been instrumental in her disappearance, but then, a few days later, they reported that she had contacted police in Hungary, and was no longer considered a missing person.

The trail being cold, there was little for them to do but wait. And why not wait it out in style?

Having arrived in the city around midday, the six of them —Percy, Joe, Althea, Leo, Cleo, and Moxie—had gone for a spot of lunch. Percy, dressed in an appallingly attractive brown three-piece suit, had soon announced he had a matter to attend to, tapped Leo's arm, and wandered off with instructions for the others to meet them in Montmartre three hours hence.

331

This was, by now, standard Percy behaviour, which got little more than an eye roll from Joe, which made Percy even less inclined to leave him, but engagement rings are serious business.

Joe and Althea, skull in hand, cat in tow, had few complaints about finishing their wine by the Seine, then meandering their way across town on an impromptu shopping spree. Althea had received her first payment from Percy, and as such, had decided, like Leo, to dedicate her life to the art of crime. She bought more gaudy clothes than Percy was likely to cope with, while Joe kept himself to too much food and a few books. Then he took Althea with him on one last errand that she was to keep top secret from Percy.

He had dressed as a priest that morning and mentioned to Percy that he wanted to call into a church alone. Percy had been the usual mixture of displeased beneath but encouraging on the surface, with a little extra of the latter, given that it would, at least, keep Joe wrapped up and well away from what he was doing.

Joe didn't take long to complete his final task of the afternoon, and when the group met again, it was on Rue Blanche, in Montmartre, where they gathered before a bright red door set into the pale stone of Haussmann's Paris. Those last three hours were all the time Percy and Joe had spent apart after two weeks recovering in London, and they were like teenagers when they found one another on the street again. Percy's hand slipped straight over Joe's belt to pull him in for a kiss. Joe's arms were around Percy, and it was a moment that Percy, back when their adventure had begun in earnest months earlier, could never have imagined coming.

Joe freed himself, only slightly, from Percy's embrace and nodded to a plaque on the wall that informed strangers they were at the onetime apartment of Edgar Degas. "We're going on an art tour?"

"No." Percy stepped forward, slid his key into the lock, and opened the red door. "We're home."

Leo and Althea went in first, running up the stairs with Moxie and Cleo, while Joe stood on the street, hands in pockets, looking at Percy. "It's his old apartment?"

"Yes."

"Yet you never mentioned that."

Percy's smile was both coy and sweet. "I don't want you to get bored of me."

Joe laughed and made his way over to Percy, stopping in the doorway, his hand toying with the top button of Percy's shirt. "Home, huh? Your little place in Montmartre?"

Percy took a few seconds to enjoy the moment, the image of him. Joe's hair in the soft afternoon sunshine. Joe with groceries, exactly like he was coming home, to their home, to spend a very normal evening together. "I told you, we'll do whatever you like, live wherever you want. But it's mine, so… that means it's yours too."

Joe smiled. Joe kissed him right there on what had just become *their* doorstep.

That sapphire ring felt hot and heavy in Percy's pocket. Maybe now? Maybe this was the perfect moment? Right now, bringing him home, right here on the threshold of their new life. So simple. So easy. What could be better?

Percy's hand slid into his pocket. "Joe—"

"Percy!" Leo shouted down the stairs. "You need to take a look at this."

The urgency that sharpened Leo's voice propelled Percy, two stairs at a time, up to his apartment. Leo stepped back, held the door wide, and Percy let go such a thoroughly unpublishable list of expletives that it cannot possibly be recorded here.

CHAPTER FORTY-ONE
HOME AWAY FROM HOME

Percy's apartment was beautiful. In its bones, it was undeniably gorgeous. High ceilings, tall windows, sublime light playing across crystal chandeliers, and a pale wooden floor that reflected it all beautifully across the enormous open-plan space. Unfortunately, that floor was now covered in just about everything Percy owned outside of his bank vault. What was there was smashed and broken, trampled, utterly ruined. Cushions were torn from the lounge, ripped apart, stuffing pulled out. Jars from cupboards and the fridge were thrown across the room, streaking the walls with mess of every colour. Every painting had been pulled from the wall, every item of furniture had been upturned and searched. The bedrooms and bathrooms were just as bad, mattresses ripped from the beds, pillows slashed, bottles emptied, leaving the whole place reeking of expensive perfumes.

Percy turned on his kitten at once. "Your witch did this, didn't she?"

The ball of fluff drew back on its haunches. "Mew!"

"I'll fucking kill her!"

Moxie let out a rare hiss, which Percy only glared at as he

kicked his way through the ruins to a beloved and broken clock. "Fuck!"

Joe stooped to pick up a canvas, kicked through, but once a Degas. "Um… This… Is this… the real thing?"

Percy managed an almost-smile of reassurance. "No, that's Lakshmi's. All the paintings in here are fakes. I keep the—" The habit of lying to Joe, to everyone, caught Percy at the throat. But only for a beat. "All my stolen paintings are in a vault. I only bring them out if I intend to stay for a long stretch. I keep the fakes here for this reason."

Joe was only half joking when he asked, "Does this sort of thing happen to you a lot?"

"No," Percy replied in all honesty. "People usually know better."

That alone was enough of a statement, but Althea ran with it, smashing a fist into her palm for emphasis. "I say we track them down and make them regret it. Get to work on them with some of those tools of yours, Percy."

Percy grinned at Joe, Joe frowned at Althea, and Leo said, "I was here a few days ago. Either she got lucky and came when I was out—"

"Or she was watching you the whole time." The ridge of Percy's back stiffened, then he climbed to his feet, striding across to Leo. "I should never have left you here. I can't believe I was so stupid."

Leo's head was pressed to Percy's chest in a suffocating embrace, through which he mumbled, "I'm okay."

"What if you weren't?" Percy pulled back, hands on Leo's cheeks to look at him, as though he needed the snapshot of a happy, living Leo in his mind. Then he smooshed his face back into his suit jacket.

"It's secure," Leo protested, gasping for air. "I set the alarm, I bolted every bolt, there's no way in here without a key."

"Unless you're a witch," Percy muttered, tightening his protective headlock. "Of course I didn't think she'd be stupid enough to think I was stupid enough to bring the sheath back here, assuming that's what she was after. But it was stupid of me to have not expected her to do something so stupid." Leo struggled against his unrelenting grip as he crossed the room with him, instructing, "Althea, you'll need to call some cleaners. Some kind of people who can fix this. And you know those companies who decorate hotel rooms and things? Have them do the lot. Today. I want it perfect by tonight."

"But…" Althea scanned the wreckage in dismay. "Um… I don't actually speak French or—"

"You'll have to figure it out. Leo's having the afternoon off." Percy wrenched Leo in a little tighter and dropped a kiss on his hair, saying to him, "I'll take you somewhere nice and we'll wait out the drama together."

"Uh…" Joe waited patiently for Leo's glare at the interruption to flitter away. That took some time. "Have you considered that Cleo's probably still in Paris? Just maybe before you go out…"

Percy's hold on Leo eased slightly. "You don't think she's gone to London looking for us?"

Althea set a phone upright, placing the receiver back on the hook. "Is there a phone book or something? In English maybe?"

"I'll help." Leo wriggled his shoulders until his head popped free, then slipped away to her side now that Joe had Percy's attention.

"Maybe," said Joe. "But if she knows this is where you live, it's probably easier for her to find you here if she just waits. But how did she know that, anyway?"

Percy gave an unhelpful shrug. "I'm in the book."

A coughing splutter of a laugh popped out of Joe. "Percy

Ashdown, master criminal, is in the book? With his address? Where he lives?"

"Well, it's…" Percy took the slightest touch of colour into his handsome cheeks. "How are people meant to call me?"

Joe shook his head, still chuckling. "Jesus Christ."

"It's nothing to blaspheme over," Percy suggested.

"How are you not dead already?"

"I ask myself every day."

"You're a walking disaster."

"I saved your ass."

"I saved your ass, too. Sort of."

"You did. Okay, let's think about this." Percy took Joe's hand, placed a fast kiss there, then called back, "Leo, stop working. It's your afternoon off."

Leo was busy talking over Althea's shoulder, his finger next to hers on the page of a phone book. "No, look, 'hôtel'. It's exactly the same as 'hotel', only fancier. 'Maison' if they're trying to be posh. And service is the same word again. Honestly, half the words are no different. Let's try this one."

"Leo!" Percy snapped.

Leo's distracted eyes wandered up to Percy. "What? Oh. I'll take it tomorrow?"

"Suit yourself." It wasn't easy for Percy to pace as he normally would have, so he shuffled around the messy room, crunching over his broken belongings, hands clasped, two index fingers meeting at the bow of his top lip, until he stopped with a clap. "Got it. What if we all go to Provence? You know, for a few days, a week at the most. Leo, could you book—"

"Or," Joe interrupted, halting Leo's hand on the receiver, "what if we just clean your apartment?"

Percy stared back, blank. "I'm sorry?"

Joe wafted a hand around the room. "What if we just do it? Now."

Percy followed the direction of Joe's hand, brow constricting. "What?"

"I mean, there are four of us." Percy's face did not clear, so Joe explained, "We could just clean it."

"But…" Percy glanced around, motioning vaguely. "The mess. Everywhere." He took a moment longer, working the problem over, then clicked his fingers, face lightening when the obvious answer popped into his mind. "What if we go to the Ritz? By the time we have maybe six drinks—"

Joe swung his groceries from the floor into Percy's chest. "You take the kitchen. Tidy it up, then make us something nice for dinner."

Percy's mouth bobbed open and closed, and he rambled out a worried, "I don't even know if she left us any olive oil."

Joe pulled the top of the paper bags a little further open for Percy to see inside. "Then it's bread and cheese and wine. We'll probably survive the next few hours."

"Wine." Percy's beautiful eyes grew unfathomably large. "The cellar. Leo!"

"On my way!" Leo's footsteps ricocheted through the hall, and they all waited in tense silence until his shout came back, "The cellar's fine!"

"Thank Christ for that," Percy muttered. "Can you imagine the sort of evening—"

Joe shut him up with a kiss.

CHAPTER FORTY-TWO
A TASTE OF ITALY

It took a solid five hours, but between Leo's expertise and a good deal of hard work by Joe and Althea, they were, more or less, settled into the sparsely but newly furnished apartment by around nine that evening.

No one said anything when Percy decided to make pasta from scratch, all being in silent agreement that he was probably better occupied there than having input into which furnishings Leo could or could not have delivered at such short notice.

To Joe's eyes, he was charmingly employed anyway, deep in conversation with grunts from Cleo's skull and mews from Moxie while he discussed how he was making his sauce. Joe couldn't tell whether he was just waffling or if Percy understood their meanings, but something in his heart popped at the choice cuts of pancetta Percy dropped for the cat he still swore he despised.

No art on the walls, door propped open to vent the smells of cleaning products and perfume, all of them a mess and exhausted, and it was already a life Joe felt completely at one with.

He made his way into the kitchen and slid two arms around Percy's waist. Percy leaned his head back for a kiss on the cheek, and Joe said, "Do you need a taste tester?"

"Fuck, no. You'll eat when I say."

Joe huffed and made to move away.

"Kiss."

He reached up and turned Percy's face for a kiss.

"Another," Percy demanded.

Joe complied.

"Another."

"Percy…" Joe did as requested, then Percy let go of his spoon, grasping Joe instead, spinning him around, pushing him back against the fridge. Joe shifted his hip forward, to be met by Percy's, and ground back. "This is better than going for cocktails, isn't it?"

"It is." Percy kissed the side of his jaw. "Do you like the apartment?"

"Yes. But I like you even more." Joe moved his lips to catch the next kiss.

"Do you know," Percy whispered in his ear, fingers trailing down his chest, "I'm a slut for you in this outfit."

"I do know," Joe replied, tilting his head to enjoy the kiss on his neck. "Why do you think I wear it all the time?"

Percy took hold of his cheek, his thumb flat along the line of his cheekbone, his fingers edging into Joe's hair, drinking in his gorgeous fiancé. Joe's hands were at his waist, gently toying with his shirt, his eyes bright and so, so content.

Everything was as calm and beautiful as it would ever be. But homely. A casual yet poignant moment. A symbol of how beautiful things would always be, from that time…

Maybe this was the perfect moment for the ring?

It *was* perfect.

Percy's hand slipped over Joe's hip, down, and into his own pocket. "Handsome——"

All words and expression slipped away when the click of a gun sounded from across the room, accompanied by the direction: "Get the fuck away from him. The wedding's off."

Joe's mouth dropped open, Percy turned, aghast, and Leo shouted a victorious, "Giordano!"

CHAPTER FORTY-THREE

WELL, THAT WAS UNEXPECTED

Giordano, handsome as ever, if a little harried-looking, gave a slight nod of hello to Leo and Althea, then advanced towards the kitchen, gun trained on Joe. "He's not who you think he is, Percy. He's dangerous."

Percy would have laughed had his ex-boyfriend not been threatening to shoot his beloved fiancé. As it was, fury rose to the forefront of the broth of emotions. "I promise you, you're grossly mistaken. Put the gun down."

Giordano directed his speech only at Joe. "Did you really think that would pass for a Roman accent? I knew I'd seen your face. That you had the balls to come back to Italy after what you did."

Joe, hands raised, wet his lips with a swift, nervous tongue. "I can explain."

"You don't need to explain a thing." Percy stepped in front of Joe, a solid mass of immovable violence. "Put the fucking gun down."

"Oh, you're going to protect him?" Giordano laughed. "Your sweet boyfriend with his pretty hair and his innocent face?" His eyes narrowed to a hate-filled glare centred on Joe.

"He's not the one who needs protection." He reached a hand around and grasped a roll of papers from his back pocket, then threw the lot onto the bench where they unfurled to reveal the grainy face of a boy—sad, scared, softly combative—unmistakably a young Joe. Old newspaper headlines bore into Percy's eyes before he could look away. 'Murderer.' 'Killer.' '*Diavolo.*'

Percy's left arm shot out and smacked the gun away. His right hand curled into a fist and punched Giordano square in the jaw. A bullet flew into a cupboard door as the gun clattered to the floor, and Percy had two fists around Giordano's collar, smashing his back into the wall. "Go."

Giordano leaned his head back to meet Percy's fury with a smile. "You don't scare me. Your bullshit might work on everyone else, but never on me." He raised both hands to Percy's chest, settling them there softly, fingers splaying out, eyes searching Percy's with an intimate confidence. "You're making a mistake. And I won't let you do it."

Percy knocked his hands away and retreated to the kitchen, where Joe remained pressed against the fridge, watching it all play out. Giordano brought his hands to his hips, catching his breath, while he surveyed Percy out of the corner of his eye. Althea snuck Percy's wine off the bench and skulked back to Leo.

"This is some truly petty jealousy," Percy laughed bitterly. "Truly pathetic."

"You arrogant bastard!" Giordano shouted. "I'm not jealous. I was happy for you. I was thrilled you'd found someone. But this…" He extended a statuesque finger at Joe. "He's a murderer, Percy. Did he ever once tell you that?"

Percy's face screwed up in utter disdain. "Have we even met? Why the fuck do you think I'd care about that sort of thing? Get out of here with your bullshit—"

"He killed his dad!"

"We all hate our fathers!" Percy rounded. "That's what makes us compelling characters."

"Percy, no, you don't understand." Giordano stalked to the bench, snatching up one of the papers, holding it high for Percy to see. "That man standing there is a monster. That man killed his own *mother*!"

A sharp silence fell over the room.

"Didn't see that coming," Leo whispered.

Percy's eyes met Joe's, and in them was a flinty flash of shock he couldn't manage to hide. He said to Giordano, "I don't care," but Joe could see right there that he did. That this was a line, one of the very few Percy had with Joe, that Joe had stepped on.

"You do, though," said Giordano, seeing exactly the same thing Joe did, advancing to the other side of the kitchen bench to be able to read Percy's reactions. "I know you. He's not right. What kind of man does that? You can't trust him—he hasn't got your back. I can see he's never told you anything. If that's not guilt, I don't know what is."

Percy turned away from the lot of them, staring out the window at the busy street below. He didn't care. Not about whatever Joe might have done. But his insides folded when he thought there was a chink in their armour. That Giordano knew, that god knows how many other people knew, something that he did not. That he was, perhaps, one of the last to know. That Joe had put him in that position.

Percy had never let another living person into his life the way he had with Joe. It wasn't something he could even have put his finger on until that moment, but all along since the very first night, Joe's faith in him had wrapped him in a shell, with Joe, where, measure by measure, he'd let Joe see everything. It was safe. It was secure. Until this crack. This suggestion that Joe, all along, hadn't trusted him the way he had trusted Joe.

He would never have made Joe tell him; he'd put himself

on the line so Joe wouldn't ever have to revisit the secrets he was keeping.

But knowing Giordano already knew hurt.

Joe's voice, when it came from over Percy's shoulder, wasn't tentative. It came as bold and kind as ever, and like a soothing gel on his sore spot, until the import of the words dug in. "I did it. He's right. I killed them both in cold blood. And I'd do it again tomorrow."

CHAPTER FORTY-FOUR
DIAVOLO

Percy reached for his wine, and when his hand met nothing but air, his eyes shot across to Althea, nursing it carefully by Leo's side. "Kids, go to bed."

"I'm nineteen!" Leo objected.

"And I'm eighteen!" Althea protested. "Now."

"Bed!" Percy snapped.

The pair climbed to their feet with a lot of muttering and scowling, and Leo whined, "Can we at least go to a cafe or something? I'm starving."

"No, you may not go to a cafe."

Leo took the time to pause and fling an angry arm towards Percy. "Literally two weeks ago you had me burn the body of some guy you shot, and now you won't let me go out for dinner?"

"The two things aren't slightly related," Percy threw back, slamming cupboard doors, searching for a new glass. He soon gave up, having no idea where anyone had put anything since the last ones had been smashed, and instead yelled across the room, "And have you forgotten there's a maniacal witch on the loose?"

"There's a what?" Giordano cut in.

Percy sent very particular eye-daggers across at him, not deigning to answer, then flicked the kettle on to boil, saying to Leo, "I'll bring you something. Go."

Leo rolled his eyes dramatically. Althea held onto her wine and followed him closely as they disappeared into his bedroom.

"And keep the door open!" Percy shouted.

"I'm nineteen!" Leo screamed. Yet the door made no sound as the pair settled down on opposite ends of Leo's bed to try to hear the ensuing conversation

Percy dumped the pasta into a pot of boiling water with a hefty load of salt, stirred, and declared, "Giordano, you're not welcome. Get the fuck out of my apartment and my life."

Giordano let go a bitter scoff, shaking his head. "Fine. It's been just as delightful as it always is."

Percy didn't turn back to see the last look. That final scan of his back, that bereftness in his eyes, mingled with anger, that said this was it. Their long, difficult, loving entanglement at an end.

But Joe, who had woken in cold sweats at the thought of living through that moment with Percy, called him back. "Stay. Please. I owe you both an explanation."

"You don't owe anything to anyone," said Percy, smashing a colander down on the bench. "What's in the past stays there. And he doesn't get to dictate whether you do or don't tell me whatever you choose to."

"I'm not going to be responsible for ruining your friendship," said Joe. "And I'm not going to let what happened to me do any more damage than it already has." He pulled three wine glasses down from a cupboard, then leaned over Percy's shoulder for the wine bottle, saying softly by his ear, "Put on some pasta for Giordano."

"No," Percy muttered. "He can go hungry."

Joe's eyes swept the empty bench. "You already put enough on, didn't you?"

Percy stirred his sauce sulkily. "I didn't want it to go to waste."

Joe smiled, then made for the photocopied newspaper articles that lay glaring and shunned by Percy. He hadn't seen that face in over a decade, but it was his and it was a picture he knew well; a frightened little boy, caught by the cameras of cold-hearted journalists as he made his way into the courthouse to be told the verdict on his case. It had been splashed across every paper in Italy for months afterwards. There wasn't a person in the country, back then, who wouldn't have recognised that face.

Giordano waited by a window in the living room, and Percy avoided any outward sign that would indicate he knew he was there. He made the food, he took some in to Leo and Althea. Joe set the other three servings on the table, with the wine and glasses, and when he and Percy were both seated, Giordano, while maintaining his distance, turned to listen.

Joe placed the papers down, spread them across the table with one movement of his arm, and calmly stated, "I killed them. My parents. Both of them."

Percy would have taken that crack in their shell before he'd ever have let Joe fall into the stoic, vulnerable place his voice indicated he was, alone and on display like that. "You don't need to say a word."

Joe gave the slightest nod as acknowledgement of the sentiment he was about to overrule, then he met the brown eyes that studied him from across the room. "I lied in court, and I got away with it."

"I knew it." Giordano's lip raised with disgust. "Everyone knew it."

Percy ignored him and went about pouring wine. "Well, obviously they were possessed or something."

"No," said Joe.

"Actual demons, then? They've been known to steal human children and—"

"No." Joe smiled and clasped Percy's hand. "They were just shitty people, Percy. Really, really shitty people. I'm not saying it was the right thing to do, from an ethical perspective, but from my perspective... It was *all* I could do. I did what was right for me at the time."

Giordano dropped an incredulous laugh. "And then lied to the whole country about it."

Joe retorted, "It would have been pretty stupid to tell the truth, don't you think?"

"Exactly right," Percy agreed, every facet of his mind fast at work building a supportive framework to keep the Joe he thought he knew intact. "Truth is only useful when it aids you or those you love. And I can't see how it aids anyone in this particular case."

No doubt that was Percy's own philosophy, because Joe had seen him live by it. But Joe wished he'd told Percy. There were so many opportunities. He knew it would come up, somehow, eventually. He knew Percy knew something was hidden, and Percy just let him have it, judgement free, that whole time. But now... Now his ex knew. Leo and Althea knew. And he had betrayed Percy by letting that happen before he found out.

Joe slid a hand over to his photo and rested a finger there, studying the boy. "I don't feel like I lied to you, Percy. Not entirely. Because that's not me. That person, who these things happened to, that's someone who lived somewhere else, long ago. And I don't think about that anymore. And I don't talk about that. It's not me, and to bring that up, it just feels like... It felt like it would have poisoned now. What we have and who I've become. I don't want you to think of me like that, or to see me as someone else, because I'm not him anymore." He glanced up at Giordano. "But clearly, I can't outrun it forever."

As Giordano's eyes slunk away across the floorboards, Joe returned his gaze to Percy. "You have strong links to Italy. I know we'll be going back… And you have a right to know."

But Percy was deep in caretaking-mode, fixing, fixing. "I know how important it is to keep those things in a lockbox."

Joe's heart pounded out a steady, calming beat with the solidity of Percy's support. He wrapped his fingers tighter around Percy's, took his hand up, and kissed it. He focused on Percy's avoidant eyes, drawing them. "I want to tell you. Because it's the last thing. The last secret between us. And it doesn't feel right to me to have anything left."

Of course, he did not expect Percy to reply, "Joe, I killed your Nazi."

Joe's strong chin tilted jutted sharply to the left. "What?"

"Back in book one. I killed him. Right after you asked me not to. I went back to the church, and I stabbed him in the throat. And brain. Sort of. An upward stabbing motion. Got both. But he's very dead, and I'm sorry I kind of went behind your back there."

A cloud crossed Joe's face, and Percy rushed out, "It's not that I *kept* lying, because I honestly barely gave him a second thought. Until just now. When you mentioned the last thing. I think he had it coming, and I understand that perhaps I should have discussed the matter with you before I killed him—"

"Yeah, you should have."

"You're right. And I take full responsibility for the rashness of my behaviour. And I would like to point out that my communications skills have improved dramatically since that time. But I wanted you to know. Everything. All out in the open."

Joe stared down at the table, a quizzical expression on his face. "You know, I wondered why he never called. I felt pretty bad about that."

Percy gave his hand a squeeze. "You did? I'm sorry."

"Well, only because I wondered if you were right, I suppose. That we should have killed him. And you know, after everything we've been through, I think maybe you were. Either way, it's done now."

Percy checked him over carefully. "Are you very mad?"

"No." Joe searched his feelings, and was surprised at just how little it bothered him. The last thing he wanted was someone else with Percy's name on their hit list. Percy was keeping them safe from the start, the way he always did. The way he was even now, when it was Joe, of all people, who had let him down. "No. I know you had your reasons. Good ones. And I'm pretty sure you wouldn't keep that sort of thing from me now."

"I wouldn't." Percy, sifting through his mind desperately, then said, "Though did I mention—

Joe cut him off with a gentle chuckle. "Stop trying to protect me, Percy. It's okay. I'm going to say it, and it's fine. Really." Percy's lips opened in a protest that Joe silenced with a shake of his head and another smile. He then raised his chin across the room. "Giordano, come sit."

Giordano waited for Percy's approval, which came in the form of half a shrug. He took his seat in a swaggering way that belied the palpable tension between him and Percy. He searched his ex-lover's face with quick, anxious eyes, but Percy was stone to him, and that empathetic pity touched Joe again. He wanted to kiss the hard edges off Percy's cheek. There was nothing good in that victory over Giordano, because Giordano was right.

"So, I'm not from Rome," Joe commenced.

"I know," said Percy, taking a sip of wine.

"I know you know. And I love that you never said a word."

"Even when I called you out," said Giordano, but he said it on a gentler note, now he understood the way Percy had chosen to let it pass when it came up in Sicily.

"I'm from Castel del Monte," Joe continued. "It's tiny. A tiny little village way up in the Apennines, and there's nothing there but sheep, a church, and an old cemetery. Or, there wasn't much more when I lived there, back in the seventies. It wasn't the sort of town you planned to get out of. You married whoever was available, and you raised sheep to milk or kill."

Joe choked down a little wine, the flavour of dirty wool and raw, hot sheep's blood forever on his palate. He glanced at Percy, who, whether he was thinking about the same thing or not, kept a neutral face. "You know I grew up poor, but when I say poor, I mean dirt poor. I mean nothing to eat for days sometimes. I mean living with an alcoholic father, who was unstable before he ever touched alcohol, and a mother who was…" Percy's deeply faithful love for his broken mother was no secret to Joe, and the bond Percy shared with Giordano's mother such that even in their darker moments the pair put it before their animosity. Joe could only try, and hope he'd be understood. "She was just as bad as he was. But not in the same way. In some ways, she was better. In some ways, she was much worse."

He had been okay, but with those words, there came a flash of that old house, accompanied by the memory of an adult hand winding him with a punch in the stomach. He felt a weight fall across his shoulders, which he tried to work out with a nervous crick of his neck. Percy's fingers pressed into his.

"I still don't know what it was," Joe said. "Whether it was a control issue for her. If being cruel to me gave her power over someone, at least. Or over something at all. Because she never stood much of a chance from the day she was born there. And that must have been hard."

He reached for his glass again, but didn't take a sip this time. He only held it there, toying with the stem. "She didn't hit me as hard as he did, because she couldn't physically do that. Even if she tried. But the thing is, he never hugged me afterwards the way she did. He never apologised and promised me he'd never do it again. He never held me and told me we'd run away together, only to tell me on the next breath he wished I'd never been born. That I had single-handedly ruined her life. Done that to both of us. It was that sort of… long-term mental abuse that really messed me up. I didn't have siblings. It was just me. So she was my only hope. And every time…" The glass raised to Joe's lips, set down again without a sound. "Everybody knew what she was dealing with at home. With my father. Everyone in town saw my mother after she'd been beaten. Saw her staggering about the place. Saw me trying to help her, with my own cuts and bruises. But no one thought she did that to me, too."

Joe could feel the tension in Percy's taut arms. The impotence of inaction. No one to take the anger out on, no means to jump in and stop Joe from experiencing it. All of it done and over, and no long-distance vengeance to be exacted. What was there, stuck inside him, circled and swirled, giving vent only in a black glower directed at Giordano.

Joe's hand slipped down to Percy's knee, and his thumb ran small circles there as he talked on, trying to get it all out as quickly and clearly as possible. "My mother would take me to church regularly, and that was a respite. Of sorts. She always acted the doting mother there, in front of everyone. Except when she thought no one was looking." He let out an empty-sounding laugh. "I used to believe her when she did that. When she would smile at me and act so kind, I thought maybe she'd forgiven me for whatever it was I'd done wrong that particular morning. But then, when no one was looking, she'd give me this death stare, from across the room, just to remind me that she hated me. Just in case I ever forgot for a few minutes. Then she'd turn back to the others, the picture of the loving mother. She was that sort of…" He reflected a moment to find the words. "She was *calmly* manipulative. And it never stopped. She'd do that at home, too. Just turn. Very suddenly. It was more stark when we were at church or around people, because at home I'd learned not to trust it. But outside… It got so… I think I didn't know what kindness was anymore. Whether I could trust it in anyone, or if there was broken glass hidden in it. I couldn't trust anything. It was…"

"Fucking hell," Percy whispered. The admission put their entire relationship into perspective, and only then did Percy really understand the depth of Joe's doubt in him so many times. He wondered if Joe even knew how far it ran. His fingers curled over into Joe's palm, and he took his hand to his lips, where he kept it, needed there for his own benefit as much as Joe's.

"It's okay," said Joe, but he didn't pull it away. He looked up into Percy's eyes. "You're the only person who'll know this, what I'm about to tell you." His eyes ran over to Giordano's, dark and hooded. "Well, you're about to be the only two people." Joe swallowed hard against the truth that was so desperate to spill out of him. So desperate, after such a long time hidden in that dusty chest.

In a low, shaky tone, he said, "I took oleander, and I boiled it down. I was only twelve, but I knew it was poisonous from history lessons. I boiled it into a concentrate, maybe a shot worth. I did it down by the cemetery, in an old tin can. I added more and more leaves and seeds and flowers and water, and boiled it again and again. For weeks, on and off, whenever I could get away. I don't know if I thought I'd really ever go through with it. It was sort of… meditative. Like a comforting daydream. I imagined how nice I'd make the place if they were dead. How calm it would be. I don't know what I thought I'd do for food or money… But it was a peaceful place, in my mind, whenever I boiled that pot."

Joe took in a deep breath, which he let go slowly, until he was completely empty. "This one night, he beat me, which he'd done before, but not this bad. He beat me until I could barely walk. They'd been fighting with each other all evening, and I tried to sneak out, but I got caught. I just remember being so scared. So, so scared there on the floor, and he made it long and sustained, and I begged her to help me. And do you know what?" Joe's eyes hazed over as he looked distantly into the past, nose crinkling with disgust, a slight arch in his lips. "She was smiling. A cruel, spiteful smile. She was enjoying every second of it. Whatever was broken in her, she'd lost all pity. She enjoyed the brutality of it. And that's the thing people don't understand. Because unless you've lived through that, Giordano, people don't think a mother's capable of that. They think she'll be there to help you. That she'll bleed for you. Every time in my life I've ever tried to tell anyone, they think I must have been mistaken. 'Mothers don't do that.' But that night, it wasn't just me being belted in the heat of passion. It was cold. And I just knew, by that look in her eyes, it was me or them."

Joe leaned back, staring up at the chandelier. "I never felt bad for what I did. I still don't. I know that's 'wrong'. It's what we're all taught from day one, 'don't murder your parents'. Or anyone, but to be specific… Anyway, that night, when they were done, I pretended I was asleep on the floor where they'd left me. This time she didn't come with a hug and an apology. She just fell into a drunken stupor in her bed. And some time in the night, as terrified as I was of what would happen if they caught me again, I snuck out. I went, and I got my oleander extract. And I poured it into their wine. Then I went to bed. Cigarette?"

Percy flicked his case open and lit two, passing Joe one, pushing the case and lighter over to Giordano.

Joe breathed deeply, in and out, with the steadying plume dancing in the soft light of the luxurious apartment, so different to the place his mind lingered. "When I woke again, which wasn't until late the next day, my mother was screaming in agony. Throwing up, so, so sick. My father was sick too, but not like she was. She was thin, frail." He tapped the smoke with a sharp strike of his index finger. "And she died the same day. I wish it hadn't been so cruel, but I didn't have a gun. I didn't have the strength to get rid of her by any other means. I was twelve, and I had nowhere to go. So I feel the guilt of her suffering. I do. But not of her death."

Percy blew out his own breath of spiteful smoke. "She deserved that and worse."

Joe checked each of their eyes. Giordano's sympathetic with a wary note. Percy's faithful. Quiet. With that spark of warmth he'd always kept burning for Joe since that first day, even when they were at their worst, in no way dimmed. The story, which Joe told with comparatively sparse detail, was only about to get worse, but that ember kept him going.

"My father, he wouldn't die," he explained. "He kept drinking until he finished the poisoned bottle, then he drank more. He kept vomiting. He was so angry and so sick. He was terrifying. But he wouldn't die. She was dead in their bed, green, and he wouldn't do a thing about it. He laid there next to her corpse because he was too drunk and too sick to care. And after three days, after he'd long since finished the poisoned wine and moved on, he slept. So soundly, once the poison let him. So peacefully, without the fever of sickness." Joe's eyes hardened in a way Percy had seldom ever seen. "And I thought, this isn't going to work. What should I do? Spend weeks making more poison? Try again? How much would I need? He was huge. And maybe it wouldn't work again. But what scared me most was thinking, *knowing*, if he gets better, and he figures out what I've done, he'll really kill me this time. And so, I felt I had little choice."

The soft touch of the cigarette on Joe's lips broke the silence. "He slept on, and I got a knife, and I did it. Like I'd seen my mother do to our sheep. I put it in one side of his neck, just as deep as I could, and ripped. He woke up, and he choked on it. And he rolled out of bed, and the last thing he ever saw was me. My hands red with his blood. And I was happy he knew it was me."

The phantom of a smile played at the corner of Joe's lips, soon broken by his sharp laugh. "I was so stupid. I put the knife in his hand when he was dead. Dabbed some of his own blood on there. It was supposed to look like he'd killed himself after finding her, but no one would ever have believed he cared that much."

He crossed his arms, letting the hand holding the cigarette tilt back. "I went to the church, and I told the priest that I'd found my mother dead, and that my father had committed suicide. I said I thought he may have poisoned my mother." Joe turned his hand over, studying it. "I still had his blood on me. It was so, so obvious, what I'd done. He went, and he saw it, that ridiculous, horrifying scene, and do you know what he did? He cleaned me up. He gave me the first good meal I'd had in months. He told me to tell the police I'd been living with him. I didn't want to lie like that. I didn't want to involve him. But he said I'd be paying him back for his kindness if I let him save my soul, and that prison would only make me worse."

Joe shifted the papers Giordano had brought about the table. Headline after headline, page after page. Giordano had done his research. Enough to convince Percy, no matter how hopelessly in love with Joe he was, that his fiancé was a killer. "As you can see, there was a huge media circus. Everyone knew about it. Everyone in town knew I did it, but just like when they'd let me go through the abuse alone, the same parochial behaviour reigned, and they said nothing after the fact either. Nothing to the police. Nothing to the media. And I went about with Father Milton, my hair brushed, clean-faced, looking like an angel. Nothing like the filthy urchin I used to be." Joe ran his fingers over one of the grainy images, as though even now he wanted to make sure that every lock of hair fell just as it should to give the right impression. "Such a respectable-looking boy."

He considered the picture a while longer, speaking absently. "I took confirmation when I was told to, and I got the Church on my side. The police investigated me, and they knew I'd done it. They pressed charges, obviously. But they couldn't pin it on me, because Father Milton swore up and down that I was with him when it happened. Had forensics been better back then… But ultimately none of it mattered. Thanks to Father Milton. He pulled strings, he spoke for me, he called in favours. And because of him, this gilded cage closed around me, and so long as I stayed there, singing the song the Church wanted me to sing, I was safe."

Percy's eyes sparked as that piece of the puzzle finally slid into place.

"I was declared innocent. Even if no one believed it." Joe glanced briefly at Giordano before returning his gaze to Percy. "And when I walked out of the courtroom that day, there wasn't any question about which path my life was going to follow from there. I'd never had any dreams of my own. And I had a debt to repay. A big one."

He watched the light reflecting in his wine as he swirled the glass around. "I would have done anything for that man. When he moved to Rome, he took me with him. When he asked me to work towards becoming a priest, that's what I did. I lived with him and he taught me kindness. He taught me trust. He made me the person I am today. When he moved overseas, I went with him, and up until the day that demon took my hands and murdered him, I was wholly devoted to him. I owed him my life, and to be the person who took his…" During the entire tale, Joe had trudged on with barely the raise or shake of his voice, until now. Now the tears rushed fast to his eyes, and he stared down at the table, his hands shaking.

The tips of Percy's fingers slid beneath his locked jaw, cupping Joe's cheek. He shifted close, turning Joe's face towards his. "Come back."

"It doesn't stop." Joe's voice broke on the words, and Percy shifted his head down, resting his forehead against Joe's, stroking his cheek, as tears forced their way through his tightly shut eyes.

"I know," he said gently. "It won't. But you come back to me." The final word was firm, and Joe opened his eyes to find Percy always, always waiting for him. Clear, capable, ready to take it all in his stride along with every other thing.

Joe wrapped his fingers around Percy's, holding them to his cheek. Joe's eyes, wet with those last memories, brightened. "That's when you came along. When you turned up at my place that first afternoon, everything was more fucked than I can ever describe to you. I was so, so alone. I didn't know what to do, because the one support I'd ever had in my entire life was gone. In such a horrible way. Then you were just… You were Percy. You lifted me out of it. It was so easy to fall for you. And when I told you how I felt, it was so simple. And when—"

"Giordano, fuck off," said Percy.

Giordano, caught up in the drama, had forgotten his own presence, and that he was the ball that had set the lot in motion. "Fuck. Sorry," he mumbled. "Um… Fuck off, like out of the apartment?"

"No, just…" Percy muttered. "Just go somewhere. For a few minutes."

"In here!" Leo called.

"And bring the bottle!" Althea shouted.

"Half a glass," Percy yelled back. Then he tapped Giordano's hand as he grasped the bottle. "I mean it. You pour."

Giordano took it in hand, then said to Joe, "I'm sorry. I should have talked to you first."

Joe, a little too shell-shocked to do much else, gave a small nod, so Percy filled in for him, spitting, "Yes, you fucking should have."

His irritated eyes followed Giordano until they were alone, when Joe called his attention back, drawing him immediately into their former intimacy with quietly spoken words. "You made everything easy for the first time in my life. It's never mattered to me once, all our most difficult moments, because it felt so right and so good to be with you. You said, let's take this holiday, and it was like you were holding an escape route there in the palm of your hand. It was you. You stepped in and you saved me. And I'm sorry I didn't tell you. I just wanted to run away. From all of it. I wanted to run away with you."

Percy caressed Joe's face, stroking softly. "I'm sorry. For everything you've been through."

"Not me," said Joe, looking back at his younger image. "Him. I did it for him. He deserved better. So I made it better."

Percy took both his hands. "I want you to know I'm proud of you. Proud of you for doing what you did. Proud of you for being so loyal and kind. Proud of you for being so pure of heart, when you were dealing with that this whole time. You were so brave. You still are. Brave and beautiful and I love you."

Joe dipped his forehead back to Percy's with a teary laugh. "How many people do you think would say that to me? How many people in the whole world would sit there and say that to me right now and mean it?"

Percy gave a shrug and a comically disgusted glance about the place. "Fuck them."

"One," Joe replied. "One perfect man, and I found him. I don't feel ashamed of what I did. I don't think I owe a debt to society. I've never felt wrong. And I told you because you make it easy. And because I knew you wouldn't judge me. You always get it. I'm just sorry I didn't tell you sooner. But I hope you can understand why."

"I do. And believe me…" Percy's words cut off abruptly with a spark of memory.

The ring.

That ring that weighed heavily against his skin now, that screamed, *This is it. This is how you show him you still and will always love him.*

Percy wanted to meld it to his finger—meld the two of them together for eternity and be Joe's outer shell for as long as he'd let him.

He leaned closer, squeezing Joe's hands between his own feverishly. "What I'm about to say has nothing to do with what you just told me. Or maybe it does, but only in a roundabout way. But I was going to say this anyway, but… Things keep happening and so… I haven't been able to get it out. And I'm not doing this right."

A flash of panic took Joe at the sudden change—a prelude to something else—something uncharted. "What? Is everything okay?"

A louder alarm sparked in Percy as he rushed to reassure him. "Very okay. Very. Very, very all right and okay and totally normal. Only… I want you to know I love you."

Joe's eyes searched his, keen, worried, but with a pleasant sparkle flickering when he heard those words. "I love you, too."

"And so…" Percy reached into his pocket. Warm, thick gold. Cool cut sapphire. "Joe—"

Just as the word left his lips, the lights were cut, and everything turned black.

CHAPTER FORTY-FIVE

THE MOST GALLING
INTERRUPTION YET

If one tenth of the anger in Percy's eyes had been physical, the entire apartment would have crumbled to dust, but in the tick of a clock, that anger changed abruptly to trepidation with the nerve-shattering call on the wind from the open window. "Doctor Ashdown?"

That voice—that sing-song lilt in the night—was all too familiar.

Percy, at the window in a few fast steps, closed his fingers around the white linen curtain and pulled it back cautiously. He felt Joe steadfast by his shoulder. Moxie sprang up onto the windowsill with a silent pounce, and Leo, Althea, and Giordano soon surrounded them to take in the scene below.

The formerly busy street lay eerie beneath them. The centre of Parisian nightlife for more than a century had dropped into an uneasy slumber. The scene wasn't bloody—not particularly—not the kind of bloody Percy and Joe had grown used to dealing with. There were cars stopped, doors open, drivers hanging halfway out or leaning on their steering wheels. There were tables laden with drinks and food, just as they so often were, but with no one to partake of the bounty,

365

because up and down the road, strewn here and there, lay… corpses? The bodies of men, women, and children lying down in the street, utterly motionless, noiseless, harrowing, and in the centre of it all, there stood Molly Tulloch, wearing Cleo's body. She took a few steps closer, a long and low-cut black dress hugging every magnificent curve all the way to the street, rising marvellously beneath the folds of luxurious black hair all about her shoulders when she lifted two arms and blew a kiss up to Percy.

Percy turned his head, and on a low breath, he whispered urgently, "See, Althea? Now that's a dress."

"Percy!" Joe snapped.

"Everything can be a learning opportunity for teenagers," Percy declared. He slipped his fingers into his pocket and pulled out his apartment keys. "Leo, the place is yours." He grabbed Leo's hand and shoved the keys into his unwilling palm, curling his fingers closed over them. "The solicitor's got my will. I've left most of it to you. Take Althea, get on a train, and don't come back for at least three months, unless you hear from me first."

Leo shoved the keys at him. "What, no—"

Percy shoved them straight back. "And don't argue—"

A loud clap sounded in the street, and, "Percy," whispered Joe, still keeping a watch out the window. He grabbed Percy's wrist and pulled him close in time to see the two figures that responded to the clack of Molly's palms. They were two figures Percy knew well, and he was a mixture of horrified and relieved to see them, because the one to the right walked tall and handsome with no shirt and no hint of a dislocated shoulder. And the one to the left had no scar where Percy had shot him in the head. Most compellingly, he now also retained two full hands. Waleed raised one of those hands and waved up at Percy.

"That fuck!" Percy growled. "How did it get itself back together? We burned the bastard! We took it to pieces!"

Percy felt a different hand slide around his biceps, a touch of gravity in the firm press. "Who's that?" Giordano asked.

Percy's voice was clipped with irritation at the interruption, but he took the time to explain, "That's Cleo. You remember her, don't you? You've met her several times."

Joe leaned forward, eyeing the pair, asking desperately, "How has Giordano met Cleo?"

"Not right now, darling," Percy tried gently. He elucidated the matter for Giordano with, "The thing is, she's *not* Cleo. She's possessed by the spirit of a four-hundred-year-old witch, and she's after… Well, I don't know. She *was* after my nice magical sheath."

Giordano let out a little gasp. "Cleo's possessed?"

"Well, obviously," Percy drawled. "Do try to keep up."

Giordano was keeping up and ready to move ahead. "No, but, I know Cleo. I want to know, who is *that?*"

All eyes dropped back to the shirtless man on the right-hand side of the witch in question. "Oh." Percy chuckled.

Althea leaned forward eagerly. "That's Tareq."

"Who's Tareq?" asked Leo, none too pleased with the sight.

"That's what I want to know," Joe returned, even less pleased.

"He's very nice," said Percy.

"*Very* nice," Althea cooed.

"He's just a little bit…" Percy thought over the predicament. Tareq certainly didn't appear to be the usual rotting, festering, slobbering, foul sort of zombie he was used to dealing with. "I don't know. He's sort of—"

"Does he… um… Is he evil?" Giordano asked, eyes fast on the beauteous face that stared straight ahead the whole time.

"He might be right now… But there could be a way he'll come good again."

"And does he… Uh…" With a casual flick of his hand in Tareq's direction, "Men? Do you think?"

Percy grinned, wide and knowing. "I got a vibe." He ignored the way Joe's mouth fell open, continuing, "We were in Libya, so he could hardly do much about it."

"There was no vibe!" Althea protested.

"There was a vibe," Percy insisted. "I just got a sixth sense about him. You know he might not even realise it."

"Oh, I'd kill to be his awakening," Giordano breathed.

Percy groaned an agreement. "The two of you together… Could you imagine?"

Joe's head spun around like a possessed child's might. "He's a zombie! Stop talking about him like he's not a zombie!"

"He doesn't look like a zombie," Giordano offered.

"No, he does not," Althea agreed.

"He looks like a zombie to me," Leo put in.

"And what are the ethics of that?" Giordano wondered aloud.

"Necrophilia?" Joe hissed.

"Don't kink shame, handsome," said Percy. "Plus, he's walking around. It's not the same thing at all."

"If you're quite done?" Molly called up. The small group shuffled themselves into a more serious-looking formation to listen. "I tried to be nice, Percy. We could have done this the easy way. The pleasant way. You could have saved yourself a lot of trouble. But you are stubborn. Which is why I've given up trying to reason with you. Joe?"

Joe said nothing, thrown to hear his name on her lips, such an inconsequential player in the whole game as he'd always thought he was. He watched her walk a few short paces to her left, where she stopped at the body of a woman lying prone on the ground. She kicked it softly, and with that one small indicator, Tareq and Waleed immediately pulled the unconscious woman to her feet.

"Joe," she continued, "it's my understanding that you're not quite so fond of bloodshed as your fiancé is. That you have a little more sense and sensibility. That you understand, whatever I'm going to do with the sheath won't be half as bad as what I'll do if you piss me off."

Molly pulled up the long sleeve of her dress, flicked her wrist back, and released a small dagger. Tareq's hands wrenched back the head of the woman he held, and as Joe's eyes flitted to the bare skin, to the flash of the blade, he yelled, "Stop! Stop it! We'll get the sheath. We'll get it now. Stop!"

Percy already had his hand on his own dagger. The group parted by instinct to give him space. But all were too intent on the drama below to notice that his movements were a little less fluid than usual. That his reactions were a little slower. Off balance. And none of it paused the sickening show playing out before Joe's eyes.

Molly's knife slid across the woman's throat, and she must have been alive, because the blood spurted free and plentiful from her freshly slit artery. Molly cupped the back of the woman's neck, and as though nothing in the presence of the harrowed onlookers worried her in the least, she dipped her lips to the scarlet fissure and drank.

"Holy fuck," Althea whispered, turning to Leo, whose pale face watched on as he ran his arms around her. Joe reeled a step back from the window, dizzy at the spectacle. Percy, who for reasons none of them could understand, still hadn't thrown the dagger, stumbled. Never off-balance, he staggered against the windowsill. The dagger clattered to the floor, drawing the attention of the entire group. With visible effort, he seemed to get his bearings, grasped the weapon, stood tall, ready to make the attempt again, even as the room swayed away from him.

"Percy!" Joe was in front of him, two hands on his cheeks, trying to look into the eyes that clouded over, unfocused.

"Joe. I need..." A stark confusion overtook him, and he

blinked back at Joe, his full weight shifting forward into Joe's arms.

Joe, holding tight to Percy, yelled down at Molly. "What are you doing to him? Stop. Please!"

All bloody lips and chin sparkling in the street lights, she called up, "If you want him back, you bring me the sheath. Montmartre Cemetery. And be quick. He won't survive long without you where I'm taking him."

Percy dropped, Joe's knees smashing to the floor by his as he tried to brace his fall. "Percy!"

"Joe…" He blinked again, this time long and slow and fading.

"Percy, wake up!" He slapped Percy's cheeks, but the face he adored fell forward onto his chest, eyes closed, gone. "Baby, no. Don't do that. Percy, don't."

In a slow, strange nightmare, Leo stumbled a step back and fell, Althea's long hair sliding across his arm as she fell down upon him, followed by Giordano, dropping against the wall, and down to the floor.

Joe, in some desperate act of hopeful defiance, took Percy's dagger and slid it into the inside pocket of his vest. He wrapped both arms around him, and pulled him with all his strength away from the window, intent on locking him away somewhere, as though the tiny latch on the bathroom door would provide some sort of obstacle to a witch as powerful as Molly Tulloch.

But he wasn't thinking straight. Because Joe's world had begun to fade in the same undeniable way an anaesthetic takes the mind. Fight, fight, but there is always the darkness, and it came for Joe callously, no matter how desperately he clung to Percy's unconscious body, trying to save him.

CHAPTER FORTY-SIX

A CRUEL AWAKENING

Joe didn't wake measure by measure, grasping his way out of the fog that had downed him. He felt the rough and wet tug of Moxie's tongue on his cheek, and he was bolt upright, searching for Percy. Fruitlessly, stupidly searching, because even before he opened his eyes, he knew the warmth was gone. His heart, his existence, his reason for living, taken while he slept.

The others roused, one by one, due to his shouts, his feet on the floorboards as he pounded through the apartment, as though Percy might have wandered off to another room and left them all there, passed out on the floor. It was an agony of fast-paced slow motion—an everything and a nothing that flung Joe from one room to another in a frenzy, some counter in his mind taking stock of his options. Whatever weapons Percy might have once had would have been taken or destroyed when the apartment was ransacked. But he would find something to use. He would get him.

Leo was up now, beside himself with the loss, Althea close, reassuring him that if it had been anyone else, they might have

371

been in trouble. But not Percy. Percy was indestructible, and Leo knew that. Just as well as she knew that.

Giordano was staggering to his feet, listening, trying to piece it all together, and Joe let Althea take over, filling Giordano in on every detail, recounting every pinprick in the map that Percy and Joe had been over together. Every twist and turn, like it was a story to be easily recounted—a tale with a start and an end—not life itself; not a moment in time before which nothing existed, after which all was void.

A sharp metallic twang sounded as he pulled the still-wet chopping knife from the dish rack, barely cool from Percy's beautiful fingers having last touched it. He searched over the counter tops and found Giordano's gun. So small. It didn't look like it could do a thing to help him, but he turned, half distraction, to Giordano, and asked, "Bullets? More bullets?"

Giordano looked regretfully at the gun. "That's it. That's all I brought."

Joe shoved it into his pocket and wrenched the kitchen drawer open with a clatter. "Where is everything, Leo?"

Leo, in tears, knew exactly what he meant. "There's nothing. There is nothing. You saw what happened to the place."

Joe pulled out anything sharp he could find, wondering if the flimsy paring knife could ever stand up to bone. "No, no, not Percy. He's smarter than that. He's got to have a hidden compartment—or, or a trapdoor or something."

Leo, pacing the floor, carded his fingers through his hair. "Anything he has is across town. In his vault."

Joe looked up, the first touch of hope easing the taut skin across his cheekbones. "Then you get it. Get it all." He slammed the drawer closed and wrenched a cupboard door open. "And that must be where he's keeping the sheath?"

"It's too far," Leo cried, the pain in his attempt at a brave voice making it crack just like a teenage boy. "You heard her. We don't have any time. We need to go get him. Now!"

Joe ripped a dishcloth to shreds and began winding a long string around his biceps. "I'm going to get him. You'll bring the sheath."

"Fuck you, Joe, I'm not leaving him."

Joe spun around, knife in his outstretched hand, and yelled, "You'll do as I say. Percy is mine, and I'm going to get him, and anyone who stands in my way is going to die tonight." He shoved the blade into the makeshift holster and strode to the door.

Althea, all this time, had been keeping one ear on the group, and one on the nightmare below. "Did you hear that?"

With his hand on the door, Joe paused, turning dark eyes back. "What is it?"

Althea scrambled for the window, and it took but one look to bring a shake of her head, and, "Joe. No. Don't go out there. It's not human. It's something else." She raised a hand, and they all waited in silence until a long and low growl cut through the air.

Definitely not human. Not good.

Joe gave a slow nod, then advanced across the room to Giordano. He shoved the gun up against his chest, Giordano's hand covering it by instinct. "Get them there. Kill anyone or anything that gets in your way."

Leo took one look at the gun, realising the inevitability of the plan that Giordano readily acquiesced to, that Joe had gone and made without him, and stepped forward. "No—"

Joe's two shaking hands pressed against Leo's face, and Joe spoke vehemently, eyes shining, locked with Leo's. "He's going to be fine. I promise you. I'm going to get him, and I'm not going to let anything happen to him. But if something happens to you, he's not ever going to be okay again. Do you understand?" Leo's face went blank at the unexpected outpouring, the protective affection. Joe lowered his voice, speaking so deeply into his heart, it was all vulnerability, with a desperate plea. "I can't do this. I can't get you both. He thinks the world of you, and you need to be your top priority now. You do that for him, and for me, and for you. I don't want a scratch on you, you got it?"

Tears rushed to Leo's eyes, and in the urgency of the moment, he knew there was no protest to be made. Joe needed the sheath—*Percy* needed the sheath. And he was the only one who could get it. Every natural impulse in him to be the one to get Percy—to not walk away from him—raised itself so violently inside and in opposition to logic that he couldn't form any utterance.

But Joe understood. He pulled Leo's head against his chest and hugged him tightly. "I promise. I'll find him."

Leo gave a small nod, pressed his back with his hands once, then pulled away to the far side of the room

"You can't go to the cemetery alone," Althea protested, trying her best to mask the fear in her voice with a deep and practical tone. "And Percy doesn't want us to give her the sheath. Let's just stick together. We'll come with you."

Joe glanced out the window at the desolate scene, another growl cutting into the night, then another, coming from a different direction. He focused clear eyes on Althea. "I'll get them out of your way. And I'll see you there. This is all we can do." He raised a hand to her cheek. "Stay safe."

He made for the door, snatching another knife from the kitchen table on his way past.

Althea called after him, "But god knows what she'll do if she gets a hold of the sheath. You're playing right into her hands."

"She can do whatever she likes," Joe threw over his shoulder on his way out the door. "I don't care if the whole world burns. So long as I get to Percy first."

CHAPTER FORTY-SEVEN
THE CRAWLING HORROR

Joe's heart thumped out a loud and stifling death knell as he pressed his forehead to the cold wood of the apartment building's front door. He both heard and felt the bangs and scrapes on the other side.

When he'd looked out the window a few moments earlier, the street was empty of all animated life. What was out there now? How many? How vicious?

It hardly mattered. It wasn't worth thinking about because he had no choice. He would go through whatever it was and he would survive. And he would get to Percy.

Joe sent a glance up the stairs, to the dark spot on the landing where he'd shut Percy's apartment door behind him. He could hear voices arguing, and his heart wrung out a thanks at the rich depth of Giordano's voice that seemed to be smoothing things over. Maybe Giordano couldn't fight at all— Joe hadn't asked—but he was tall, and strong, and he loved Percy. Joe could never doubt that, and he trusted it, and so he trusted him to keep Althea and Leo safe.

He faced the entrance, brought his knife up in preparation, took a deep breath, then flicked the latch open. He leapt back from the doors that slammed inwards with a deafening bang. White and damp flesh pressed into him, suffocating him. Claws and teeth and wide, round mouths. He could decipher no more in the mess of hot skin and bad breath and the din of hungry growls. His knife slid into stomachs and necks. Lost in a clamour of legs and arms and sharp, grasping fingers, there wasn't time to aim. He slit, and he hit, and he kicked, and he was as well satisfied with a broken leg as he was with pierced skin. The beasts let out screeches of agony with every attack. Their blood was warm on his fingers—not like the dead things he'd tangled with in the past.

He fought his way forward, shoving one to the side, cracking a skull on the pavement. His knife ran deep into another's throat and he slid it free, cracking his elbow into a cheek when one clambered up his back, its nails slitting the skin down his shoulder blade. His boot smacked down piteously on a kneecap, and inch by inch, he made his way into the street, bleeding, gasping for air, denying the pain that already screamed through his body.

The creatures pursued him, some down low and agile, ready for attack, others dragging broken limbs, some breathing hard and already dying from the first onslaught, but they all followed.

Joe's relief was palpable at the sight of the crawling, clawing things coming for him, leaving the entrance. He needed them away from that door. Away from Althea and Leo. He slowed his pace, waiting in the street for them to close in, backing up, backing up, catching his breath.

They were almost white, their flesh anaemic and translucent. They were humanoid of some sort, but they crawled along the ground. Not zombies, not humans under whatever sort of spell Molly seemed able to cast upon those close to her. These things showed no more intelligence than intent. Intent to destroy Joe and only Joe, their drooling teeth set on his flesh alone, ignoring the bodies that were strewn all over the street.

There were maybe seven of them now, some leaving red pools as they went, bleeding heavily from his knife, their elbows clambering high as their misshapen limbs propelled them forward.

A claw grabbed onto his hurt shoulder from behind, and he heard Althea's shout somewhere above. He doubled over, flipped the crawler to the rough asphalt, kicked a boot to break its rib, and dropped to his knee to slit the throat wide open. He spun away from the carnage, knocked off his feet by another of the beings. He moved with it, fluid, and his other shoulder hit the ground hard, tearing a rip in his shirt and his skin, but he kept going and rolled over onto his back, kicking two legs up into his assailant, which he knocked back into another. Just as he got halfway up, another flung itself upon him, digging claws into his chest, cutting four vermillion streaks deep into his skin. Joe took two hands to the shoulders of the powerful beast in an attempt to restrain it, but its head flicked and its teeth gnashed all the more violently as it lunged for his neck.

A flash exploded to his left, a shot went off, a splatter of hot gristle painted his cheek and his chest, drenching him in the brains of the thing.

Joe scrabbled to his feet and looked up to find Giordano at the window, gun smoking. He let off a shot to Joe's left, smashing another's head open before it could complete its vicious pounce. The final crawler jumped, Joe wrenched his paring knife free from his arm holster, and smashed it deep into the mouth that opened to devour him, stabbing the creature through to the brain, killing it instantly.

It splatted to the ground, he heard a sharp "Mew!" and a second later, tiny claws dug into his already-bleeding shoulder, where Moxie landed with an unsteady thump. His aching fingers ran over her coat as he made his way a few steps back up the street, and slammed the apartment door closed.

"Thanks," he called up to Giordano.

Giordano gave a sharp nod, wary eyes scanning the road for more of the predators.

A fresh growl sounded some way down the street, in the direction of Montmartre Cemetery. "All right, Moxie," said Joe, wiping the blood from his knife onto his sleeve. "Let's go get your master."

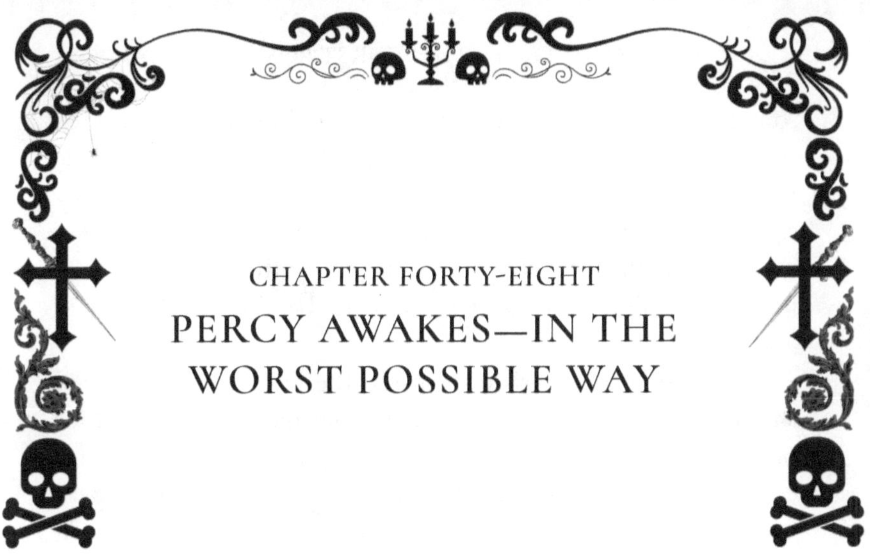

CHAPTER FORTY-EIGHT
PERCY AWAKES—IN THE WORST POSSIBLE WAY

Of all the ways Percy had ever imagined dying, this was by far the worst. After all, there's hardly a person alive who hasn't thought, at least once, about what they might do if they ever found themselves in the same predicament. For all of human history, the slim possibility of that fate has hung over almost every member of the species, and Percy had come up with no better solution to the problem than all the rest of us, even if circumstances had given him greater reason to dwell on the idea than most.

As such, when Percy opened his eyes to the dark, when he reached out his hands and felt the smooth satin overhead, when he ventured his arms out to his sides and met more satin, when he breathed in the musty, dusty, dank air, he didn't shift. He didn't panic. He stayed still, and let his heart sink, because he knew he had time. Plenty of time. Too much time. Because when you're buried in a coffin deep beneath a tonne of earth, there is nothing but time. Nothing you can do but wait and try not to go mad.

Percy's heart smashed so hard in his chest, he felt the shake of it in his shoulders. He was hot. Burning hot, and cold somehow at the same time. His ears were drowned in a rush of blood and horror, and he tried to listen for some sound outside the coffin, but he couldn't hear a thing above the emergency signals his body was sending out.

Fight or flight… Neither. Neither. For the first time since he was a child, there was nothing to be done but lie here and die.

He wanted to smash his fist into the lid—tear the satin to shreds, then try to force his way out. But having meditated for bored hours on this very eventuality, he had long since concluded that the slow march to death would be better spent without broken fingers and nails hanging bloody and loose. At least until he lost control. He wondered, would he feel the pain then? Or would it all be a miserable blur, like walking home drunk after missing the last bus?

Joe, he knew, would be cutting his way across the city to him. But where was he and what signs could possibly lead Joe to his… grave?

And if he didn't come in time, was this it? His final resting place? Where his body would always remain?

He quite liked the idea of ending up in Montmartre Cemetery—which is where he guessed he was, considering Molly's request for Joe to meet her there—but not like this. Not in someone else's grave, which it had to have been, because the place was full to the brim, overflowing. Bodies upon bodies and no space for new ones.

So what had Molly done? Was this coffin resting on someone else's? Had she had the hole prepared before she came to see them? How long had he been interred? How deep? How much oxygen was left?

Percy shifted, aware now of something digging into his back. Something sharp and hard just beneath his shoulder blade. It shifted away with the movement of his body, but he gave it only the spectre of a thought as the idea of his being in someone else's grave closed in on him. Closed in tight like the walls of his coffin.

It was pitch black. Black and cold. He could have eased his lighter out of his pocket if it was still there. But if the satin caught fire... He shuddered at the thought.

He reached out once more and yes, satin, definitely. But it wasn't flush with the lid. It sagged, and it came too close to his face and he didn't like it. Nothing unusual there, for who would like to feel the sagging satin of their own death box on their cheek? But something about the idea struck Percy as disrespectful. Disrespectful beyond the fact of being put to a grisly death via premature burial. It was a sort of... final kick in the teeth. A way of saying, you're not even worth a new box. Not even the most basic model. Just dig up one of the old ones, damp and mouldering, and throw the bones in a ditch somewhere.

He deserved better.

He deserved his own nice new——

A sort of crick about the back of his thigh shifted his leg down a notch. That brought a jab into his left hip. He shifted by instinct and a crunch and crumble under his left arm brought his head across, and his cheek brushed something hard. Cold. Rough.

A shudder shot through every inch of Percy. A deep rejection of fact and a revulsion of reality.

No.

She had not emptied out an old coffin.

She had simply closed Percy inside with the owner.

It was a thought too harrowing to admit so readily, and he closed his eyes against it, though it made no difference there in that dark box. He saw nothing, eyes open or closed, but now he felt it. Maybe it lay clothed in a suit or a dress that had cushioned him somewhat, all mildew and tatters. Perhaps there was some leathery skin left. But he felt the bones now. He felt the arch of the ribs as his mind mapped out the body. His hips were settled down on top of the pelvis, and with another involuntary shift, the leg bones of the corpse popped over to lie flush with his own.

"Fuuuuuuuck!" Percy whispered.

And just then, he felt a soul-shattering breath of putrid air on his face.

CHAPTER FORTY-NINE
JOE CUTS A SWATH

The distance from Joe to Percy was only a few city blocks. But Montmartre is a strange and terrifying place at night when it's deserted and you're being hunted by pale crawlers. Every lane and byway is a hiding place. Dumpsters and cafe tables leer out of the darkness with equal menace, and it doesn't matter how many gorgeous twinkling lights sparkle overhead or how romantic such a quiet stroll would ordinarily be; every touch of Joe's shoes to the cobblestones echoed back a thousand noises that weren't really there and augmented those that were terribly.

The growling had never stopped. Not really. There was a pause here and there, the direction it came from changed frequently, but it was always somewhere close by. It was as if the creatures were watching him all the while, and Joe felt the constant prickle of hunters' eyes trained on his back.

He wondered why they hadn't attacked again. Maybe they'd learned something about the gun Giordano had. But though they gathered around, more and more, until the soundtrack of his walk was a low and ravenous hum, they seemed to be following.

Joe worried over what Molly had done to the people that still lined the streets outside Percy's apartment. He'd taken several pulses as he went by. They slept. Or seemed to be asleep. They lay there warm and unconscious, all except the woman whose body was still crumpled in a heap on the ground, her throat gashed, her blood drunk. He wanted to return to her corpse. What if one of the sleeping children was hers? What if they awoke to find her like that?

He slowed, looking back down the long street. An echoing snarl curled around the buildings, as if in warning. *Keep moving.*

If he turned back now, would they follow him still? Would they start picking over the bodies he led them to? Eating people while they were unconscious, unable to even try to defend themselves?

That consideration, coupled with his restless desperation to find Percy, propelled him onward.

The timing of the murder hadn't escaped Joe—that Molly had performed the horrifying act seconds before the attack, which, he imagined, must have taken enormous power to perform. That thought, coupled with what he knew about Althea's abduction—that she too had been drained of blood regularly—ticked over in the back of his mind as he walked.

It looked exactly like blood magic. Like she needed that blood to access her powers to their full extent.

He hadn't seen another animated soul all the unnerving walk to the cemetery. Nothing human at least; just the occasional flash of that insipid skin. He wondered how far the sleeping sickness spread. Was all of Paris asleep like this? Could Molly do that?

And how were Leo and Althea to get to the sheath without a train to catch? How were they to drive through the city streets when they were packed with stopped cars and bodies?

They would just have to find a way.

He had qualms about giving Molly the sheath, of course he

did. But it wasn't something he had to think twice about. She didn't have the Spear of Destiny—the lance that would make the sheath magical once they were reunited—if the rumours were even true. That was still at Percy's place, overseas, back where their journey together began. Without the spear, the sheath was all but useless. She didn't have anything but Percy. And if Joe could only get him back, he would give her whatever she asked for, just as obligingly as he could.

Until he could get a clean shot.

And that was entirely too bad for Cleo. And for Percy. Because if he got that one shot, he was going to take it.

Joe thought over how close Percy had come to throwing his dagger earlier, though he didn't think for a second it would have been a head shot. Or a heart shot. Not by Percy's hand.

How he wished it had been. That this whole nightmare was over before it ever began. Another bullet for each of her zombie off-siders, and then some celebratory champagne.

But no. It was cruel to think that way. Percy had grieved his friendship with Cleo for so long now. Joe saw it in the hotel room the night she tried to seduce him—the shock and hidden worry at the change in her. He saw it in her house, the tense regret as Percy walked around, taking in the remnants of their long history together. The way Percy had been so sure, when they did the séance, that Cleo couldn't have been at fault for any of it. And he'd been right.

He'd played it off in front of Joe as though he had the lot under control. As though it wasn't eating away at him. But every night since they found her skull, Percy had sat her down to dinner with them. He was always talking to her, took her everywhere decent he could. He cared for her in the quiet way he always did with those close to him. All the unspoken kindnesses that had made Joe fall so deeply in love with him.

And Joe had developed some kind of fondness for Cleo, whoever or whatever she now was, though he wasn't anywhere close to seeing the soul in that skull as the woman who owned her body. That woman he could have killed easily, despite the state it would leave Percy in. Because Joe had seen first hand, more than once, that Percy's one and only weakness was the people he loved. And what would he let the possessor of the vessel of such an old friend as Cleo get away with in the hopes of reuniting her with her body? Freeing her from the madness of being trapped inside that skull?

He would put himself on the line like he always did. Joe knew it. And it was a risk Joe couldn't bring himself to take anymore.

Perhaps Joe would destroy the skull. Kill Cleo's body first, then smash Molly's skull to pieces. That would send her off to Heaven or Hell or wherever she was destined to be, wouldn't it? She'd be out. And Percy would be free. Free and safe and back in his arms. And then they would retire from all this. Whatever this life was that they were suddenly leading. Because for all the talk of being in the eye of the storm, that only held when he was by Percy's side. When it was the two of them to face it together. He'd have died so happily that way. But not like this. Not torn from Percy.

And where the fuck was Percy? Was he even alive anymore? Was Joe simply marching to his own death, perfectly, horrifyingly ignorant of the fact that he was already half in the grave? Because there was no life without Percy. There was nothing to return to, or to go on for.

A bridge, supported by a thick, blue, and ornate iron frame, stretched out ahead. On either side of it, a near-opaque darkness spread and spread wider again, nothing but void beneath. Off to his right, stairs dropped down to the entrance of the burial ground. Joe stood at the top, surveying the scene. The gate below was high and flanked by green metal spikes, adjoining a long and unceasing stone wall that circled the area. Keeping the living out, and thankfully, hopefully, keeping the undead in. At least until someone came to open those gates tomorrow morning. Assuming the people of the city ever woke again. But for now, how was he to get in?

A small "Mew" broke the taut silence. Moxie tilted forward, pressed her paws to Joe's chest, and before he could catch her, she sprang to the ground. She bolted a few feet ahead, and from the street, jumped onto the iron fence of the bridge.

"Moxie! Wait!" Joe hissed just as loud as he dared. He ran the few paces to her, but she was gone, over the edge of the bridge into the black below. Joe approached, taking in the sight. One stone grave after another, row upon row upon row, all pillars and sharp angles, and piled up all around, like the aftermath of a game of Jenga. But only the tips of that mishmash of stone memorials were visible. A fog rolled through the valley of the cemetery, set low beneath the streets. It was edged with trees that were black and formless patches of obscurity in that gothic and forbidding resting place.

He knew the only way in was to follow Percy's kitten. To take the same leap straight over the edge of the bridge into the dark, and hope nothing reached out for him when his feet hit the ground.

He readied his knife, climbed over the guardrail, and without even the thought of saying a final prayer, he slipped into black.

Joe's feet hit solid concrete, which, despite the pain it occasioned in his legs and back, was a welcome surprise. The rolling fog, a sickly yellow, was so dense, he could only see a few feet ahead. Of that, there was little more than the suggestion of leaves, the silvery arms of grasping trees, and looming high above him, shadowy, sharply lined monuments of the long deceased.

He glanced back over his shoulder at the sinister darkness beneath the bridge. More graves, skulls and faces chipped into their dimly glinting granite surfaces, seemed to study him, this creature of the living, stepping uninvited into a metropolis of the dead.

Joe knelt down, and with a soft click of his fingers, whispered, "Moxie."

Not a peep of sound met his call.

He tried once more, and with a new, curling sickness in his stomach at the thought of losing Percy's kitten, had to remind himself that it was not really a cat, but a thing of evil that had decided to befriend them.

The path forked forward and left, and Joe, with little guidance but his faith that he would somehow find Percy, walked straight ahead into the blanketing fog.

CHAPTER FIFTY
BURIED UNALIVE

There was nowhere to go. There wasn't an inch of space Percy could back himself into to get away from the thing he had awoken.

To keep still? To lie there trying not to breathe in the flakes of its rotting and aged skin? To will his pulse to stop lest it felt that beat of a living being next to it, that it would undoubtedly want to snuff out?

Or… to get it over with. To let it strangle him, pulverise him, tear him apart—whatever it wanted to do—and be carried swiftly to that savage and ignoble death, thus putting an end to the horror once and for all.

But Joe would be on his way. Percy was sure of that. And so he had little choice but to try to survive this. Because he'd be damned if he'd let Joe find him like that.

Percy took in shallow breaths, the kind that made him feel lightheaded with the lack of oxygen, and he kept still. Very, very still. But he felt a rise in the chest of the thing beneath him, and he wondered at it. It had no lungs to expand, but he knew it was breathing, because he could smell it. He could feel it. It was cold and vile and it ran across his cheek and down his neck like a spider.

The thing shifted. It placed its one free hand against the wall of the coffin. Percy heard it. Rough bone on old satin, the threads tugging at the pull of the movement.

Was it realising? Did it understand?

The other hand, the hand he lay upon, tried to reach out. The shoulder hitched up, softly, then more violently. Should he move? Was it better to give it two hands—let it explore its fate and see what it might do? Perhaps it might think him nothing more than another corpse thrown on top, or an old blanket?

A strange grunt came from the thing, and with it, Percy began to feel an odd affinity with the creature. A sympathy. Percy considered, if he died there, now, he might not come back to life. But this thing... How long was it to spend there beneath the ground, having been so cruelly roused from its eternal slumber? How aware was it of this atrocious fate?

He decided to move, just a little. To brace his feet against the bottom of the casket and arch his back, rolling his shoulder to the outer edge, allowing the thing the opportunity to slip its arm free to explore its confinement.

That was a mistake.

Skeletal fingers clamped down on his neck just as quickly and easily as if the thing had been able to see him lying there. The power of it surprised him, as did the bold and firm intent to kill in a thing that had been dead so long.

Percy had very little to work with. His chest was almost pressed against the lid as it was. Just as if his attacker were human, he went for the face, not the hand, as experience told him a jab to the eyes or throat would disable that hand faster than his yanking at it. But of course, it had no eyes. Percy's desperate fingers dug into holes and dusty, ragged, leather-like remnants of skin. He sunk his fingers where he could, grasping for anything that might inflict pain, but how do you hurt a dead thing with no nerves?

A strangled cough sounded in Percy's throat, the noise of his own voice strange in the dark and claustrophobic heat his body gave off in the small cavity. He groaned again, as a subconscious reminder he could even hear anything—that he wasn't already dead and in Hell.

The bony hand tightened, and he felt the face turn in his grasp, felt the bumps on the surface against his forehead. He flattened his palm and jabbed up, trying to hit a jaw, trying to knock the head off. He heard the teeth smash together, felt a shower of small hard lumps fall onto his shoulder, and heard the thing seethe out an angry breath. The arm beneath him shoved its way to the outer edge of the coffin and wrapped itself around him. The other shoulder came across, its left leg curled over his own, and that toothless mouth chomped at his ear as it gathered all of whatever supernatural strength it possessed, and pressed the lot down on Percy's neck.

His air was gone—completely cut off—whatever little bit of it had been left in the coffin. His body arched violently as he tried to find some escape, as it begged for oxygen. He ripped at the thing's wrist, which seemed held to the hand by nothing at all, but it would not give. His chest burned for a breath, as though his lungs must collapse in on themselves.

His other hand pulled at the fingers, too strong, too tight, and he rammed his shoulder up at the creature's chin. Lifting his chest flat against the lid, he slammed down hard, intent on breaking the ribs of the thing. His adrenaline made the black space scream with movement and white noise, and in the horrifying commotion, he didn't feel the coffin slip.

The bones cracked beneath him when he came down, just as he'd wanted, but those that broke away left six sharp and jagged points cutting into his back. He wondered, if he did it again, would he pierce his own lung? And what the fuck kind of state would he be in when Joe found him?

Percy tried to turn away from the creature, but his shoulders were too large to turn in the coffin. He slammed his body back down again and cursed the scream that couldn't escape—the stuck cry that was somehow even worse than the pain that ripped through his back when the old bones sliced into his skin.

He grasped for the hand again, putting all his ebbing strength behind it, but his sweating fingers couldn't take hold, slipped free, smashing his elbow painfully into the side of the coffin.

And it slid.

And this time, over the agony and terror, he felt it.

The other way now, desperately, Percy rammed his arm back, and he and the skeleton were jostled to the left.

It was precious little hope, but it was hope.

He did it again, back the other way, and there was definite movement. More movement than he could ever have dreamed of. Enough movement to tell him maybe he wasn't underground at all. Maybe he was still lying on the grass of the cemetery. Of Montmartre Cemetery, only metres from his own home. Only metres, perhaps, from Joe, searching grave to grave for him or for Molly. Within shouting distance, if only he could shout.

Percy kicked his knees up into the lid. Smashed his feet down at the base, trying to knock the old wood through. He slammed two hands up on the lid, and with the last gasp of energy in his dying frame, he turned as much to his left as he could, then rolled his arms and his legs and his entire body against the other side of the coffin with enormous force.

Everything veered away from him in a dizzying tumult that brought his stomach to the clamp at his throat, and he was upside down, over and around, and a sharp pain ripped through his right arm as he smashed down upon it, the coffin and the skeleton and all of it on top of him, then a bang back down onto his back. His hands formed a battering ram, and both forearms came with his fist up against the lid and it flew back.

Frigid air, dank and thick, swept over his skin. It was still dark, still pitch black, but he sensed he was in some sort of room. The excitement of it—of anything but being in that coffin—revived him. He hauled himself over and the full body movement was enough to rip the arm upwards and force the hand to slide. Painfully, ripping into his flesh, it moved around his throat. Percy pushed himself back and flung his body over the edge of the coffin, his back smashing hard into a stone wall. The arm came, still holding on, but it felt light. Not the weight of an entire skeleton. It was but an arm and a head and it disappeared into nothing somewhere about the smashed ribs.

He scrambled to his feet and threw the skeleton and himself into the wall. The bones began to break apart. He felt them fall onto his shoes, heard them clatter across the floor. He did it again and again until the wrist cracked open. Then he sank to his knees, dug both hands under the fingers, and, finally, forced them free.

He smashed them to the floor as he doubled over, holding them there, writhing against the cold ground, as he gasped deep lungfuls of air into his chest. A virulent weakness ran through his body, and he almost let go of the searching fingers in the whole-body relief of being able to breathe again. He collapsed onto the floor, rolled onto his side, his back hitting the coffin. With this came the reminder, something was still inside, maybe soon to reach a second hand for him, and he clambered back up and against the wall, holding those wriggling finger bones all the while, eyes closed against the nothingness, not hearing a sound but the clacking movement of the dead hand.

"Why does this keep happening to me?" he whined.

A few moments longer he stood there, fear and duty fighting exhaustion, then he shoved his own hand down deep in his pocket, relieved to feel the cool steel of his lighter. He flicked it open and held it high, taking in what little there was to see.

He stood upon a stone floor next to the coffin, with its lid hanging open, in a small and rectangular room. There was little space between him and the casket, for the centre of the room was taken up by a large stone plinth, upon which the coffin had rested before he knocked it to the floor in his death throes.

There was nothing more, except a stone ceiling and stone walls, and one black door at the far end.

He was in a tomb. A small tomb, designed to hold a single body.

He made for the door, still gripping the bony appendage in his hand. He searched around for a handle, but there was none. He slammed into the door with his shoulder and hit cold steel. He almost smacked a hand down on it, called out for help, but then realised… What if Molly were just outside? Waiting right there with Tareq and Waleed?

It went against his nature to do nothing, but he knew it was wiser to take the time to think his options through.

Percy threw the hand down and snapped the coffin lid shut on it. He took a seat on top to keep it closed, as he could easily see the latches that would have kept it sealed had been broken in the fall. He lit a cigarette and deeply replenished his lungs with unsavoury air.

He wondered briefly at the necessity of being able to lock a coffin from the outside. At the person who had designed that coffin and what their train of thought had been when they screwed the latch on there. Presumably they'd known it was going into a tomb, to sit here on its plinth forever, all alone.

And that idea drove one further moment's reflection.

A tomb of their own. Right in the centre of Paris. Who might have been able to afford that?

Just whose tomb was he in?

He set to studying the grey edge of the stone podium behind him, holding his lighter close. He slid to the end of the coffin, keeping the lid down always, but running his eyes all along the expanse, searching. At the end, he was forced to stand and stretch, keeping one foot on top, but from there he found the front of the plinth and moved the light of his flame close.

He saw it written there, but still his fingers traced the etched lines in disbelief, as though he needed to prove to himself that it was real and solid.

He stared at the words.

His eyes flitted back to the coffin.

He read the words over again.

Edgar Degas.

His eyes latched onto the coffin.

He whispered, "Oh, no. What have I done?"

Percy fell to his knees and wrenched the lid of the casket back open.

CHAPTER FIFTY-ONE
STANDARD ZOMBIE PROTOCOL

Joe felt like he'd been walking for hours. Too long. Far too long, with no sign of Percy.

He began to wonder if the sheath was a red herring, and Percy was Molly's true goal all along. That she'd only sent him here to distract him, while she took Percy far away, somewhere Joe would never find him. But why bother? Why didn't she kill him when she had the chance?

Yet another turn, and up on the right of the path, a captivating, gorgeous grave came into view. It was that of a man, his full, life-sized body represented in copper, dead and laid out long with the folds of a sheet covering his legs and feet. His head lay back, lips parted from having taken his final, painful breath. An elegant and heroic figure, the green of the oxidised copper dripped like blood from the effigy of his person, down over the concrete plinth that supported him.

The darkness shifted somehow, and Joe's eyes fell upon the black and barely visible form that lay out long atop the grave.

As though waking from a nap, Molly rolled onto her side, stuck a hand beneath her head, and sighed out, "You didn't find him, did you?"

The knife was weighty in Joe's hand. But what use would it be? She was right. He couldn't kill her yet. Not in this sea of graves that he'd traversed for so long already, without any sign of his beloved.

"And I guess you don't have the sheath, either?"

"Where is he?" The words were hollow on his lips, plainly desperate. If he'd hoped to gain an upper hand, a chance at bartering, it went with the pathetic plea in his voice.

She pushed herself up with a weary groan, sounding like someone who'd been interrupted for the dullest of reasons. Her legs dropped over the front of the statue, and she leaned back on two arms, stretching out her spine. "You'll never find him. And you're almost out of time." She glanced around the overcrowded graveyard, at nothing in particular so far as he could see. "Or maybe he's already dead. Though I probably shouldn't tell you that."

Joe's grip tightened on the blade. He wondered at the way she left herself so completely exposed, but he was thankful for what he took to be her stupidity. "If he's dead, you're next."

Molly laughed, but even in the thick of the unnerving interaction, it struck Joe as a sad sort of laugh, short and lack-lustre. "If only you could."

Joe edged a step closer, foot rolling from heel to toe with practised silence.

Molly paid him scant attention, searching the night sky through wisps of fog, head languid, eyes flat and glazed. "If only anyone could. I think this may be it. And it's not much. This world of yours, four hundred years of it, and it's still not much."

He couldn't kill her yet, but if he could get closer, get a hand on her, there were other ways. "You don't think you can die?"

Her head snapped across, darkly focused, as though she'd forgotten for a moment that he was there. "I can't. Not ever."

She delivered it in an accusatory, disappointed, provoking sort of way. Almost a challenge. The insinuation in her tone surprised him, and he couldn't help but ask, "Is that what you want? You *want* to die?"

"No." She shook her head, just a little, her voice soft. "Yes. Yes and also no. I had a life, a long time ago, and I want that back. And I can't have that back. Because I don't remember it. Does that make any sort of sense to you?"

Joe, unsure, wanted her talking, so he gave a slight sound of understanding while he closed the distance.

She stared at the ground, brow contracted in thought as she explained, "I have memories of memories. I remember remembering things, you understand? Because I've thought about those things over and over. And when they took my head, and they hung me up... my hair fell out, strand by strand. My skin flaked off my skull. I didn't feel it, but I knew it was happening. And I thought..." Joe froze as her eyes slid back to him. "Why was I a dead thing to them? Why did they watch it? Why did they listen to my screams, and drink their drinks, and go home to their beds? And my hair would fall on the floor. And I would scream, and my skin would flake, and they would drink. Then they would go home. And my hair would fall... It was long and black, just like Cleo's."

The tale of Molly's death, the horrors of her torture and demise, the feeling of her skull in his hands, while he was surrounded by people who saw her as nothing more than an entertaining ghost story, were all still with Joe. He'd felt her history viscerally. And even in his anger, his desperation, her past conjured the same note of sorrow and sympathy in him. He said, "Cleo's trapped in there now. In your skull. Just like you were." It was an appeal to humanity in something that he wasn't certain was human at all. In any form anymore. But his soul had latched onto her sadness. Her loneliness. The hurt. All the emotions that ran in parallel with his own from long ago, that he'd discovered so recently still hadn't left him.

Joe thought he felt a common thread running between them, just for a moment, therefore he was surprised when she replied, "And why shouldn't she be? She's better off in there."

A chill sank over Joe with the statement, given with clear eyes, like it was an obvious truth. "Better off like you were?"

Molly spoke indulgently, much as a mother might when explaining a simple concept that her child had failed to grasp. "She loved him, your Percy. She does love him. Adores him. And so she never told him so many things. All the things her husband did to her. A prince. So powerful. But I remember." She raised a hand some small way into the night air, as though listening to the memories trailing on the faint breeze. "Four hundred years. And nothing changes. She's trapped safe, or she's trapped unsafe. But she's always trapped."

Joe gave the words straight from his chest. "Percy can stop it. He can do anything. He's..."

But how useless it was to speak in the face of Molly's coolly mocking eyes. Cleo was rich. Powerful by a normal person's standards. And she was too scared to even tell Percy the whole truth. Who could know better than she did what lay in store for her, or for Percy, if he tried to help?

Molly seemed to read his thoughts. Her head tilted, like she was observing the black ball of guilt and shame forming in his stomach. "You have so much faith in him, don't you?"

He lifted his head to meet her gaze. "I do."

"It hasn't got you far. To a graveyard in Paris. While he bleeds and dies, maybe metres away." She leaned forward, eyes keen for his reaction. "How does that feel?"

"Why are you doing this? You want the sheath? I'll give it to you. Percy doesn't need to be involved. It's coming, it's on the way, and I'll hand it over, no questions asked, so long as you give him back alive. He's done you no wrong, and you must..."

How Joe hated to admit it, to tap into those memories, but he felt he had little choice. "If you remember that Cleo loved him, then you must remember him. He's good, and he's kind, and he's strong, and he doesn't deserve this."

Lifting her chin, she looked down her nose at him. "Deserve what? What is it you think I'm going to do to him?"

Perplexed, trying to figure out just exactly how mad she was, he shouted, "To die! Here, tonight, alone in this cemetery. To be taken away from me. A man who loves him. Deeply and forever. He doesn't deserve that, any more than I do!"

"Oh, but Joe, Percy won't remember a thing afterwards. You needn't worry about that. He won't remember the pain, or his death, or you. Not really. It will be a memory of a memory of a memory, and nothing more. Until one day, he'll wonder, did any of this really happen? Were you ever real? Or were you just a daydream?"

"What?" The word came weak, eking out of his gut, his brain joining the dots before his mind would allow him to accept the horror of Percy's fate.

"He won't die tonight," Molly went on. "Not forever. Just for a short, difficult time, much like I did. Only not as painful as when I did. And then I'll fix him. Because I do remember." Her voice was silken as that of any lover, silken as his own was so many long mornings, by Percy's side, his arms around him, pouring out a thousand heartfelt promises of unending love and devotion. "I remember him. I remember his body. I remember his smile. I remember that Cleo wasn't his one, any more than he was hers. But you are. You're the one for him. His great love in this life that I'm choosing to cut short. Or, you *were…*"

Molly slid down from the grave, and Joe, despite himself, took a step back. She clicked Cleo's long fingers, and her two zombie off-siders appeared out of the darkness.

"But now he's mine. And when I reunite the sheath and the

spear, when I tear this world of yours apart, he'll still be mine. When I've dismantled your governments, your monarchies, your entire society, and rebuilt it all by myself, he'll be by my side. And you'll be gone. You, and all those like you." Molly ran her eyes over Joe's black cloth, from his shoes all the way up to the collar at his throat, that for the first time in his life felt like it was choking him, as he remembered he was a walking, talking vision of the Church. A symbol of the beliefs and people that had set Molly's body on fire, strangled her, tortured her, taken her head and set it on a plaque in a pub for four hundred years.

Her voice seethed over her lips with a hatred she'd kept under wraps until that very moment. "Tell me, how does that *feel*, priest?"

Tareq and Waleed closed in on either side of Joe, and even as his subconscious instincts prepared his muscles to fight, the shocked words ripped out of him, "Wait, you think *I'm* the morally questionable half of this relationship?"

Waleed's strong fist, recently reattached to his body, but thoroughly functional again, swung at Joe's stomach at speed, to be blocked by his strong wrist. "I killed one guy! One! Deliberately. But he left me with no other choice."

Tareq looped an arm around to take Joe's neck. Joe ducked, ramming an elbow beneath his ribs, eliciting not even a breath of pain. Waleed's arms slammed down on his shoulders from behind. He thrust his wrists across each other like a cross, slammed Waleed's full weight against his back as he bent, and threw him over his head to the concrete.

Joe backed up, Tareq in fast pursuit.

What would Percy do?

He'd aim to kill and not think twice about it.

And that was the only way Joe was going to get to him in time.

Standard zombie protocol.

In one smooth motion, he flipped the blade, raised it high, and rammed it down. With a flash, it smashed straight through Tareq's right eye. His head slammed back, his body followed, and he landed on the sharp corner of a grave, his shattered brains spilling out onto the ground with a squelching smack.

All the force of Waleed's powerful form came at him, but he still had the paring knife in his arm holster. It took but the simplest twitch of Joe's wrist to grab the thing, twist it, and drive it sideways straight through Waleed's ear. He slowed, stumbled, then fell flat at Joe's feet.

Molly's voice drifted across the silent path. "I didn't expect that from you—"

Another knife came from his pocket and missed her by an inch. It was his last, and he ran for it, but by the time he had his hand on it, she'd slipped behind an enormous gravestone. He was quick in pursuit, but the graves were thick and many, and the dark hid her from his sight.

She showed little fear beyond a basic self-preservation instinct when she called out, seemingly from where he'd just been, "They won't be happy now."

They?

Blood running like ice in his veins, Joe retraced his steps towards her voice, knife at the ready, hoping to take her out, but already aware of what horror he was likely to find instead.

A sliver of moonlight sparkled on the chunks of brain that lined the pavement—glinted and shivered, as the pieces twitched, trembled, vibrated in place, then flipped, flopped, and made their way slowly but as one mass towards the half-empty cavity of Tareq's skull.

"No," Joe whispered. "No." Then he spun around, searching fruitlessly for Molly, and yelled, "This isn't a fair fight!"

But Waleed was already climbing to his feet with the uncontrolled, grotesque movements of a puppet on a string.

Joe slashed again, hitting him in the stomach this time. He barely even bent. Joe raised the knife a little higher now, but that was when he felt the wet slap on his cheekbone.

He knew what it was before he dared to look. But it was look and understand or die, so he forced his head down to where a puddle of brain sat scrunching and squelching, with clear and disturbing intent.

It was the sort of sight that would hold most men in its thrall long enough for a piece of animated brain to get one good leap in. But Joe knew better, and by the time it made the foul flight, it met only his shoulder, then he was gone into the trees.

"Percy!" he screamed. "Percy? Where are you?"

No call came back for him, and he swore furiously at the enormity of the surrounding cemetery. Avenues and avenues, graves and graves, labyrinthine and surreal. Percy could be anywhere. Was he too laid out on a grave like Molly had been? Nearby? Or was he stuck in one of these tombs? Or worse?

"Percy!"

Tareq and Waleed were behind him, recovering fast. He knew it logically and intuitively. His only direct foes until they found him, that he was aware of, were pale crawlers and Molly. He hadn't heard a growl since he touched down on consecrated ground. She was half his size, no match for him physically should he be able to get her within his grasp, he thought, so he was quite surprised when she stepped lithely from a black parting between two graves, raised a fist, and floored him with one hard punch.

The air was knocked out of him by that well-aimed jab straight to the diaphragm, and his knife clattered to the concrete. Gasping, he pushed himself up on scraped and bruised fingers, pain shooting through his legs and arms, which was doubled when merciless hands clenched tight at his biceps and wrenched him to his feet.

Joe struggled against their hold, his lungs howling for a full breath of air, as Molly fronted up to him. "He's around here somewhere. In fact, I think he could probably hear you if you screamed just a little louder."

Feeling the uselessness of struggling against his two zombie captors, now fully reformed just as though he'd never touched them at all, Joe let his body relax, concentrating only on getting those desperately needed breaths back into his lungs to clear his dizzy, oxygen-deprived mind.

But his mind did clear, and in record time too, with alarm that set every nerve to horrified attention when Molly said, "Boys, let's have a cook-up."

CHAPTER FIFTY-TWO

THE RIB BONE'S CONNECTED TO...

Percy had set his lighter upright on the floor, flame at a medium burn. It threw a meagre and flickering light about the tiny space, and blew out frequently with every gust of wind that drifted beneath the tomb's door. But Percy barely noticed. As quickly as the fire flickered and died, he clacked it back to life, and zeroed in on the task before him with no thought of the likely dire consequences of his actions. He'd cross that bridge when he came to it.

He was no expert in human anatomy. Yes, he knew which arteries to strike for the best payout of blood. He knew just how to gash them, long and jagged, so they'd be irreparable. He knew how to aim for pain, to maim, and to disarm with the least impact, rarely as he chose that latter option. But the sorting of broken and dusty bones back into the shape they'd held in life was close to beyond him.

Ribs are easy enough. Smallest to largest, isn't it? But was that a humerus or a tibia? How tall had the man been? Would any of this hurried arrangement help his cause?

Percy reflected, even if the creature was a malignant

407

demon of the damned, would that have made him so very different from so many artists who came before?

His expectations for Joe were shifting fast. No longer did his partner need to arrive in time to prevent him from suffocation deep beneath the ground in an unmarked grave. Now he only needed to arrive in time for Percy to escape from a newly resurrected zombie Degas until they could figure out what to do with him.

Percy's mind ticked over the possibilities as he moved what he hoped was a shard of hip into place. This would be the grandest art restoration he'd ever had a hand in. And what knowledge would Degas bring back from the dead? Where had he been? What had he seen? Did a living skeleton need a brain for higher cognitive function, such as art conception, creation, and appreciation? If they could think to kill, why not to paint? And why had this idea never once occurred to him? And just how soon could he talk Joe into a hunt for the lost *Necronomicon* so he could use it to hone his skills of necromancy to the level that Molly seemed to have honed hers? Would it bother Joe if he started raising the dead for such an altruistic purpose?

A rustling came from outside, calling Percy from his thoughts and task. He cut the light and rushed to the door, ear pressed close, fingertips on cold steel for stability. The rustling approached. Dry leaves disturbed, crunching, and not a breath of sound besides.

It could have been Joe. That would have been Percy's first conjecture, but there was no call for him. It would have been smart to stay quiet, of course. Molly was out there somewhere, hot zombie and average zombie in tow, and surely Joe would be trying to find Percy on the down-low.

Perhaps he should signal somehow? But what if that only drew attention to Joe, and left him exposed, with no help from Percy, locked up in here? Or what if it wasn't Joe at all? What if it was Molly, stopping by to listen for his scratching on the casket lid? Or, finding no sound, coming to gloat over his death while she awaited his fiancé?

Percy made the decision to keep quiet. It felt like a lump of obsidian in his chest, but it was safer that way. If not for him, then for Joe.

He waited regretfully by the door, the darkness of the room seeming to settle on his shoulders as the sound of life stilled, dissipated into nothing. Then he dropped back to the floor to carry on with his morbid task.

He'd done most of the reconstruction as correctly as he could. What was left in the bottom of the coffin, he scooped up, hands covered in body dust and scraps of old cloth, and he sifted out the solid material. Which bits were fingertips or toe bones, he knew not. The teeth, at least, that he was ashamed to admit he was responsible for loosening from their frame, were easy enough to pick free, and he'd arranged maybe five, when there came a new sound at the door.

A sniffing, snaffling sound, which blew a spray of fine dust into the air, accompanied by a great shadow cast by the meagre light without. This came with a rasping growl that was amplified tenfold by the architecture of his tomb, swirling on the misty rays.

Percy's eyes were glued to the door. His heart doubled its pace, and he wrapped his fingers around the sharpest shard of broken bone within his reach.

There was a clank. The screech of metal. Some external latch released.

The door began to move…

CHAPTER FIFTY-THREE
CRISPY-FRIED PRIEST

Molly had come prepared, and within minutes, Joe, though he fought valiantly, found himself strapped immobile to an enormous statue of the virgin Mary. His back was pressed against hers, and where she looked out over one half of the cemetery, hands clasped in prayer, his own were tied painfully tight behind him, his last vision of the earth to be a sea of death.

Tareq and Waleed didn't have much to do now they'd delivered him to his fate. The pyre had been set in advance. The rope that was wrapped around his chest had awaited him. All the long walk to and through the graveyard, his short talk with Molly, all of it had been a meandering, easy, casual line with which she had reeled him in to die.

And how simple he'd made it. Not a thought for himself. Not a thought for anything but Percy.

"It hurts," Molly called up, careless of his struggles against the unforgiving binds. "A lot. You think you can imagine what it is to burn to death, but you have no idea. When was the last time you maybe… burned the tip of a finger?"

"Let me go. Please. I'm not like them." To this plea, he added the billionth desperate shout of, "Percy!"

"It's so painful that all at once, you go a little bit mad. You almost leave your body, in a way. But you don't. You feel it all, but you feel nothing else. There is nothing but pain. Nothing but the madness of unrelenting, burning horror."

"Molly, please," he tried, struggling against the rope. "I can help you. I'm sorry. I'm sorry for what they did to you. But I didn't do that. You can't—"

"Fire!" she shouted, her voice echoing all throughout the cemetery, bouncing off every stone surface in the vicinity and back into Joe's ears like a metal skewer.

"Molly, stop! Percy!" The graveyard became a blur, swimming in his panicked vision as he scanned the darkness desperately, tried the blank faces of his captors, couldn't even capture the attention of Molly, busy rifling through Tareq's pockets like he was another of Cleo's expensive handbags. Until she found what she was after…

It was a match. One small match. One tiny movement, one tiny spark, and one tiny flame. But the sticks at his feet were dry and crisp and thirsty.

Molly enjoyed the fear, the way Joe's eyes latched onto that little match. She took her time. She lit a cigarette with it, took a deep drag, and let the match burn almost all the way to her fingertips. She tilted the small stick, so the flame was just as long and strong as the speck of kindling could make it, then she dropped it.

The flame took hold with terrifying speed, growing bigger with every meagre breath of night air. The tendrils of fire licked Joe's legs, the soles of his shoes burning molten against his feet within seconds.

"How does it feel, priest?" she yelled, the black of his religious garb glowing orange in the light of the flames, bright in those hazelnut eyes as he refused to look away, even as the fire burned up all but his last shred of hope: that Percy was out there somewhere. That he had escaped from whatever trap she'd put him in. That Joe, who had done everything exactly right this time, had at least been a distraction for long enough. That he hadn't let him down, and doomed him to an empty half life, living as a mindless zombie.

His head fell back against the statue in defeat, in desperation. The rubber of his shoes melted and bubbled. He could feel the leather warp beneath his feet, pain searing at his ankles, up his calves, as his clothes began to catch. "Percy," he whispered. "Oh, god, please."

Molly leaned her head back in cool amusement, took another drag and puffed out a long plume into the night, mingling with the smoke of Joe's pyre. "God?" She laughed. "Look around, priest. Does it look like anyone's coming for you?" Molly tapped a tip of ash to the ground, and with a cruel smile and dead eyes asked, "Where's your Saviour now?"

The glowing tip of that cigarette drifted silently into the air, then extinguished itself into nothing, having been hewn sharply with a soft whistle of movement that was so fast, it was imperceptible to the eye in the semi-darkness. The movement kept on, a ruffle on the wind and nothing more until the rope that held Joe to the virgin Mary snapped, and Percy's bejewelled dagger clattered to the ground. Joe dropped, shoving off the statue just in time to save himself from falling into the fire, landing instead on the cool stone of a grave, his eyes finding Percy's, sharp, determined, and more murderous than he'd ever seen them before. "There he is."

A long rib bone slid into Waleed's gut and ripped from the base all the way up and across, letting his intestines spill to the ground before he was shoved down onto them. Tareq got it in the throat the second he went for him. The side of his neck gashed open with a ribbon of blood that splashed across Molly's unmoved face. Molly watched the lot, head high, horribly sure of her body's place in Percy's mind. That he wouldn't raise a hand to her, despite the glint of pure violence that still terrified Joe somewhere deep inside.

Percy never paused. Red-handed, jagged hunk of bone dripping with the blood of her zombies, he was within striking distance in half a second. Joe's stomach coiled like a snake, and all the venom of it—the still-hot soles of his shoes and the crackling sticks on the ground by his grave—almost stopped him, almost stole that thread of humanity that, in Joe, was irrepressible. But it wasn't Molly he was thinking about.

The weapon shone white and cruel as Percy raised it, and "Percy, stop!" Joe screamed.

But it was already too late.

The shard sank, so deftly, straight into her chest. Through the skin, blood easing its procession, it pierced her heart all the way through, until that once-pale tip of Degas's rib burst out the other side.

And then Joe saw what he knew was coming. The deed done, Percy's hand let go of the makeshift dagger with a tremble. All the malice gone, he stared, horrified, into the eyes of his friend. He said nothing, for what could he say? She was all shock, pain, hurt clearly written in every line of her face. And perhaps it was that. The way Percy could see the crushed expectation there. The sense of betrayal. As though she was actually Cleo.

Scarlet ran full and voluminous over her chest, soaking the black dress, dripping to the ground in a pool that glittered in the moonlight. She stumbled back, one step, two, three and four in quick succession, then caught herself with an unsteady wobble. Her eyes dropped from Percy to the bone still sticking out of her chest. She returned them to him, shocked, but now with a modicum of offence. "Ouch!"

Percy's face cleared a touch at the unexpected response, taking on a shade of bafflement amongst the horror.

Breathing hard, for the blade was true and did not pierce her lungs, Molly wrapped her hand around the bone and pulled. Her body twitched and trembled with the effort, the pain she must have felt, but she didn't shed a single tear.

Both Percy and Joe stared in stupefied silence. Now, indeed, would be the time to attack again, but the backs of their minds were alight with the questions—what was this thing? If that didn't stop her, what on earth would? Exactly how fucked were they both? But at the front, that usually conscious part of both minds simply watched.

Long was the bone she drew forth. Long and curved and scarlet. She tripped a few steps further back with the volition of release, then she raised the rib up, examining its sharp tip.

She dropped it, the crack of the bone hitting the ground finally breaking Percy's and Joe's stunned trances.

All three looked at the rib sitting there, then her eyes drew Percy's back, and she said, "I really didn't think you'd go through with it. And to think... I didn't have the heart to kill you myself."

Percy had no opportunity to make a reply. Molly threw both hands up into the air, and the pavement lifted beneath his feet, cracked in two, and he was thrown to the side and into a jagged row of graves.

The concrete of the grave beneath Joe cracked open. He rolled to his side, falling onto a flowerbed. He shuffled to sitting, hands still tied behind his back, pushing himself against the stone, using it as leverage to try to clamber to his feet. He pulled one foot back, shifted his weight onto it, pulled the other leg for support... But that leg didn't move.

It was stuck.

Caught.

Held.

Joe looked down in terror to find a white and bony hand

reaching up out of the ground, fingers twisting around his ankle, clasping him in a death grip.

"Fuck! Fuck, fuck, fuck, fuck!" Joe hissed under his breath. He yanked at his captured leg, fruitlessly, for another skeleton hand stuck up out of the dirt, taking his shin in the same painful hold. A third came up around his other leg, and he heard, with some consternation, a scratching at the top of the broken grave above him. He struggled against the fingers that dug into him, pulled at him with a pressure that spoke of so much more beneath the ground, trying to push through the dirt.

Another hand rose up with a tuft of earth, and this took his thigh. Joe fought against his binds, the rope burning into his wrists, on the verge of tears at the stupid helplessness of it all, when if he'd just had one hand free, one leg free, what he could have done then.

A fifth bony hand settled on his shoulder from above, crept down and down his chest, then around his throat. And that was it. The moment Joe thought he would die, silent and strangled in Montmartre Cemetery.

A crack sounded, that of strong, human flesh meeting a bony skull, and Percy's fist knocked the head clean off the thing that still had a hold of Joe's neck. He threw the arm to the ground with a clatter, stomped a foot down on the bone that held Joe's thigh, wrenched the other from his bent leg. Joe kicked it out, knocking both remaining hands off, and in a second, he was standing, pulled to his feet. His chest hit Percy's, and Percy's strong arm slid around his back, holding him tight against him, his eyes searching, scared, then his lips on Joe's.

Joe's entire body fell into the kiss, and the sound of graves cracking open, the clack and scratch of bones seeking them out, all the terrors of the night sank away, and Joe didn't care anymore. If they died, right then and there, he'd do it in Percy's arms, the two of them together, and none of it would matter. Paris could burn. The world could end. So long as he went down with Percy's kiss on his lips.

But Percy broke it, turned him, slit the rope that held his hands with his trusty dagger. Around again, dizzy with speed and complete displacement, Percy caught Joe's cheek with his hand. "Are you all right?"

Joe laughed, smiled, could barely form an answer, but the concern on Percy's face and in his voice demanded one. "I'm fine. Totally fine. Percy…"

Joe threw his arms over his shoulders and kissed him back, tripping forward over another hand that came for them. Percy crunched another as he braced himself against Joe's adoration. Percy's fingers shifted to the back of his neck, fingertips sliding into his hair, where Joe loved them, remembered them, wanted them always.

Breathless, Percy dipped his forehead softly against Joe's. "When I saw you like that…."

Joe shook his head gently, refusing to break the contact. "Nothing happened. Thanks to you."

"I love you." It came out like a plea. A desperately sad, almost broken sound that made Joe take Percy's face and kiss him even harder, as if to prove that he was still here, flesh and blood and in his hold. Their two bodies pressed together, as though no closeness, no touch, would ever be enough again.

"I love you," Joe whispered, both hands squeezing his biceps. Still he kissed him, not unaware of the crumbling of stone monuments around them, but eventually he forced himself to draw back just far enough to ask, "Are we going to do this?"

Percy gave a firm nod, and Joe pulled away.

But Percy caught him around the waist, and pulled him straight back, one hand gripping his dagger, one hand holding Joe against him, one thigh sliding against the inside of Joe's, with such strength, and such a gorgeous love for Joe in his smile. "One more, handsome."

Joe gave the kiss with all his heart.

Percy released him and said, "I found this." From his jacket pocket, he produced his own favourite kitchen knife. The one Joe had long since lost somewhere in the cemetery, searching for him, fighting for him.

Joe accepted it, forcing it into the cloth holster on his arm. Then he took Percy's hand to lead him… he had no idea where.

But it hardly mattered to Joe now. They would fight. They would kill. Maybe they would die. But finally, they were back together.

CHAPTER FIFTY-FOUR

PERCY AND JOE REGROUP

To say Percy was shell-shocked would be an understatement. He'd thought of Joe the whole time he was trapped—been desperate to get to him—but he never once imagined he'd come across the sight he had. The revulsion of knowing what Molly was doing to him, the thought of his screams, the deep-seated hatred he felt for himself that he wasn't there. As though he could have fought whatever spell put them all to sleep. As though he could have broken down a solid iron door with his bare hands. But that failing sat deep in his gut, regardless.

Then he'd killed Cleo. Maybe she wasn't dead, and maybe she wasn't Cleo, but he'd killed her. Sunk a blade into her heart as though she was nothing, and he felt it, the blood still sticky on his fingers, a constant reminder of his coldness. His inhumanity. When even Joe had found it in himself to try to stop him.

"Are you all right?" The hand that tugged at his lifted him, just like it always did, from the muck and filth of his regret, and there he was. Joe. Beautiful, vital, alive.

Percy clasped his hand tighter, escaping with him into a tuft of trees, one of the few spots they could find away from the erupting graves. Rather than worry him even more with his dark thoughts, he said only, "I don't know how to kill her." Because even if bile swam in his throat at the idea, he knew he had little choice but to do it again.

"She's mad," said Joe. "Completely mad. She wanted me here alone. She set this trap. It's some kind of, well, I guess you'd call it religious trauma, but of a pretty significant magnitude."

"She's got a good motive," Percy conceded, meaning it more as a discussion of what they were up against than any sort of forgiveness.

Even so, Percy could feel the searing heat in Joe's eyes, which he refused to meet when Joe snapped, "They were Protestants!"

"Totally different, I know. Nothing like the Catholics burning witches on the continent." Joe took a breath to interrupt. Percy didn't let him finish. "For the record, I don't think it's okay that she tried to burn you."

"Thank you!" Joe replied, about as sarcastically as he'd ever said anything.

"But now we know what we're dealing with. Somewhat. Someone who has a very good and very strong reason for wanting to see you dead."

"I didn't do anything to her!" Joe vomited out.

"I'm not saying you did. *I* don't want you dead."

"Well, thank you very much, Percy, that makes me feel so much better."

"I'm just saying I understand why *she* would want to kill you."

"For fucks's sake." But as always, it was said with all the warmth and humour Percy's ridiculous outbursts always brought about in Joe.

"And now we're getting somewhere. So she has a vendetta against you, the Church—"

"And humanity, in general, by the sounds of it," Joe hurriedly explained, checking over his shoulder to see if any skeletons had managed to dig themselves fully out of their graves to give chase. "She has some plan, that if she can get the sheath and the spear together, she'll destroy everything. Tear society apart and rebuild it, which is obviously a bit outlandish."

"Not at all. Not if the mythology around those artefacts holds true, the power she would wield is beyond anything we could imagine."

"That's worrying."

"That's an understatement."

"And she remembers everything. She remembers dying, she remembers being trapped in that skull, but more than that, she remembers everything Cleo remembers. And I know you said she'd had a hard time. And that seems to be what Molly's zeroed in on. Had she taken someone else, someone with no problems and an easy life, someone who thought the best of people and the world—"

"The type of person who would never have been drawn to Barmiston Hall the way Cleo was." A very matter-of-fact state-ment that carried an air of melancholy, and Joe knew what Percy was thinking. And just then, he loved him even more for it. Joe squeezed his hand. "We were just friends," Percy added, as though he were a doll and Joe had just pushed the voice acti-vation button.

"I know." Joe's smile was hidden in the dark as they trudged on, silent and moss-covered graves almost black around them. "But that explains why she didn't kill you. I really believe she never thought you'd do it. She thought she was some kind of safe with you."

"Well, she'll be pissed off now."

"Big time."

"She did try to have me killed, though. In a roundabout way."

"What happened? Where were you?"

"She stuck me in a coffin with a zombie."

Joe stopped, spun Percy around, examining him all over. "You didn't get bitten, did you?"

"No, I took his teeth out." Joe wondered at the averted gaze, the almost guilty look that came over him when he said it. "And he was very dried out. No saliva. I'm guessing that's how it spreads."

"I never thought about that. Does it have to be a fresh zombie? Can they even turn us?"

"I don't know."

"But where were you? How'd you get out?"

Percy's face softened with a sheepish grin. "It was Moxie. She used her powers to let me out. I don't know where she is now. I heard you call, and I ran as fast as I could to get to you. I'm sure she's around here somewhere." He recommenced their walk, saying, "I'm just glad I didn't let you get rid of her."

"You were the one who wanted to get rid of her!"

"Details. Anyway, there's something else I should probably tell you, and it's nothing to worry about. We're in a graveyard full of reanimated skeletons, after all, so what's one more?" Still he walked, but suddenly he gave Joe the impression he was trying to get away from more than skeletons.

Joe stumbled forward to keep up and to read his expression. "I'm sorry? What do you mean?"

"It's more of a philosophical question at this stage," Percy waffled, eyes ahead. "I would need you to consider art, and the question of what art is. Is it in the eye of the creator? The beholder? And you know, if we took all the dead-inside pricks out of the art world, just kept the virtuous, can you imagine the saccharine array of utter bullshit we'd be left with?"

Joe slipped under a branch that Percy held back for him. "What are you talking about?"

Percy paused there, hands expressing whatever he wasn't quite coming to. "I'm just saying that if I'd done a thing——"

"A thing?"

"An art project——"

"Is this important right now?"

"No." Because how could it be? Right here, this second, chasing a witch, the dead rising around them… "No, it's nothing," Percy agreed, relieved. "All that matters is we're here together, and we're going to end this now. Even if I don't know how. Maybe I can appeal to her hatred of the Church and general misanthropy? I feel like we identify somewhat——"

"Or maybe not?" Joe suggested.

"When we find her, let me do the talking."

"I'm not sure that's a great idea."

"Trust me, handsome. How about we find her, tie her up, take her back to the apartment, and we'll work at it until she sees things our way and gives Cleo her body back? I've done it once before, you know."

Joe laughed. "That's true. You did well."

Percy took a hand to Joe's cheek and kissed him. "We'll be fine. The important thing is that she never got her hands on the sheath." As the words shot a shard of ice into Joe's veins, Percy chuckled out, "Because in that case, we'd have been royally fucked."

"H-how fucked, exactly?" The two stepped out of the trees into the scant moonlight of a small clearing—a circle of grass, surrounded on all sides by tall and teetering graves. "It's useless without the Spear of Destiny, isn't it?"

"Yes. But if I were Molly…" Percy gave brief hesitation, but must have decided it wasn't worth troubling Joe about what he would have done if he was a powerful witch with a four-hundred-year vendetta against mankind. "Well, it doesn't matter. I knew you'd never give over that kind of power, even for me. Because you have the heart of a saint, handsome. The bigger picture, humanity, that sort of thing comes first. You're just not the sort to risk all of human existence for—"

"Percy!" Leo's shout across the small clearing cut into Joe like a knife. He, Althea, and Giordano tumbled out of the darkness, Leo beaming at Percy, running, until he threw himself into his arms, knocking him back several steps.

"Leo?" Percy wrapped his arms around him, disbelieving, but still he kissed the top of his head, and though smiling, said harshly, "What the fuck are you doing here? You need to leave, all of you."

"But we got it," said Althea, smile just as wide and proud as Leo's. "The sheath. It's right here, just like Joe said."

Giordano's strong arms lifted the box. He offered a nod and a grin, and Percy's eyes turned on Joe. It was but one short, shocked, unreadable moment before Molly's voice sang around the open space. "Finally."

She stood atop one of the higher-set graves, bloody, beautiful, and with Percy's ancient and rusted Spear of Destiny turning over and over in two hands.

Percy's eyes locked onto it with sickened recognition. "Fuck."

Tareq and Waleed stood on either side of Molly's grisly stage. Waleed's entrails dragged along behind him, and Tareq's naked chest was awash with blood that still gushed endlessly, relentlessly, from the gash Percy had made in his neck.

But for all this show of gory power and intimidation, Percy's eyes flitted uncontrollably to Joe once, again, and on the third with a grin that was both sly and deeply adoring. "You really do love me, don't you?"

Joe, always and again, on that edge of whether to cry or laugh, gave into the latter, with the helpless admission, "I do, Percy."

Percy yanked him close, leaned closer still, and said, "I guess we'd better save the world, then."

CHAPTER FIFTY-FIVE
MURDER IN MONTMARTRE

Percy raised his dagger to point at the Spear of Destiny, which Molly held between her fingers. "You'd better not have touched my Caravaggio when you took that."

With a smile, she replied, "I'm not in the habit of destroying beautiful things, Percy."

The comment set Joe's blood to boil, hating the way she could tune in to all Cleo's knowledge of Percy. But Percy replied, as though it was in any measure similar to the Caravaggio, "You almost burned my fiancé."

Molly's eyes ran over Joe, disdainful.

Percy added, "And you almost killed me."

"Oh, Percy," she cooed. "You wouldn't have stayed dead for long. I would have brought you back, just like these boys." She looked him over, with nothing but hunger in her gaze. "But unlike them, you would have had a special position. As my own *very* personal assistant."

Althea made a choking, vomiting sort of sound, Joe, a huff like a jealous fiancé might, but Percy's face softened into a slightly bashful smile. "You would have brought me back? To be your slave?"

Her nod was expressly enthusiastic. "Yes."

"Forever?"

"Of course."

Grin now spreading from ear to ear, Percy turned to Joe as though he'd just won top prize on a scratch-it card and expected Joe to celebrate with him.

Seeing Joe's expression dimmed his own somewhat.

Gruffly, Percy replied to her, "That would have been horrible. So disrespectful, to expect a man like me to spend his afterlife… like that. Awful. Horrible." He added, for Joe's benefit, "She's a true villain."

"Back to the point," Joe spat.

"Yes," said Percy, trying very hard to remember where he was going with any of it. "Molly, I like you a lot—"

Joe actually stomped his foot.

"Which I'm only saying," Percy enunciated at Joe pointedly, "to make it known that I don't want to kill you. You're clearly very smart, very tasteful—"

Joe let out a long and loud and perfectly involuntary groan.

"—and I hate the Church too—"

"Is this really how you're going to deal with it?" Joe whisper-snapped.

Percy shrugged it off with a small eye roll, finishing, "And people. A lot of them. But not all of them. And there are good people here, tonight, and in this city, who don't deserve whatever you think you're about to do to them."

She twisted the rusted shard of metal in her fingers. "With this blade?" She smiled to herself. "Do you remember when you told me how useless the sheath is? Asked me what Christ's blood had ever done for me? Shall we find out?" Her eyes cut a path to her right. "Althea? Is that your name?"

Eyes just as black and dark as the ground she stood upon, Althea snarled, "*Is that my name?* You fucking bitch."

Molly gave a goading shrug. "I'm not the one who convinced all those little girls to come away with a murderess."

Althea started straight forward with her knife, only to be wrenched back by Leo's ready hand. "Al, no. Percy, why the fuck are we talking? Why haven't you killed her yet?"

Rather than admitting to the group, especially Molly, that he had indeed tried to but actually had no idea how to kill her, Percy meandered over his words, until Molly explained instead, "Because one must run distraction. Skeletons are slow and stupid, and it takes a while for them to dig themselves out of their graves."

"What?" asked Giordano, suddenly, unnervingly aware of the echo of a clicking and a clacking behind the trees.

Percy stepped forward, moving into the centre of the small clearing, looking up at his once-friend. "Stop them. Put them back where they belong. We'll talk this out. I'll even let you keep the spear."

"How kind, Percy," she trilled. "I think I will keep it. And just for that, I'll keep you, too." Flinging her arms out long, the seal on every grave in sight lifted. The crunch and snap of breaking concrete filled the air with dust and dirt as dozens of coffins cracked wide open. With a white flash of bones, the lot clattered to the ground.

"Everyone here," Percy shouted, and in the next second, all four were in the centre of the ring, back-to-back with Percy, weapons at the ready. "You three need to head south. She hasn't opened the graves there. Be quick, take the sheath, get on a train—"

With a clap of Molly's hands, a rumble of noise came from the south side of the cemetery, this accompanied by a "Fuck!" from Percy.

The bones that lay among the freshly disturbed earth and splintered coffin shards began twitching, as though each piece had been given its own sentience and drive to form itself back into one whole. They slid and rolled, and with no sinew or muscle to help them, began to build one upon the other, toe after toe, feet, ankles, piece by piece. Some had flakes of skin attached here and there. Some took with them the ancient remnants of once-best dresses and suits. All quickly and clearly shared the same goal.

Giordano was still 'keeper of the sheath', being taller and stronger than Althea and Leo, and while he kept it tucked safely under one arm, this left him one hand only to hold and aim his gun. He'd already discharged it several times earlier in the evening, getting Althea and Leo safely past one or two pale crawlers (not that he knew what they were called), which left him now with only a few bullets and far too many targets.

Althea had desperately wanted to bring a crossbow she'd discovered amongst Percy's belongings, but having insufficient arrows, she, like Leo, had settled for knives. And like Leo, she had no real idea what to do with them other than slash at hard bone, its own special armour.

And Leo, while he unerringly believed Percy would fix everything, did not at all like the way Althea's eyes remained almost always on Molly, as though she were assessing the distance with every step, waiting for her chance to attack a woman who seemed as though she'd rip her in half as easily as look at her.

Both Joe and Percy were aware of the hopelessness of the situation from the second the group arrived on the scene. The two of them, they could fight it out alone, but their meagre resources were stretched protecting their friends.

"We'll all go," Joe decided. "Let's stick together, fight our way to the closest wall, and get you over it."

"East then," said Percy. "Let's move."

Percy and Joe advanced on the unsteady, still-reanimating skeletons. Percy was first with a strike that took the head off one of the newly raised creatures. Joe, improvising, picked up a long and sharp shard of a coffin, just the right size to wrap a fist around. He slipped it between two ribs, then forced his end down, prying the ribcage apart in one blow. Althea fell back against them as a skeleton lunged for her, but this was soon knocked back by Giordano, thrown down by Leo, and had its arms and legs broken by Althea as payback for the affront.

"Do you remember——" Percy started, only to be cut off by Joe's laugh.

"How could I forget?" He tripped up a skeleton and smashed its pelvis into so many pieces with his boot that it would never stand again. "I thought we were about to break up."

"After a first night like that?" Percy replied, slapping a skull to the left and then slicing down on its neck. "I was never going to let you go."

"Percy…" Joe blushed hotly as he knocked the legs from under another skeleton.

And in just such a manner, they battled on, Percy never letting his doubts show behind a facade of fond quips and occasional vulgarity, Joe confident in the steadfastness of Percy's words and actions. But they made it only a very small way, constantly pushed back by a multitude of white coming through the trees, crawling out of more and more graves, and the whole group woefully underpowered from the get-go. And that's when they heard the growls, low and mean, and all around, from beyond the skeletons.

"What the fuck is that?" asked Percy.

"Pale crawlers," Joe replied. "Easy to gut, but they're fast and they have big teeth."

"This is useless," Althea said breathlessly, punching and stabbing at the encroaching horror closing with every second. "There isn't a way through."

"If she's the lead villain, we need to take her out, right, Percy?" called Leo.

"They're not vampires," said Joe. "She's a witch and I'm pretty sure her spell will hold whether we kill her or not."

"It's worth a try, isn't it?" shouted Giordano, having resigned himself to one fist to fight off the onslaught.

Molly hadn't moved from her spot, nor had her hot and average zombies, watching on impassively, waiting for the skeletons to do her work.

One made a grab for the sheath, a move that took them all by surprise. Evidently, they had purpose beyond the destruction of their little group. And this made Leo snap, "Just give it to her. You don't believe that bullshit, Percy. It's just junk."

"It's two thousand years old. It was worn by a Roman soldier, who—"

"Saint Longinus," Joe offered.

"That's apocryphal," Percy spat.

"You're apocryphal," Joe threw back.

"It doesn't matter who he was. It's my only Roman sheath and she can't have it. Now on the off-chance it did hold those powers—"

"Then you'll be wanting that spear back." Althea stated the words coolly before breaking rank with startling efficiency. Small, she weaved beneath arms, cracked a tibia or two on her way past, shoved at ribcages, and made her way through the conglomeration of death, full pelt, in the straightest line possible towards Molly.

Leo was after her like a shot, ducking and criss-crossing, leaving the three hulking men little alternative but to turn back and start smashing their way through the pile in the other direction to get to them.

"Althea, don't!" Leo screamed after her, but she was already at the foot of the monument Molly stood upon. Waleed and Tareq slammed skeletons to dust in an attempt to stop her. She was nimble, athletic, a born survivor, and she fronted up to Molly with all the nous of a Surabaya girl from the wrong side of the tracks. She got in one punch that was so hard, so well-aimed, that even Percy and Joe flinched at the sound it made when she cracked Cleo's cheekbone.

"Ah, fuck!" Althea yelled, trying to shake the pain out of her hand.

"She's got super-strength," Joe shouted.

"She's got what?" Althea ducked the punch that came back for her.

"You're just mentioning this now?" Percy rounded.

"There are skeletons!" Joe screamed.

"Doesn't—" Althea doubled Molly over with a sharp elbow to the ribs "—seem that—" she smacked Molly's face down with two fists, directly into the knee she raised hard and fast bringing a gush of blood from her nose "—that tough—" she wrenched her up by the hair "—to me!" This final phrase she punctuated with a punch to the throat, at which instigation Molly dropped the spear to the concrete below, where it bounced twice, then slipped into darkness down the side of the grave.

"You're getting a raise!" Percy called.

"Don't encourage her!" Joe yelled.

Althea was wrenched off the plinth, not by Molly, but by Waleed, who finally got an arm around her waist. She grabbed for Molly to take her down with her, but he was too fast. Even so, she got a solid touch to the concrete beneath her feet and pushed back as hard as she could. Waleed stumbled but would have held, had Leo not tackled him, forcing all three back with a crash that caved Waleed's head in on a decorative spike, just as effectively as it cushioned the fall of the other two, except Leo's hip, which came down on the flat side of the Spear of Destiny.

Leo snatched it, reached for Althea, and scrambled to his feet as he pulled her up with him. On solid ground, he took both her hands, searching her over for wounds. "Are you okay?"

Her head snapped up, straight back to her target. "I'm gonna kill her." She lunged for Molly, and was out of Leo's reach, halfway back up the plinth, when she felt the crack of Molly's fist. Althea was knocked into a full spin, Leo jumped and missed, and it was Giordano's arm that came out just in time to stop her being impaled on the broken bones of the skeleton he'd most recently dispatched.

Giordano couldn't offer her a second more help than that, and she tripped back into a mass of snapping skulls when Tareq threw all his weight against Giordano. The sheath was knocked into the ever-growing pile of bones at their feet.

Using the full and considerable power of his enviable physique, Giordano rolled, taking Tareq with him, until he was on top. He locked his fine thighs over Tareq's and reached for the sheath, straining. Tareq's fist closed around his shirt, and he tried to pull him down, but Giordano had already braced against such an attack and all it did was rip the shirt clean open, exposing his sweaty, muscular chest. Tareq tried again, firm abdominal muscles firming even more as he fought his way upright, wrapping an arm around behind Giordano's neck. He pumped his pelvis up, forcing Giordano to grab him by the shoulder with one hand to steady himself, bringing the back of the other across his face with a resounding slap. Tareq only wrenched him closer, until their two naked chests were pressed together, Tareq attempting to force Giordano onto his back while Giordano struggled against his grip.

The snapped and sharp arm of a skeleton would have pierced Percy's head straight through, had it not been thwarted by Joe giving Percy a good shove. "Stop watching them!"

"I'm not!" Percy spared him a glance, then lost it back to Giordano and Tareq. "Can't you see he's… he's struggling? Wrestling him? Like that?"

Joe dodged a plank of coffin-wood that came at his chest. "Are you going to help, then?

With a vague shake of his head, eyes on the hot man and the hot zombie, "No, I don't think so." This time, a curled fist of bone got him square in the jaw. "Fuck! When did they learn to punch?"

"Serves you right!"

Joe made for the pair and soon had his fingers sunk into Tareq's hair. He raised his enormous fist, and was about to break his jaw, or worse, when Percy yelled, "Maybe not the face!"

"You slit his throat!" Joe yelled back, fist frozen in readiness.

"You did what?" Giordano shouted.

"I've had more time to think things through now," Percy called as he threw down a skeleton that had launched its entire body at him from a high gravestone. "Just break an arm or something."

Joe was only too happy to grab the arm that clamped down on Giordano's throat that very second and wrench it backward with such volition the shoulder made a loud crack, then hung loose. He was no more sympathetic with the other, soon leaving Giordano relatively unencumbered, whispering, "But his nice shoulders…"

Joe slammed a foot down on a skeletal wrist that guided bony fingers towards the sheath, snapped it upwards, and broke the hand off. He took up the sheath, muttering, "I've had enough of this."

He wrenched his knife free from its holster and began to cut a clear line for Leo, hoping he still had the spear. Percy, anticipating his move, made for the same place.

Leo, having found an enormous rock in a garden bed, had smashed his way to Althea. She was back on her feet with nothing but malice in her eyes and heart, but the revival of

Waleed, pieces of brain crawling up his shoulder and back into his broken head, made Leo throw himself in her way before she could launch her next attack, pinning her behind him. And just as well, as that very movement was the only thing that stopped a swath of pale crawlers slamming down on top of her as they poured through a gap in the graves and set upon them both.

Waleed clocked Joe, slicing fast and vicious through the crowd. He waited, as though still capable of thought and strategy, until Joe was within striking range. He raised his fist high, gathered all his strength and brought it down hard and fierce. Joe reacted instinctively. He wielded Percy's expensive and ritually sharpened kitchen knife with precision, defending himself from the dark shape that he barely caught from the corner of his eye. The blade moved swiftly, cleanly, through Waleed's wrist, as smoothly as if it were a hock of well-cooked ham.

Percy watched on in abject horror as that hand flew, spinning, flinging drops of blood as it went, around and around, to where it flopped down right by his foot.

He stumbled back so fast he tripped and fell. He was prepared for a dozen skeletons to clamber on top of him. Prepared for the hand to be back at his throat. But not remotely prepared for the timid "Mew" that sounded at his shoulder.

"Moxie!" He scooped her up, took her to his cheek, and kissed her furry face. "All right. Kill them. Use your powers and destroy the lot."

Joe fought on, making fast progress towards Leo, where Molly continued to wait, watching him with a worrying smile. Then he halted, wrenched a step backwards. Percy saw first the look of fright on Joe's face, then the glistening spectacle of Waleed's slithering entrails slipping over Joe's chest, alive, terrifying, and utterly repulsive.

"Now, Moxie!" Percy shouted, but the kitten did nothing but put her little feet on his cheek.

Giordano was busy with Tareq, who evidently had the use of his arms again; Leo and Althea were all but lost in flashes of pale skin amongst the dust, fighting desperately; and Percy was too far away from Joe to help, his hands desperately pulling at the entrails that tightened around his neck, a sea of writhing bones between them.

More and more skeletons clambered from their broken graves, more and more shapes, luminescent in the distance, closed in, the growling only got louder amidst the cacophony of groans and gasps and scratches and punches, and above it all, Molly stood, lip and cheek bleeding, watching, waiting, looking like someone who had no doubt that her enemies were about to be brutally crushed.

And why not? She had the entire graveyard. Her unable-to-be-killed zombies. Her own immortality. And then who knew? How many other people would she kill and reanimate? The whole city might be at her beck and call.

It was a completely unwinnable situation from where Percy stood, fighting on only to spare those around him a little longer, because if they also realised they were beat, not one of them showed it. But Percy knew. It rarely, very rarely, happened, but he knew when someone had got the better of him.

And he knew he had only one weapon that might work.

Not his dagger.

Not the powers Moxie suddenly seemed reluctant to use.

He had only Moxie herself.

Percy closed his eyes. He took Moxie from his shoulder by the scruff of her tiny neck. He tried to go to his dark and isolated place, the place he could always go before Joe. But Joe was a life so rich and so beautiful. Joe was the light that shone on everything, bathed everything and made it so gorgeous that his place of refuge, of dissociation, would not come. And his hand shook as he raised that dagger. His fingers barely held the fur. He knew and felt what he was going to do and it was a depth of depravity even he had never thought himself capable of.

He raised Moxie higher and higher into the air and shouted, "Molly! Stop it now or the kitten gets it!"

Her head turned sharply with the expression of one deeply perplexed at the unexpected interruption. She focused on the kitten, hard.

"Don't do it!" Joe yelled, straining at the intestines strangling him.

Percy pressed the sharp end of the dagger to the kitten's round and fluffy belly. His eyes burned into Molly's and she, in response, brought up a finger of command that saw everything stop dead. Skeletons clattered to the ground in piles of bones, Waleed's intestines turned loose and flopped in a foul heap at Joe's feet, Tareq sat as lifeless and unresponsive as ever. All was silence, every living eye on Percy and his beloved kitten, and the only sound that broke it was Moxie's purr, so happy was she to be held again by her master.

Molly was the first to speak. "Why do you think I'd care if you kill that kitten?"

"Because…" Percy glanced at Joe, who had absolutely assured him that Molly's familiar's presence in the kitten's body could turn any tide with her. "Because. Look at her. Don't you recognise her?"

Molly's head tilted to the side with the effort of her investigation. "It's a cat."

"It's not just any cat. Look at her! Look into her beautiful, big," his voice began to shake, "loyal, loving eyes."

Molly did, but she made no sign of recognition. Only seemed to be enjoying the novelty of the drama.

"I'll gut her," Percy threatened. "Little kitten entrails spilling out everywhere. I'll slit her wide open."

"Go ahead," she replied with a shrug.

Percy looked at Joe, Joe looked at Percy, and Percy hissed, "You said this would work."

"She's bluffing!" Joe declared loudly. "Spill some blood and see how she feels about it."

"Yeah," said Percy. He nodded. Firmed his grip on the dagger. "All right. Um…" He loosened his grip. Tightened it. Shifted the dagger around a bit. Then, on a cough, "Joe?"

Joe glanced at the tense and horrified crowd, then back to Percy. "What?"

Percy tilted his head sharply away from Joe. "Could you, uh, come here? Just for a moment."

"But—"

"Please. Could you?"

Joe took a moment to get moving, then picked his way awkwardly across the clearing, bones crunching with every step, until he finally made it to Percy's side. Percy whispered, "I actually can't… um… do this. So, could you?"

Joe's eyes grew larger than the full moon just now setting close to the horizon. "No. No, I don't think I can."

"Well, one of us has to."

"I will," called Althea.

"You stay the fuck away from Moxie!" yelled Percy. Then to Joe, "She's vicious. Did you see?"

Joe nodded his stern agreement.

"Look, you can—just—like this…" Percy pushed the kitten into Joe's hand, and Joe, reluctantly, sympathetically, took hold of her. Percy passed the knife across and said, "There." He called out, "Now Joe is going to kill Moxie," his voice breaking sharply on her name.

Joe whispered across, "I don't think anyone believes I can actually do this. Least of all you."

Guilty, Percy searched for a response that was anything but

the admission of his complete failure, but then Molly spoke up. "Okay."

Percy looked up hopefully. "Okay?"

She shrugged. "Okay." Molly jumped down from her grave and walked, nimble between the bones, to the centre of the clearing. "You're right. I don't want you to kill the kitten. I may have murdered dozens of children, and quite a few adults, but…" She sighed. "You win." With a motion to the bundle under Joe's arm, "You have the sheath." Then to Leo, "You have the spear." And with her eyes on Moxie, "And I have my companion. And immortal life. And magical powers. I'll tell you what…"

Joe lowered the kitten, pulling her back against his chest, where she clawed into him and scrambled straight back to Percy's shoulder.

Molly said, "You give her to me, let me go, and we're done."

Percy had been expecting it. Joe had too. It was exactly why he'd convinced Percy to keep the kitten. But it was so sudden. So easy. Too easy.

Joe said, "How about you leave and we'll bring her to you later?"

She countered with, "How about I just reanimate my skeletons and zombies?"

Percy knew it was a stupid risk to take. But he could see his friends were exhausted, cut and bleeding, close to breaking point. If she did that, it was over. So he did the only thing he knew to do, and, cradling Moxie, he moved towards Molly.

The kitten clambered up to his chin, burying her head there, purring, and breaking his heart. But he didn't let it show in any way beyond the unconscious stroking of her fur and the protective hands that held her tight by his heart.

He stopped in front of Molly, who, in her expression, looked so much like Cleo. Whose face had softened, who had an expectant sparkle in her eyes, who showed a clear fondness for him and the cat.

"You won't hurt her, will you?" said Percy, trying halfheartedly to get the tiny claws out of his shirt.

"I promise you. She'll be safe with me." She watched on, that same knowing smile playing around her bloody lips. She tried to sweeten the deal a little, revealing, "You know, I had a cat once. I loved it dearly. More than you can imagine."

Moxie nuzzled her head against Percy's chin, and for all the rest of the world, he never would have done it. But for Joe, Leo, Althea, and Giordano, he picked her off his chest, kissed her forehead, gave her one final stroke, and with wet eyes and shaking hands, placed her in Molly's upturned palms.

It was the most vulnerable Joe had ever seen Percy, as he watched Molly, frightened, desperate, horribly subjugated. The guilt Joe felt at seeing Percy like that. He wanted to be in the middle of it, protecting him, never again watching Percy step out onto that ledge. But that's what he did every time, for all of them.

Molly picked the kitten up, examined her, then brought her face in close and kissed her cheek. "She's gorgeous," she said. "Thank you."

Joe could see the way Percy's shoulders lightened, that smile that was so, so beautiful. The very essence of the man he loved so deeply. And Percy looked for him. Always for Joe first to see that Joe was happy. That Joe thought he'd done well, and that Joe loved him. That look of complete and pure love that had turned the whole world upside down for Joe in the best and most glorious way.

Then his head snapped sharply to the left with a gut-pulverising crack, and Percy dropped down dead on the wet grass of Montmartre Cemetery.

CHAPTER FIFTY-SIX

YES, YOU READ THAT CORRECTLY. THAT REALLY JUST HAPPENED. SORRY.

Joe heard nothing. Saw nothing but the limp body of the man he loved—the man he was going to marry—lying there on the ground, sharp bones sticking into him, that he did not pull away from. No breath moved his body, and it was over in the blink of an eye. Too fast. Percy was gone, and it wasn't something Joe had the ability to process.

That thing, that heap on the ground—that wasn't him. It simply wasn't. Percy was absent from it, the soul of him, the essence of him, and Joe could not fathom that change, because Percy had promised. He said he would always come for Joe. He said he would do it again and always, and it was eternity, and Percy had promised. And Joe never doubted him.

Althea was screaming, crying, Giordano was pacing somewhere, his head in his hands, and Leo, still clutching that spear, stared at the corpse in much the same way Joe did, but with more anger, more loss even, because Percy had never made him that same promise. Leo didn't know in his heart the way Joe did that Percy could not possibly be dead.

Molly tossed the kitten to the ground, and Moxie, in her animal way, seemed also to know that he was gone. She skirted the body, sniffed at his cheek, but she didn't huddle into him the way she had before. There was an emptiness in the air, in the cemetery, in all of Paris, it seemed. Everywhere but in Joe's heart.

"No," he said, shaking his head, unaware of the tears streaming down his cheeks. "No. He's fine."

"Joe…" Giordano started towards him, and Joe flinched away from the approach, holding up a hand to repel him. "No. She didn't. He's not…" But he couldn't say the words. If he didn't believe it, then why couldn't he even say it?

A sob broke out of Joe, and the sound of it felt like a betrayal. The sound of mourning someone who wasn't gone. Not at all. Because Percy would come for him. Just like he would for Percy.

Joe searched over the ground, his friends, the graveyard, trying to put it all together. Trying to find the missing piece of this bizarre puzzle that would finally make it make sense. He searched wildly, desperately, until he settled on Leo. Or more correctly, on what Leo held.

He extended the open palm of his hand. "Give me that spear."

Leo was shocked to remember that he even had it. He looked at the object with such revulsion, a pure hatred of this thing that Percy had been murdered for—even if it was what he'd lived for. He hated it for existing, for taking Percy's passion and his body and his mind. All the dangerous adventures, that drive to preserve these lifeless things that he had died for. That he'd let himself be torn away from Leo for.

He looked at the spear, then at Joe with the sheath, and he hated them all. "He's dead," Leo wept. "What the fuck are we doing any of this for?"

"For him!" Joe yelled. "He wanted—he *wants*—he *needs* this! He doesn't want her having these things, this kind of power—"

"He's fucking dead, you fuck!" And Leo might have thrown the spear straight at Joe's head, had Molly not spoken just then.

"It wouldn't be smart, Leo. Watch."

Tareq, sitting on the ground, exactly as a zombie might, staring directly ahead at nothing, suddenly became animated. Really, truly animated. His eyes cleared, his expression took full human affect, and for the first time since the night Percy had met him in the hotel in Libya, he spoke. "What… Who… How am…" He looked down at his shaking hands, then they stilled. His head raised, and he was blank again, and not one of them could fully process the idea of Tareq having been in there the whole time, stabbed, shot, beaten, slashed, broken, and still alive through it all.

"Do you want Percy back?" Molly asked. "Simple. Give me the spear."

"Percy needs that." Joe spoke through clenched teeth, angry and scared. "Don't do it."

"It's very easy for me," she said, eyes never leaving Leo's broken face. "But I'm getting tired. I'm running out of energy. If you want him back, complete, just like he was before, give me that spear."

"Give it to me," Joe insisted, flicking his fingers eagerly. "I've got the sheath. I can stop this. I can fix it."

"Otherwise," Molly interrupted, moving a little closer to Leo, who held his ground. "I can borrow your girlfriend for a while. Drain her of blood. You can watch. Before I kill you in front of her."

Joe moved in too, wary gaze shifting between Molly and Leo. "Leo, I know you don't like me. I know you haven't ever trusted me. But Percy loves me. You have to know that. He trusts me. He believes in me."

"A lot of good that did him." Leo's words were salt on an open wound.

Molly enjoyed the moment, and she ran with it, flashing

Leo a wide and confident smile. "I can put him back exactly as he was. And I can get rid of this priest for you too, if you'd like. Say the word, and you'll have Percy all to yourself, as good as new."

Leo's head turned down, the reflection of his tears on the spear catching the early rays of dawn. "I don't want you to kill him. I don't… Joe, he's dead. He's dead. How can I—"

"Leo," Joe cut in, clear as the morning light burning up the graveyard fog. "What would Percy do?"

A sad, hopeless ghost of a smile rested in Leo's gaze when he looked up. "Probably something incredibly stupid."

"That's exactly right."

"Fine." With the word that came out like venom, but which had a backbone of all the secret fondness he'd always felt for Joe deep down, he flung the spear in Joe's direction.

Heavy, true, the two-thousand-year-old blade twirled and spun and Joe caught it with the precision of a warrior.

He looked up at Molly, victory written in every beautiful feature, from the vengeful smile on his tear-stained face to the virtuous spark of glory in his eyes. "Prepare to fucking die."

It felt like triumph in Joe's hands, the sheath and the spear together at last. It felt so exactly right, the two made for each other, immaculately crafted, the blade ready to return to its home for the first time in millennia. It felt like a promise. Like all his years of service to the Church, all that time he'd spent fighting evil, all the demons and horrible things he and Percy had put their lives on the line to kill through the years, finally, all this would be recognised with this one precious gift from God.

With renewed vigour, the flame of hope—more than hope—*belief* alive in his heart, Joe slammed the blade down into its sheath. It slotted in smoothly with a satisfying *shink*, and…

Nothing happened.

But what had he been expecting? A magical fire from

heaven to shoot down and smite Molly on the spot? Percy to jump up alive and well?

But there was nothing.

A complete and utterly useless nothing.

There was no power there. He sensed it. He knew it. He realised a complete and vast emptiness, and that chasm of loss threatened to swallow him whole in the instant. Tears flooded fast and hot to his eyes, and that look on Leo's face… That look of betrayal, pure grief, hatred, all of it mingled together.

And Percy, still limp on the ground. Dirty from battle. Just left on the grass as though he was so much rubbish and rubble, refuse to rot and be gone, as though that whole beautiful life, that beautiful, beautiful being, that precious mind and soul and heart were meaningless.

Molly's mocking laughter broke into the bereft scene. "Wrong decision."

Leo had his back to her, held in Althea's arms, crying. He probably didn't even hear her, but Althea did. She radiated unalloyed hatred back, but she stayed there, arms around Leo, offering the only morsel of comfort she could in what she knew was a blow Leo would never recover from.

"And you," Molly said. Joe lifted his eyes from Percy's body to meet her hateful glare. "It's over, priest." She stretched out her fingers, and Tareq's head began to turn. Waleed's body began to twitch. Thousands of bones recommenced their macabre dance. Sure of her power, her victory, she surveyed the resurrection of her dead, as she stabbed at Joe with her final thoughts. "You've lost your friends. You've lost your love. And now, you've lost your faith."

"Oh, no," Joe said softly. "I'll never lose my faith." He took one step towards her, and Joe drove the Spear of Destiny deep into Molly's neck. A choking gasp of shock gargled in her torn throat, and her wild black eyes begged for escape, but Joe had her by the hair. He ripped her head backwards, and just as he'd seen her do some twelve hours prior, he put his lips to the gaping, haemorrhaging wound, and he drank.

There was a scream, gasps around him, but he didn't notice any of it. He drank deep of the blood that gushed free and plentiful, salt and iron and sickening, gut-twisting belief, not in the light, but in the dark. The darkness he had always lived in, fought in, refused to let Percy die in. It was visceral, real, undeniable, and Joe gave his soul over to it—to dark magic—the promise of Hell. Because from there, whenever the time came for him to be condemned, he'd fight his way out. And he'd do it with Percy by his side.

But it wouldn't be today.

He drank until the blood stopped flowing, and he threw Cleo's pale and drained body down with all the carelessness Molly had let Percy's fall. Then he turned towards his fiancé's corpse.

This time, he felt the power. He felt potency in every atom, vibrating the pure energy of life and of death, and he understood it intuitively. He flung a hand out and dashed every just-standing skeleton into powder. In the same move, Waleed and Tareq burst apart into piles of broken skin and organs. Leo, Althea, and Giordano watched on, stunned and nauseated, not sure whether he was good or evil, or something else entirely. And in the centre of it all, surrounded by utter destruction, graves ripped apart, blood and broken bodies, shards of smashed coffins, stood Joe. His priests' vestments were blacker than black, wet through with blood, the white of his collar red, like his neck and his chin and his hands and his teeth.

Joe staggered forward, to where Percy lay slumped on the ground, and he fell to his knees. He lay on his side, face to face with the only man he would ever love, who made no movement, no sound. He placed a hand on his cheek and he whispered, "Please come back to me."

He curled closer, Percy's skin ice-cold beneath his touch, his forehead on Percy's, and his body shook with the tears, with the racking, desperate pleading of his entire being. "You promised. You promised me. Eternity. Percy, please. Please come back to me."

Joe's trembling lips touched Percy's, once, twice, again, and those lips remained cold and unmoving. "Baby, please. You promised," Joe wept. He pulled Percy's limp arm over his shoulder and moved his head down under his chin, shrinking in the way he did whenever he had a nightmare. Whenever he needed Percy. Percy's protection. Percy's love. Like no one else in the world could ever give him. Because they two were pieces of one unique puzzle. Nothing would ever fit the way they did.

Joe's hands scrunched into Percy's shirt. Joe bathed it with his tears, and he shook so violently, cried so hopelessly, that he didn't feel Percy's fingers twitch, then press gently into his back. He didn't feel the breath return, and it wasn't until he heard the words, gently murmured, as if they were in bed, just waking, "What's wrong, handsome?" that the air came into his throat, and he lay perfectly still, not daring to move a muscle.

Percy's hand drifted to his cheek, and Percy kissed his hair, eyes not yet open.

Joe shoved away from him, crawling several feet back at lightning speed, where he stilled, staring back at Percy.

Percy, bewildered by Joe's sudden flight, opened his eyes, and began to realise where he was. He pushed himself up on one arm, bleary-eyed, looked around, then, seeing the blood all over Joe, "What happened?"

On a trembling breath, "Percy?"

Percy looked down at himself, back up at Joe, and, "Last I checked?"

"Percy!" Joe very nearly broke Percy's neck a second time when he leapt on him, knocked him backwards, and peppered him with kisses. "Percy! You're…" Joe pulled back, hands pressed into his surprised but pleased face, examining every inch of him. "Are you all right? Are you evil or anything?"

Percy gave a vague shake of his head, as best he could in the vise-like grip. "No more than usual, I don't think…"

"Oh, Percy!" Joe kissed him long and hard, pausing only to reassure himself again that those bright blue eyes still sparkled with life, with soul, with everything that was Percy. "Baby, you died. You died, and you came back." Joe wrapped his arms around him. "I knew you'd never leave me."

Percy returned the embrace, arms enfolding Joe as tightly as he was held, but his gaze ran anew over his friends, wan, ashen, trails of tears cutting through the bone dust and dirt that covered them. None of them approaching, and Leo, most of all, holding himself back.

Percy reached out an arm for him, and Leo was bundled against his chest in a second, wrapping his arms around Percy's waist. Percy held them there, Leo and Joe, and surveyed the devastation, trying to put it all together. The sight of what had been Tareq and Waleed, utterly unrecognisable, had he not known it was them, nearly turned his stomach. But he was soon pulled away from that by another vision.

Molly lay gasping at the base of a grave. Her hand covered her throat, and the wound was healing fast. Not that Percy would ever have been able to gauge just how big it once was. All he could see now were red fingers, pink bubbles of froth leaking over them, and Cleo's body so close to death. And sitting on the ground near her, perfectly unharmed, Moxie. "Please tell me what happened."

"It was Joe." Leo spoke proudly, looking at Joe with more love, more admiration than Joe had ever imagined he would see on that face. "He brought you back."

Percy's brain ticked the matter over fast. The blood at Molly's throat. The blood at Joe's lips. Joe in his arms when he woke, and now his eyes searching Percy's, waiting. At the alarm that screamed quickly, loudly, Percy said, "That's dark magic, Joe. That's blood magic."

"I don't care."

"I can't get it out of you."

"I don't want you to." Joe's fingers slid into Percy's hair. "I got you back. That's all I care about. I got you back."

"You did." Two small words, but all he could get out to reassure Joe, as the chill fear of what Joe had done to himself, for Percy's sake, began to overwhelm him.

Molly's rasping and gargled words cut into his mounting dread. "It's not what you think it is," she said, head leaning back on the cold concrete of the grave, sucking in thin breaths. "Someone will find out. They'll come for you. They'll cut you down and take him away… Eternity can't protect you. It's life that you need to escape. Not death."

"Are you still here?" Joe pushed himself to his feet, throwing a glare over his shoulder at the tall statue of the virgin Mary peeking over the tops of the trees. The place of the pyre that was meant for him. "Then maybe it's time we had our own roast."

Percy let out a half-shocked, half-amused chortle at the unexpected comment, but said, "Slow down there, Darkside." He held out a hand, and Joe pulled him to his feet, his dagger-like eyes on Molly all the while.

Percy dusted off his expensive suit and straightened himself. He discovered his knife on the ground and took it up before setting his sights on Molly.

They all watched him, all except Molly, wondering just how far Percy would go. Nothing was going to kill her. The only viable option would be to disable her somehow. Would he tear her limb from limb? Take this head and mount it on a new wall in a new bar somewhere? Secret it away in one of the graves, just as she'd entombed Percy?

Joe hated her, violently, but even then, after everything, he was not without empathy, nor would he ever be. The story of the events that had led her to become what she was that day still rang in his ears, and a tired, bruised and bleeding hand reached out and caught Percy's arm as he walked past.

Percy paused, his eyes met Joe's eyes, and his heart just about beat out of his chest at the look on his face.

Joe and his saving the sad ghost bullshit.

Even after Bruges. Even after letting himself get possessed at Barmiston Hall. Even after he'd just watched Percy die at Molly's hands.

Percy brushed gentle fingers over Joe's, the slightest pressure acknowledging and reassuring. Then he slipped his dagger into the inner pocket of his jacket.

Looking rather like a slightly roughed up gentleman who'd just enjoyed a good ten hours of sleep, he bent down and scooped up his kitten, who purred loudly at his touch, working her way onto his shoulder. He settled down on the grass opposite Molly, and he explained, in a voice much like that of a brand new and not yet embittered university professor, "You'll come back to my apartment. We'll find you a new host. You'll give my friend her body back. After you heal it."

"I'm not doing shit for you," she croaked, throat awash with the red that talking forced through the slit.

Percy's vexed eyes sought Joe's. Joe gave a little nod, Percy clacked his tongue softly, then pushed forward on a sigh. "Look, I'm really not in the mood to torture you out of there. I'm tired. You killed me, apparently. It looks like Joe's just about done the same to you. So this is… This feels like a stalemate." She turned her head a little further away in response. "Unless I take you apart piece by piece. But despite what you might think, I don't want to do that."

He thought over what he could say, thought over what he believed Joe wanted him to say or do, but more than that, he searched through his feelings—his true feelings about the whole mess they'd all found themselves in. How they got there. Every action that needed to slide into place for the lot of it to occur, a horror hundreds of years in the making and every person there in the cemetery that day caught in the crossfire of shots launched by cruel and idiotic men long since dead. He thought over all the things he'd seen and done with Joe those last few months, especially those last few weeks, and he said, "The problem is, I agree with you."

He met her incredulous gaze with one that was sombre and grave, and he spoke softly. "I can relate to you in more ways than you know. I won't pretend I've been through the same things you have, but I've wanted to destroy all of it. Every last bit. I've wanted to smash the lot apart, and a few months ago, I probably would have joined you willingly, had you asked nicely. But I've learned a thing or two since then."

Allowing a sardonic smile, "What's that? Play nice?" She looked down at her blood-coated fingers, and Percy felt all the anger simmering just below the weary, barely alive surface. "You've seen what happens."

"No," said Percy. "This is what happens when you don't trust people who care about you. When you don't let anyone in. It's very hard to make it through this life all alone."

Her brow narrowed, and she scrunched the bloody hand back down on her wound. She closed her eyes, waiting to heal, waiting for her powers to come back in full, or waiting for Percy to either attack or go away. Whatever might happen first.

But Percy revealed, "I met your familiar."

Her reserve switched to disbelief, but the idea was clearly turning over in her mind that Percy wouldn't have known to lie about that had it not happened. Still, she whispered, "You didn't."

"I did. And now I know what you did. You locked them in your basement. You promised you'd take them with you, didn't you? You double crossed them, took the powers they gave you, and then you ran out, leaving them locked away in a demon's body, starving."

She shook her head bluntly. "No. I left them safe. If they get out— It's what happened last time. People found out about us... That's why they did it. I had to protect them. I had no choice."

"Your familiar took Joe's body, then they took my cat. I've spent a lot of time around the fucker, and they did a lot of damage. They did that trying to get back to you. Because they're in love with you. And if what they say is true, you love them just as much."

She scanned Joe, as though wondering if he still had about him somehow the proof that he'd been touched by her familiar. She found Percy's eyes, and in a confiding, barely audible voice, shared, "I'm keeping them safe until I fix everything."

"You can't lock someone up to keep them safe." He said it just as gently as though there were no argument or animosity or history of abject horror between them. "I've lived it, and I know it." He brought the kitten down onto an arm, stroking her back as she nuzzled against him. "Listen to me. You have one person—one person who understands you. It's more than so many people ever get in this life. One person who'd do anything for you. Kill for you, steal for you, tear the world apart for you." He looked over at Joe, ever-blooming adoration in his eyes. "That's true love. That's not something you walk away from."

Molly leaned forward, and when she spoke, she was more earnest than any of them had ever seen her, as though desperate for Percy's acceptance of her words. "You can't understand what happened to me."

He held her gaze and replied, "I know. I would never claim to. You've been through things no one should ever have gone through. It's unforgivable. It's a dark cross that's going to sit over all of us for as long as life goes on. But it's not the only one."

He rubbed the kitten's chin, her head tilting up, her warm purr filling Molly's silence.

"What's the end game here?" he asked. "Go through the world smashing things up until there's nothing left? Until either the anger burns you out or someone finally finds a way to destroy you once and for all? Because Joe and I aren't going to stop. We won't back down. And now you've seen what he can do." Percy only caught the smallest flash of Joe's becoming blush before he was drawn away by Molly's cry of frustration.

"I want revenge!" She threw her hands up into the air, a rain of blood dripping across the grass. "I don't know. Some kind of… *Something*! Something to make up for it. Something to make up for four hundred years—"

"Nothing can," he said bluntly. "And that's brutal, and it's life. Nothing can ever atone for a past wrong like that."

"Yet you expected me to give up and walk away in exchange for a cat?"

"I'm not asking you to give up. And you're not having my cat either." She scowled, he scowled, and he continued, as patiently and succinctly as possible, "People want to tell you that anger is dark and that it's bad. It's not. It's energy, and it's power. When you let go of your anger, that's when you become complacent. That's when you become a victim. I would never ask you to do that."

Percy reached for her hand, which surprised her enough to look up at him, large and frightened eyes meeting those that had known the fathoms of deepest love, and deepest pain. "If I could change it, I would. I've wanted to burn this world more times than I can tell you. But I'm glad I couldn't. Because if I wasn't here to fight, if Joe wasn't, what then? Should we just hand this world over to people like that? We can't choose our pasts or our families or the people we're surrounded by, any of us. But you can choose the people you love. You can choose to fight for them. They're worth every bit of it."

Molly gave a breath of a laugh, so much as to say she felt only the crippling fury, and none of whatever else Percy hinted at.

Without a trace of malice in his tone, Percy said, "Your anger is valid and justified. But you can't just blindly take your fury out on anything and everything. You need to target it, and I can help you. You'll get your revenge. And it won't be through 'living your best life' or any of that trite, pacifist horseshit. It will be real, and cold, and viable. Precise. But you can't give in and throw it all away by making a mistake like this. You can't do them the favour of taking yourself out of the battle before you take some ground. Even though the odds are stacked against you, you fight, and you never stop. Because unless you fight, nothing changes. Just being here is a fight. Just existing. You stay and you be a thorn in their side until you split them wide open. There's too much beauty in this world, too much love, to sacrifice it like that. That's what they want. Don't, after all this time, don't let them take that from you."

Her eyes fluttered closed, and the first tears she'd cried for four hundred years slipped free, down onto Percy's fingers that still held her hand. She cried, long and piteously, and Percy's kitten sank her little claws into him over and over, and Percy stayed right where he was, holding onto both of them. Molly yielded to his touch, moving her arms around his neck, pressing herself against his chest, and he ran a hand around her, stroking her hair, much like he would have stroked Cleo's hair.

He could never have said how he might have reacted, what he might have done, had she looked any other way—had she taken the body of someone who meant nothing to him—but as it stood, Molly had chosen that one step on her path to near-world-destruction wisely. Just as she had when she'd chosen Percy and Joe to be the people to stop her.

Percy pulled back to look at her and said, "I really do believe that sometimes violence is the answer. Often. More often than not, in fact—"

"Percy!" Joe interrupted.

"But sometimes, the softer way works even better." Percy raised his eyes to Joe and offered a loving wink in return for his smile. "I never would have gotten here if I didn't have someone to take my hand and show me the way. And I would have been broken. Hurting. And I didn't think I was ever going to find my way out of that. I didn't even know there was a way out." Taking Molly's hand again, he said, "That's why I'm offering it to you."

Molly tightened her fingers around his, and Percy enclosed hers with his other hand, and she said, "I'm sorry I killed you."

Percy responded with a grin. "It's okay. A lot of people want to do that."

She laughed softly, then found Joe. "Sorry. For everything."

"Fuck you," Joe retorted.

Percy stifled a laugh, settling into how much fun Dark Joe already was.

"She's a murderer," Althea threw in, having been waiting for the appropriate time to remind them all of that small fact.

Percy gave a harried nod of understanding. "To be fair, a lot of us are murderers." Her understandably outraged response was cut off when he focused his attention back on Molly and said, "I need to know. Can you bring those girls back? Not bones and ashes—can you bring them all back, full and alive again?"

"I can," she said. "And Cleo too. Get me to the skull, and I'll do it."

Just then, a low and morbid groan echoed up a long avenue. All eyes snapped down to a shady path, where one final skeleton ambled their way along. More than a skeleton. A corpse in remarkably good condition for a body that had lain in its coffin for so very long.

"Oh, shit," Percy muttered under his breath. He freed himself from Molly with a squeeze of her fingers, jumped to his feet, grasped Joe's hand and pulled him some small way from the others. "Please don't be mad."

"What?" Joe did a double take of both the skeleton and Percy, not sure which one was worrying him more. "What did you do?"

Percy vomited out, "You know we were discussing art and morality, and, and, the philosophy of—"

Twice as loud, twice as urgent, "What did you do?"

Molly's head turned, and she cried out, "Puss?"

"Urrrrrrrh!" came the groan in return.

"Oh, Puss!" Molly bolted full speed down the path to the zombie, and all five watched on as she kissed the dusty walking cadaver, every bit as passionately as Joe had kissed Percy when he too was a freshly woken ex-corpse.

"That's disgusting," Leo offered.

"I'm going to need bleach," said Althea. "For my eyes. And for... everywhere."

Puss pulled back and addressed Molly with more 'urgs' and 'arghs', and Molly, who seemed to understand every utterance, threw back a defensive, "It's nothing I can't fix!"

Puss doubled down, it appeared, groaning more loudly, to which Molly responded, "It's all still there. All the pieces of them, all in the house. Even their souls. I trapped them there. They haunt the place. But they have each other, you see?"

Percy's eyes narrowed at the twisted logic regarding the many girls she'd bled and murdered at Barmiston Hall. "That's fucking dark."

"I know, but..." She ran supplicating eyes over to him. "I wouldn't have done it if I couldn't bring them back. It wasn't…" Fingers twisting in the tatters of what had once been Degas's burial suit, "I thought they'd be better off, in the house there, together. Away from things. They were all… They were all so sad. Like Althea. And this world, it takes girls—"

"You took them!" Althea shouted. "Percy, what the fuck is this?"

Percy gave a stern nod of agreement. "Althea's right. Althea deserves a big apology and—"

"An apology?" Althea yelled. "What the fuck is going on? Why are you being nice to her? You should kill her! Where's Percy? Meanwhile, Murder-Joe-Nosferatu's over here, looking really fucking scary—"

"Sorry," said Joe. He wiped at the blood on his chin with a sleeve. "I'm still me. Want a hug?"

"No!" She visibly reeled back from him. "And… And there are bodies all over the ground. And how does she get to get away with this?"

"I literally can't kill her!" Percy threw back.

"But that's your whole thing!" Althea shouted.

"I know!" Percy also shouted. "It's not the ending I expected either, but there we have it."

"For fuck's sake!" Althea spat.

"I'll make it right," Molly said, patting down zombie Degas's mess of a jacket. With that, she slipped away from him, two weak and shaking arms stretching out towards the scene of destruction, and with a touch on the air, the pieces of Waleed and Tareq that Joe had torn apart squelched back together.

It was early daylight now, and the sight was beyond all recorded revulsion. It went on for some time, several minutes, during which Percy sidled up to a horrified Giordano and a bewildered Leo, Althea allowed Joe a bloody arm over her shoulder, and the five of them regrouped.

Last of all, the two former zombies regained consciousness, both harrowed, both deeply confused.

Giordano immediately stepped forward with a supporting arm for Tareq. "You've been through a lot. Can I help?"

Tareq, taken aback at the beautiful, bloody man holding out his arm, took it tentatively.

Percy caught Tareq's eye as he searched his unexpected surroundings. "Remember me?"

It took a moment, but eventually Tareq uttered, "You shot me."

"You shot him?" Giordano gasped out. "How could you?"

Tareq continued, confused, "I was…" He looked around again, and finally clocked Waleed, who appeared to be just as lost as he was. "How did we get here?"

"We were in the hotel…" Waleed said, tracing over his most recent memories. "Where are we now?"

Percy, delighted that they seemed to remember nothing of their ordeal, supplied only, "Paris."

"How did we get to Paris?" Tareq whispered.

"I'll explain everything." Giordano moved a hand around his waist to help him across the field of bone dust. "First, we should get you to a hospital and make sure you're okay."

Tareq acquiesced easily enough, too befuddled to put up an argument, while also somewhat dazzled by the rich brown eyes that took such a concerned interest in him. He brought an arm over Giordano's fine shoulder, because he did need some support after all.

"Can I come too?" asked Waleed.

Giordano glanced back at him, then to Percy. Percy gave a nod. Giordano's lips twisted. "All right."

But any move that might have been made to depart the cemetery was then paused by the grotesque sound of wet kisses on crumbling and putrid, half-rotten skin. The increasingly heated display in front of them eventually forced Percy to call out, "Enough of that! At least until you give Cleo her body back."

When Molly turned to face them again, she was positively beaming. She led her zombie up the garden path, where Percy stepped forward to take a closer look at him. "Puss?"

"My cat," said Molly.

"Your familiar," finished Percy with an exasperated eye roll. "A lot of fucking use, you were."

"Urrrrrrrh," Puss protested.

"What the hell is going on?" asked Tareq.

"It's probably best we just go now," Giordano said hurriedly. Then to Percy, "We're good? We're done here?"

"Cocktails later?"

"I'll call." And with that, he led the way out of the cemetery, half carrying the exquisite and uninjured Tareq, Waleed trailing dazed and normal-looking behind.

"Leo," said Percy, "locate some local morgues. We'll need to steal a body for Molly. And possibly another for Puss."

"On it." He pulled out his notebook to jot a reminder down, and Althea let out a cry of furious exasperation in response, immediately stomping off towards home. "Al, wait!" Leo ran two steps after her, then turned back to Percy and declared, "I'm taking her out for dinner. Somewhere really expensive. And I'm putting it on your card. And you can't stop me."

Percy gave a small nod. "All right."

"Okay." He made to dash away again, but Percy called him back.

"Leo?"

"Mmm?"

"Thank you. I love you." Leo almost visibly melted, and his full body smashed back into Percy's with an enormous burst of love. Percy held him for as long as Leo could stand the thought of Althea getting further away, then Percy, feeling him pull back, whispered, "Run."

He gave Percy and Joe each one final, thankful glance, and was gone.

"Right," said Percy, dropping Moxie, his unpossessed and slightly abnormal kitten into his pocket, "Let's get these two home and body-swapped—"

"No," said Joe, reaching in and picking the unwilling kitten back out. "They can meet us there." He handed the kitten to Puss with a glare at Molly. "She knows where you live. And we've got something we need to do."

Percy, none too pleased to see his kitten back in Molly's company, glanced around with a lightly annoyed shrug. "The council will clean it up."

"Not that." He said to Molly, "Go. Revive anyone you killed on the way, and when you get there, go into one of the bedrooms. Leave Althea alone."

She gave a guilty tilt of her head and ambled away with her familiar.

As soon as they were out of earshot, Percy turned to an anxious Joe. "What is it? It's not like you to let an arch villainess and her zombie lover walk the streets of Paris unaccompanied. Certainly not with my cat. Are you all right?"

"I am," Joe assured him. "Really. But there's something important we need to do. Right now. It can't wait another minute."

CHAPTER FIFTY-SEVEN
A RELIGIOUS RENDEZVOUS

Joe led the way out of the cemetery, across early morning, still-quiet streets, where he was relieved to see a few people out and starting their day. Normal. Looking at them like they were the strange and abnormal element of the city, no memory of their supernatural slumber.

He paid scant attention to them, pulling at Percy's hand, racing as fast as he could walk, almost a run, across one street, down an alley, over another wide road.

Percy kept up as best he could, worried for Joe, asking the occasional question that went unanswered before resigning himself to the mystery of the short and silent trip, until finally Joe brought them to a small garden.

The garden was cool and lush, grown high with elms, an oasis in that part of Montmartre. Percy recognised it, having walked past on occasion, but he'd never been beyond the black iron fence. Joe went through as though he knew the place intimately. He walked along a curving stone path, hidden beneath a tunnel of curling branches that met overhead, and directly to a little wooden door, arched, set in a stone wall.

He looked back at Percy, as though confirming he was still there by his side, then he took a long, black key from his pocket. He slid it into the lock, and the door opened at his command.

Taking Percy's hand tighter now, he led him inside. Percy tripped over a step, and was caught and steadied by Joe, as his gaze drifted upwards to row upon row of soaring stone beams overhead. A rainbow of light filtered through beautiful stained-glass windows, set high, so, so high above. Joe closed and locked the door behind them, then clasped his hand again and brought him to the centre aisle of the ancient church they found themselves inside.

It was probably the last place Percy thought Joe might have taken him that morning. Perhaps a hospital or a patisserie. An all-night bar? But this… Was he having a crisis of faith? Was he turning to God?

The thought unsettled Percy's stomach, but his aesthetic eye, his heart and soul, responded with the expressive ardour he could never subdue where such beautiful things were concerned.

The church sat silent and reverential, evidence of all the faith humanity had in a greater something there in every stone, every column, every gorgeous curve and line, and, "Do you like it?" Joe asked. His eyes were as keen on Percy as Percy's were on the walls and windows and carvings and artworks.

"It's magical," Percy whispered. It was. Utterly. Beyond spectacular.

"It's the second oldest church in Paris," said Joe, suddenly sounding a little nervous. "I, um… I think it's prettier than the oldest one. And because it's so old, it's not… What would you call it? It's not 'cloying'." Percy let out a small laugh as Joe spoke on. "And I knew you lived in Montmartre. And it felt right."

Percy looked at Joe. Tired. Worn. But Joe. Beautiful, always, to Percy. More than anything. And not because of the way the morning sun lit the edges of his hair like a halo. Not because of the lips and the eyes and the curves of every feature that had first drawn him into the gentle and distant obsession that had marked their earliest days together. He was Joe. And he could have been one hundred years old, and Percy would have thought he was just as beautiful. "You planned to bring me here?"

"I did. Not right now, of course." He gave a soft, bashful laugh, then turned serious again just as quickly. "I thought you'd love it. And I wanted to, but... after everything that happened last night... Percy..."

Joe raised his gaze to Percy's. The intensity in his eyes, the something he was holding back—Percy could see it was close to overwhelming him. "What is it?"

"Come." Joe led him up the aisle, to the front of the church, where he paused by the altar. A square altar, large and flat, made of stone but gilt in shining copper. A thing of history. Like the church. Like the city.

Joe took both of Percy's hands in his and looked deep into his eyes. "I fell in love with you. Percy, I'm so in love with you, and I don't know what to do with it. Sometimes it feels like there's too much. And there are so many things I want to say to you, and..." Joe dropped his gaze to their hands, folded together, Percy clasping his just as tenderly as he held Percy's, and when he looked up, that smile. Percy's eyes loving and proud. Like they always were.

"I wanted to bring you here last night," Joe explained. "I thought, maybe after dinner, I'd take you for a walk, and surprise you. I got the key yesterday because I thought..." Joe looked down the long aisle, drinking in the glorious details that lay before them, just for their eyes. "This place, I thought it represented us in a way. It's so exquisite. And things like that, they're like air to you, and I know that. I thought—I *knew* you'd love that."

"I do," Percy said softly, an acknowledgement and an encouragement. He wondered what the meaning of it all was, but Joe seemed to be warming to his task, to Percy's acceptance of it, moment by moment, so he waited, and let Joe say what he needed to.

"I thought it was like these two worlds. Our worlds. What you believe in, and what I… What I *did* believe. I think. For a while. I tried to…"

Percy's smile slipped with the confession, with his sadness for what he imagined Joe must be feeling, but Joe spoke on, faster now, getting it all out. "I used the sheath. The sheath and the spear. When you… When *that* happened, I got them, and I put them together. And I got nothing. Not a thing."

No atheistic quip met the admission. No lightly mocking joke. Only the firm, "That's no proof of anything."

Joe laughed. The idea of Percy, of all people, trying to help Joe keep his faith, was amusing. He said, "You'd try to protect me from anything, wouldn't you?"

"Forever."

"Forever," Joe whispered. He brightened a little. "I'm not sad about it. I always doubted. I've always seen horror, and darkness, and these terrifying things, and I tried to be good. But the life I was living, it was a half life. It was a half understanding. Every day was like that until I met you."

Joe smiled, a touch of his nervousness morphing into what seemed to Percy to be mounting excitement. "When I met you, you opened up a new world. One I'd been blind to my entire existence. One I'd locked myself away from. You showed me love and passion. And you showed me anger and hate. You showed me the filth and the dirt of this world, and you made it beautiful. You make everything so, so beautiful. You, even in your most ridiculous, most appalling moments, Percy, you bring me a peace and a happiness I didn't know I could ever feel in this world. And that's why I wanted to bring you here, and why I wanted to give you this."

He dipped a hand into his pocket and pulled something out. He held it firmly in his fist for a moment, as though considering whether to go ahead. Finally, he turned over a shaking hand, stretched his fingers open, and there in his palm shone a stunning ring.

The band was gold, newly polished, though the ring was old, which Percy could see at a glance. Gold detail, complicated and exquisite, curled and coiled up the side of the band, rising ornately around a black inlay of pure and polished onyx, that glinted and glittered in the morning light.

Percy's heart was hammering in his chest. The hand that held that ring… The ring that was for him. He was speechless.

"Percy…" said Joe, turning the jewel over. He looked up into Percy's eyes, bright and hopeful. "Percy, I want you to marry me."

Percy's fingers curled around Joe's palm. He brought his other hand to his cheek and dropped a gentle kiss on his lips. "Darling, you know I want to marry you. I proposed, and I meant it."

"No." Joe shook his head. "No, I don't mean one day. I don't mean when courts catch up and change their rules. I don't mean one distant maybe, and planning, and suits, and… Percy, I want you to be my husband. Forever. I want you to marry me right now. Right here. With me as celebrant."

Percy's hand moved to his open lips, covering them briefly, then, "You would do that? Really?"

Joe let out a gasp of laughter. "How can you ask me that? I love you. I love you so much and when I saw…" Joe's voice broke. The grief was so close to the surface that it didn't even need the words to uncover it. He turned his face away, tears sliding down his cheeks.

Percy pulled him back, the touch of his hand catching the tears. "It's been a long night. It doesn't have to be now. We can think about it—"

"I'm done thinking. I just want to live. With you. I want this with my whole heart, but I don't know…" He swallowed, gathering himself. "I don't know what I did last night. I… I don't know what it makes me now that I drank that blood. But I don't feel different." He took Percy's hand and placed it on his chest. "Not in my heart. I feel like I love you, and I want you, and if you would share your life with me—"

"Oh god, of course I would." Percy took his face in both hands, kissing the trails of tears away.

"I've never told you enough," said Joe, shaking his head softly against Percy's kisses. "I always think you know already, because I never thought you'd consider me. Because you're Percy. And I always thought you must know how much I love you, how grateful I am to have you, but if I didn't tell you, just one day, then you were gone—"

Percy kissed him and kissed him. "I'm right here. I would never leave you."

Joe's hands closed on Percy's shirt. "I know. And that's why I have faith. In you. I will always believe in you. And I will always love you. And now I've done this thing. And I don't know what it means, but if it means I watch you grow old and die, and I don't die, and I go on…"

"Joe, no. No." Percy moved closer, taking Joe in his arms, holding him to his chest, letting his tears fall on his shoulder. "What did I say? Where you go, I go. There's no stopping that. I meant every word. I won't let you go. Not without me. And that's why…" He took Joe's chin in his hand, and brought his eyes up to meet his own. "Joe, I thought about this, straight away and on the walk over here and… That's why you're going to give me your blood."

Joe's lower lip quivered, his brow drew deep, and he whispered, "No… I can't do that."

"Eternity. It's not just a pretty word, it's a promise."

"Percy, this isn't something you do lightly."

"You did it lightly."

"You were fucking dead!" Joe shouted.

"And now I'm not fucking dead and I don't want to be dead! I want to drink wine and smoke cigarettes. I want to drive fast cars and steal things. I want to do it all with you. Forever. If you're going to marry me, if you're going to join our lives and our souls—"

"It's till *death* do us part," said Joe.

"Fuck death!" Percy yelled. "Fuck parting. I'm yours and you're mine and that's an end to it." He grasped Joe's arms as he tried to pull away. "I'm not doing this lightly. I'm not doing this again with someone else ten years from now. You're it, Joe. You're my soulmate. You're my only one. The way we fit together, no one else can fill that space. You're my world. You're my heart and my existence, and I'm never letting you go. I told you that. I promised you that. Even death can't keep us apart. You said you want to get married, then let's make it official. It's you and me, Joe, forever. Us against the world, for all eternity. Do you want to marry me or not?"

"Of course I want to marry you. I just asked you to marry me!"

"Then marry me, goddammit. But do it properly!"

"Percy!"

"Joe." Percy kissed him, a goading smack on the lips that ended in Percy's hopeful, sly, gorgeous, irresistible smile. "I'll make a great husband. You'll see. Five minutes from now."

As he so often did, Joe tried and failed to repress his own smile.

"Marry me. Do it now. Pronounce us."

"But—"

"If you don't do it, I'll cut you and take your blood in the night, and I don't care if that's a consent issue."

"Percy!"

"Come on." Percy bundled Joe's hands up against his heart. "I want your ring. I mean, obviously I want your ring, but specifically, right now, that one, there in your hand. Put it on my finger."

Joe laughed, blushing that way Percy had always loved to make him blush. Would always love it. Would devote his life to making it happen and loving it again and again.

And that's when he remembered.

He remembered the weight that had been burning a hole in his pocket some twelve hours earlier, and he slapped a hand down on his thigh to make sure it was still there. The small, round bump remained, despite the fight and the fire, the blood and the bones, the death and the resurrection.

And if ever Percy needed a sign, that was it.

He squeezed Joe's hands, and he commenced: "I take you, Joe Bruno, to be my unlawfully wedded husband. To have and to hold, from this day forward. In good times and bad. In sickness and in health. In the filth of a graveyard or the private castle of a playboy billionaire." Joe let out a chuckle. "Until forever. Eternity. Joe…" Percy's voice wavered, and Joe melted at the tears that came into his eyes. "Joe, I will honour and adore you, for all my days. I promise you that. With this ring…" Percy reached into his pocket and pulled forth the stunning, ancient, irreplaceable, eternal sapphire and gold ring.

Joe's gasp echoed throughout the church. "You didn't…"

"Joe, with this ring…" He slipped it onto Joe's trembling finger, where it slid into place, a perfect fit. "I thee wed."

Joe turned his hand over, staring open-mouthed at the beautiful blue ring on his finger, staring at Percy, then he launched himself at Percy, kissing him with such force Percy stumbled against the altar to support them both. "Handsome, that's supposed to come after."

"Oh, right. But…" He stared again at the ring on his own hand. "How?"

"That's where I went yesterday. I was going to give it to you last night, too. Or as soon as I could. I wanted you to have it. I thought it would look so beautiful on you. It's two thousand years old. It's also Roman, but now I wonder if that was in slightly poor taste—"

"Percy, I love it. I'm never taking this off. Never."

Percy used the outstretched, be-ringed hand as leverage to pull himself upright. "Do me."

"Okay, okay." Joe moved back to his position in front of the altar, taking Percy with him. "I take you, Percy Ashdown, to be my husband, from this day forward. To have and to hold, in good times and bad, in sickness and in health, no matter what ridiculous bullshit you pull next." Percy, having the best time of his life, laughed with a hearty slyness that Joe devoured. "I promise to honour and adore you, for… Are you sure about this?"

"Now!" he snapped. "Do it now!"

"For eternity! You and me. Forever. With this ring, I thee wed." He slipped it onto Percy's eager finger, and he didn't think he'd ever seen Percy as happy as he was just then. Percy gave a nod, hands shaking with excitement, and Joe said, "By the power vested in me, I now pronounce us husband and husband."

Percy let out a cry of pure and unadulterated joy, took Joe's face in his hands, and kissed him. And kissed him. And kissed him again. Until finally he stepped back and looked at the ring. He snuck Joe a delighted glance. "Sixteenth Century?"

Joe grinned widely. "Yep. Venetian. Not that I probably need to tell you that."

"It's marvellous. Look how well it fits. It's like it was made for me."

"It is. Look." Joe reached for Percy's hand, slipped his finger along the edge of the ring setting, and the top popped open on a delicate, hidden hinge.

"Oh my god," Percy whispered, caught in his admiration for the exquisite jewel. "It's a poison ring!"

"Do you love it?" Joe asked desperately, as though he needed the answer.

"I love it so much! I love you so much!" He kissed Joe again, then said, "I can't believe you're my husband. I can't believe I'm this lucky."

"No," said Joe, a curiously decisive note in his voice. "Not yet. There's one more thing we have to do. To make it official. In the eyes of God."

"Oh…" Percy's face dropped, and he looked around warily. "Is it going to be very religious?"

"Very," said Joe.

CHAPTER FIFTY-EIGHT
PERCY AND JOE MAKE IT OFFICIAL

Percy straightened himself, put on a smile, and said, "If it will make you happy, I'll do it."

"It will." Something in the way Joe looked at Percy just then cut the intimacy with tension. His hand moved slowly but deliberately up his chest, his fingers slipped beneath his clerical collar, dark red with dried blood, and he pulled it free.

This wasn't simply undressing. Percy could see it in his eyes, clear and serious. This was more. This was symbolic.

He watched Joe stare down at the stained collar, watched his fingers open, watched the thing drop to the stone floor.

The action was so decisive, so pivotal, Percy felt the need to stop him—to prevent whatever sort of pain he imagined might be tied up in that decision. "It doesn't have to change."

Joe's fingers wrapped back around Percy's. "Can't you see? There's only one thing I have faith in now." He kissed him. "And it's not God." He kissed him again. "And it's not the Devil." Once and again, then he stepped away.

Joe walked to the baptismal font. He pulled the black cloth of his shirt over his head, and Percy surveyed him as he bent over the water, washing his face, his chest, the scars on his back, his skin red and purple with new wounds just made, just healing. But when Joe stood, when he turned back to Percy, cleansed, beautiful, dripping, his eyes were warm, and he had a confidence about him Percy had seldom seen. A purpose. A happiness.

Joe returned, taking his place in front of the altar, and he placed his hands on Percy's chest, running them down the expensive fabric of his suit jacket. He pulled one side open, and there, in Percy's inside pocket, he found his dagger. He drew it forth, holding the hilt with one hand, the blade with the other, and he settled it carefully, reverently, on the altar.

Percy watched on, curious, enamoured, as Joe's hands shifted to the inner seams of his jacket. He took a hold, and eased it back over his shoulders, while Percy moved his arms, compliant, wondering, softly aroused.

The jacket was laid out long upon the altar next to the dagger, and now the increasingly confident, increasingly determined fingers moved to the buttons on Percy's vest. Joe stepped closer as he worked, his thigh brushing against Percy's. Percy wasn't sure how sexy any of this was supposed to be, so he tried to hide his interest in case he let Joe down by not showing proper decorum for whatever strange Catholic ceremony this was about to be.

Joe's eyes were fast on his work, disrobing Percy of the vest, then beginning on his shirt. Percy followed every move intently, fixed eyes, dark lashes, searing heat building between them, as it always, always did, almost corporeal, alive with each passing moment that he held himself back from touching Joe.

Down his chest, the gentle press of fingers slipped each button free. A sensation close but not quite against his skin, down his abdomen, Joe refraining from reaching into the open shirt, though his eyes drank Percy's body in all the same. He pulled the remaining portion of Percy's shirt free and loosed the final fastenings. This too, he made to slide over Percy's shoulders, but Percy's hand clamped down on his wrist, shocking Joe, forcing a flash of his eyes to Percy's.

Percy said nothing, awaited him. Joe tilted his lips up and kissed Percy. He kissed him and he did not stop kissing him as Percy yielded, let Joe push his hand down, let Joe take his shirt over his arms where it dropped in a crumpled heap on the church floor.

Percy slipped a hand around his waist as Joe began to pull at his belt buckle. "What are you doing?"

"I need you," Joe whispered, fingers more frantic now, kisses on a tremble of lips. "I need you. And I'm going to have you."

Joe took his lips to Percy's neck and wrenched his belt open. It uncoiled like a snake, dropped to the flagstones, trodden beneath Joe's feet as he got closer to Percy, spreading his hands over his pecs, feeling the hard shape of him as his chest expanded, as his back arched into the sensation of Joe's teeth.

Joe bit him, hard, and "Oh, fuck," Percy groaned. He was just about gone already, sunk under Joe's spell that he'd thrown over him so easily ever since that first night. And all those memories mingled in Percy's mind behind his closed eyes. Joe shoving him against the wall of his own house, soaked from the rain. Joe kissing him for the very first time. Joe fucking him as he held onto the golden bars of his own bed posts. Joe's unerring and complete control of him that he wanted to give in to completely. The way he wanted to be his slave.

Joe pulled his head back and looked deep into Percy's eyes. "Kneel."

Percy's knees hit the ground fast, but the pain barely registered with the tingling of anticipation flooding his brain and body.

Percy stared up at Joe, bathed in a shaft of morning sunlight that cut through the church dust like a message from

God. He was everything to Percy. He was worth living and dying for.

Joe reached across to the altar, and Percy, captivated, followed the curve of his body, every line of every rib, his brown nipples, the precious hairs on his chest, the arms, cut and bruised and bulging with strength.

He took up Percy's dagger, long and silver. The jewels on the hilt glinted in the light, and Joe ran his long fingers across the blade. It sparked a flare in Percy's eyes when he turned it over, then he drew the blade across his body, closer and closer to his skin, until the tip touched down at the inner edge of his right ribcage.

"Joe…" Percy grasped him by the hips. Joe pressed the dagger into his flesh and cut, his skin ripping open in a long, clean line.

"This is my body…" Joe whispered. He took two fingers through the blood that came plentifully, leaving a vermillion smear across his rippling body. Those fingers, red and wet, he brought to Percy's eager lips. "My body, which I have broken for you."

His fingers traced the line of Percy's beautiful lower lip. Percy's mouth opened for him, and Joe felt the erotic warmth of his tongue sliding beneath his fingers, taking him deep into his mouth, hungrily. His thumb and ring finger, the latter newly augmented in sapphire, pressed against Percy's beautiful cheeks, and he forced his fingers deeper, his cock straining against his pants as Percy sucked.

Joe raised the dagger in a shaking hand, brought it to the left of his navel, and slid it into his flesh, opening a fresh wound. He pulled the dagger away, blood dripping onto the church floor, blood dripping onto the altar where he placed it down, blood running down his firm flesh. "This is my blood, which I have shed for you."

Percy's eyes raised to meet his, black, heated, and he relinquished Joe's fingers with a slide of his hot mouth. His tongue traced a line beneath Joe's navel, slowly, up and up, never breaking that eye contact, until his head tilted and his tongue ran across the long slit. Joe shuddered in ecstatic agony as he lapped at the wound, drank his blood down, and Joe said, "I will be your saviour, Percy. I will lift you up, and I will be your protector. I give eternal life to you."

The potent effect of the dark magic flowing in Joe's blood took immediate and heady effect on Percy. The heaviness of his heartbeat, the vigour in his veins, the clouded, reality-altering obsession that he'd always had with Joe, rolled his eyes back as he let the blood pour down his throat. He drank until the blood stopped gushing. Then his hand moved to the fastening on Joe's trousers. He ripped them open and wrenched Joe's remaining clothes to the floor.

He stared up, worshipful, and just then, beneath Joe's enormous and erect dick, Percy had his awakening.

This man, flesh and blood, was the way and the life.

Percy, of all people, had finally found his religion.

Percy took Joe's dick, fabulously sleek, deliciously hard, dripping for him, and he closed his lips around it, slid his tongue all the way along the base and sucked. The rasp of pleasure that ripped out of Joe echoed off the church walls. And Joe stood, naked, at the head of the church, the light of the new day glorifying him and Percy in its warmth, one ecstasy piling on top of another. His thick thighs flexed, and he held Percy at the nape of his neck, hands following the movement of his keen mouth, ears attuned to the sounds, the lick and the breath, heavy, his own mingled with Percy's, which was amplified by the high ceilings and stone walls, an altar of pure and unmitigated sex.

Percy was in heaven. Joe's complete devotion to him made him want him all the more, which he hadn't thought was possible. His husband, his partner, his lover, for eternity. Finally, Joe had overthrown his God, his religion, for Percy, and that filled Percy with a determination to bring Joe to his knees with pleasure every day for the rest of time. But especially that day. Percy would bring him to his knees, and from there, would push him down and fuck him right there on the floor of the church. He was resolved to make him lose himself entirely, every piece of him unravelled and fallen apart and Percy's alone to put back together.

But Joe said, on a shaking breath, "Rise."

"No," Percy responded around a mouthful of cock.

"Percy!" Percy only increased the suction, leaving Joe a shuddering, trembling mess, holding on for dear life as Percy took his ass in hand and really went to town. His lips smacking, Joe's gasps, Percy's pleased groans, and that would have been exquisite. Joe could have come right there in Percy's mouth, and they both would have been perfectly satisfied with the morning's events.

But it wasn't quite enough.

It wasn't right.

Not yet.

Joe threaded his fingers into Percy's hair and made a slow fist. He pulled firmly, but in no rush. Percy fought him, and Joe tightened that grip, pulling, pulling at the thick hair, while Percy's head tilted, while the muscles in his neck resisted, but Joe didn't relent. And that wasn't easy, because Percy was a masterful cocksucker. And how Joe wanted to come—fill his mouth to the brim—make him drink his cum down right then and there.

His whole body racked with the closeness of his orgasm, Joe forced Percy from his dick, love-drunk, sex-drunk, blue eyes staring up at him.

"Rise." Joe pulled, Percy rose, a mass of half-naked muscle at his beck and call. Joe forced Percy's mouth to his with the one hand, loosed his pants with the other, and let them drop, turning Percy, shoving him backwards, kissing, stumbling, until he hit that low, flat altar, where Joe took a hand to Percy's chin and held him, looking hotly into his eyes.

He didn't need to say a word. Percy wouldn't have moved for all the world. He was caught on the edge of stopping Joe, asking him, really, is this what he wanted? But he was in too deep. He was drowning in pleasure, and blood, and dark, magical energy pulsing through his veins, and he only waited, following Joe's lead with bated breath.

Joe leaned past him, reaching around the edge of the wooden pulpit that stood by the altar. How the fuck he knew it was there, Percy didn't think to ask, because the golden sunlight hit a small glass jug of anointing oil, lighting it up like a city of lost gold.

He tilted the bottle, and a trickle of oil ran down Percy's chest, and more and more, as Joe let it pour. The scent of cinnamon and myrrh flooded Percy's senses as the oil heated on his hot skin, then Joe took the pour into the palm of his hand, set the bottle down, and slathered his precious dick.

Percy's shock at the act cannot be understated. He was lost in the sight of Joe's big hand on his big cock, oily, glistening, glorious, and he only snapped to when Joe's hand slapped down on Percy's ass, the sound ricocheting off the walls. He shoved him around, pushed him over, and Percy just had time to grasp the cool metal of the altar before a stream of oil ran down his back, before Joe's fingers entered him, and curled.

"Jesus Christ!" Percy's body shone with oil as he arched against the artful movement. Expert now, Joe knew how to get him off in seconds. He applied every facet of his hard-earned skill until Percy was a writhing mess on a pillar of sparkling copper, muscles quivering, begging Joe to fuck him.

Joe leaned a knee on the altar, his dick gliding over Percy's ass, and how he wanted to slide in, enter him and fuck his hole just like that. But Percy, there on that gilt canvas, that face that to this day outshone all others Joe had ever laid eyes on… That look on his face when Joe fucked him. He would not miss that.

Joe's hand locked onto Percy's neck. He wrenched him back up and around. His slick fingers took Percy by the thighs, digging into him, lifting him, and with the brute strength that had caught Percy from day one, that he'd come to worship, Joe lifted him, wrapped an arm around his shoulder, and pulled him down onto his cock.

"Oh, fuck!" Percy hadn't been remotely prepared for the sudden, welcome incursion. Not mentally, at any rate. Joe settled him onto the altar, leaned forward to hold Percy to him, while Percy arched his hips, giving Joe full, delicious access. Joe thrust forward, slowly, forcing a cry from Percy that Joe felt in his heart.

"Christ, I love you," Joe groaned against his neck.

"Forever," Percy whispered on a trembling breath.

Joe's eyes devoured Percy as his dick slid exquisitely into him. His hand was grasped, Joe's fingers crushing his. Percy sucked air over his teeth against the pain of the delicious, determined hold. He raised his eyes to Joe's, hot, possessive, about as sexy as anything Percy could ever have imagined.

It was one thing to be married. Quite another to have the man you love claim you as his own by fucking you on the altar of his religion right after illegally marrying you. It did things to Percy that Percy didn't know could be done to him. His heart rate and temperature rose dangerously. His need for Joe over-flowed to madness.

Joe's fingernails dug into his shoulders, a bruising clasp of him while he fucked him, harder, harder, his back flexing, a groan on every breath, like Joe couldn't ever get his fill. He kissed Percy, feasted on the glorious spectacle, his pupils blown with pleasure and blood and magic, Percy's entire being responding to the sight and taste of him. And how he loved being fucked by his priest on that altar.

Joe reached for his dick, and Percy slapped his hand away, wrapping one around Joe's firm ass, reaching his legs over his hips, pulling him in, willing him to come, to let it all go, every last bit right there at the head of the church.

Percy shifted his hips, forcing Joe's pleasure, giving him no control as he tried to hold back, fucking him more brutally, powerfully, his ass so tight around Joe's dick, until finally, with one enormous thrust that ripped a cry of pleasure from Percy, Joe let go, his orgasm filling Percy, his head falling on his shoulder, exactly where Percy loved it best, his body a trembling wreck.

Percy gave him precious seconds, time for the waves of ecstasy to roll through his limbs, for the tension to ease, for the shuddering to slow, and the briefest moment for Joe to look up with his smile, wide and loving, satisfied. Then Percy took a hold of his ass and wrenched him up onto the altar, spilling his cum beneath them. He lay back, head against cool metal, Joe's knees pressed into it as he straddled Percy.

Oil, glistening in the sunlight, poured into his hand, dripped golden over Percy's belly, and Joe slathered it over his dick, overwrought and begging for Joe's ass. Percy ran his fingers through a swath of liquid, wrapped a hand around Joe's neck, and pulled him down to his chest. Reaching fingers over his ass, Percy found his hole and sank in. Joe tried to work Percy's dick at the same time, but soon found himself a mess on Percy's chest, fingernails in his skin, sighing against his ear, Percy stretching him wider, finger-fucking him deeper, until he could barely take it anymore.

Percy's strong hands lifted him, and Joe wrapped his hands around Percy's ribs as he settled him. Joe rose up on his dick like an idol, covered in blood and anointing oil, his rib sliced, his side cut, his hair a glistening, thorny crown, tips sharp with blood and sweat, close to exhaustion but always fighting. A picture of all the things Percy loved about him. The place light and darkness met, the unerring bravery and beauty, the naked, gasping vulnerability of him in Percy's arms, their wild devotion to one another.

Percy shifted his hips with one hand, the other feeling over his thigh, loving, savouring the sensation of his skin beneath his fingers, the sensation of him molten around Percy's cock, the look of him taking it, loving it, not a shred of doubt or sadness in his decision. Rising up into the light, a rainbow of stained glass windows behind him, pure, heavenly, like he was straight out of some renaissance painting... Like he was...

The sexy Jesus.

Percy almost let go, almost came at the very thought of it—his own saviour, cut and broken, in an ecstasy on his dick, falling apart for him.

But Percy always demanded aesthetic perfection.

"Touch yourself," he whispered.

Joe's eyes opened slowly, hazily, upon Percy's expectant, filthy half smile. Joe was spent, assuredly, but that dick fucking into his ass, that smile. He took his still-hard cock in hand as directed, slid lazy fingers down, smooth with oil, sending a new and welcome shot of fire through his body.

How the blue eyes gazed up at him, unguarded, dark against the shining altar, that unkempt hair thick, nearly black, his pomegranate lips setting hard about the white teeth with every stroke, every thrust, that he had begun to fight.

The vision and the euphoria took Joe, and he began to fuck his dick into his hand just as Percy fucked harder into him, eyes fluttering closed, head tilting back to reveal the long, tender neck.

"You're so beautiful," Percy whispered. "I wish you could see yourself like this."

"Percy..." Joe breathed.

"Say it again."

"Percy..." he moaned.

"Tell me how good it feels."

"You're a god. Oh, Christ. Percy, you're a god to me. You're everything."

Percy wrapped a hand around his shoulder and slammed Joe down onto his dick and he thrust upwards and he pulverised Joe, relentlessly, watching him all but crumple, helpless at his hands, working his dick for Percy, assailed by pleasure on all sides from the sight and scent and feel of his beautiful husband.

Joe was lost in the same dream. His husband. Here, now, and he made Percy slow, right on the precipice. Made him take his hand from his thigh, red with his iron grip, and he pulled him up.

Their chests met. Percy's hand pressed firm into Joe's back, taking him close, and Joe dropped his forehead to Percy's, their breath mingling, eyes burning into one another's, Joe taking Percy's cock with a helpless whimper of exhausted happiness.

"I love you," Percy whispered. "My husband. My beautiful, beautiful husband."

He took a hand to Joe's cheek, and Joe leaned into it, rising up, riding him. He leaned his head back and Percy kissed his neck, wrapped a hand around his cock, worked him, firmly, gently, faster, until his hand clamped down with an involuntary movement, gripping tight, letting out a cry as his orgasm came for him.

"Percy, fuck," Joe gasped. And Joe let go, for the second time, only with Percy's hand placed just so to send the cum bursting out the sides between his fingers, coating Percy's hand, the pair of them, and the bloody, sweaty altar. Percy kissed Joe, cum, anointing oil, and blood mingling on their chests, and he finally, after he'd seen every shared tremor of bliss through to the last, pulled him down next to him to lie on the cool copper, the mess they'd made spilling down the sides of their altar, onto the church floor, as they lay heedless of anything but each other.

Percy placed an arm beneath Joe's head, and the two of them rolled onto their sides, facing one another. He traced down Joe's jawline with the side of his index finger, storing away the sight. Something to remember for the rest of his life. Then he said, very seriously, "I'd like you to take me to church every Sunday from now on."

It was incredible to Percy that Joe could still blush after everything he'd just done, but he turned bright pink, hiding his smile against Percy's chest and moaning, "It's too soon for that kind of joke."

"Who's joking?" Percy returned.

Joe gave a small, almost argumentative but well-humoured enough huff, and submitted to having his hair stroked by his gorgeous tormenter.

Joe.

Too sweet for words.

Unchanged, deep down. The one solid thing in Percy's life, for the first time ever, and for always. Percy hugged him closer.

They lay there, basking. Joe stared up at the ceiling, his beautiful eyes illuminated and more golden than ever. Percy wondered what he was thinking. Eventually, he took a breath to ask, but his voice drifted off with his inability to hit whatever it was on the head.

"Am I thinking about which thing?" Joe supplied. "Watching you die, damning you to eternity, losing whatever shred of faith in God I may have had left, filling us both up with dark magic, or quitting the priesthood?"

"Which one?" Percy asked, bracing himself for reality to slip back in, which he was used to. Which he hated.

But Joe said, "None of them. Percy, I'm so happy. It feels like… Like this is the end. Like this is how it was all supposed to work out. And I'm so, so happy."

Percy kissed his temple. "I feel the same way." His arms around Joe were solid, and his sigh was deeply contented. His head shifted against Joe's, warm and loving. "I think it was terribly romantic of you to bring me here. It is perfect. Perfect for us."

Joe stretched out his hand, forever examining Percy's ring on his own finger. "Two thousand years old?"

"Roughly."

"It's special. Beyond special. I don't feel like I should be wearing it. It's irreplaceable."

"So are you. Hopefully, it will last you the next two thousand."

Joe laughed lightly, a touch of gravity behind it, then quieted for a few minutes, until he asked, "Do you really think we're immortal now?"

"Who knows?" Percy contemplated the matter. "There was something in that blood. I can feel it. That sex was…"

"Mmmm," Joe agreed heartily.

"But besides that… I don't know. But I wonder if Puss… Are we really calling it 'Puss'?"

"For now? I guess."

"Very well. I imagine if Puss could grant it, they would also know how to take it away."

Joe's head tilted against Percy's arm as he looked up into his eyes. "Is that what you want?"

Percy kissed his forehead. "I want whatever you want. I'm with you. All the way to the end. Whatever it is. Whether there's an end or there isn't." Joe snuggled in against Percy, who continued, "We don't have to decide right now. If we're to stay this way, I have no complaints. There's a lot I'd like to do, and I don't think I'd have time otherwise."

"Ah. So you're not planning to slow down and enjoy life? Take it easy?"

"I'd like to go back in time."

Joe's head snapped up. "What now?"

"I'm just reflecting. If you can open a portal to Hell, then why not to the past? Wouldn't it be fun to go back and spend the weekend with Byron? Or commission a painting by Caravaggio and stash it away to be discovered tomorrow? Or we could attend a Regency ball and really fuck things up. Go down in the history books."

"I already have regrets," Joe sighed out.

Percy nudged him with his shoulder. "No, you do not."

"I don't." Joe chuckled. "Why not? I gave up normal a long time ago. We could do that. Or anything, I suppose."

"Or we could just lie here all day." Percy stretched out his back. "It's surprisingly comfortable, actually. How long have we got the place for?"

"Oh, shit!" Joe whispered. "Oh, fuck!" he hissed, pushing himself up to sitting, with an urgent, "What time is it?"

Percy, about ready to drift off to sleep, offered a languid, "Fucked if I know."

"You, but—" The bells of Sacré-Cœur cut into his speech that very second.

"That makes it seven," Percy said.

"Fuck!" Joe was up, gorgeously naked but running around like a madman.

Percy rolled onto one arm to enjoy the show.

"Aren't you going to help?" Joe panicked. "Look at this mess! Jesus Christ, what did I do? They'll be here any minute!"

And so it went, Joe ranting and raving, Percy watching his new husband with a smile until he really couldn't leave it a second longer, when he finally got up to help Joe clean away every sacrilegious trace of the utterly magical morning they'd spent in church together.

CHAPTER FIFTY-NINE
PARIS WRAP

Percy and Joe used their shirts to wipe down the altar and the floor of the church. The blood stains were impossible to remove entirely from the stone flags, but they did a very fair job given the precious few minutes they had.

When they finally made it back to Percy's apartment, it was to Leo's immediate and horrified, "What the fuck happened to you two?"

"Were you in another fight? You look so…" Althea stopped right there.

Arguably, at first glance, Joe looked incredibly hot, wearing only Percy's open vest over his bulging chest. But another moment's observance brought the eyes to the dried blood, then to the rest of the oily, powdery mess that coated his skin. Percy was able to hide a little more than Joe with his suit jacket, but he, too, was covered in the telltale signs of their surprisingly holy tryst.

"Jesus Christ," Giordano groaned, hiding his face in his hands.

Tareq, luminous in the morning light, right by Giordano's

side, took in the sight with an open mouth and blooming cheeks. And if Giordano was about to be a more abrupt sort of awakening, Percy and Joe were almost certainly the catalyst.

Waleed said, "I'd like to go home."

Percy replied, "Sorry, no. We've got a lot to do, and no one's to disturb me or Joe until four o'clock this afternoon. Leo, I assume you found those bodies?"

"I'd like some sleep too," Leo offered.

"We'd all like things," Percy dropped, leading Joe into their bedroom.

Molly sat at the foot of the bed with Cleo's skull in her hands, having some sort of conversation with her. She'd long since finished making apologies, and was now doing her best to become personally acquainted with the woman she knew so well. Zombie Degas was in a chair in the corner, still looking like a desiccated corpse, but far more like a living human than he had before. And Moxie, a relatively normal kitten now, jumped up at the sight of Percy and leapt into his ready arms.

Percy kissed her little head, muttering, "Out. All of you."

"And stay away from Althea," Joe added.

Percy and Joe showered, climbed into bed, and with Moxie breathing softly on Percy's chest, which Joe didn't mind at all anymore, they slept the entire day.

Given the many hurdles Percy and Joe jumped daily, stealing a woman's body from a morgue was a relatively simple feat. The one they chose was thirty-five years old, her name had been Anaïs, and she had died at her ex-partner's hand. Her story had fleetingly made the papers that day, and knowing she left no family behind, and that she likely had a post-death vendetta, she was selected to be possessed.

There was no need for much of a ceremony. The body was laid out on Percy's floor, Molly lying down next to it, the skull between them. Percy slit his own arm open to volunteer the blood that would give Molly the energy to complete the transfer, which she did willingly, easily, and a little too enthusiastically for Joe's liking when she put her lips to Percy's cut. But Joe only needed the consolation of a few knowing looks transferred between him and Althea before the wonder of the thing began to replace his animosity.

The eyes on Cleo's body shut. The silence of death passed through the room. Then the corpse's eyes opened. Then Cleo's eyes opened once again, and both women sat up.

Percy dropped to his knee by her side. "Cleo?"

"Percy!" She immediately burst into tears, clasping her arms tight around his shoulders. He held onto her, ran his fingers over her hair, but it wasn't long until she pulled back, searching over the group for the face that she guessed must have been Joe's. "I'm sorry. I'm sorry for everything."

Joe was speechless. He could see she was a different woman. It was in the fluid movement of her limbs when Percy helped her to her feet. The way she held herself. Her relation to Percy. It was everything about her, her voice, her tone. "Don't be," he managed.

"Althea?" Cleo found her, her own face stricken, mortified and sympathetic, but Althea made no response, struck dumb.

Cleo, in the skull, had been carried in her arms. Althea had talked to her, she'd heard so many conversations. She knew what she was going to wake to, in theory, but as though her own ordeal wasn't enough, the accusatory faces that rested on hers now, totally innocent, were a special horror.

Leo said, in a practised sort of way, "It's good to have you back, Cleo." Which got a thankful smile from both Percy and

Cleo, before Percy's arm sheltered her, and he led her away from everyone.

But Joe was in fast pursuit. He descended on the couch Percy brought her to, dropping to her side with, "I'm Joe. It's good to meet you."

Cleo laughed with a softness that was both kind and miserable as she studied him with her own eyes. "I think this is the worst way we could possibly have met."

"Probably." He also laughed, nervously. But he stayed there while Giordano brought her tea. He stayed while Althea circled around distantly, trying to get a feel for her. He stayed even longer than Percy, who was eventually pulled into an argument about whether it was okay for Molly to take out the body of the recently deceased woman and commit the murder of her ex.

Percy eventually overruled any arguments by pointing out how amusing the look on the killer's face would be when she turned up at his door. And with that, he got his coat to accompany her. Joe was left little choice but to go along, and it was during this long walk that Molly, softened by the features of the dead woman, filled them both in on some of the blanks of Cleo's past, and her relationship with her husband. And that set their next plan in motion.

The decision was made for the entire group, except for Tareq, Waleed, and Giordano, to return to Scotland.

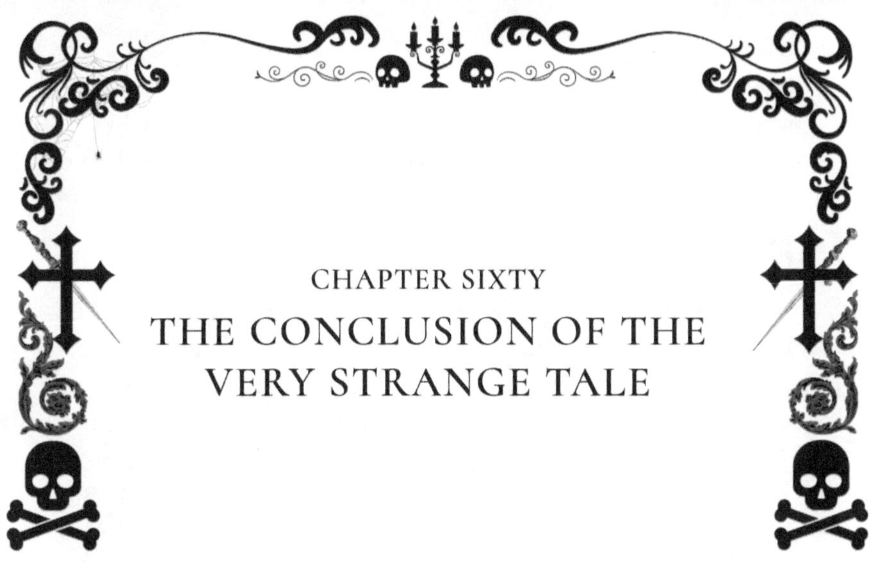

CHAPTER SIXTY
THE CONCLUSION OF THE VERY STRANGE TALE

Althea insisted on returning to Barmiston Hall to oversee the resurrection of the kidnapped girls. It was a work of awe-inspiring magic that took several months to complete, and she was there to receive every one of the newly risen, to talk them through the situation. Each reacted differently to finding themselves in that strange house, but all were thankful in their own way to have her there. Althea made it her business to get them home or wherever they wanted to go, sparing no time or effort or money to make sure each was settled back into the world in a better position than they had left it.

Leo worked by her side, a master of logistics, and he got her whatever she needed. He knew better than to ask Percy where the money came from. He always checked in before he made any major purchases, but any concerns he raised were waved away.

Percy had money. A lot of it. And it flowed plentifully, with unprecedented ease.

Barmiston Hall was tidied and polished and returned to its former glory, only warmer and more full of life than it had ever been before. Percy and Joe stayed on and on with Cleo, as did Althea and Leo, and Molly and Puss, who now looked, and painted, exactly like Degas. It was a marvel, and many late nights were spent between Puss and Percy, enjoying too much wine, discussing art and Hellfire and dark magic.

Molly and Althea never did heal their rift entirely. Althea developed a solid sympathy for her, honed some quiet evenings when Molly would talk about her past over dinner, recalling, as best she could, the time when she was the owner of Barmiston Hall, back when it was a small cottage. Recalling the very short, very different life she'd spent on the small island. But there was too much blood under that bridge. The two had a tacit understanding that they would never be alone together, and Molly played her part by leaving any room Althea unwittingly entered, unless there was a group to cushion the sharp-edged tension between them.

And after all, Molly had plenty to do elsewhere in the house. Specifically, in the basement.

The work of the mass resurrection took unrelenting energy and labour, and it took magic. *Blood* magic. And one of the reasons it took months to complete was the need to wait for the supply of blood to be replenished. Daily. For there is only so much blood one man can make in a day. Even strapped into a chair with intravenous fluids being pumped into his veins. And Cleo's husband, Prince of Jordan, was no exception to this rule.

Percy and Joe had abducted him, then brought him into the basement under cover of darkness, two days before Cleo was due to return to the house. They soundproofed the area and sealed it. Cleo was never told he was there. All she did know was that she suddenly had unfettered access to any money she requested from her lawyers, and not the slightest interruption to her freedom. No phone calls came from her husband. No instructions for her to do this or that. If she suspected anything was amiss, she never said a word. Nor did Percy. Nor Joe. Nor Molly. Letters were written and official documents were signed by the prince, and all the rest of the world thought only that he had taken a long holiday.

When he finally returned to the public eye, months later, all who knew him remarked how changed he was. They were surprised when he quickly granted the divorce Cleo had been seeking for years. Even more surprised when he gave her an enormous parting settlement. But nothing astounded them more than when he suddenly declared his undying love for a mysterious French gentleman, some thirty years his senior. The court hushed the scandal up as best they could, and when the prince disappeared to live his years out with said gentleman, it was thought best to let the fifth in line to the throne fade into obscurity.

A close observer might have noticed the string of murders —namely those of objectively unpleasant men—that seemed to follow the couple wherever they went. Happily, no one was observing them that closely.

The time of the prince's disappearance was around the time a woman called Anaïs became Percy's new personal assistant in Paris, which was around the time Leo was accepted into Cambridge University. He eventually earned a PhD in Art History. He was never lonely or out of place there, not least because Althea soon joined him. She studied International Relations and Criminology, specialising in human trafficking and modern slavery, and went on to do a lot of very real, very legal, very good work in the world.

She and Leo married shortly after graduation, had four children, and lived happily ever after, no one ever discovering their mutual penchant for necromancy and extreme violence.

All the while, Giordano had chosen to remain in Paris, in Percy's empty apartment, with Tareq. He got a job as a barman, at the Ritz in Paris, not long after everyone left for

Scotland. He was hired on the spot on account of his vast experience and fine forearms.

Tareq, knowing no one in Paris but Giordano, made a fast habit of coming into the bar at the end of Giordano's shift each night to walk home with him, via some cafe or other, for a late dinner. This went on for months, and the two grew closer, measure by measure.

One of these nights, when Giordano was required to stay back at work to do a stock take, he brought Tareq down to the cellar for company. It was there, deep in the dark and secret recesses of the hotel, with Giordano high on a ladder calling numbers down to him, that Tareq finally realised he could never do without that voice again. And when Giordano climbed back down, Tareq let himself touch Giordano's hand for the first time. Giordano asked if he could kiss him, and Tareq said yes.

Two nights later, Tareq experienced his first ever blowjob holding tightly to that very ladder. Not long after, the two committed to remain together, as boyfriends, permanently. They stayed in Paris, happy and in love, for the rest of their lives.

Waleed went back to his job as a security guard in Libya.

THE END

CHAPTER SIXTY-ONE

JUST KIDDING. PERCY AND JOE: THE FINAL CHAPTER

For Percy and Joe, eternity was not to be. Not in the way they'd imagined, at least. During one of the many late-night sessions Percy spent with Puss, the question neither he nor Joe had broached with the others finally came up. Percy opened the subject tentatively and quietly, for he wanted only to gather information so he could break whatever news there might be to Joe by himself.

As it transpired, and not unexpectedly, it takes a little more than drinking the blood of a powerful being to hold those same powers forever. Indeed, Percy and Joe could have supped at Molly's cut throat repeatedly, and thus revitalised the temporary magic on a regular basis, but even given Percy's inclination to forgive natures as dark as his own fairly readily, neither of them liked Molly so very much that they could commit to that sort of lifestyle long term.

Puss explained that Molly had earned her place among the eternal through a combination of expert witchcraft and a special 'alliance' with her familiar. Puss offered, at some later date, if Percy and Joe worked very hard at their craft, to allow them the same opportunity. But Percy summarily decided he'd rather be dead and in Hell than see Joe fucked by the corpse of Degas, a scene that could only be marginally worse than the look on Joe's face if he actually suggested it.

These matters, Percy dutifully related to Joe late one grey afternoon, during a long walk around the misty lake.

Joe took it about as well as could be expected, which is to say, with a mixture of sadness and relief. He meandered some time, trying to voice a reply, while Percy skipped stones along the glass-like water, waiting for him.

But what to say?

He knew now that he would have to say goodbye to Percy one day, in this life, at least. Which he'd already known was probably coming, but it had been nice to pretend it wasn't there.

On the other hand, that one rash decision to drink Molly's blood hadn't condemned Percy to eternity, after all. He no longer had to worry that when Percy drank his blood in the church, it had been out of some sort of duty, or regret, or being caught up in the moment. He no longer had the fear in the back of his mind that he'd somehow forced Percy into it.

And ultimately, he'd brought Percy back. He'd really done everything exactly right this time.

Percy cut into his deliberation, saying, "I'd like to find another way."

At that, Joe's face and heart lifted. "To be immortal?"

"I'm happy to devote my life to figuring this out. To you. I'm sure we can do some deals. Search for the Necronomicon or the Holy Grail."

Joe accompanied his reply with a melancholy laugh. "I think my days of believing in the power of religious relics are done."

The whole time they'd been in Scotland, Joe hadn't once brought up the subject of returning to the priesthood. Or of leaving it. But he hadn't visited the lonely church up on the hill. Nor had he, as far as Percy knew, been in contact with any Church members about his position. He'd simply dropped the lot, just as he'd dropped his collar on the floor of Saint-Pierre de Montmartre.

For the first time, Percy asked, "What are you going to do?"

Joe knew what he was referring to. Yet he had no answer. He hadn't had one since that night.

"You know," Percy threw a stone, which skipped well and far across the water, "the Lord's Prayer scares ghosts."

Joe threw his own stone in response, which skipped even further. "Maybe they don't know any better."

"It's possible," Percy replied. "But it might suggest something is out there."

"It's not that." Joe turned the pebbles over in his fingers as he recommenced their stroll. He needed to walk, and to stare down at the mud along the edge of the lake, to distract himself while he sorted through his knot of thoughts. "I feel like I'm letting him down."

Percy knew he was referring to Father Milton, who had raised him. Percy walked by his side in silence, listening.

"I never really believed, I think." Joe tried to laugh, but instead sighed out a defeated breath and gave a sidelong glance at Percy. "But I wanted to. I really, really wanted to. And it's not as though I don't know that exorcisms evoke the protection of God for the victim. It's not as though supernatural lore hasn't grown up with two halves. Good and evil. And that's what I tried to put my faith in. Because, if he… I don't know, what if Father Milton's watching? What if he knows, and I've let him down?"

"Joe." Percy took his hand and slowed him to a stop. "Then he must know the rest. He must know what that's done to you. Being in the Church. Denying yourself everything you might have wanted for so long. Do you really think he'd want you to be unhappy?"

Joe shook his head, turning to face the lake. "No. He wanted to help people. That's why he did what he did for me. But what if he was right about God? About faith? What if he's up there, and he's watching me, and he knows I've... I don't know... betrayed him? I promised to follow the path of light, then I embraced dark magic to bring you back. And here we are, talking about going to find the Necronomicon, the Book of the Dead, the most evil book in existence, to gain eternal life... How do I come back from that in his eyes?"

"Darling, I'm not convinced these things are so very different."

"No, you wouldn't be," Joe laughed out.

"I mean it. You did what you did with a purity of heart. You did it for love. And what ghost or god couldn't understand that?" Joe made a mouth-movement like he was about to interrupt, so Percy talked on. "If we start down this path, chasing the dark arts as a means to thwart God's grand plans for us, well, what of it? We're hardly going to turn into villains tomorrow because of it. And we've done our time. So what if we buy a few more years to enjoy ourselves? Listen." He pulled Joe's full attention over with a gentle hand on his chin. "You've been nothing but good and kind your whole life." Joe tried to turn away again, with a pained expression, but Percy refused to let go. "You're the best man I've ever known, and I love you for it. And I know that will never change. I know it with all my heart. I trust you, and I love you, and anyone who's ever known you knows that just as well as I do. Joe... I never thought I'd say this, but I don't think you should leave the Church."

Joe pondered Percy for a time, eyes wide, then he took one small step back from him. "Did you do a séance without me?"

"What?"

"Are you possessed right now?"

Percy broke a handsome, slanted smile.

"Where's Percy?" He scanned their surroundings. "There aren't any sheep around here, are there?"

Percy looped an arm around Joe's waist and manoeuvred his head to his shoulder as he led him on. "You know it's all bullshit as well as I do. So why not one less bullshitter in their ranks? You did good work there. You believed in *that*. What's faith got to do with exorcisms, anyway? I can pull them off just as well as you can."

"That's true," Joe conceded.

"You wanted a place in this world to make a difference, and I've seen you do it. It's how we met. It's how I fell in love with you. And you look so good when you wear that—"

"Percy!"

Joe gave him a shove, but Percy was right back at his side. "And I really want to rail you in the confession booth while you're wearing it."

"Jesus Christ." Joe stepped away in the other direction, bright red, but Percy tripped in front of him, halting him with a kiss. It was authoritative and loving, and when he looked at Joe again, Joe knew that was the one true and unerring thing he could always put his faith in.

He fell onto Percy's chest. "How far is it to the Witch's Head from here?"

"Not far," said Percy. "Shall we go for a drink?"

"Did you return the skull?"

"Of course. Secretly. Though I'm pretty sure they knew it was me."

"And I bet they forgave you, too."

"It's not as though the place burned down."

"Then yes. Let's go for a drink and…" He looked back at Barmiston Hall, across the lake, as dark and brooding and atmospheric as it ever was. And not at all where he wanted to be. "Do you want to take the night off? Away from the Hall? Maybe stay at the inn?"

Percy's head tilted back with a smile. "No fish heads?"

Joe laughed. "No fish heads."

"Let's do it. Then…" He raised Joe's hands up and kissed his fingers, his thumb toying with the ring he'd given him, watching for his expression over the top. "What do you say we go home?"

"Home? Home as in… *home?*" Joe had all but given up the idea. The resurrections had taken so long. Percy's necessity to be the cash cow, Althea and Leo's apparent reliance on him… It wasn't something he'd thought was an option. "But the Necronomicon. It's in Japan, probably. And the Holy Grail, if that's something you're serious about—"

Percy's voice was low, calming Joe as he spoke. "I am serious. But what if we just take a bit of time? Settle in? I meant every word—I'm determined to find a way to fight this thing with you—"

"'This thing' being natural human lifespans?"

"Yes, that kind of thing doesn't apply to us anymore." Joe only laughed in response, so Percy went on, "We'll find our answers, and we'll get our ending… Or our *not*-ending. Our never-ending story. But for now, let's move into your cottage. You can take your position back, and while you do it, I'll be there every day. I'll be your houseboy."

"You'd be bored in five minutes. I don't think you're capable—"

"How about you let me decide what I'm capable of? I'm capable of loving you." He kissed Joe's cheek. "I'm capable of supporting you through this." He kissed his other cheek. "And I'm capable of helping you redecorate the cottage." He stopped Joe from protesting by kissing his lips. "I'm going to have Leo book the flights in the morning, and then the money will be spent. And I know you won't let me throw it away."

Joe, who wasn't deeply inclined to argue, agreed, "They're expensive flights."

"They are." Percy turned on his heel and began to trudge towards the inn, throwing over his shoulder, "And I'm determined to fuck you in that confession booth."

"Percy!" Joe called after him. "Percy!" he yelled. He ran in pursuit, shouting, "Do you know how small those booths are?"

"I wouldn't have a clue. I've never been inside one. We'll have to get it widened."

"You're going to renovate the church, too?"

"I'll do it in line with the original architect's vision. Very tasteful."

"Pretty sure that didn't include a fuck bunker for the priest."

"The Church needs to move with the times, Joe."

Joe, having caught up, said, "Hey, Percy?"

Percy paused his march across the mud and turned back to look at Joe. Beautiful Joe. Joe, who'd given his life and love and religion for him. Who loved him now and for all eternity. And who said, "Thanks for marrying me."

He took Joe in his arms and replied, "Handsome, I wouldn't have it any other way. It's you and me. Forever. That's a promise."

"I believe you," Joe whispered. "You and me. Forever." And he kissed his husband.

THE END

CHAPTER SIXTY-TWO
AN EGREGIOUS EPILOGUE

Joe's cottage was small and stone and adorable. It resided in a courtyard, hidden from the world on all sides—on three by tall stone walls, and on the fourth, by the soaring bluestone of Joe's church.

The courtyard was paved with sandstone slabs, shaded by an arbour of overgrown grapevines, decorated by quaint wooden seats and tables, and the lot was replete with terracotta pots in which grew healthy and vibrant herbs and flowers.

The exterior of the cottage was painted white and set off by a vine of scarlet roses that had taken over half the house. The door was red to match the blooms, with a little golden lion's head door knocker. The ceilings inside were low, with wooden beams stretching across the expanse. The two bedrooms were tiny, and Joe and Percy and Moxie could not have been happier.

Joe resumed his position at the church, only now he did it with more purpose, more strength in his heart and body than ever before. He was already well liked in the small village; now he became beloved.

He and Percy slowly and sympathetically redecorated Joe's

cottage, keeping many touches that would have made Percy's toes curl out of context, but seeing the way they pleased Joe, they took on a fond significance for them both.

Percy successfully discharged his duties as houseboy, while seeing to the sale and distribution of a series of 'recently discovered' paintings from Degas's previously unheard of 'dark period'. Percy found he rather enjoyed his new, quieter lifestyle. Especially once he'd gained access to the church after hours and discovered that, in fact, the confession booths were already a perfectly reasonable size.

But, despite all of this, the world turned on and on, and Percy was still, and would always be, Percy. His mind and his heart were aflame with the same passions that had made Joe fall in love with him—a fact which Joe understood and accepted when he married him.

Therefore, the following might not have come as a huge surprise to Joe, had he been awake…

The pair occasionally stayed over at Percy's house, and it was during one of these nights, some months after they'd returned home, that Percy slowly, carefully, shifted his arm from beneath Joe's beautiful head. He had worn him out, thoroughly and deliberately, and at that time, two o'clock in the morning, Joe was deep in a blissful, ignorant slumber.

Percy slipped from the ash-coloured linen sheets and pulled on pants and a robe. He made his way into the living room, and though, as a rule, he considered it vulgar to smoke in the morning, he hadn't yet slept, and decided the cigarette he lit was still part of the evening's usual ruination.

He took a long drag, and stared off into space for a minute or so, going over what he was about to do.

Picking up a notepad and pen from the coffee table, he scrawled a quick message:

If you've found this, I'm already dead. Don't go into the basement. I love you.

He rested his cigarette on the edge of the ashtray, then crossed the room to his weapons cabinet. From there, he took out a long, thin, Japanese blade—terrifyingly, supernaturally sharp.

Shoving the cigarette into his mouth, he threw back his thick white rug, which decorated and warmed the wooden floorboards in front of his gigantic stone fireplace. He looped a finger through a silver hook and pulled up the trapdoor. It moved silently on its well-oiled hinges, and he stepped down the ladder, closing and bolting the door behind him.

He hit a switch, and light after flickering light illuminated the long walk through the underground tunnel, to a reinforced steel door at the far end. He took it slowly, still meditating on whether he should or should not be doing what he was doing, but when he got to the door, he slipped his key into the lock. The latch gave a jarring clang as it sprung open, and a soft thunk as he closed and locked the door behind himself.

It was pitch black inside, but Percy knew his way by heart.

Running a hand along the bare-earth wall, he found the fireplace and lit it. Gas. What a marvellous idea that had been. The room was aglow with warming orange in seconds, lighting the weapons that lined the walls, the gigantic candelabras decorated with dried wax, the spell-casting tables littered with books and herbs and spilled potions.

All faded into obscurity as Percy focused on the object of his desire right there on a table in the centre of the vast room.

He took up a crowbar and eased out the nails, one by one, from around the edge of the large, pale, beaten-up pine box. He stood it on its side, and using the very tips of his fingers, tapped its lid down onto the packed-dirt floor with a crash.

Percy took a few steps back, tilted his head to the side, and breathed out a long plume of smoke in contemplation of his treasure.

His very own, very original copy of *Death and the Child* by Edvard Munch.

Mother and daughter, locked in their eternal, horrifying, suspended animation.

"Ladies," he said, an elegant index finger tapping the ash from the tip of his cigarette, "time to come out and meet your new master."

THE END
(Or is it?)

THANK YOU FOR READING! (AGAIN!)

I hope you loved **Sinful Crimes for the Artistically Inclined** AND **Monstrous Travels as Wicked as Sin**.

Thank you so much for reading both books and for your support! As an indie author, it really means the world to me.

While you're here, I would be so thankful if you're able to leave a review of *Monstrous Travels* on Amazon, or Goodreads, or your favourite review site.

And if you still can't get enough of Percy and Joe, please pop on over to join the discussion in my Facebook reading group, WH Lockwood's Book Club, or sign up for the newsletter at whlockwood.com!

There's some very big book news coming soon, so be sure to follow me on Instagram where I tend to announce most things first.

ALSO BY W. H. LOCKWOOD

Coming soon:

Do you like your men French and hot? How about if he has a *very* big axe?

Details to be announced early 2025...

Did you know Percy and Joe first met in the Endymion College trilogy? Check out those books to discover a different perspective on their story from Percy's too-sweet brother and you know who…

Endymion College 1: A Lesson in Love and Death

Endymion College 2: A Study in Survival

Endymion College 3: An Education in Evil

Visit www.whlockwood.com for more information or come find me on Instagram @w.h.lockwood.books

ABOUT W.H. LOCKWOOD

W.H. Lockwood writes MM and MF gothic romance, action-romance, historical fiction, dark academia and cosy horror.

Raised on a diet of teen horror books and Pepsi, only willing to leave her den to attend chess club at public school, W.H. Lockwood started writing at a young age and has kept this passion throughout her life.

Always a voracious reader, she obtained an undergraduate degree in literary studies from a gorgeous sandstone university, following that with a master's in publishing and editing, then a master's in astronomy, thus uniting her two great loves of the arts and science, leaving her utterly unqualified to cope with the real world.

These days, W.H. Lockwood can often be found aimlessly wandering the coffee shops and bookstores of the beautiful city she calls home.

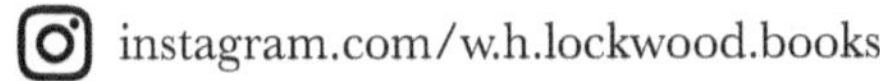 instagram.com/w.h.lockwood.books